THE MONK'S GRIMOIRE

THE MONK'S GRIMOIRE

BETSEY KULAKOWSKI

BABYLON BOOKS

For Runex, Vortai, and all of **One Exodus**. *This hunter is nothing without her hunting party.*

Do not be overcome by evil but overcome evil with good.

— ROMANS 12:21

"Petre? What was that? Did you see it?" The detective froze beside his partner, pressing his back against the wall of the ancient cathedral. Both were breathing hard. Both had their weapons drawn. "I know I saw … something."

"Take it easy, Demetri," Petre said calmly. He put a hand on his partner's arm. "I saw something, too."

"But what was it?"

"I'm going to find out," he said. "Cover me."

Petre slid along the stone wall, making his way to the gate that led to a courtyard where a statue of the Virgin Mary glowed in the moon-kissed fog. The night had gone cold. Reports of a break-in at the Church of Our Holy Lady, the Victorious, had gone out shortly after midnight. The two detectives had been the closest.

It wasn't normal for detectives to follow up on a simple break-in, but at such an historic site, Petre had insisted on responding. He had been baptized in this very cathedral, as had his father, grandfather and great-grandfather. His great-aunt had chosen the consecrated life of a Carmelite Nun and had lived in the monastery here until her *ascension to grace* earlier this spring, at the age of 106.

Petre had spent many hours here at the ancient gothic cathedral. This was where he learned to pray. He had served as an altar boy as a child, and a torch bearer in his teen years. He had even been chosen to aid the priests in the preparation of the Holy Sacrament on Palm Sunday, the same day he turned eighteen.

At that time he had considered the priesthood, but then he met a girl, and he chose another path. He didn't marry her, but she was the one who nudged him to pursue law enforcement. He joined the police academy because she did. While she washed out early in the process, he thrived. He discovered a love for law enforcement and felt called to protect and serve. His own teenage son was now on course to take up the Mantle of the Lord and would begin his studies in the seminary soon.

"Petre," his partner called in a high whisper.

"Shh!" Petre whispered back, watching over his shoulder as he found the gate unlocked. He eased it open, but the ancient wrought iron groaned and creaked as he slipped into the garden and secured the latch.

He herd footfalls behind him, knowing his partner would reposition to keep his back protected. The experienced detective did his best to keep to the shadows as he made his way through the courtyard. He paused and genuflected in reverence to the image of the Holy Virgin. A quick *Hail, Mary* ran through his head and found its way to his lips, despite the urgency of his task. *Hail Mary, full of grace. Pray for us sinners, now and at the hour of our death…*

This was one of his favorite images of the Madonna. He'd prayed to her when his wife was ill with childbed fever after the birth of his son. She had been brought to full health *as if by some miracle*, the doctors had said. If he had time, he might have stopped here to pray a while longer, but now wasn't the time.

As his knee straightened and his eye lifted, he saw something move in his peripheral vision. The door at the end of the long pathway to his left rattled as it latched. He turned and signaled his partner. Even though he couldn't see him, he knew he was there. He pointed towards the entryway before quickly making his way to the door.

This door, he knew, lead to the apse of the cathedral. He waited, listening for sounds of shoes on the marble floor, but only silence came from within. With a nod to his partner, he pressed the door open and slipped inside. The apse stood opposite the main entrance of the cathedral, leading to the ambulatory and on to the quire. He moved silently, aware of the whisper of his own leather-soled shoes on the white marble. Half-tempted to remove them, he found his way to the nave and skirted along the side where the hidden buttresses projected into the room. Each provided a shadow in which to hide, and he had to suspect if someone were inside, they would make use of these shadows, too.

As he neared the altar where a single candle burned, he observed it illuminated the Holy Sacrament. His eye scanned the rows of pews. A priest sat in the third row, with his head down. At this hour of night, he could be praying, but he may have also fallen asleep on his watch. He knew no one would leave the Sacrament unattended. Priests would take an hour's watch at all hours of the day and night to guard the Blood and the Body of the Lord Jesus Christ. But to fall asleep on watch was highly frowned upon. There was a shuffle at the back of the nave, but the priest never moved.

The hair on Petre's neck rose. He came to kneel at the priest's knee and put his hand on the man's arm as it rested in his lap. His rosary hung loosely from unmoving fingers. Petre recognized him by his rusty red hair.

"Father Jerome?" He spoke softly. The priest's hand was cool beneath his own. "Father ..." he moved to lift the man's head but fell back with a gasp. The front of his plain black cassock was drenched in something dark. It was sticky to the touch but gleamed in the candle light. The echo of a drip on the floor beneath his feet resonated in that quiet hour. The same dark, sticky fluid trickled down his hand and dripped off the rosary. The puddle that formed on the floor behind the priest's feet reminded Petre of chocolate syrup, and his stomach churned. Upon closer inspection, he observed the man's throat had been cut. The wound was deep, nearly to the spine; ear-to-ear.

Petre didn't have time to mourn. This was no longer just a simple break-in. A killer was on the loose.

He rushed to the vestibule where he'd heard the door slam but found nothing. There was no one on the streets outside the cathedral. The fog was growing thicker. The full harvest moon was obscured behind glowing cloud-cover, which gave the night an eerie glow.

"Petre?" The radio on his belt squelched. He turned down the volume before unclipping it from his belt. "Where'd you go?"

Something moved in the shadow beside him as he lifted the mic to his lips. He froze. A man stepped out of the darkness beside the stairs. He had a scroll tucked under his arm; his fingers clutched the document. Petre recognized it immediately.

The church housed a large collection of sacred documents, but it also protected what were considered apocryphal texts. These scrolls were stored in an alcove behind a tapestry near the quire. He had only found them himself while playing as a child, hiding from the older altar boys between their lessons. The one he had taken down and opened had been hand written, in a language he didn't understand. What he remembered most was the sketch of what he could only describe as a demon; an effigy of *Old Nick* himself.

"Drop your weapon," Petre said, leveling his own gun at the killer.

"You have no authority over me," the man said, his accent different from anything Petre had heard. *Swiss? Italian?* He couldn't be sure. "I am an Agent of The One True God himself."

"No Agent of God would take the life of a priest in his prayers, not in God's House." Petre felt sweat build on his brow, despite the falling temperatures.

"I did what I was called to do," he said.

Petre considered this man as a shaft of moonlight broke the clouds. He was young, maybe the same age as his own son. His eyes, as blue as the fog-shaded moon, glowed eerily, as if illuminated by his own internal fire. His blond hair was cropped short in the back, but hung over one side of his face. The hand holding the gun trembled.

"You're too young to ruin your life like this." Petre started toward him. Somehow he felt sorry for the boy who'd lost his way so young. Maybe it wasn't too late for him. Petre wanted to help.

The echo of gunfire broke the uncomfortable silence of the night. It resonated off the tall stone walls, crackling into an echo as it was carried on the still night air. Petre saw the flash of the discharge from the weapon in the man's hand. It blinded him for a moment. He had not felt the bullet pierce his flesh. He staggered back a step before regaining his balance. It never occurred to him to pull his own trigger.

The young thief stepped closer. "Go with God," he said and fired his gun a second time at point-blank range.

The cop crumpled, falling into the thief's arms. The boy caught him and lowered him to the ground, gazing into his eyes. He knew now he had been shot; knew it was a fatal wound. "No." He reached up and caught the scroll, pulling it from the man's hand as he sank to the stone stairs.

The thief snatched it back and tucked it under his arm, freeing himself from the detective's death grip.

"Petre! Petre!" The radio squawked. "Where are you? I'm coming!"

A moment later, the front door flew open. Demetri

dropped at Petre's side. The detective clutched a hand to the wound in his abdomen, but his blood flowed freely from beneath this fingers. "He ..." Petre grabbed Demetri's arm. "He ... took ... a ... scroll ..."

"Who?" Demetri was busy trying to staunch the flow of blood from his partner's body. He took out his radio. "Officer down, repeat, officer down..."

"Just ... a boy ..." Petre fought for breath. It gurgled in his chest as Demetri found the second bullet wound, just beneath his breast. There was a sick sucking noise as he tried to breathe.

"Officer down!" Demetri screamed into the walkie talkie, tears pouring from his face. "Officer down! I need an ambulance!"

1

<hr>

The Ancient Gods would be angry. The Great Deceiver had been at his old tricks, and the infant godchild was in peril. The High Priest of the Serpent King had been listening to the whispers the Dark One had been spreading in the hopes that the priest would become afraid. The Deceiver was good at putting doubt into the hearts of those whose spirits were weak.

"It's a monster." The Deceiver planted a seed. "You can't trust those who call themselves *gods*. They're trying to trick you; so they can destroy you."

At first the priest didn't believe him, but the Deceiver was patient. He was good at growing deceit and patiently tended it as it grew. "It will destroy you," the Deceiver said.

"But it's a … child," the priest said. "Hardly more than an infant."

"An infant who will grow in size, and power," the Deceiver insisted.

"It is of no threat to us."

"It will be."

The priest initially refused to act, protesting. "But it was … a gift …"

"Meant to destroy you."

"How could an innocent child destroy us?" The priest cried.

"Children grow."

"But the gods will be angry if we act."

"The gods will never know," the Deceiver insisted. "I will show you the way."

"Tell me what I should do."

The Deceiver had the priest beneath his thumb at that point. "When the moon is dark, you must take the child deep into the cavern below the city, where the water collects and where you may purify yourself. Use an obsidian blade. Take off the child's head and leave the body deep beneath the ground. Cleanse yourself, and wrap the head in straw and mud, place it in a basket and take it to the temple. Bury it beneath the altar and tell no one." The priest paused to study the child who watched the Serpent King's armies as they trained for battle, enraptured at the concept of war.

WAR WAS AN ALIEN CONCEPT TO THE GODCHILD, YET THE ancient memories of its people – carried in the child's DNA – included memories of an ancient war between the great forces of the universe. The All-Father had wept as brother fought brother and the concept of war spread to the creatures Enlil created … creatures whom the godchild had been sent here to save.

The All-Father had given his own son to protect these creatures. The humans might not be worthy of such a gift, but it was not the godchild's place to decide that. He was made to be a teacher of men; a bringer of peace. Before he could bring peace, he had to learn the concept of war, and it made the godchild tremble to watch even the simulated conflict meant to prepare men to fight.

The godchild languished in the company of these barbarians. Few had true compassion in their hearts and most knew only hate. The priest bore the most hate of all. The godchild could feel the man's disdain growing each day. When the All-Father returned, the godchild would have little good to say about the hearts of these people. As it was, the gods had already sensed the pervasive wickedness and were prepared to deliver their retribution. When their wrath was complete, rain would not come. Crops would not grow. Children would starve at their mother's breasts. Only when they allowed their hearts to find goodness would the godchild be able to teach them what the All-Father wanted them to know.

This was not the first time the All-Father had tried to teach goodness to mankind. The gods had tried before and failed. In retribution, the highest of all gods sent an abundance of rain, so much that the world was consumed by water and many – nearly all – died. The All-Father was not without mercy. One worthy man was compelled to save the animals and his family. His descendants now faced the great and terrible wrath of the gods.

It was part of the cycle of the universe. Chaos, creation, existence, destruction, and regrowth made up all aspects of the galactic circle of life. Life in general mimicked this cycle. From the smallest atom to the largest constellation, the universe ebbed and flowed; beat in the same rhythm as the human heart. The magnitude of the great cosmic processes was more than these mere mortals could comprehend. Even a teacher as small as the godchild knew that. There was no one here worthy of the gods' mercy, and the godchild would tell The All-Father as much when the gods returned.

THE GODCHILD WAS ALWAYS WATCHING WITH THOSE LARGE black-green eyes that rarely blinked. The alien being was barely bigger than a human infant, but it already was growing in wisdom and power. It had raised an injured feral dog from the dead, a dog that now lay at its feet, guarding it from anyone who approached too closely. When it lifted its hands to the sky, the clouds gathered, and rain came. When it touched fertile ground, crops sprang from the ground and grew lush in a matter of days. It healed the sick and the lame. When angered, its touch could wound. Destroying it would not be easy.

The priest had been entrusted as its care-giver; its protector. It followed the priest wherever he went. The godchild seemed happiest when they were outside. The priest would notice its eyes lifting to the heavens; its eye drawn to the morning star. When it wasn't visible, the godchild was often left searching the sky as if it were lost and seeking a landmark.

Soon, the people would celebrate the Festival of Q'ollort'i, the Return of the Stars. They would go to Apu, the sacred mountain, where the air was thin, and the gods closest. There, at the foot of a huge glacier, they would commune with the heavens. By the thousands they would come, from hundreds of miles, to welcome the Seven Sisters as they returned to the skies above. The Sisters would bring with them, the Sun Beyond The Sun and they could find the road to the sky that led to the umbilicus of the universe, a luminous chord that connected the solar plexus to the sky.

It was at this time of the year that The People were closest to their gods. The gods would bring the Light of wisdom and higher consciousness to them. Through the gods they would learn the forbidden arts, such as math, art, astronomy, astrology and even healing.

The Deceiver continued to whisper in the ear of the priest, chanting a curse upon the godchild. The priest knew he could do nothing about the godchild before the Festival. The gods would need to see their child, and know it safely protected by The People. However, once the Seven Sisters left the sky, the gods would not be able to find the child and they would not return again for another cycle, and by then, he'd figure out how to explain the godchild's absence.

Children died all the time. They fell from trees. They ran out in front of armies. They choked on food or died of disease. Children rarely lost their heads unless they were sacrificed to the gods … he could explain away a death in such a manner, but his orders were not so simple and there would be repercussions if he was not careful.

No. He couldn't do it. The godchild was a gift from the gods. The priest was charged with protecting it, that it might become a teacher of the ancient mysteries; the gods' ambassador on earth. He couldn't do it.

"You must," the Deceiver whispered in his ear as his gaze returned to the godchild. "But yes, timing is everything, or the gods will be angry. You will not be punished. I will protect you."

THE PRIEST CARRIED THE CHILD IN A BASKET ON HIS shoulders as he made his way to the top of the Sacred Mountain. The moon shone brightly, casting a brilliant blue-white pallor on the landscape below. The gods had been welcomed and worshiped and all the rituals were completed as required.

The priest stood at the foot of the great glacier, his alpaca serape wrapped around his shoulders to warm himself and the godchild as he told the story of the gods' promise to the multitudes. His voice rose strong and deep over the valley.

"In ancient days, before the reign of the Serpent King, the world was made of darkness. There was no light or warmth; no land nor sea. The world was without form and The People were cast adrift into a void of nothingness. There was no hope; no peace." He spoke with authority, having received the story from his own grandfather's father, who was the High Priest before him. "Then the gods spoke the world into being, and made a place for mankind, for plants and for animals. He made mankind cunning and strong so that they could take their place of dominion over the fish of the sea, and the animals of the land, and even the birds of the heavens above. And when mankind grew lonely, and cried out to the gods *why have you left us incomplete?* The gods realized they had made man with no soul – no heart. The gods split the ancient men in half and gave a heart to one half and a soul to the other. Man was commanded to find his matching heart, now in the form of woman, so that when man found what was split from him, he would be happy. He would be complete."

The People listened intently, even though most had heard the story before. "But man was foolish and impatient. Some men could not find their matching half, so they settled and took the woman meant for another. For a time, they might be happy, but a mismatched pair would eventually grow dissatisfied, disgruntled. Some men would take another man's woman hoping it was his other half. Women would bicker and argue with men who did not match them, and discord entered the world. As the world became full of the offspring of these unhappy, unnatural unions, war came into the world. Men killed men. Women killed women. Children fell at the hands of parents, and even siblings. It was something the gods had never intended, but by the time they returned, it was too late to repair."

The People cried out. "No! The gods can bring us peace!"

"Yes," the priest answered. "But man must be patient. Man must find the one woman that is meant for him; is made for him … made *from* him. This is the secret to man's happiness and to a lasting peace in the world."

"But how will we know? How will we find our split-apart?"

"A wise man will know," the priest assured the multitudes. "A wise woman will give herself to him and their union will be blessed. Their offspring will be the most useful of peacemakers, teachers, and healers. This is the will of the gods."

"Glory be given to the gods."

"So it is written." The priest nodded. "So it is done."

"We pray to the gods for peace!"

"So the gods have answered," the priest said. "The gods have sent us their child. He comes to be a teacher to us all. The godchild will bring peace to the world if we believe, and if we can show we are worthy."

The women called out, "Let us be worthy!"

"Let us give thanks to the gods!" The men answered.

"We must give to the gods what belongs to the gods." The words came unbidden to the priest's lips, before he even knew where they had come from. "Man is made from corn and blood. Our sacrifice will appease the gods."

A man brought a basket of dried corn in its husks and lay it at the priest's feet. He knelt before him and held out his arms. "May the gods have mercy upon us all." He bowed before the priest, taking the obsidian blade from his belt. He slashed his own arm, then drug the razor-sharp blade across his chest. Blood ran freely from the wounds and the man held his arm over the basket of corn, letting it drip from his body.

The priest turned and took a twist of herbs and held it into the fire, then brought the flaming punk to the basket of corn and held it to the dried fibers until smoke arose. The basket erupted into flames and the aroma of burning corn and singed blood filled the star-dappled sky.

"May the gods have mercy upon us all," the priest repeated. "Your sacrifice will be known to the gods. May they smile upon you and bring you peace."

2

"After you, Mr. Pierce," Dr. Aziz said.

Rowan stood with his hands on his hips looking dubiously at the small entrance to the burial chamber. By Rowan's calculation, his broad shoulders would be his undoing. Even after dropping nearly thirty pounds over the past year, he was still a big guy. Big guys hated small tunnels, no matter how svelte they were. *He'd never get Lauren in that hole,* Rowan mused to himself. Her claustrophobia grew worse with each passing year. She refused to enter tight spaces as a rule now. Maybe it was the cave in Washington State; maybe it was the cenote in Mexico. Rowan had no idea what had spawned her fear, but it was palpable whenever they were faced with entering a cave or tunnel. She wasn't simply scared, she was terrified.

At this moment, he wasn't about to go down in that narrow tunnel either. "We need to test the atmosphere before we make entry," Rowan insisted. "Confined space entry protocols and all. The air might be bad."

Dr. Aziz eyed him suspiciously. "I have been an archeologist since before you were born," he sputtered. "I have never once had a problem with *bad air*."

Rowan stood fast, his brow creeping towards his receding hairline that was hidden beneath his straw hat. He wasn't trying to be difficult, but he felt like it was a fair request considering it was his life on the line.

"You have a choice, Mr. Pierce. You can go in and be the first to see the contents of the tomb, or you can stay out here and fail my class. The choice is yours."

"There's a third option there, you know?" Rowan offered. The rest of the class stood back waiting to find out what was going to happen to their much older, and much more famous classmate.

"Oh?" Dr. Aziz glowered. His bulging eyes narrowed. His pencil-thin mustache twitched.

"I can go in there and suffocate from a lack of oxygen, and you can go explain to my pregnant wife and my two small sons how you refused to follow protocols and why her husband and their father isn't coming home." It still gave him goosebumps when he thought about Lauren being pregnant ... *again*. Baby number three wouldn't be here 'til late summer. They hadn't told the boys yet. Lauren wanted to wait ... just in case. She argued they were too little to understand. Henry might, but John Carter? No he probably wouldn't. He was just two.

Rowan had suspected she was pregnant even before Lauren did. She had a glow about her ... a green one. She kept having to run to the restroom to throw up. She blamed it on the Egyptian food. Even after a year in Cairo, she had yet to become accustomed to mutton or the rich variety of spices and seasonings that were so common in the Middle East. Tima had been teaching her to cook and they were often guests in his professor's home, but nothing had helped her acclimate.

He hadn't said anything to her about his suspicions. When he came to her one afternoon with and found her with tears streaming down her face, and a pregnancy test on the coffee table in front of her, his suspicions were confirmed. "What is this?" He feigned ignorance.

"I can't look," she said, the stick turned over to hide the results. "I haven't been feeling myself lately … and Tima asked if I was … *pregnant*."

"Are you?" he asked, sitting down beside her, pulling her into him. She was trembling.

"I can't look." Her voice came out in a squeak. Rowan didn't need to. He already knew.

Aziz grunted, bringing his focus back to the moment. Rowan stood fast. The professor's face turned three shades of red as his eyes bulged in their sockets. "Miss Bouchard?" He turned to another student. "Would you care to make the discovery?" He pointed towards the entrance with the tip of his walking stick.

Rowan's classmate took a step back. "No thank you … sir," she said. "My fiancé is a safety officer for his company. He would insist on testing the air as well. I agree with Mr. Pierce's assessment."

Just when Rowan was confident Aziz couldn't turn any redder, he was proven wrong. "Anyone else? Or are you all cowards?" He turned, pointing his walking stick at each of the class members as his voice rose into the alto range. His eyes bulged even larger. Sweat trickled down the side of his round face.

Rowan gave a nod to Angeline Bouchard, who'd backed him up. The rest of the class stood fast. No one stepped forward.

"Fine!" Aziz said. "Then you all will receive a failing grade on this assignment."

"Dr. Aziz." Dorian Stewart, another of his classmates, a Brit from Oxford stepped up. "Are you aware, the International Board of Higher Education has regulations prohibiting instructors from placing students in harm's way in exchange for a grade? You can't threaten to fail us for refusing an assignment due to unsafe conditions."

"Don't cite regulations to me, young man." Aziz looked as if he were about to have an apoplexy right then and there. "I have been an archeologist since before you were born … before you all were born!" This was the professor's standard line when confronted by a student. They'd heard it before.

"Mr. Stewart is right," Rowan crossed his arms. "I believe Dr. Badr will take issue with threatening students with a failing grade for refusing to enter an unsafe space." Aziz's mouth twisted, his mustache now contorting and undulating beneath his flat nose. "Look, once it's safe, I'll happily be the first to go in." Rowan glanced at the other students. Several of them nodded. Clearly, they were all behind the international superstar and *Travel Adventure Magazine's Man of the Year*, an accolade he'd won three times now.

"It's safe now!" The professor nearly spiraled out of control.

"Then prove it," Dorian said. Rowan had to force back a smile as several of the other students nodded in agreement.

This wasn't Rowan's first run in with a confined space. When he was still a rookie on his wife's television show, he'd gone into an underground chamber on an island off the coast of Nova Scotia in search of Captain Kidd's treasure. Legend said the treasure included large quantities of gold and precious gems. The entrance hadn't been much larger than the one he stood facing now. Brash and headstrong, and maybe a little *treasure-hungry*, he hadn't hesitated to crawl in, despite Lauren's vehement protests. Everything seemed okay at first, but by the time the camera crews followed him in with their equipment, he began feeling light-headed. Thinking it had more to do with the excitement of the hunt than the conditions of the underground cavern, he didn't say anything. Standing in knee deep water that was black and covered in slime probably hadn't helped any either.

It was Jean-René who'd saved his life. When Rowan's words began to slur, and he slumped to his knees, the cameraman took immediate action. He and the crew wrestled their much larger coworker back to the entrance and got his head up to fresh air. He'd already passed out before the crews topside were able to extract him. The lack of breathable air began to affect the rest of the crew one by one. In the end, three of them had to be taken for medical treatment. Rowan had a headache for over a week. He was lucky, and he knew it. He also knew better than to make the same mistake again. *Lessons learned, and all.*

"Fine." Aziz groaned, turning away.

TWO HOURS LATER, THEY FINALLY HAD THE EQUIPMENT THEY needed. Rowan made sure the monitor was calibrated and performed the required bump test before sending the probe into the space. He measured the air every three feet, just to be safe. The tunnel wasn't that long, fortunately. Once everyone had seen the test results, Rowan wasted no time making entry. The entry was a tight fit, but with his arms over his head, he managed to squeeze through. He clipped the air monitor to his belt, and the probe to his collar, to make sure he was alerted to any changes in the oxygen levels.

With a video camera and lamp clipped to a band on his forehead, he made his way through the narrow entry to the chamber. He had to turn and twist to force his way through the narrow break in the crumbling bricks. Once inside the chamber, he had enough room to sit on his knees. He felt a rush of adrenaline as he took in the site. Grave robbers had been here before, but it was clear that the violation had taken place decades, if not centuries before. The crypt had been ransacked, the mummy was gone, but clay jars in the corners remained in excellent condition. He moved closer to study them.

Every inch of the walls were decorated with hieroglyphs. Some of the symbols were embossed in gold. A statue of Anubis guarded the tomb. The jackal-headed god's eyes were also lined in gold. Tomb raiders had defiled the god, the tip of its nose had been broken off, and an ear was missing.

Mummified bodies of cats were stacked in the corner of the tomb. A stone statue of a leopard stood beside the niche, intact. There, he found stacks of crumbling papyrus scrolls and stone tablets. A glyph that looked like a palm tree was cut into the stone over the niche. Beside it, the second glyph, the half circle configured like a setting sun was placed next to a glyph of a west-facing woman. This told him it was an altar to the Goddess Seshat. Rowan's heart raced as he realized this was in fact the tomb of a priestesses of the Goddess Seshat herself. He didn't have to be fluent in Egyptian hieroglyphics to put the pieces together.

Rowan scanned the room making sure his head-cam recorded all of it. He wanted Lauren to see it. While he could make out the names of the goddess, and the priestess who had been entombed here in a place of honor by the Pharaoh she had served, he had little gift for the language or the hieroglyphs. That was Lauren's strong suit.

"What do you see, Mr. Pierce?" Aziz's voice broke the eerie silence.

"Mummified cats … probably leopards, and an altar to Seshat." Rowan relayed information on the scene. "Tomb raiders have been here before. The tomb was defiled, and the mummy is gone. The canopic jars are intact though."

"What does this tell you, Mr. Pierce?" Any hint of a grudge from Rowan's earlier protests seemed forgotten.

"It gives us a date," Rowan said. "Or at least a range of dates."

"Continue, Mr. Pierce."

"These types of funerary jars were used from the time of the Old Kingdom; I think, but no later than the Late Ptolemaic Period."

"And what is the origin of the term *canopic*?"

For a moment he wished Lauren were there. She'd know the answer to that off the top of her head. Rowan hesitated, trying to think. "I know it has to do with Canopus." It came to him suddenly. "But they made a mistake. Early Egyptologists confused the legend of Canopus — the boat captain of Menelaus who was buried at Canopus where he was worshiped in the form of a jar."

"Very good, Mr. Pierce," the professor said. "Now, let us talk about how to document a find such as this."

Rowan sat on his rump, scanning the room with the camera on his headband, knowing the class was watching the feed on the monitors. He listened to Aziz provide instruction to the team on proper management and preservation of an archaeological dig site. All the while he drank in the effort the ancient Egyptians had made, just to honor a priestess after her death.

The engineering of the tomb alone was a marvel. The chamber was built from blocks of limestone that appeared to have been polished before they had been painted. How the ancient builders had accomplished such feats was difficult for his modern brain to comprehend. They had no cranes; no diamond saw blades and no college degrees. Yet, here beneath the shifting sands, the ancients had constructed a marvel. He couldn't wait to get home to tell Lauren all about it.

THE SUN WAS SETTING OVER THE DESERT WHEN ROWAN emerged from the tunnel. Sweat poured from his brow and his clothing was soaked. He wasn't sure what was worse, the sweat running down his back, or the grit that clung to it. Even below ground, the temperatures hovered well over 100 degrees. The sand dunes and mountains rising around them shown golden in the fading light. The cheers of his classmates greeted him. Even Dr. Aziz appeared pleased as he offered him a hand up. "You just made your first major archaeological discovery, Mr. Pierce," Aziz said. Rowan didn't have the heart to correct him.

"I need a shower," Rowan said, groaning as he got to his feet. Dorian handed him a bottle of water. Rowan nodded thanks. "And some food."

"Let's load up the equipment. We are going to be getting home late," Aziz said. "Well done, everyone."

3

"Lauren, dear." Dr. Fatima Badr opened the door, reaching for her as soon as she saw her. "Welcome. Come in. Come in. How are you, dear?"

The older woman rattled when she moved. Dozens of gold bracelets lined her arms. She embraced Lauren, hugging her firmly. She always smelled of frankincense and patchouli. It made Lauren's stomach churn. She backed away quickly. "Dr. Badr." She hadn't known the woman all that long, but Rowan's professor had taken a liking to his family. She was extremely affectionate, and always hugged, touched, or rubbed everyone within arm's reach of her. Lauren didn't mind much, usually, but lately she was extremely sensitive to being touched. She wasn't sure why but her whole body ached from recent waves of nausea that had taken over her life. She'd never been sick with Henry or John Carter.

"Don't be ridiculous, dear. You know you may call me Tima." She patted Lauren's cheek, then bent over to pick up John Carter, hugging the toddler fiercely. Henry waited patiently for his turn. "How are the sweetest boys today?"

"Wearing me out, if truth be told," Lauren groused. "Have you talked to Rowan this afternoon?"

"You know his class went out with Dr. Aziz on a dig, right?" She carried John Carter into the living room and sat down so she could hold Henry, too. Lauren followed and took a seat, unbidden. "They probably won't be back until late. Didn't he tell you?"

"He told me he'd be home for dinner," Lauren said.

Tima glanced at the clock and smiled. "He must have meant Egyptian dinner, Lauren, dear."

Lauren sank back in her chair. "Oh." She deflated. "I'll never get used to eating so late."

"Are you hungry? I can make you a snack."

"I am. I'm hungry," Henry said brightly.

"Me too," John Carter chirped.

"Auntie Tima will make you a snack. Would you like a *ful* sandwich?" A mischievous smile crossed her face. Both the boys recoiled. "Maybe some *hummus* or some *kibbeh*?" Henry's face lit up. John Carter looked to his brother, then reacted similarly. "I'll make both." She kissed each of them on the cheek before she sat them down. "Lauren, dear?"

She looked up. "Sure." She rose and fell in behind her husband's professor.

In the kitchen the two women went to work while the boys went to find one of Tima's daughters to play with. Tima set out everything to make *a'aish baladi*. It was the first thing Tima had taught Lauren to make after they moved here. The recipe made a simple bread. Lauren had it down pat. She measured out the whole-meal and all-purpose flours, then added a portion of dried yeast. She tossed in a generous pinch of salt and a drizzle of olive oil. Lauren mixed it by hand in a flat wooden bowl while Tima started on the other dishes.

Kneading dough was cathartic, Lauren decided. She thought about making this bread while out camping, trying to decide if she could bake it in a cast iron skillet or griddle, maybe even on the grill. She missed camping. She missed pine forests and aspen trees; she missed mountains. Egypt was hot, arid, and crowded. But the people were lovely, and generous. She smiled, glancing at Tima as she started cutting lemons and chopping herbs. The fragrance of the citrus blended with mint was comforting and it seemed to settle Lauren's stomach.

Working the dough took Lauren's mind off Rowan. She wasn't even sure why she was worried. Over the past year, he'd gone on numerous digs with his professors and classmates. Soon, he would have his master's degree and then, they'd re-evaluate their future. The hiatus had been good for their family. It was growing much faster than she'd ever expected, and Rowan was a straight A student.

Lauren had busied herself with caring for two little boys under the age of five, but she'd also been reading everything she could get her hands on, in any language she could find. She needed some form of occupation to keep her sanity. It wasn't that she didn't like being a wife and a mother. She loved it. She just felt a need to use her own education, and the gift given to her by the ancient gods, to the fullest of her ability. After her experiences working with her brother, Michael, several years before, they had gone on to put together an amazing season for the Escape Channel that allowed them to research not just Rowan's family tree, but several other members of the team, and even a few of the Escape Channel stars.

John Carter had been born during that time, while they were working in Virginia. Lauren had decided she needed a break. About that same time, Rowan got his acceptance letter from the University of Cairo.

After first contact with the alien race, Michael's girlfriend, Dr. Kitty Donovan, had gone on to facilitate a major peace treaty, even as the worlds' governments denied or remained silent on the topic of extraterrestrial life. The United States Government had declassified some of the records on unidentified aerial phenomena. It had been a nine page report that came down to little more than a statement saying, "We don't know what we don't know." Lauren could have written tomes on what *she* knew about extraterrestrial life, but as usual, it was a secret she couldn't tell.

Kitty's job wasn't easy. In some regions, like South Korea, the peace that had been brokered was tentative at best. Middle Eastern Countries had been the most affected. Taking advantage of the improved relations in the Middle East, the Pierce family had packed up and moved to Egypt to be closer to Rowan while he worked on his education.

The Network had been less than pleased when the Pierces didn't renew their long-time contract. Rowan assured them they needed to take a temporary break, and the additional education would give him better insight into some of the mysteries they wanted to research next.

Henry was almost old enough to start school, but with two studious parents, he'd been homeschooled, practically since he was born. Having a biological anthropologist for a mother, and a soon-to-be archaeologist as a father, the boy would have been out of place in a traditional school setting. He was already reading books at the fourth grade level and was excelling in math. He loved history and geography too. John Carter hadn't been left out of the studies around the kitchen table. Though he wouldn't turn three until spring, he already knew his ABCs and could count to fifty without help. He was just learning to read and knew a few easy words.

Lauren used this respite for her own personal edification too. At Tima's insistence, over the past year she'd read everything she could get her hands on in Latin, Greek, Hebrew, Egyptian, Farsi; anything to challenge her abilities and hone her skills. Tima had been impressed with her knack for languages and encouraged her to continue her education with another degree in ancient languages. She'd seriously considered taking classes herself, but between raising two boys and Rowan's busy schedule, she'd convinced herself there was no way she could make it work.

Of course, the dire warning of a coming galactic war, and the need to prepare had not gone forgotten. Lauren's reading of early tomes spanned the entire breadth of ancient Sumerian history before she moved on to apocryphal texts from the Dead Sea scrolls and beyond. She didn't know what she was looking for, but the thirst for knowledge was all-consuming. She knew when the time came, she'd have found wisdom in those ancient writings that would serve her well.

"What do you think about coming to lecture at the college some time?" Tima asked.

Lauren looked at her blankly. Sometimes she wondered if Tima had gifts of her own. She seemed to read her mind and usually knew what Lauren needed. She seemed to know of Lauren's pregnancy, even before Lauren suspected it herself.

Tima was the best friend Lauren could have in Egypt. Without Bahati, Egypt was a lonely place. Tima made it somewhat better, but she missed her long-time friends and co-workers. Their sudden departure from *The Veritas Codex* hadn't been without drama. Feelings had been hurt.

Bahati and Jean-René had returned to San Diego where Network was keeping them busy. Jean-René was doing free-lance photography, taking jobs as they came. As a result, he'd been nominated for a dozen or more awards for some of his photos that had been published in National Geographic. He'd earned several cover spots and as his credentials grew, so did his price tag.

Bahati's daughter had been born just a week before John Carter. Now, Bahati was writing and doing research for other shows, when and if she wanted to. Lauren had been heart-broken by how their decision had impacted the Toussaints. The Network hadn't been happy about their sudden depar-ture, and as a result, had cancelled their contracts; all of them, including the contract Rowan had negotiated for Jean-René and Bahati. It had been a slap in the face, but when a competing network got wind of the turn of events, and began pursuing the couple, the Network circled back around and made them a decent offer, and a bidding war broke out. Last Lauren heard negotiations were still underway. It had been a strange turn of events when she heard the hot-headed Bahati was prepared to walk away from the Network altogether; but Jean-René was still trying to get Jacob to reconsider.

"Lauren?" Tima nudged her as she moved past her to get the chickpeas from the pantry.

"That might be nice," Lauren said, still working the dough under the heel of her hand.

"I think that's probably enough," Tima said. She put her hand on Lauren's arm and slid the bowl of dough out from under her. Lauren let go of it, realizing the dough would go tough if she continued. "Are you troubled, dear?"

"No," Lauren said. "Yes. Maybe."

"Well, which is it, Lauren, dear?"

"I'm not sure what it is," she wiped the flour from her fingers.

"Tell me," Tima said.

"It's nothing." She started cleaning up her mess. She'd gotten flour all over the counter and the front of her black t-shirt. "Maybe it's just being …" she glanced down at John Carter as he ran through the room with a rocket over his head. He made sound effects as he ran on down the hall. "You know."

"Maybe." Tima knew what she meant. She handed Lauren a can of garbanzo beans to open and drain. "Save some of the aqua fava."

"*Aqua fava*? Bean water?" Lauren scowled.

"Yes, when you drain the beans, save some of the water. The starch will help smooth out the hummus."

Lauren nodded and did as instructed. Tima took out the food processor and set it up. Soon, the tantalizing bouquet of baking bread and spices filled the home. The children came to the table and were waiting for the bread to come out of the *tagine*. They could barely wait for it to cool enough to tear off pieces and dip them into the spread. Lauren realized she was starving too. She made a plate for herself, including a few *kibbeh*, which were fried patties of bulgur wheat stuffed with minced lamb and pine nuts.

"What are you reading now, Lauren, dear?" Tima asked when the women sat down to eat at the kitchen table. The children sat on stools at the high counter, feasting on their Auntie Tima's cooking.

"Huh?" Lauren was caught yawning as she ran a piece of bread through the bowl of hummus beside her plate. "Oh, I started the *Curse of Agade* this morning before the boys woke up."

Tima considered her for a moment. "Have you been sleeping well, dear?"

"Huh? Why do you ask?"

"You've been yawning since you got here." Tima observed. "And, if I may be so bold, you look exhausted."

"The curses of being … you know." Lauren leaned back in her chair. She felt as tired as she thought she looked. "I've been having bizarre dreams."

Tima gazed into her eyes sympathetically. "Sweet girl," she reached forward and ran her hand along Lauren's cheek. "Hormones will do that, you know." She lowered her voice.

"I have heard that," Lauren said. She didn't want to share details of the bizarre dream with Tima. She couldn't even tell Rowan.

She'd dreamt of the godchild she'd found in Peru so many years ago. But it wasn't a vision of the headless corpse that had been abandoned deep within a cavern. These dreams showed the life of the alien being among the people of the region before it had been killed; before the gods had punished them for its death. She had a vivid image of what the child might have looked like, before the ancient men took its head. It reminded her of a smaller version of the alien being she'd met working with Michael. But this was just a dream—a disturbing one—but still, just a dream.

"Why don't you let the boys stay with me over the weekend?" Tima said, bringing her back to the moment. "Shemi and I will spoil them and take them to the museum or the park. You need to rest. I know what it's like to chase a two- and four-year-old around."

"Damn near impossible to rest." Lauren yawned again.

"You need to take care of yourself, dear. Finish your food. I will pack a meal for you to take to Rowan. He will be hungry when he comes home. You should take a warm bath and go to bed early."

Lauren hesitated to say yes. It seemed too great of a favor. "Are you sure you don't mind?"

"Please. I miss having the giggles of little ones in the house," she said. "Until my older children make me a grandmother, I will be content to be *khala* to your boys … if you will permit me."

Khala … aunt. Tima was the closest thing they had to family in Egypt. *Why not?* Lauren glanced over at the boys who'd stopped what they were doing in anticipation of their mother's answer. "Do you want to stay here with *Khala* Tima and the girls this weekend?"

"I do," Henry said. "I do!"

"Me too," John Carter added.

"Is that all you can say, John Carter?" Tima asked.

"Uh huh." The dark-haired boy stuck a piece of bread in his mouth, clearly enjoying the meal.

"Can we, Momma?" Henry asked.

"Will you behave yourself?" Lauren asked. "And will you keep an eye on your little brother?"

"Yes, ma'am," he said.

Lauren looked back to Tima. Expectation and excitement was written on the woman's round face. "Okay," she said, resigning herself. Lauren knew Tima was right, but she hated to admit she needed help. "But only if you're sure it's no trouble. And only if you'll promise to call if they've outstayed their welcome."

"Don't be ridiculous, Lauren, dear." Tima laughed. "They are wonderful boys."

"Thank you, Tima."

"Think nothing of it, sweet girl." Tima beamed. "It's nothing at all."

~

ROWAN HADN'T EXPECTED TO FIND LAUREN ASLEEP ON THE sofa when he crept into the house much later than he'd intended. She stirred, then startled awake. "You're home ..."

"Sorry I didn't call. The battery on my phone died." He came over and pulled her into his arms. "And our truck broke down."

"Are you sunburnt?" He was sure she could feel the heat radiating off of his arms. He'd had his hat on while they'd milled around waiting for the air monitoring equipment to arrive. He'd put sunscreen on, but it hadn't survived the day. It was the curse of his Anglo-Saxon heritage; his kryptonite.

"Yeah." He winced at her touch on his forearm. "Just a little."

"Let me get the Maui Vera." She started for the stairs. He caught her hand and pulled her back into him. Rowan enveloped her in his arms. She melted into him, even though he smelled of sweat, sand and ancient mysteries. "Find anything good?"

"The burial of a Priestess of Seshat," he said, with exhausted exuberance. "The canopic jars were even intact." He sighed as she rested her head on his shoulder. "I got video of the hieroglyphs for you to look at later."

"Lucky you," she said. "And lucky me. I look forward to seeing them."

"I about got kicked out of the archeology program today."

"What? Tima wouldn't let that happen." She leaned back.

"It's a long story, and I'm too tired to tell it tonight."

"It can wait 'til tomorrow."

"I take it the boys are asleep?"

"The boys are at Tima's," she said, as his hands moved lower down her back.

"Oh really?"

"I was so tired I could barely get through the evening. She offered to keep them over the weekend."

"Still tired?"

"Exhausted," she said, lifting a brow. He had something in mind, she could tell.

"Well then," Rowan said. "Let's get you tucked in."

"How about a shower first?"

"Capital idea, my dear."

LAUREN WAS KNEELING WITH HER HEAD OVER THE TOILET when Rowan found her the next morning. "Again?" He knelt beside her, pulling her braid back out of the way. Her hair had grown so long. It almost came to her knees, even when braided.

She gagged again. Her whole body tensed as she barfed. Rowan winced and reached over for a washcloth. He ran cool water and soaked it. He wrung it out and pressed it to the base of her skull. She reached up and toggled to flush the toilet, then sat back on her heels. "Ugh." She groaned as he mopped her face. "I was never sick like this with either of the boys," she added.

"Go back to bed. I'll get you some tea and crackers."

Lauren held out her arm so he could help her up. She barely took three steps before she turned abruptly and puked again. "God, this sucks," she gasped, turning to the sink. She flipped on the water and collected a hand full of it, bringing it to her lips. She swished it then spit.

"Think you need to see the doctor?" Rowan asked.

She shook her head. "No." She curled up and he pulled the cool white sheet up over her shoulders. "I don't think so. I ate too much at Tima's last night."

"Well, rest and I'll be right back to check on you."

IT WAS NOON BEFORE SHE WAS ABLE TO GET OUT OF BED. Lauren dragged herself downstairs looking for her husband. The house was empty. She went to the kitchen, knowing it was a futile endeavor. Even if she could eat something, it probably wouldn't stay with her long. Looking around, she had the distinct impression something was wrong, but she couldn't put her finger on it. Then she realized, the coffee pot was missing. She turned and went to the door and opened it. Lauren found him sitting at the table in their gated patio, which served as the entrance to their home. It was the only outdoor space they had in the multi-family housing unit they rented in the heart of the city. Lauren was a patient gardener and planted the decorative pots with colorful flowers; a palm tree in a large container provided greenery. The gurgling fountain on the wall, cooled the entire space.

Rowan had half a pot of coffee, an empty cup, and a stack of textbooks on the table beside him. He looked up when she came out. "Feeling better?"

"Eh," Lauren said as she shrugged. "Isn't it a little hot out here?"

"It wasn't when I started," he said. "I was afraid the smell of the coffee would trigger your morning sickness."

"I think I'm okay. Why don't you come back inside?" Lauren suggested. "Did you find the leftovers Tima sent home with me?"

"I had them last night after you fell asleep," Rowan said, gathering up the coffee pot and his dishes. She collected his books. He followed her into the house. "Have you eaten?"

"Ugh." Lauren rolled her eyes as she set his books on the bar. "I may never eat again."

"You need to eat," he said, his voice heavy with concern. "Maybe some toast?"

"Maybe."

She started to go back to the patio to get his laptop and the rest of his things, but as she reached for the doorknob, a knock nearly made her jump from her skin. She opened the door.

A tall man with distinct vampiric features greeted her. "I'm looking for Dr. Pierce," the man said in a thick Slavic accent.

"I'm Dr. Pierce," she said, swallowing hard. "How may I help you?"

Rowan came up behind her. "What's up?"

"Dr. Pierce, my name is Dr. Masa. I am from the Antiquities Department at the Museum at the University in Prague." He nodded politely. His accent matched his appearance; his voice rich and melodious. Bela Lugosi had nothing on this guy. His hair was as black as his coat and his skin as white as his teeth. Lauren caught herself looking to see if he had fangs. He didn't. "Please forgive the intrusion. You are not an easy woman to track down. I have been looking for you everywhere."

"You found me," Lauren said impatiently.

"How can we help you?" Rowan moved closer behind her. His hand went around her waist protectively.

"Dr. Pierce, have you ever heard of the *Codex Gigas?*" he asked.

"The *Devil's Bible?*" She recoiled.

"Yes," he said.

Lauren swallowed hard. The hair on her arms stood on end. "I've heard of it."

"You have heard the legends of how the Codex was created, yes?"

"I vaguely recall something about it," she said. The Devil's Codex was allegedly written in one night by a monk who'd been condemned to be walled up and forgotten. He prayed, not to God, but to the Devil to help him finish a book containing all of mankind's knowledge in one night. As a thanks to Lucifer for his aid, a full page sketch of the Devil had been included in the grand grimoire. "I hate to be blunt, but if there's a purpose for your visit, I do wish you'd get to it."

He reached into his satchel and produced an 8x10 glossy. "Some months ago, a man came into our museum and presented himself as a retired police detective who had come into the possession of the document. He said the artifact had been evidence in a murder case, the murder of his partner. He wanted to get rid of it, saying it was cursed. He feared it was placing him in great risk to keep it, that it needed to be protected from dark forces. He begged us to take it. We received it but had no reason to believe the man's claim. We never even asked his name. After several months of study, we have reason to believe the page may be lost from the *Codex Gigas*. There's only two things we haven't been able to comprehend."

"What's that?" Rowan asked before Lauren could.

"Firstly, there is a section that had been added into the margins in a font we do not recognize. The language is something we haven't been able to identify. The original *Codex Gigas* was written entirely in Latin, so this initially made us question its authenticity," Masa said. "Secondly, Dr. Pierce," he addressed her directly. "We are at a loss as to why or how your name was inscribed onto a page from one of the most significant books in the history of the world."

4

Lauren's jaw fell open as she took the picture the professor held out to her. "My name?" Her vision blurred as she glanced down at the image. Rowan's grip on her tightened as she swayed, supporting her as he looked over her shoulder. There, in the lower left corner, written in perfect 12-point Latin font — a form of calligraphy from antiquity — was Lauren's full name neatly printed. The image only showed her name, and the unusual font no one else recognized—none of the other text. *Dr. Lauren Grayson-Pierce, PhD.* The unusual font in the margins was Cherokee. *Tsi stu wu-li-ga' na-tu-tu'n une'gu-tsa ge-se'i. The rabbit was the leader of them in all the mischief.*

"Can you explain this?" Masa asked.

"Photoshop?" Lauren looked up. She could feel a mist of sweat forming on her upper lip as he scowled and shook his head. Lauren shrugged. "No. I can't."

"I've heard of the Devil's Bible, but we've never investigated it." Rowan could tell she wasn't telling everything she knew. "Dr. Masa, why don't you have a seat so we can talk? Lauren, come sit." Rowan stepped back and invited the man in. Lauren's heart leapt in her chest. *Dammit Rowan, you never invite a vampire in! Didn't he know better?*

Rowan played host, offering coffee or tea, but the visiting scientist declined. "Is this ... part of the original text or is it some kind of ... vandalism?" Lauren asked when she found her voice.

"And you're sure it came from the *Codex Gigas*?" Rowan added.

"We're not certain," he said. "We thought perhaps it would be best to begin by interviewing you before we went to the expense of further testing ... most of which is destructive. We hoped to spare the page from any further damage."

"What clues do you have to suggest it might be genuine?" Lauren asked breathlessly as she studied the picture.

"The original Codex was not written on paper, but rather on vellum, made from animal skins. The legends say the hides of 160 donkeys were used, but perhaps it is calf skins. We haven't tested this page. The original tome is three feet long, two feet wide. There are 320 sheets in the existing document. We know some were subsequently removed. We don't know why, or what happened to them. Altogether, the ancient manuscript as it exists today weighs more than 165 pounds. The pages are sewn together by hand. This missing page appears to show all the same characteristics of the original. It is the same size, and the ink, at least visually, appears to be consistent with the Codex. It appears the page has been torn out. Such an act would have taken a great deal of effort, even for an aged manuscript. The print containing the unknown language and your name appears, at least on the surface to be the same ink, and your name is written in the same print."

"Is this ... blood?" Lauren pointed to a smear across the script just above her name in the photo.

"We think so, but we haven't had a chance to test for that either."

Rowan took the picture, wishing it showed the whole page. "You mentioned there had been previous examinations of the Codex?"

"Scientists have studied it for centuries, Mr. Pierce. A team from Frankfurt had unprecedented access to the Codex for a National Geographic documentary a few years ago. They are the only ones who have had access to it in the past half-century."

Lauren ran an unsteady hand over her face. Her hair was disheveled and while she didn't wear make-up often, Rowan thought the dark circles under her eyes made it look like her mascara had run. It could have just as easily been the weariness from having been sick. "I'm at a loss, Dr. Masa ..." she finally said, taking the picture from Rowan, handing it back to the man. "I have no explanation for why ... how ... my name might have turned up in an ancient document. Surely, it's some kind of a mistake. Some *hoax-monger*, perhaps ..."

"Dr. Pierce," he said. "There has been much discussion about this having been some sort of fraud, but I have my reservations. I do not suspect you were personally involved, but I have orders to investigate the matter. If there is some criminal element at play, the museum will turn it over to the authorities."

Lauren said, glancing at Rowan, "What do you need me to do?"

He sat back and gazed at her a moment. "Dr. Pierce, your reputation is wide-reaching. If you are willing, I want you to come to Prague. I suspect you will wish to see the page for yourself."

"Prague?" Lauren gasped. "I can't go to Prague."

"Dr. Pierce, after your amazing find in the Yucatán, and your more recent work in South Africa, your reputation as a scientist and linguist has not gone unnoticed. We had hoped you might be able to decipher the text. That you might help us authenticate it."

"Can't you just send her pictures?" Rowan asked.

"I'm afraid that is something the museum is not willing to do," he said. "We cannot risk the information contained in the text being disseminated before we know what it says. Please do not think us unkind or that we do not trust *you*, Dr. Pierce. But the legend of the *Codex Gigas* makes us untrusting of *anyone*. The knowledge contained — rumored to be contained — could lead to the destruction of all mankind."

"Dr. Masa," Lauren started, but hesitated.

"We'll pay for your travel, and ... for your time."

"It's not about the money," Lauren said. "I have two little boys. I'm ..." she stopped. "I ... I can't go off and leave them. Rowan can't go with me. He's got classes. I can't just pick up and take off any time I want to. I have responsibilities here."

"Lauren," Rowan lowered his tone as he stood. "Dr. Masa, will you excuse us a moment?"

"Of course." He stood when Lauren got up. "Perhaps you need some time to consider." He reached into his pocket and retrieved a card. "I'm staying at the Luxor Hilton. I'll be returning to Prague in three days' time. I'll allow you to discuss. Please, call me when you have decided. I will take care of all your travel arrangements." He jotted down some additional information on the back of the card. "Here is the fee we are willing to pay for your trouble." Rowan took it and flipped the card over. His jaw fell slack.

"You needn't bother," Lauren snapped at her husband, without even seeing the figure. "I can't go."

"We'll call you." Rowan walked Dr. Masa to the door, offering his hand. The man accepted it. "Thank you for coming by."

ONCE THE DOOR CLOSED BEHIND THE PROFESSOR, ROWAN turned to face her wrath. Lauren's hands were clenched, her lips were pursed. Her eyes were practically on fire. "Have you lost your ever-lovin' mind?"

Rowan held up the card and his other hand in self-defense. "Just think about it, honey. This is a lot of money. We could really use this right now. With neither of us working, we've put a significant dent in our savings. With a baby on the way, this would give us a nice nest egg until we're ready to go back to work. This would cover almost a full year of living expenses and allow for all the extras we might want." He reached out for her, but she took a step back. Clearly, she would not be placated by a soft touch. "Aren't you the least bit curious how your name ended up in the *Codex Gigas*?"

"Curious? I'm absolutely terrified!" She shivered, turning away.

"What? Why?"

"This isn't about money, Rowan. Do you know the legend of the *Codex Gigas*?" She screwed up her face a moment, but her anger seemed to abate. Her whole countenance imploded on itself as she sank into the chair behind her.

Rowan sat down across from her. "I've heard of the book, but I don't think I know the whole story."

"It was written in the early 13th century at a Benedictine monastery in Bohemia. That's now part of the modern Czech Republic. It contains the complete works of the Bible as well as the entire content of human knowledge up to that point in time. It is said to include Josephus' *Antiquities of the Jews*, and *De belle iudaico*, *Isidro of Seville's encyclopedia*, *Etymologiae*, the chronicle of *Cosmos of Prague*, medical works and two books by Constantine the African. It's handwritten in perfect script. No errors, no typos. No sign of any corrections having ever being made. Pristine, exactly as the original works are found."

"What's so scary about that?" Rowan shrugged.

"According to one version of the tale, the scribe was a Benedictine monk who broke his monastic vows and was sentenced to be walled up alive."

"You mean, bricked up into a room and left to die?"

"More or less, yes," Lauren said. "The story goes that he pleaded for his life and in order to avoid such a long and miserable death, he vowed to create — in one night — a book to glorify the monastery forever. He vowed the book would contain all human knowledge. Near midnight, knowing he could not complete the task, he could all but smell the fresh mortar being mixed. He prayed, not to God, but to the fallen angel, Lucifer. He pleaded for the ability to finish the book and offered his soul in exchange."

"And let me guess, the Devil took him up on the offer?"

"The Devil gave him the power to complete the manuscript and the monk added a sketch of the Dark One out of gratitude for his aid," she said. "It's probably the most disturbing representation of Satan you'll ever see."

"I take it you've seen it before?"

"Pictures on the internet," she said. "When we were working to name *The Veritas Codex*, Jacob suggested we should do an episode on the *Codex Gigas*, but I declined at the time."

"Why?"

Lauren turned and looked at him. "I'm not really sure," she said. "The whole idea of the Devil's Bible has always been frightening to me. I'd rather go back to that cavern in Peru than go to Prague now, especially after everything that happened in South Africa."

Rowan considered this for a moment. "I hate that I am saying this, but … if it's your destiny to face Enlil, the Dark One … this may be part of the preparations that need to be made."

"All the more reason I don't want to go." A shiver washed over her, and her hand went to her arms, rubbing her chilled flesh. "Especially now."

"How do you think your name got on that page?"

"It has to be a hoax of some kind," Lauren said. "The Devil's Codex was written before 1299, before the monastery was destroyed in the Hussite Revolution. At the end of the Thirty Years' War, it was plundered and taken by the Swedish army. Legends say it's cursed, and it was nearly destroyed in a fire in 1697. The wooden and metal binding was damaged then, and several pages went missing when a vicar tried to save it by throwing it out the window. It landed on an innocent bystander and nearly killed him."

"But if one of those pages has your name and that strange writing on it," Rowan said. "How can you not go?"

"What about Henry? John Carter?" She furrowed her brow.

"I can take care of my own sons," Rowan said. He was almost offended that she hadn't even considered that.

"What about your classes?"

"I'll see if one of Tima's daughters will come by and watch the boys when I have to go to a lecture," he said. "Maybe Shemi could just come and stay with us while you're gone."

Lauren grimaced but sat back in her chair. The thousand-yard stare she got so often when she was thinking overtook her face.

"Look." Rowan reached out and took her hand. "If I know you … and I do, you will want to figure this out," he said. "You'll regret it if you don't go."

"I wish you could come with me," Lauren said, her voice trembling.

"Me too," he said. "But … knowing the powers you have, knowing the gods protect you, I feel only slightly better about sending you alone. I have classes and the boys to take care of. I know you. You can take care of yourself." She couldn't believe he was saying that. He'd been so over protective of her since Washington. He'd come a long way in understanding what had happened to her, and his confidence in her gave her comfort.

She returned her thoughts back to the discussion at hand. "But … why would a monk pray to Lucifer, rather than God?" She thought aloud. Her voice sounded small and frightened.

Rowan leveled his gaze at her, tilting her chin so she'd look at him. "Go find out."

5

Lauren came out of the ladies' room at the airport, feeling woozy. She'd been sick three times since getting up at 0500 that morning. She dreaded leaving her family behind, but with Rowan and Tima insisting she go, what choice did she have? She knew she could never fight them both.

"You named your show *The Veritas Codex* for a reason. Now you must find the truth of the *Codex Gigas*." Tima's logic was infallible. "Don't worry. I will see to Rowan and the boys while you're gone. Shemika will help me." Her second oldest daughter was seventeen, and the boys adored her. She loved to play games with them and teach them Egyptian songs. Knowing Tima, they'd be well-fed. Lauren tried to reassure herself she need not worry about the boys — or Rowan.

"Dr. Pierce?" Masa found her at the water fountain splashing cool water on her face. She'd already spotted a trash receptacle a few feet away, just in case. "Are you ill?"

"I'm okay." Lauren used her scarf to blot her face dry. The cool water had helped.

"Is there anything I can do? May I get you anything?"

"I'm sure it's just nerves," she lied. "I've never left my sons before." She wasn't ready to tell anyone about her pregnancy. While she was certain Dr. Masa was an intelligent man, he didn't seem to suspect anything.

"I understand your husband is pursuing his degree in archaeology," Masa said, making polite conversation as they walked.

"Yes," Lauren said, finally able to keep her stomach in check. "Rowan has tried to convince me to enroll as well, but … someone has to stay home and raise the children."

"But you already have your degrees?" Masa seemed surprised that she might want another one.

"True," Lauren said. "But lately, I've been considering a degree in linguistics." She needed a cover story to explain her *almost magical* ability to read and understand languages. Over the past four years, she'd been interviewed a dozen times about the Maya calendar and her ability to understand ancient languages. She had no good explanation for the gift of the ancient gods. She felt like she needed one.

"From what I hear, you should be teaching the classes rather than prostrating yourself before inferior instructors." His tone sounded almost condescending.

"One can always learn *something*," Lauren said as they walked. "I may not be enrolled in classes, but the Dean of my husband's department has been encouraging me to read some of antiquities greatest works, in their original languages. She has asked me to lecture to one of her classes."

"How many languages do you speak, Dr. Pierce?"

"Oh, well, not all that many." She tried to feign a blush. "I read more than I speak."

"How many do you read, then?"

Lauren knew she had to deflect the question. She couldn't possibly be truthful. "Oh, I've lost count." Lauren waved him off casually. "What about you, Dr. Masa? Why are you interested in this lost page?"

"Not just the page," he said. "The entire Codex."

"Oh?"

"It is my goal to see all the pages restored to the book. It is a shame for it to be an incomplete document, considering the goal of its creator was to assemble all the world's literary knowledge to that point."

"Fair enough," Lauren said.

"I must confess," he said, hesitating. "My ancestors came from Podlažice, near Chrudim. That is where the Benedictine monastery stood until it was destroyed. It is where the *Codex* was supposedly penned. It is my family's history. My great, great, great, great — I lose count of how many generations back — grandfather was killed during the Hussite Revolution. The legend of his death has been handed down for generations until it has become something of a folktale."

"Sounds like an interesting story," Lauren said as they found a seat to await their flight. "Do tell?"

"The Hussite Revolution was also called the Bohemian Wars. You may also know that the Hussites were also called the *Calixtines* … from the Latin for …"

"Chalice," Lauren said. She didn't need him to translate.

Masa's nod showed his approval of her abilities, but he continued. "This was a Holy War, of sorts, between the Holy Roman Army and a number of factions, not just the Hussites. There were also the more radical *Taborites*, *Orebites* and *Orphas*. The *Utraquists* were eventually reunited with the Holy See and defeated the radical factions at the Battle of Lipany in 1434. My ancestor fought with the Bohemian League. His name was Jan Čapek ze Sán. He was the cavalry commander, a general. Jan lead the army when they crossed the borders for the crowning ceremony, as he was elected king of Hungary."

Lauren had a very vivid mental image of him in her head. Masa took out his phone and skimmed through some pictures. He handed it to Lauren. "Scroll through these," he instructed. The first was a painting of a man on horseback, leading an army. A banner flew over his shoulder. Lauren tried to zoom in on it. "Scroll to the next image." Masa seemed to recognize her interest. The second image was a cut out of the banner. The background was white. In the foreground, black briars entwined into a crown, surrounding a red cup.

In the top right-hand corner, which extended out into a triangle beyond the border of the flag, in red lettering was the motto *Veritas Vincit*. "*Truth prevails*," she muttered.

"Or *truth wins*, if you prefer the more colloquial. In Czech, *Pravda vítězí* means the same thing, it's the motto of the Czech Republic."

Lauren sat gutted, realizing she was on yet another journey to find an ancient truth. She could feel the blood draining from her skull and the room spun. A mist of cold sweat broke out on her flesh and dots danced in her eyes.

She and her brother had made first contact with an alien race. It was yet another mystery she couldn't tell. They had been *abducted by aliens*, in truth, the ancient gods. Michael had been gone for years, serving as their ambassador, but as far as anyone knew, he was still on the International Space Station working on a new space-bound telescope to replace Hubble that had suffered a catastrophic failure last spring. His intercession had given NASA everything they needed to actually build the telescope he was allegedly working on, and it would launch in the summer. Jacob had hounded them about coming back to do a special for Space Week on the launch, but Lauren finally had to put her foot down about the interruptions. Rowan had come close to packing them up and heading back to San Diego between semesters more than once. Lauren feared if he left Egypt he would never return; never finish his degree. She was *not* going to let that happen.

The thought of Michael made her heart ache. They'd made peace before he left, and his absence made her long for the closeness they'd found in those final days before his … *ascension*. Kitty continued to communicate with him and would convey messages occasionally. Lauren envied Kitty's ability to go visit her brother when it was deemed appropriate. She would call or text Lauren from time to time, but Kitty was overdue with an update. Lauren wondered how their relationship fared considering Michael's higher calling. Kitty kept her feelings close to the vest, if she had any love left for her brother.

"Dr. Pierce?" She looked down and realized Masa's hand rested on her arm. "You've gone off-white. Are you quite sure you're all right?" Lauren shook off the overwhelming dizziness. "Are you sure I can't get you something?"

"Oh, I'm fine." Lauren forced a smile. "I have to confess. The thought of finding my name in the *Devil's Bible* has me feeling … apprehensive."

Masa sat back. "I can only imagine," he said, rising with a cat-like grace. "Let me get you some tea."

Before she could protest, he left her trying to swallow down the contents of her stomach. There wasn't much. She hadn't eaten more than tea and crackers for the past few days; hadn't been able to. Despite the constant rumbling of her stomach, just the thought of food made her head spin. She sat with her eyes closed, breathing through her nose to try and still the spinning.

"Here." The professor pressed the cup into her hand. It nearly startled her out of her skin. He moved so silently; she hadn't realized he'd returned. She took the cup and held it between unsteady hands, inhaling the perfume of it. It was chai. Not just tea, but a blend of milk and spices. It smelled like Christmas. Surprisingly, even the aroma soothed her. She sipped cautiously at first, finding it sweet and spicy. Once she was certain she could stomach it, she drank the whole thing, one small sip at a time.

By the time they boarded the plane, she felt renewed. The honey in the tea had been just what she needed to raise her blood sugar, without upsetting her stomach. Seated in first class, a fact which hadn't gone unnoticed, Lauren was pleased to find when lunch was served, she was able to eat it … and keep it down.

∾

Prague was an ancient city of legendary origins. Lauren had done her homework. She knew it was founded in the 8th century. A Czech duchess and prophetess, Libuše, and her husband, Přemys founded the city. Legends said that Libuše climbed out to a rocky cliff high above the Vltava and spoke the prophecy: *Here I see a great city whose glory will touch the stars.* She commanded that a castle and a town be built on the site. Today, Prague was the 9th largest city in the European Union.

Like Chichén Itzá, Prague was a UNESCO World Heritage Site. The old city-center was resplendent, topped with the heaven-reaching spires of the gothic Metropolitan Cathedral of Saints Vitus, Wenceslaus, and Adalbert. It was beautiful, and haunting. The whole city center was. She could almost feel the ghosts of ancient souls wandering the streets among the crowds of modern-day tourists and residents who mingled and paused to take in the scenery.

"Dr. Pierce." Masa brought her back to the moment as the car pulled up under the portico at the hotel. "You will have a room here. Your expenses are fully covered, so please take advantage of whatever comforts you may need. The hotel has one of the few remaining Michelin four-star restaurants in Prague and the spa is fantastic. I hope you will enjoy a nice supper, perhaps take advantage of room service," he suggested. "Don't think I haven't noticed; you haven't eaten much today."

Lauren turned to him as the valet came towards the car. "Thank you for your generosity," she said.

"I will send a car for you at 9:00 tomorrow. Will you be ready?"

"Yes, of course," Lauren said. "I'll see you then."

The hotel was elegant and comfortable; a far cry from the type of place she was accustomed to. Despite the age of the façade, the furnishings included all the comforts of the modern world. The pillow-top mattress was dressed with crisp linen sheets, topped in a down comforter. The duvet cover, reminiscent of the Byzantine style, was elegant. Her room was high above the surrounding buildings, and it gave her a full view of the steepled cathedral nearby. She stood at the arched doorway that led out to a small balcony. Clouds gathered in the sky behind the church. It was gray, and the chill of the evening washed over her. She gazed out, contemplating the history of the holy temple as the rain began to fall.

She took out her cell phone and tapped out a text message to Rowan. She knew he'd worry if she didn't let him know she'd made it safely.

Made it to Prague. Nice city. You'd like it here. Miss you. Kiss the boys for me. Save one for yourself.

She hit send. Lauren debated striking out on her own to discover more about the city around her, but the deluge outside quelled any plans she might have considered. Instead, she decided to take Dr. Masa up on his offer and order room service.

She found the menu and sat down in a comfy chair to study it. Glancing at her watch, she confirmed what her stomach was already telling her. It was dinner time; American dinner time. Egyptian dinner time wasn't for several more hours. The menu, however, indicated dinner was served from 6:00 pm until 9:00 pm.

She picked up the phone and called down to the restaurant, placing her order for *pečené vepřové s knedlíky a se zelím;* pork roast with dumplings and cabbage. She took a bottle of spring water from the micro-fridge and sipped it as she waited. She knew she'd have to take it easy on the rich meal, but she was so hungry, and it sounded delicious.

While she waited, she decided a bath was in order.

Travel always left her feeling icky, and a soak in the tub was just what she needed to feel refreshed. The bathtub wasn't as large as the copper tub in their house in Cairo, but it was sufficient for her needs. She lounged in foam-capped waters, letting her hand run over the emerging swell of her stomach, feeling happily at peace. When her meal arrived, she had on her night gown and the bathrobe she'd found in the closet.

Vepřo-knedlo-zelo was a traditional meal in Prague. One of the things Lauren loved about travel was experiencing the culture through the menu. It smelled warm and rich, even before she sat down at the small table where the porter served her. She could almost taste the yeasty dumplings on her tongue even before she picked up her fork.

The food was good and there was plenty of it. Despite having been ill that morning, she was ravenous now, and she devoured more than she should have. She could only hope it would stay down.

When she climbed into bed, it was with a contented heart and a full stomach. A good night's sleep was what she needed — and that's what she got. She drifted off to the sound of the rain tapping against the window.

❧

"Okay, Henry. Go brush your teeth. It's time to go to bed," Rowan said. He already had John Carter tucked in.

"When will Momma be home?" Henry asked, his lower lip sticking out. His dark blue-green eyes glistened with impending tears. He was somber and had been pouting all day.

"Momma had to go to Prague," Rowan said. "Remember?"

"But when will she come home, Daddy? I want her to come home."

"Not for a couple of days," Rowan said, trying to console his son. "She explained this to you, didn't she?"

"Yeah, but … I want her home. I want her home now." He hesitated. "I don't like her gone."

"Well don't get any ideas about bringing her home early," he said. "Remember what we talked about …" Rowan put his finger on his nose and wiggled it, mimicking Samantha on *Bewitched*.

Henry's displeasure showed on his freckled nose as he realized his dad had already figured out his plan. He crossed his arms and refused to go upstairs and brush his teeth. Rowan was still trying to finish up the dinner dishes so he could return to his own homework and hopefully get to bed before midnight. He had an essay due the following morning, and though he had the outline complete, he still had several hours of work ahead of him.

"Come on, son," Rowan pleaded, but Henry was steadfast. "Pick out a book. I'll read to you for a while." It was a peace offering he hoped his son would take him up on.

"Any book?"

"Sure." Desperation made him fold. Henry wasn't usually so willful, but he was also accustomed to having his mother read to him every night. Rowan took over the role on rare occasions, but Henry and Lauren had a routine, and it didn't take much to set the child off when the ritual wasn't observed. "Let me finish the dishes while you brush your teeth and pick a book out. I'll be up in ten minutes."

"Okay." Henry acquiesced. "Ten minutes. Not eleven."

"Not even twelve."

When Rowan went upstairs, he found Henry sitting on the edge of his bed, with a book in his hand. "That was only nine, Dad."

"I can go back downstairs for a minute if you're going to hold me to it," Rowan offered.

"No." Henry handed his dad the book. He turned and drew back his blankets and climbed into his small bed, pulling the navy-blue comforter back up as he got settled. Rowan pulled the chair over. John Carter was already asleep in the toddler bed across the room. He was a solid sleeper. Not even the Armies of Asgard could wake that child once he dozed off.

"What's this?" Rowan looked at the book his son had selected.

"Heinlein," Henry said, pointing to the name on the cover.

"You want me to read you … Heinlein? Do you even know what this book is about?"

"It's a classic, Daddy. You've read it, right? *Glory Road?*" Henry asked. "It's about a man who is and is not a coward. That's what Momma said. She promised I could read it when I got older, but I want you to read it to me now. Will you? Please? I'm older today than I was then."

Rowan lifted a brow, considering him a moment. This young man was a marvel. Wise beyond his years, he was always begging for bigger books. He'd already read every Edgar Rice Burroughs book in Rowan's collection. Burroughs was a gateway author, Rowan supposed. Now the child wanted some hard core sci-fi. This one wasn't a bad place to start. Not too much sex or foul language. Rowan could edit that out as he read, he decided. "You sure you don't want something better suited for someone your age?"

"I'm not a baby," Henry retorted. "I'm big enough. Please, Daddy. You said *any* book. I want this one."

"Oh, all right," Rowan said, taking his glasses out of his shirt pocket. He set them on the bridge of his nose before he cracked open the spine on the hardcover book and began to read.

～

TWO HOURS LATER, ROWAN LOOKED UP FROM THE BOOK'S pages to find his son asleep, finally.

He would have liked very much to take the book back to his own bed and read for several more hours. The story of a soldier coming home from war to a world he never expected to find had been engrossing. Rowan could relate, but he had other obligations.

A paper on the *Order of Anubis* beckoned him back downstairs. He drew the covers up over Henry's shoulder, switched off the lights and left the boys to their rest. He was relieved to have survived the first day without Lauren. *Six more days to go.*

6

Lauren realized she was awake when a rumble of thunder shook the room. Darkness blanketed the void around her, but the lights on the street below caused the rain drops on the window to sparkle and cast shadows on the opposite wall. Lightning flashed and she could see it was coming down in sheets beyond the arched windows. She lay in boneless rapture, comfortable beyond all measure; happily drowsy. It was the first morning in weeks that she hadn't launched herself from her nest to race to the lavatory.

She wasn't sure what was different today, but she was content to drink it in and savor the moment. She reached over and picked up her phone, and it nearly blinded her when the clock came up on the lock screen. It wasn't quite three. She didn't have to be up for five more hours. She lay her phone down, tucking it beneath her pillow and contented herself to watching the rain until sleep returned.

"Momma," Henry's voice filled her ears. A small hand patted the bed, reaching for her. She didn't think twice about it.

"Yes, baby?"

"I miss you, Momma," he said. She rolled over and lifted

her blanket, inviting him in. The little boy climbed up and tucked himself into the warmth of his mother's arms and Lauren sighed in welcome. She was just as happy to have him snuggle with her as he was. She could feel the firm swell of her stomach against his back, and it made her smile.

"I have missed you, too." She sighed. She could smell the baby shampoo's perfume in his hair. Abruptly, her eyes opened. "What are you doing here?"

"Don't worry. Dad's asleep on the sofa," Henry said. "I just wanted to check on you, Momma. Are you still sick? Do you feel better?"

Lauren's brow narrowed. "Yes," she said, hesitantly. "I do feel better."

"Are you gonna have another baby?" he asked.

"How did you know? Did your dad tell you?"

"No, Momma," Henry said. "I just know. I knew when you had John Carter in your tummy, too."

"Oh, you did, did you?" Suddenly her head hurt, and she tried to convince herself she was dreaming.

"Do you want me to take you home, Momma?" Henry rolled over, his hand found her cheek, as if he could sense her distress. "I can take you home."

"Oh, baby. I have work to do," she said. "I have to solve a puzzle."

"I understand," he said. "Don't worry. Daddy's doing a good job taking care of me and John Carter. We're gonna stay with Shemi today."

"Just be sure you behave," Lauren said.

"I solemnly swear I am up to no good," he quoted from Harry Potter like an oath.

"Henry?" Her tone raised in caution.

"Don't worry, Momma. I'm just kidding. We're being good."

"That's better."

"Go back to sleep. I'll check on you again later. Oh, and

don't be mad at Daddy. He started reading me Heinlein last night. Maybe we'll have it finished when you get home."

"Oh? That's nice, son." Lauren yawned and sleep came over her. She sighed as she surrendered back to the dark.

❧

LAUREN WAS SITTING IN THE HOTEL LOBBY SIPPING A CUP OF Lady Gray tea the following morning. There was no chai on the menu, but the light bergamot flavor of the tea was comforting and so far, the polish pancakes she'd had for breakfast were staying with her. She woke early and thought for sure she'd talked to Henry in the night, but of course, that should have been impossible. Henry was in Cairo. Lauren was in Prague. A ten-and-a-half-hour flight and the Mediterranean Sea separated them. Henry's *powers*, however, made it extremely likely that it hadn't been a dream, even though he knew he wasn't supposed to do things like that.

They'd had numerous talks about what he *could* do, and what he *should* and *shouldn't* do. Lauren now understood how she'd ended up in Mexico when Rowan was in trouble. Henry's powers were sure to be strong if he could do something like that, even before birth. He'd been responsible for the incident in Hilo, and the black sand beach with the sea turtles. He'd disappeared a few times on his own. It had terrified Lauren, but before her heart could leap out of her chest, he returned. The scolding he'd taken from his frantic mother had been enough to discourage any blatant violation of their *no magic* rule; most of the time.

"Madame." Lauren glanced up when the valet found her. "Your car has arrived."

"*Děkuju,*" she said in thanks.

His brow lifted. It was only then that she realized he'd spoken to her in English. "You speak Czech?" he asked in his own tongue.

"Only polite phrases," she replied in English.

He gave her a bemused smile. "It is supposed to rain something awful today. Do you have an umbrella? A rain coat?"

"I've just come from Egypt," she said. "I barely have warm clothing."

"Please." He took an umbrella from a receptacle by the door. "Feel free to use this while you are here."

"Oh, thank you. *Děkuju*," she said, grateful for the small gesture of courtesy. He opened the door and led her out beneath the portico where a black sedan waited for her. The driver tipped his hat politely as she buckled her seat belt and sat back for the ride.

IT WAS JUST AFTER TEN WHEN SHE ARRIVED AT THE MUSEUM. The morning traffic had been heavy. Rain had surely delayed the journey. Grateful for the borrowed umbrella, she made a dash from the car across the long sidewalk to the entry of the Czech University's Museum of Antiquity.

Inside, she paused, finding a coat rack where she could leave her umbrella to dry while she met with Dr. Masa. As she moved through the vestibule, the museum felt empty, almost abandoned. The soles of her sneakers squeaked on the marble floors. The sound echoed in the high ceilings as she walked down the long mezzanine. Gothic paintings hung on the walls in gilded frames, tiny brass plaques identified the name of the painting, the artist, and the date. Lauren didn't recognize any of the names.

She stopped at a painting, in a gilded frame, gazing up at the massive piece. The image knocked the wind out of her. It looked like an angel, bedeviled by tiny demons. One had her by the leg, her skirts ripped, its teeth sunk into her calf. Another hovered over her shoulder, yanking on her long dark hair. Her wings drooped behind her, as another beastie swatted at a broken feather like a cat batting at its favorite toy.

The angel's face was twisted in agony, the tortured eyes cast down, watching in horror as a third — larger demon — came up under her arm. Its claws dug into her hips. Blood ran from wounds in her side, as well as injuries to the palms of her hands. The stigmata was disturbing enough, but the look in her eyes was heartbreaking; tears of crimson ran down cheeks that were exact replicas of her own. It was like looking into a mirror; a horrifying mirror.

She gasped and took a step back, her vision blurring. Dots danced in her eyes, and her stomach churned. She turned away, staggering towards a blurred form that came towards her. "*Dobré ráno*," the man greeted her in Czech. "*Mohu vám pomoci?*"

"Yes, you can help me," Lauren said, recovering somewhat. "I'm here to see Dr. Masa. He's expecting me."

"Dr. Masa?" The man puzzled. "The name doesn't sound familiar. Does he work here?"

Lauren's vision suddenly cleared, but her head was still spinning; still throbbing. "He ..." She swallowed back the contents of her stomach. "He told me he worked here."

"Come," he said. "Let's go to the office and see if anyone knows him. I'm only a volunteer. I just come in a few days a week."

"I appreciate your help ..." she managed.

"My name is Vincent," he said. "You are?"

"Dr. Lauren Pierce." Glancing back at the painting, she hesitated, but decided she'd rather go with him.

"Rowan, darling," Tima said as she opened the door. "You're late," she added, waving him in. She took a sleepy John Carter – still in his pajamas – from his arms as he went over to the counter and dropped the boys' backpack on the floor. The Buzz Lightyear toy in the pack started making laser noises inside.

"I know. We overslept," Rowan said, his voice gruff. It had taken most of the night to write his paper. He was operating on little sleep and no coffee. "I'm so thankful to Shemi for keeping an eye on the boys today."

"Shemi is waiting for them in the library." Tima inspected him, setting John Carter down. "Go find her, boys. Take your toys." Henry hoisted up the bag and followed John Carter to the other room. "Do you have time for a coffee?" Tima asked.

"I'm afraid not. I could use one, but I'm going to be late for class if I don't hurry." He turned for the door, but she caught his sleeve and looked down her nose at him dubiously.

"I'll write you a note. Let me make you one to go," she said. "It'll just take a moment." Rowan couldn't refuse. "I will be at Uni at 10:00. What time is your first class over?"

"Depends on how long-winded the professor decides to be. Class should be over by 9:45 though. I have another lecture at 3:00 and lab at 4:30."

"My lecture starts at 11:30, if you care to come," she said. "Join me for lunch afterwards?"

Rowan smiled as she handed him a paper cup with a lid. Her kitchen smelled like coffee and spices. "I would love that." Rowan agreed. She reached up for his face and pulled him down. She kissed his cheeks before letting him go. "You know you are my favorite student, yes?"

"I was pretty sure of it after the first semester," he grinned, with a lift of his cup in thanks. "I wouldn't miss your lecture for the world."

"Perfect," she said. "I'll see you at Uni. Plan on coming for dinner tonight."

How could he say no?

"Henry, John Carter! Come in." Shemi met them at the door to the library.

"Good morning, Shemi," Henry said.

"Shemi!" John Carter squealed reaching for her.

She scooped him up and he hugged her fiercely. "I haven't seen you in three whole days."

"Our momma went to Prague," Henry said. "Do you know? Prague is in the Czech Republic."

"I did know that," Shemi said. "That's why you get to spend the day with me. What shall we do first?"

"*Pway wockets*," John Carter said. Even for a little boy, he had a deep voice. He looked just like his mother. Henry, on the other hand, looked just like his father. If someone didn't know they were brothers, they wouldn't have even thought they might be related.

"You want to play rockets?" Shemi asked. "Sure. They should be in the toy box."

"Buzz!" He rummaged through his backpack.

"I'll build a launch pad and mission control with my LEGOs," Henry announced.

"Every astronaut needs a launch pad," Shemi said, and came to sit down on the floor with the boys.

"Shemi? You know my Uncle Michael is an astronaut, right?"

"That's what your mother told me," she said. "It must be very exciting."

"We've never met our Uncle Michael. He's been in outer space since before John Carter was born. I was just a baby when he left." Henry had met Uncle Michael, but he wasn't supposed to tell anyone. That was their secret and he'd taken an oath not to tell.

"That's kind of sad," Shemi said. "Will he be home soon?"

"Momma says he's doing important work."

"I'm sure he is." Shemi changed the subject. "Maybe this afternoon we can go to the park and get a *kunafa*."

The boys' eyes lit up. Only Shemi would take them to get *kunafa*. The boys loved the local pastries and sweets. Shemi knew she could use the promise of a treat to make them behave. Not that they were ever bad, but they did tend to be rather rambunctious at times — John Carter especially.

The boys scattered the toys across the floor and were happily playing when Tima came in to check on them. "So, what did your father feed you for breakfast?"

"Boiled eggs and toast," Henry said. "I wanted cinnamon on my toast, but we are out of cinnamon. Do you have cinnamon toast, Shemi?"

"Still hungry?"

"Yes!" John Carter stood and jumped. "Eat!"

"Let's go see about a snack then," Tima suggested. John Carter rushed over to her and wrapped his arms around her legs and hugged her fiercely. Tima grabbed the door jamb to prevent him from taking her down. She scooped him up. "Henry? Are you coming?" Tima turned but paused when the older brother sat staring at the floor. His expression had gone distant, and he didn't seem the least bit interested in food. "Henry?"

Shemi put a hand on his back, and he nearly came out of his skin. "Henry? Are you okay?"

Henry nodded. "I just miss my momma. I want her to come home."

Shemi looked to her mother, who lifted a knowing brow. Tima put John Carter down but held his hand as she dropped to one knee, running a hand over the older boy's head and down his cheek. She lifted his chin, his eyes coming to hers. "You know your mother is going to be okay," she said. "She has a job to do, and so do you."

"I do?" Henry sniffed.

Tima pulled John Carter into her arms so she could

address them both. "Yes," she said. "Respect for one's parents is the cornerstone of morality, and the most fundamental duty of the eldest son is to care for your parents," she addressed Henry directly. "All children must honor their parents, for their behavior reflects on them. A child who is willful or misbehaves shows that his parents are of no worth. We know your mother and father are good parents. Your behavior shows us that. We know you to be good and honorable sons."

Henry brightened at that thought and nodded. "I *am* trying."

"And you are doing well," she beamed. "Now come, let us find something to eat."

7

Lauren found herself laying on a bench in an office she'd never seen before. A large mahogany desk filled half the room. An old computer, with a sepia tone screen, flickered in the fluorescent lighting. It took up a large portion of the right return on the L-shaped desk. The blinds were open on the wall-to-wall windows. She could see it was raining furiously outside. The chill of it reached her as she sat up and tried to gain her bearings. Her internal gyroscope was out of whack, and it took a moment before she found her place in the world and her spinning brain settled.

The last thing she'd remembered was ducking into the ladies' room just in time to vomit in the first stall. She should have known better than to eat so much. She put her hand to her head, shivering as a chill raced over her. The feeling of waking up somewhere she'd never been was disconcerting. Unfortunately, it seemed to happen to her all too often. *Had she fainted?* She must have.

She froze when the doorknob wiggled. It squeaked as it turned, and the heavy door swung open with a groan. A woman entered the room. "Miss?"

"What … what happened?" Lauren asked, swallowing hard.

"Someone found you passed out in the ladies' lavatory," the woman said. "My name is Dr. Eliška Kominsky, I'm the director here. Do you need medical attention?"

"Sorry, Dr. Lauren Pierce." Lauren shook off the miasma of confusion. "And no, I don't. I'll be perfectly fine in about seven or eight months."

"You're expecting?"

Lauren nodded. "Just found out a little over a week ago."

"Your first?"

"Third," Lauren said. "I'm terribly sorry to be so much trouble." The woman brought her a bottle of water. Lauren took it with thanks.

"Vincent said you were here to see a … Dr. Masa?"

"Yes," Lauren said. "Do you know him?"

She seemed to hesitate a moment, looking dubious. "I'm sorry to have to tell you. There's no one that works here by that name, Dr. Pierce."

"What?" Lauren gasped. Panic raced through her. She knew she hadn't been talking to ghosts. He'd come to her house, flown with her from Cairo. She'd felt his hand on her arm, and knew he was flesh and bone. "But … he came to my house in Egypt. He checked me into the hotel last night and sent a car for me this morning."

"Perhaps you have the name wrong?" Dr. Kominsky said.

Lauren shook her head. "No, it was Masa." Lauren spelled the name for her. "I'm certain of it."

"Why are you here, Dr. Pierce? What was the purpose of your visit?" The woman spoke curtly and stared down her nose at Lauren.

"He said you had one of the lost pages of the *Codex Gigas* and he wanted me to see it," she said.

The woman's mouth twitched as she leaned her hip on the edge of her desk. She crossed her arms and seemed to consider Lauren for a long moment. "Part of that story is correct," she said. Lauren's pulse quickened. "We do have a page that is *allegedly* from the *Codex Gigas*. Why would you be interested?"

"He said my name was written on it. He showed me a picture. You see, I'm a linguist," Lauren said. "Not by education, but by trade. My degree is in biological anthropology. I also have a knack for ancient languages. I've been studying them and anyway... Dr. Masa asked me to see if I could translate part of the text."

Dr. Kominsky scratched behind her ear. Her brown hair was pulled back into a tight twist. She wore an impeccably tailored suit and heels that were several inches high. Her nails were perfectly manicured. She wore a string of pearls around her neck. Lauren never dressed like that, but she admired the look. The Director was polished. "Could you identify this man?"

A wry smile pressed tightly into the corners of her cheeks. "He looked like ... a vampire."

"A vampire?" The director eyed her warily. "You know we take that kind of thing quite seriously here."

"He was tall, pale ... he had dark hair pulled back tight in a queue at the base of his neck. He wore a black suit and he looked very ... *Slavic*."

Kominsky nodded. Lauren thought she saw a glint of recognition in the woman's eyes, but she couldn't be certain. "Yes, that's often how vampires are portrayed. Are you feeling steadier now?"

"Yes," Lauren drained the bottle. "Thank you."

"Come with me," Dr. Kominsky said, adding, "Please?"

THE MUSEUM DIRECTOR LED HER DOWN THE WIDE HALL TO the elevator. She said nothing as they went down to the main gallery. Dr. Kominsky stopped at a wall full of portraits, most were older men, all were distinguished. "Does anyone here look familiar?"

Lauren inspected the portraits and older paintings, pausing when she found a familiar face, and gasped. "That's him." She pointed to a painted portrait.

"That's Bartolomeo Masa," she said. "He was a wealthy benefactor who passed away recently. This portrait was commissioned in 1938, when he was a young man. He helped the museum acquire many of our most precious pieces."

"Does he have a son? Or … a grandson?"

"He died without an heir," she said. "Thanks to him, we have an endowment that will fund our mission for many more years to come."

Lauren clenched her jaw and heaved a deep sigh. "I'm not crazy."

"No one suggested you were," the director said.

Lauren's brow narrowed, not so much at her host, but in deep thought. "There's a painting in the lobby I want to ask you about."

"Ah, this is the work of Milana Muclia, a Slovakian painter. It was painted in the 13th century and was quite rare for its time." Lauren didn't want to look at it, but she found herself unable to look away. Her knees quaked and the thought of how uncharacteristic that was for her came and passed just as quickly. It took a lot to shake her, but she was definitely shaken.

"How so?" Lauren asked, her hand over her mouth.

"What do you know of angels, Dr. Pierce?" Kominsky asked. "Are you Catholic? Christian at least?"

Lauren had to consider her rapid-fire questions for a moment. She knew more than most, but that wasn't something she cared to talk about. "I have studied religion for the sake of history, but … as a scientist, I consider myself … neutral."

"In the Bible, angels are neither male nor female in a human sense because they belong to a different order of beings." Lauren's brow lifted as she considered this. Michael had spoken of Enki and Enlil as fallen angels, but they were referred to as brothers, which seemed pretty gender specific to her. "Still, when biblical writers try to describe angelic appearances, they consistently use masculine pronouns and male attributes." *Well, that made sense then*, Lauren thought. "Artists too, struggle with how to depict them. This piece is called the *Rape of Phanuel*. She is the fourth angel who stands before God in the Book of Enoch — after the angels Michael, Raphael, and Gabriel. Because angels have no gender as we know it, the artist painted the Divine Being as female. Her name means *the Face of God*, but that may be an inaccurate translation. Phanuel was actually the *Hand of God*. Her duties include standing beside God's throne, ministering Truth, and serving as the *Angel of Judgement*."

The words made Lauren's heart race, the room tilted, and she swallowed hard. Memories of her experiences some years ago with her brother came racing back at her. Michael had been chosen as an ambassador to a race of beings that some might call *aliens* – others might call *gods*. He served as the ambassador of the gods, their voice. They had referred to her as *their hand*. Enki, the alien god, had told her to prepare for a coming war between the forces of good and evil; heaven and Hell. Lauren chilled just thinking about it. In the years since Michael had been *called* … she hadn't seen him, nor had she been visited by the gods, whom he served.

Her own spirit guide, Tsul'Kalu, a shaman of the Bigfoot tribe, had been absent from her, too. He had served in judgement for the *rabbit* in Washington State, a double-dealing diamond thief who'd been causing torment for the race of bipedal primates who dwelled in caves around Mt. St. Helens. Tsul'Kalu had been judge and the very hand of judgement when the thief had attacked Lauren and her team. Now, as she gazed into the angel's tormented eyes, she wondered why her own face appeared in this horrifying image.

"Dr. Pierce," Dr. Kominsky nudged her. "You've gone pale. Are you sure you are well?"

Lauren looked at her host sharply. "Am I crazy, or ... or does she look like ... like me?"

The Director answered without much thought. "One of the beautiful things about art is our ability to see ourselves in great works."

Lauren's scowl deepened. She didn't know what to say — what to think. "I suppose so." She stared at the painting a moment longer.

"I'm terribly sorry, Dr. Pierce. I wish I could have been more help." Dr. Kominsky put a hand on Lauren's upper arm, then turned to leave her.

"Wait," Lauren called after her. "I've come all this way ... would ... would it be possible to see it? The page ... the Codex that is."

Dr. Kominsky hesitated a moment before she turned. When she did, she looked dubious. "It's not that easy. It's been transferred to a safe. I'll have to coordinate with Security and the archivist. If you can make an appointment, I'll see what can be arranged."

"I can come back tomorrow." Lauren offered.

Dr. Kominsky folded her hands and hung her head. "It might take a few days," she said, sadly. "Perhaps it would be better if you left your number. I can have my assistant call you with an appointment time."

"My flight leaves in a few days," she said, fishing a business card out of her handbag. "I don't have much time."

"I'll do what I can. In the meantime, enjoy our beautiful

city. Try the food, see the sights. You will not be disappointed."

Lauren's brow knitted and she glanced back at the painting, then to her host. "Call me and I'll come back." Lauren gave her the card. Kominsky nodded. "Thank you for your help earlier." Lauren offered her hand.

She tucked Lauren's card in the pocket of her suit jacket, before accepting her handshake. "I do hope you are feeling better, and … congratulations."

ROWAN GOT TO HIS SEAT ON THE SIXTH ROW JUST AS THE lights in the auditorium dimmed. Tima made a grand appearance in the spotlight on stage, to the applause of her students. She was dressed in the attire of an ancient Egyptian woman, a sheath dress known as a *kalasiris*. The red garment bore striking similarities to ones Rowan had seen depicted on the walls of the tomb of the Priestess of Seshat. Tima wore a circlet of gold with inlayed red stones, a blue feather in her crown. She carried the scepter and ankh of a queen.

"I am called Ma'at, I am the goddess of truth, balance, order, harmony, morality and justice. I personify these concepts and regulate the stars, the seasons. I wield power over the actions of mortals and the deities who brought order from chaos at the moment of creation."

Rowan sat, spellbound. Tima had missed her calling. She was a splendid actress.

Tima continued. "In the *Duat* … the Egyptian underworld … the hearts of the dead were said to be weighed against my feather. It is a symbol representing the concept of balance and can still be found in the *Hall of Two Truths*. This is why hearts were left in Egyptian mummies while their other organs were removed, as the heart … called *ib* … was seen as part of the Egyptian soul. If the heart were found to be lighter or equal in weight to the *feather of Ma'at*, the deceased had led a virtuous life and would go on to *Aaru*, or paradise. A heart found to be unworthy was devoured by the goddess *Ammit*. Its owner would be condemned to remain in the *Duat* for all eternity."

He wished Lauren were here. She held steadfast to the power of truth, even more so since her bizarre experience in Washington State. She'd clung to it just as diligently after the ordeal in Mexico. Since South Africa, peace and balance joined to form her own personal ethos; a trilogy that was engrained in her spirit. Lauren would like Ma'at, he decided, especially Tima's depiction of the goddess.

Rowan hardly took a single note, even though he had his iPad at the ready. He found himself so enthralled in her performance, he completely lost himself in the story. He had a new goddess to add to his list of favorites.

Yes. He had a list.

LAUREN WAS AT THE TOP OF THAT LIST. AS HE SAT IN THE BACK seat of the car with Tima, he couldn't stop thinking about her. She still hadn't called. That wasn't like her. He typed out another message and hit send.

"Still no news?" Tima seemed to be able to read his mind.

"Not yet," he said. "I'm starting to worry."

"She'll call when she can." Tima tried to reassure him.

"That's what worries me," he said. "I know she'd respond if she could."

"Maybe her battery died." Tima shrugged.

"Yeah, silly me." Rowan sighed. "That's probably it."

AFTER A FUTILE EFFORT AT THE MUSEUM, LAUREN FOUND herself at a café in the old city center. The rain had finally abated, and she'd been seated on the patio. The pavement remained damp, but the furnishings had been dried off. The air was cool, perfumed by coffee, baking bread and sweets. She'd already finished her cup of soup and smiled to herself when the waitress brought her a cup of tea and a pastry.

She was enjoying watching people as they rushed by or strolled along the promenade. The food was good. The tea was strong. She hadn't kept the little food she'd eaten down, and she was surprised now that she could eat. While the aroma of the coffee was overt, even over her floral tea, it hadn't triggered her nausea. Rowan's morning grog usually set her off. Maybe she'd pay for it later. At the moment, the tea was just the balm she needed after her odd encounter at the museum that morning.

The thought of Rowan reminded her to check her phone. She'd texted him some pictures from the gothic cathedral she'd toured earlier, knowing he'd want to see them. *Still no response.* That wasn't like him. She hoped everything was okay.

She lay her phone on the table beside her cup and sat back, sipping it as she watched people passing by. A man went by with two Great Danes that were almost taller than he was. There was another man in a rumpled business suit shouting at someone on the phone as he passed. Lauren only caught part of the conversation. He was arguing with a coworker about the division of labor and how he always had to do the hard assignments. A red and white cable car passed on the railway, full of passengers.

A group of teenage girls in their baggy pants and over-sized flannel shirts came and took the table next to her. One had a nose ring. One had a tattoo around her neck. Yet another had one side of her head shaved and her hair was dyed dayglow pink. Lauren sipped her tea and sighed deeply. She was grateful that she had boys and they were still little.

Her thoughts went to the one she carried now, wondering if it would be a boy or a girl. She wondered if it would look like Rowan or more like her. Presently, they each had a mini-me. Henry was the spitting image of his father, while John Carter was olive-complected with a head full of thick dark hair, the exact shade of raven-wing black hers had been when she was younger. Threads of gray were beginning to appear amongst the dark as she aged.

The image in her mind's eye coalesced into a little girl with cinnamon curls; a little girl who looked like her daddy. She sighed as a happiness she could have never imagined over ten years ago washed over her. She loved being a mother. Her boys were her pride and joy and though they hadn't been trying, a third wasn't unwelcomed in the Pierce family. Lauren just worried about how they would manage and if she'd ever be able to go back to work. She missed filming *The Veritas Codex*; she missed her friends and the crew.

"Dr. Lauren Grayson?" A stern voice snatched her from her happy daydream. Lauren turned and found two men in black coats standing behind her. A third stood across from her. "Are you Lauren Grayson?"

"Yes." She looked up at the man. "May I help you?"

"Come with us." The man caught her under her arm and practically lifted her out of her chair.

"What?" She stiffened but didn't resist. "Wait!"

It all happened so fast she couldn't even get the words out. She was shoved into the back of a van with two of the three men pinning her arms to her side. The third jumped in the driver's seat as the back doors closed. The van began to move, and she might have been upended had the men not held her so tight. "Who are you? Where are you taking me?"

No one answered.

Panic gripped her throat, squeezing the air out of her. She found herself struggling to breathe. The more she tried, the harder it became, and that familiar feeling of impending unconsciousness washed over her. Her stomach churned.

Please, don't let me puke or pass out now. The thought wasn't a prayer, or — maybe it was. Either way, it didn't help.

~

"STILL NOTHING FROM LAUREN?" TIMA ASKED AS THEY SAT down in the faculty dining room. Normally, Rowan wouldn't have been allowed in here, but no one told Fatima Badr what she couldn't do or whom she could or couldn't dine with, including the service staff. They were given the best table, with the most efficient waitstaff.

"No, she hasn't called since she left," Rowan said. "I texted her earlier, but …" He took his phone from his pocket and pulled it up. "No, she hasn't responded."

"I'm sure she's been quite engrossed in her work," Tima said. "Perhaps the museum doesn't allow cell phones in their vaults for security reasons. We don't allow them in ours."

"I hadn't thought of that," Rowan said. "Everyone has a camera in their hip pocket these days, don't they?"

"It's so true," she said. "I talked to Shemi a few minutes ago. The boys have worn themselves out this morning and were napping."

"I hope they don't nap too long." Rowan reached for his tea. "It took forever to get Henry to bed last night."

"It's to be expected." Tima patted his hand as she looked at him over the top of her menu. "They miss their mother."

"So what am I? Chopped liver?"

"Oh, Rowan, darling," she scoffed. "You are their best friend, but you are not their mother. You would be wise to appreciate the significance of a mother's place in a son's life. My boys, well, they will never love a woman more than they love their mother."

Rowan's brow lifted. *That's what you think*, he thought to himself. He loved his mom, but Lauren was his goddess, his North Star; his *Deja Thoris*, his Princess of Mars. He never felt complete without her. Perhaps Henry and John Carter felt the same way. She was the glue that held their little family together.

"I enjoyed your lecture," Rowan said, as he took up his own menu.

"The Egyptian Goddess Ma'at has always been my favorite," she said. Ancient Egyptian beliefs and religion were her specialties. As Dean of the Department, she could teach any class she wanted. *Whatever Fatima wanted; Fatima got.* She didn't have to teach if she didn't want to, but she loved to lecture, and she was good at it. Her classes were always booked in the main auditorium and were usually packed. Rowan even considered she might have missed her true calling. She was a performer on the dais and her students — and even a few who sneaked in that were not *her* students — were almost always transfixed by her presence.

Rowan knew he had a strong presence on camera. He'd quickly become a fan favorite when he took over the #2 spot on *The Veritas Codex*. The previous co-host, *Big Ron* Riggs, and Lauren had suffered from — *creative differences*. He had been a famous big-game hunter from Saskatoon, turned paranormal researcher. He played the role of the perpetual fly in Lauren's ointment. She lacked the ability to hide her emotions from her face, so it was clear to everyone except *Big Ron* that she loathed him. Of course, on camera, she fought to hide how much she truly hated the man. Rowan recognized the restraint on her face in the old episodes. He'd watched every episode before he started rallying to get himself hired.

Rowan could only describe his predecessor in words he couldn't use in front of his children. While Lauren used terms like "*evidence suggests that this would be ideal hunting grounds for a species such as the Sasquatch,*" Big Ron used more — colloquial terms. His catch phrases were more along the lines of, "*I seen me a ghost,*" or "*Smells kinda squatchy out here.*" But no, he and Lauren did not get along. Not one bit. Oil and water. Salt and vinegar. Now, his name was never spoken in Lauren's presence. By anyone. *Ever.*

It had been while they were working at the Stanley Hotel that he'd come straight out and called her a *witch* — well, something that rhymed with that — to her face. Ten minutes later, she was laying with her leg wrenched nearly backwards at the knee. The bone broken and sticking out from the skin, with her foot — practically hanging. While all the evidence pointed to her having been pushed down the stairs by a ghost. Rowan had another suspect. One he couldn't prove, but then again — he didn't have to. He got his revenge by taking his job and winning the girl. *And what a girl she was!*

"By the way, I wanted to tell you how much I enjoyed reading your paper on the parallels between the Egyptian and Mayan creation stories," Tima said after the waitress had taken their order. "Perhaps I shall have to visit Chichén Itzá someday for myself."

"Let me know when you want to go," Rowan said. "I have an excellent guide there that I worked with. His wife makes the best tacos in the Yucatán. I'll meet you there."

Tima smiled. "Have you thought about pursuing your PhD after you complete your Masters? You could finish in just a couple of years."

"I don't know," Rowan said. "One know-it-all in the family ought to be enough, right?"

Tima laughed at that. "The quest for knowledge is never-ending. You of all people should realize that."

"I'm not saying I'm not considering it," Rowan said. "But I can see it in Lauren's eyes. She's got the itch to go back to work."

"No one said she couldn't work," Tima said. "She didn't seem to hesitate about going to Prague."

"Oh, she hesitated all right," Rowan said. "I had to talk her into it. Thank you for your help, by the way."

"Well if she didn't want to go …" Tima started.

Rowan shook his head. "She wanted to go. Trust me. That woman doesn't do anything she doesn't want to do." He chortled. "She just needed to know the boys would be taken care of. She's never left them before."

"That is the duty of every mother," Tima said. "You are lucky to have such a devoted wife."

That made Rowan smile even more brightly. "Yes, I am."

8

"Did you see that?" Bahati's urgent call woke Jean-René from a dead sleep.

Jean-René lifted his head and looked blankly at his wife. "See what?" The sailboat was anchored in a harbor for the night, and the gentle waves were hypnotic. It'd been a long day of sailing, scuba diving and fishing, and after a supper of fresh-caught fish and a couple — okay, more than a couple — cocktails, he was exhausted.

"Jean-René." She slapped his leg. The urgency in her voice suddenly had his full attention as he sat up, looking at her. He turned his gaze towards the sky where Bahati pointed.

"What the …?" He stood and took two steps to the shelf where he'd set his camera. He'd taken a couple dozen shots of Bahati in the sunset. He lifted the camera to his face and zoomed in.

"It appeared on the horizon and shot overhead so fast I thought it was a meteorite," Bahati said. "Then it took a hard left turn and I realized it wasn't." She came and peered over his shoulder to see what he'd zoomed in on.

The object hovered 50 meters above the surface of the

sea. The moonlight gave it a shadow and illuminated one edge of the triangular shape. As they stood, mesmerized, the craft shot straight up into the air and hovered a moment as if it had stalled, then rolled over and descended in freefall, a vapor trail building behind it just before it contacted the surface of the water with an audible splash.

"*Tabernaque!*" Jean-René gasped. The water seemed to churn as the object traveled beneath its surface, then shot back up in the air, arcing across the sky, shooting over Catalina Island. The object disturbed the calm of the evening air, and the force of it created a disturbance on the surface that made the sailboat rock against its anchor line. A mist of water sprayed them, and it made Jean-René's ears pop. He grabbed the rail to steady himself. "*Merde!*"

He sank back down to his spot on the deck, running a shaking hand over his head. The velvet fuzz left on his scalp was coarse against his hand. Bahati stood at the bow, still watching the sky. Jean-René watched her for a moment, admiring the play of the moonlight on her strong features, before turning his attention back to his video. He replayed it on the small view screen.

Hours later, he was still puzzling over the video. Whatever it had been hadn't come back. Bahati kept her eyes on the dark above, even as he replayed the video over and over again. She rose and came over, running her hand along his arm. "It's late," she said. "Let's go to bed. We can't do anything about it tonight anyway."

"Hey," Jean-René said, catching her hand. She sank down beside him. "I … I don't want to turn this over to the Network."

Bahati looked surprised at his statement. "What? Why?"

Jean-René hesitated to answer. He knew she would understand, but he couldn't believe he was saying this. "I don't want them taking credit for our work," he said. "And you know

Jacob. He's dying without Rowan and Lauren. He's desperate for anything to bring the ratings up."

"So?" Bahati put a hand on his arm and leaned her head on his shoulder. "What are you going to do with it?"

Jean-René shrugged. "I think Lauren and Rowan need to see it," he said.

"But ..." Bahati sat back. "We have orders."

"I know what the Network bosses said," Jean-René wrinkled his nose and curled up his lip. "They have a lot of nerve telling *me* what I can and can't do. Rowan is *my* best friend. Lauren is *yours*. They can't order us to stay away from our best friends."

"You don't think ... that Lauren put the edict in place, do you?"

"Oh, I absolutely think she did," he said. "But I don't think she meant for it to apply to us."

Bahati chewed on her lip. "I have tried calling her, but ... she doesn't answer." Her voice faltered, and Jean-René put an arm around her. "She isn't responding to any of her social media accounts, and she's not answering any of my emails."

"Rowan, too." Jean-René hated how things had gone between them. He understood Rowan and Lauren's need for some down time. He respected Rowan for wanting to study and finish his degree. He could understand them moving halfway around the world to do it.

But it left Jean-René and Bahati in an awkward position. When the Pierces didn't renew their contracts after their tremendous success with The Escape Channel, the Toussaints were left to fend for themselves. Rowan had done his best to get the Network to take care of their friends, insisting this was just a temporary sabbatical and determined to get the *Veritas* gang back together when he finished his degree, but the Network had quickly turned on their heels, leaving the Toussaints in a tight spot.

~

THINKING BACK ON THINGS, BAHATI HAD TO WONDER WHERE the trouble initially began. She and Lauren had been friends since Bahati joined the Veritas Codex team. Over the years they had grown close and when they both got pregnant at the same time, they'd been elated. Bahati had always wanted to be a mother, but it hadn't been that easy. She'd had a hard time just getting pregnant. Lauren already had one baby before Bahati had, and she'd been envious. Two miscarriages made the envy all the more intense. Then Bahati began to have complications and ended up having to endure an emergency C-section at 29 weeks.

The baby, a big-eyed little girl they named Nyota, weighed less than four pounds at birth. Their daughter had breathing issues and spent the first three days of her life on a ventilator in the NICU. No one could tell her if her daughter would even survive. The odds were roughly 50-50.

Meanwhile, Lauren herself, was a week past due with John Carter, and had been trying her best to help her friends through their ordeal. Bahati suffered from early post-partum depression which only made things worse. Lauren made every effort to be supportive and rarely left her side. Jean-René wasn't much better off — unable to do much for his distraught wife, or his premature infant daughter and Rowan did what he could, too.

A week later, Lauren finally went into labor herself. She was already at the hospital sitting with Bahati as she waited to get into the NICU to see Nyota. Lauren was in denial and did her best not to let on. By dinner time, even Bahati had noticed the pain in her back had started to come and go every few minutes. When she said something, Lauren brushed it off and insisted she was just having Braxton-Hicks contractions.

Late in the afternoon, Lauren decided to walk the halls

until Rowan arrived. Lauren's mother had come to visit them there in Virginia and was taking care of Henry while they were otherwise occupied. When the new baby arrived she'd need her mother even more.

LAUREN HAD TOLD BAHATI THE WHOLE STORY, LONG AFTER Nyota had been released from the NICU. Rowan had taken her down to the cafeteria to get something to eat but Lauren had done little more than push her food around on her plate with her fork. He'd been watching her, noting something was *off*. Rowan narrowed his eyes at her as she shifted uncomfortably in her chair.

He'd recognized the signs of labor even before Lauren had. She'd paused what she was doing and rubbed her back or tried to stretch almost every two minutes. He began timing her.

"What?" Lauren's brow tightened as her hand went to her back. "Well, excuse me, but ... my back hurts," she snapped. "I've got this twenty pound watermelon in my lap."

"Are you sure you're not in labor?"

"Do I look like I'm in labor?" she snapped, her voice rising.

"Yes," two of the nurses at the next table over piped in, unbidden. Lauren's head whipped around, and she stared daggers in their direction.

"She's not in labor," another nurse said in a thick Indian accent. "I have been a labor and delivery nurse for forty years. I know a woman in labor. She is not in labor."

"Wanna bet?" The first nurses challenged.

TWENTY MINUTES LATER, MEDICAL STAFF WERE SCRAMBLING. The doctor on call was in the middle of a difficult delivery with twins and the poor resident had three other women come in at the same time. For a small town hospital, it was more than they were accustomed to. Rowan found himself scrubbed and gloved, delivering his own child; another boy.

Their second son came into the world weighing in at eight pounds and nine ounces. Lauren hadn't even gotten a dose of Tylenol much less an epidural. Henry's delivery had been almost as quick, but he'd been almost three pounds smaller.

JEAN-RENÉ MOORED THE SAILBOAT AT THE MARINA THE following morning, still puzzling over the strange object he'd videoed over Catalina Island. Bahati gathered their things from below deck and set them off onto the pier as Jean-René made sure everything was secured. "Did you call McKenzie?"

"I did," Bahati said. "She said Nyota had a good night, and they were having breakfast." The couple had hired a college student as their nanny, and she didn't have classes on the weekends, which allowed them some liberty again. Jean-René had always wanted a sailboat, but Bahati was terrified Nyota would fall over-board. This had been the first overnight sailing trip they had taken since he got the boat, and it had been a good chance for them to reconnect and discuss plans for the future. The strange sighting was … unexpected.

"Here," Jean-René said, taking the heaviest bag when they were ready to leave. "Speaking of breakfast, I'm starving."

"Me, too." Bahati grinned.

They hadn't gotten to the car when Jean-René's phone rang in his pocket. He reached for it. "Why is Jacob calling on a Sunday?"

"Answer it and find out." Bahati stopped in her tracks.

"Hello?" Jean-René put the phone on speaker.

"Jean-René! It's Jacob," he chirped brightly. "Hope I didn't wake you."

"No," Jean-René said. "I'm always up early on my day off."

Jacob didn't recognize his sarcasm. "Oh, good," he continued. "Look, I hate to bother you on the weekend, but I just got confirmation from the Network. The Director of Photography on one of our projects took ill and we need you to take over for the field production. We have an assignment for Bahati, too," Jacob said. "If she's interested."

"And it can't wait until tomorrow?" She piped up, leaning over the phone's speaker.

"Well," Jacob said. "I can get Jean-René on a flight tomorrow morning, if he wants to work." Bahati detected something in Jacob's tone that came across as a challenge. Since Lauren and Rowan had left the Network, he'd been more passive aggressive than usual.

"What's the project?" Jean-René asked.

"YOU'RE REALLY GOING TO LEAVE ME?"

"What choice do I have?" Jean-René snapped. "I have to go where the work is. You've got an assignment, too."

"But ..." Bahati protested. "I have to stay behind and work with a two-year-old? With no one to help me?"

"You have McKenzie," Jean-René said, shoving his clothes into his suitcase. "I'll only be gone a couple of weeks."

Tears flooded down Bahati's dark face; desperation evident in the cry that escaped the back of her throat. "This isn't fair!"

Jean-René stopped, running a hand over his head. He let out a deep breath, then turned and pulled her into his arms. "I don't like this any more than you do, *ma petite*." He kissed her head. "I can't take you with me, but I have to go."

Bahati sniffed, nodding. "I know," she managed. "But I don't like it. It isn't fair."

"No," he said. "It isn't, but what else can we do?"

"I'll talk to Jacob," Bahati said. "Maybe I can work from home."

9

D r. Eliška Kominsky called down to the antiquity's lab as soon as the American woman left. She'd had two inquiries on the mysterious page in the past week. Eliška decided she better go see for herself what the hubbub was all about. She grabbed her lab coat off the hook on the back of her office door as she passed.

The volunteer who'd brought the American woman's presence to her attention was in the hallway when she came out of her office. "Victor? Is it?"

"Vincent," he said. "Is our visitor okay?"

"She's fine," Eliška said. "Probably back at her hotel resting comfortably."

"She was as white as your coat when she staggered from the ladies' room," he said, nervously wringing the umbrella in his hands. "She forgot her umbrella."

"Just put it in my office. She'll be back. I'll make sure she gets it," Eliška said.

"Thank you, Dr. Kominsky."

"Thank you, Victor."

"Vincent."

"Vincent," she blushed. "Sorry."

"It's okay."

~

THE CHIEF CURATOR HAD RECEIVED THE VELLUM SCROLL AND taken it to the lab for a quick evaluation before it had been secured in the vault. His initial assessment had been that it was most likely a forgery, but he had other projects that took priority over a fake scroll. Eliška didn't believe in myths or legends. She knew the story of the *Codex Gigas*. Everyone in this region did.

"Dr. Zmolek?" She knocked on the door as she entered the lab.

"Ah, good afternoon, Dr. Kominsky." The assistant came into the room with a wooden crate.

"Is this the scroll everyone's losing their minds over?"

"Yes," he said, checking the inventory tag, confirming he'd gotten the right artifact. "This is it."

Eliška reached for a pair of white cotton gloves from the box on the work bench and pulled them onto her long, elegant hands. She'd gone into administration almost twenty years before and rarely got to touch a relic or artifact these days. Still, she remembered how it worked. Zmolek would do a majority of the handling, but she was still required to wear gloves … just in case. One never wanted to contaminate a piece especially before it had been rigorously examined. Even then, human skin cells and oils could contribute to significant deterioration of most antiquities. It was especially true for any biological object, like vellum.

It took several minutes for the curator to document the examination and longer still before he removed it from the crate. Eliška impatiently waited for him to unroll it onto the work board. There were clips at each corner of the table he used to secure it without damaging it.

He stepped back and allowed the director a moment to

inspect the piece. He handed her a magnifying glass as he moved to the other side of the table.

"While this piece is exquisite, there's nothing specifically that calls this out as a lost page from the *Codex*," Zmolek said. "There are a few similarities, but nothing definitive."

"What are the similarities?" she asked, moving to get a better look.

"The size of the vellum is the first similarity. It appears to be torn along the *folio recto*. It's approximately 2.5 centimeters off centered, which suggests a portion of the page is actually missing. We are confident it is vellum, animal skin, but we haven't tested it yet to determine the species." He flipped a switch and the worktable illuminated. The light shone through the vellum as a soft ivory glow. In the top right corner, an image appeared in red and blue ink. This was a symbol of some sort. It looked like an S with an infinity symbol bisecting it.

"What's this?" Eliška asked. "Is this a… a water mark?" She pointed to the mark.

"This appears similar to the angelic sigil for *truth*," Zmolek said. "The writing in the known pages of the *Codex* is Latin; meticulously handwritten, according to the legend, by a single scribe. This part is not written in Latin, I don't recognize the language or the iconography, but otherwise, the page appears remarkably similar to images I've seen of the Devil's Codex. But again, I haven't had a chance for a cryptographer to analyze it."

"If it's not Latin, what is it?" She studied the writings. Not only was the writing not in Latin, English or Greek or any of the twenty other languages she was familiar with, the font itself was completely foreign to her. She had never studied the *Codex* in question though.

"Again, a cryptographer might have an idea, but … I remain as confused as you." He took the magnifying glass from her as she folded her arms across her body. "The *Codex* has a unified look throughout. The nature of the writing is unchanged from beginning to end. While legend says the fallen monk completed his grimoire overnight with help from the Devil, scientists currently think that it could not have been completed by a single person in less than twenty years."

"So they think a single person completed it?"

"Hard to say, but it is rare that a person's handwriting does not evolve over time. In the Codex, it is consistent from beginning to end."

"So how would this page have disappeared from the Codex? Presuming it's authentic, of course."

"We know there are several pages missing," he said. "The Devil's Codex contains every known text at the time, including almost the entire Christian Bible, but the beginning of Genesis is absent. There was supposed to be a page with the *Devil's Prayer* along with several pages of apocalyptic prophesies. These are among the known missing pages, but there's no complete list of the contents, missing or otherwise."

Eliška turned as the door behind her opened. Two men in black coats entered. "This area is off limits to—"

The first man was tall, with a head full of pale blond hair that was disheveled; eyes like ice water. The second was a villainous-looking creature, reminiscent of the legendary vampire. *Masa?* "Who are you?" She took a step back, recognizing the American scientist's description of the man who'd summoned her to Prague. Her breath sucked in and froze in her chest as he paused, an arm's reach away from her. His black eyes were piercing. The blond man came around behind her and caught Eliška by the arms, turning her around. She gasped, feeling a hand wrap around her throat. Her body turned to lead, and she couldn't move. The black-draped figure moved past her, turning his attention to the curator, who stood; dumfounded.

Zmolek took a few steps back and gasped before the most gut-wrenching sound echoed through the room. Eliška wanted to scream but the blond man put his gloved hand over her mouth; so hard she almost couldn't breathe. Blood splattered her white coat, and she could feel it strike her skin. The Curator's body hit the tile floor with a thud. He didn't have a chance to cry for help any more than she had.

The crunch of bone and tearing of flesh reverberated in her ears as Eliška pinched her eyes shut. It was like listening to a wild animal feeding. She felt her heart thundering. Her pulse pounded in her ears. He took her hand in his; his hand cold. She could see the smear of blood on her white coat out of the corner of her eye as he moved. He came to stand in front of her, wiping his chin on his sleeve, smearing blood across his face. His teeth flashed behind ruby-coated lips. "Do you know who I am?" His words trailed out into a hiss as his goon removed his hand from her mouth. She was too frightened to cry out; too terrified to struggle. He ran a bloody nail down her cheek. "I am called by many names. *Asmodeus. Shiva. Abaddon. Al-Shaitan. Antra Mainyu. Diablos, The Slanderer. Beelzebub, The Lord of the Flies. Ballein. Mephistopheles. The Evil One. Nergal. Lucifer. Satan, the Father of Lies.* I am … the *Dark One; Enlil … the Great Deceiver.* I am the Morning Star. But I was the one who was deceived. Once, I was a god, demoted to the Prince of the Grigori — the Watchers. I was deceived by those whom I loved most dearly."

"Deceived? By whom?" she gasped, fighting to breathe. The monster moved as his henchman took a step back. He brought her into his arms, and the goon seemed to fade into the void around them.

"My father, my brother … my own race." His raspy breath was cold on her skin. "I bore my father's standard into battle. But when the tides turned, I was tricked by sorcery into taking arms against the All-Father. He cast me aside, giving my brother dominion over what I had created. I was banished into the world of mortal men, where I was forgotten. My brethren fell from glory as well. Here we dwell in exile. Forgotten. Betrayed." His hand cupped her cheek, and she could feel the blood, sticky against her skin. "We found ourselves bewitched by mortal women who seduced us." His other hand ran down her arm. "We lay with them against our will and found ourselves cursed forever. The spawn of our sin — the *Nephilim* — became heroes to the mortals. As they were exalted, we were hunted, tortured, and tormented by humans who feared us. Our own children turned on us. We were betrayed in Heaven. We were persecuted on Earth. I knew what we had to do." He tipped her head to the side and let his lips trace the thin flesh behind her ear. His breath was icy on her skin, but she could smell the brimstone burning in his soul. She trembled but could not move. "We raised an army to destroy The All-Father who betrayed us. It was a jihad against the gods; a fight we felt assured we could win."

"P-p-please." She managed a weak whisper. Her cry made the monster smile as he brushed her hair aside.

"They all betrayed us, and the All-Father smote us with his hand. His wrath was cruel and without mercy. I was cast here … into Purgatory, banished. Here, I have plotted my revenge. The time comes now for my plan to be executed. When my book is restored and the stars align, the spells can be cast. The fall of the gods and mankind is at hand."

"Please." Her eyes begged. "I … I'll do … whatever you want…" A single tear ran down her cheek. Her body seized and a flood washed down her legs and pooled on the floor beneath her. The Dark One glanced down, realizing she'd voided her bladder. The terror his grasp elicited fed him even more and a wicked laugh erupted from him, as sobs pealed from her chest. He gazed upon her with a moment of sympathy. His thumb grazed her cheek as he wiped the tear away.

"Anything?"

"Any … thing …" She gasped, desperate to save her own life.

"I only ask one thing of you, my servant." He took her

into his arms and held her to his body, tracing the outline of her chin with his sharp claw. She yielded, melting into him. She had meant what she said. She'd do anything to avoid the same fate as her curator. He leaned in and whispered into her ear. His icy breath stung. "Die for me."

His claws splayed and her flesh tore beneath his hand. Blood gushed from her throat. It filled her lungs. Her breath came in labored gurgles. He released the spell holding her. Her weak hands went to her throat. She collapsed to the floor. Despite her best efforts to staunch the bleeding, it was of no use. The Dark Lord knew where to cut and how deep. It seemed to take forever for Death to come. In truth, the director bled out in a matter of seconds.

The Deceiver stepped over her dead body as his accomplice collected the page from his master's book. He rolled it back up, returning it to the wooden case. He latched it shut, handing it to the Dark One who transformed into a more presentable figure. "Do the work I have commanded of you, my faithful Simon. When my battle is won, your reward will be the greatest of them all," Enlil said. He waved his hand and released his minion from this place in time and space, returning him to another task that needed to be done in his name.

Pausing at the mirror in the hall, the monster checked his visage and was bemused by the face that greeted him. He dabbed away a speck of blood from the corner of his lips with his thumb. Then, with the box tucked under his arm, he walked out of the museum. Doors locked behind him as he passed. Lights dimmed. Even the rain parted to allow him passage as he stepped outside and disappeared into the effluvium of nothingness.

10

Lauren wasn't sure what'd happened. She might have passed out, or … they could have drugged her. She couldn't say for sure. The throbbing in her head was exacerbated by the ache in her shoulders; the muscles in her back cramped and seized. Maybe they'd clobbered her. Lauren pushed herself up and forced her vision to clear.

She sat inspecting the room, realizing she couldn't possibly stand. Not yet. She struggled to stay calm. The room, she brought her focus back to the small space, was painted a pale off-white, unadorned with any decorative furnishings. She was sitting on a bench that was spartan to say the least. There was a table and two chairs by the window. The blinds were closed.

That gave Lauren a thought that required her to stand. She did and felt her knees tremble beneath her. She allowed a moment to steady herself before she took the first tentative step, then all but staggered to the table. Lauren reached for the cord to the blinds and raised them. Outside, the shade of night had fallen She had a view of the city below, at least ten stories up. All hopes of escape were lost. The windows were not designed to be opened, and considering the industrial chair, she knew she would never be able to throw one through the window. She wasn't even certain she could crack it.

The other tall buildings around her gave her a sense of place. There were cranes rising above two buildings and she'd seen them before. The driver who'd taken her from the museum to the café had taken her on a tour of the old district, and she'd seen downtown from a distance. If she could get out, she at least knew which direction to go to find her way back to her hotel. There was a metro station entrance at almost every corner in the city center, and taxis weren't hard to find either. Lauren just needed to get out.

She went to the one door into the room and tested the knob. Hope shriveled in her heart as it refused to turn. It was locked from the outside. Like a caged animal, she paced a few breathless moments as her mind raced. *How could she possibly escape? What did those men want? Who were they?*

The door opened as if in answer to the racing questions in her mind. She was tempted to charge them, hoping to catch them off guard, but when all three filled the doorway, she knew it was futile.

"Take a seat, Dr. Grayson." The tallest one ordered. He was an older man, possibly in his early fifties. His hair was thin, dark; probably dyed. He reminded her of her high school algebra teacher. His formal tone and deep voice gave him the power of authority. Lauren backed up and sank down on the bench. She said nothing. *Let them make the first move.*

"Over here," he said matter of factly as he walked over to the table and pulled out a chair for her. She looked over at the others. The one on the right was older, more muscular, and seasoned. His hair had probably been sandy blond when he was a boy. Now, his hair was pale-blond, not quite white. What stood out on him was the color of his eyes. The diluted blue was closer to the color of ice than water, but he had a wicked countenance that made her recoil. He stared her down as if in challenge, daring her not to obey so he could intercede. The third man was shorter, balding, with glasses and a sour disposition. He wasn't as buff as the other, but he was wiry, and she felt the need for caution as she gaged her enemies. While the first one might pull a gun on her, this one probably had a knife in his pocket. He probably had the skills to use it, too.

"If you please, madame." The leader spoke with a saccharin-kindness that was bitter to Lauren's senses. Still, she rose and walked on unsteady legs, stoically, to the chair he held out for her, sinking as gracefully as she could. He pushed the chair back in as she sat down at the table. He took the seat across from her, staring her down.

The leader reached into his coat and took out a tattered photograph. The picture was grainy, like a grab from a security camera. The image was black and white. Lauren recognized the man at once. "Do you know this man, Dr. Grayson?"

Her mouth had gone dry, and she swallowed hard, nodding. "He came to my house in Cairo. He said his name was Dr. Masa."

"Did he say why he came to see you? What he wanted from you?"

"He said he worked for the museum at the university here. Something about an ancient text he wanted my help with." She took a deep breath. Suddenly she felt weak. *Something told her not to tell them everything. She would appear to cooperate, but …*

"Why would he come to you for help?"

"I have a knack for languages," she said. "He wanted me to translate."

The man glanced ever so quickly to the men by the door. Lauren noticed the look passing between them. "When did you last see him?"

"He took me to the hotel after we landed in Prague." She noticed the leer that crossed the man's face and realized how that must sound. She refused to give him the pleasure of confirming his suspicions. She didn't have to explain anything to anyone, except Rowan. He didn't need her explanation. "He said the University was paying the bill and all my expenses were covered. I was supposed to meet with him this morning at the museum, but …" She swallowed back the bile rising in her throat. "They'd never heard of him."

"I don't believe your story, Dr. Grayson. You would be wise to tell us the truth."

"But that is the truth." The room spun. She clutched the edge of the table to steady herself. "Who are you people? I don't even know you. Why would I have any reason to lie to you?"

"We work for a very … powerful man," he said. "One who answers to no one. One who has given us the authority to do whatever it takes to get the answers we seek."

"Well, you have them," Lauren said. "I don't know anything else." She crossed her arms and sat back in her chair like a defiant child.

The man narrowed his eyes at her and pounded his fist on the table. Lauren startled but did not yelp. She remained stoic on the outside. Inside, her mind was spinning. Her guts were in knots and her heart was galloping against her sternum. The racing of her mind kept her from making sense of it all.

"Answer the question truthfully, Dr. Grayson. I will not ask it again."

For a split second she wanted to retort, "*What do you know of truth*?" But she held her tongue. "I have been truthful." The words came out so easily. She *had* told the truth.

"You are a liar," he snapped.

"Then we have nothing more to discuss," Lauren said, crossing her arms.

"Dr. Grayson," the man across from her said. He lifted his hand, and she noticed the blond one at the door start toward her. The leader waved him off. "What was the text this man wanted you to see?"

Lauren paused a moment before she answered. "He didn't

say." She swallowed hard. "He only said it was torn from an ancient manuscript. 14th century, I think he said. He didn't give me many details."

"Yet you came from Cairo to Prague? At the bidding of a man you didn't know. To see a document … a document that he did not identify? This is what you expect us to believe?"

"It's not for me to say whether or not you believe, Mr. …" she hesitated. He didn't offer up a name. "It is the truth of things. A truth that I can't change."

"You take me for a fool, Dr. Grayson."

"You take me for an idiot and a liar, sir." Lauren retorted. "I can assure you. I am neither."

ROWAN SAT BACK FROM TIMA'S TABLE FEELING BLOATED AND miserably stuffed. The food was good, and there was plenty of it. He'd made a pig of himself, and he knew he'd pay for it later. He glanced over at John Carter sitting back in the little chair that had once belonged to one of Tima's children. John Carter stuck out his gut and put his hand on his belly. "Dat was good," he groaned in a perfect impression of his father.

"Yeah it was," Rowan laughed. "I'm going to have to go for a run before bedtime."

"Well," Tima said, standing to clear the table. "You'd best hurry. Daylight is burning, and *that* one isn't going to make it much longer." Henry was already dozing at the table. He was like his mother. He wanted to eat early and was usually ready for bed when she was.

Rowan stood and gathered up his plate, then returned for the rest of the dishes. "Rowan, darling," Tima scolded. "Go. I will take care of the dishes."

"That was a fantastic meal. The least I can do is help with the dishes." Rowan refused to be shooed away. "Besides, it's still hot outside. The boys like it when we go for a run after the sun sets." They often fell asleep in the jogging stroller, so he didn't worry too much about going for a run after their bedtime. Sometimes, it was the easiest way to get them to sleep.

"Just be careful," Tima said. "Not everyone in Egypt is as nice as your professor."

Rowan leaned down and kissed her cheek. "No one in Egypt is as nice as my professor."

"Okay guys, load up." Rowan called up to Henry and John Carter. The boys came to the top of the steep stairway and sat down. John Carter scooted down each step on his backside. Lauren had been so afraid they might take a tumble that she required this method — at least of John Carter — to come down. The boys thought it a fun game, so Henry often joined in

Henry stopped at the bottom and waited for his little brother, taking his hand as he reached the last step. Together they bounded out to the patio where Rowan had the jogging stroller set up, ready to go. They'd had it shipped over from the States because there wasn't one tall enough for him here in Egypt. The boys loved to go with Rowan when he went running and it intensified his workouts.

Rowan was never much of an athlete, even as a boy. He would have preferred to read or play video games. He liked to tinker with computers, and even built his own gaming rig while he was stationed in Afghanistan so he could play *World of Warcraft* with his buddies state-side. Of course now, he had little time for such diversions. His health had become an issue over the years of constant travel, eating in restaurants, and having to catch-as-catch-can. Now, with Lauren cooking at home — even in spite of dinners at Tima's — he was much more fit. His stomach was flat, and his muscles were visible beneath his skin. Lauren didn't seem to mind his new physique; not one bit.

Taking the boys with him to run was a bonus. They spent many happy hours together. He loved to hear them laugh. It made his heart light and made his feet feel like they were floating inches from the ground.

Lauren refused to run. She was happy to walk. She loved doing yoga or playing with the boys. She'd always been slender but having two boys had changed her physique over the years. She was still slim, but her hips were gloriously wider, and she carried a little more weight in her buttocks and chest. Rowan loved her new physique. She was never sexier to him than she was now. He didn't have to be anywhere near her for the thought of her to turn him on. It was a blessing … and a curse.

That reminded him to check his phone. "Hey, guys," Rowan said, before they got started. "Let's call Momma and see how she's doing," Rowan said.

"Momma's sick," Henry said. "Did you know Momma was sick, Daddy?"

Rowan came around to the front of the stroller and knelt down in front of his oldest. "What?" Rowan furrowed his brow. "How do you know she's sick?"

"I talked to her," Henry said. "She has another baby in her tummy."

Rowan's jaw dropped and he sputtered, taken aback. "Did she tell you?"

"No," Henry said. "I just know."

"Oh," Rowan said, standing.

"She's looking for the devil."

Henry's words struck Rowan in the gut. "What?" He sank back to one knee. "Why do you say that?"

"Cause its true," Henry said. "I heard her telling Auntie Tima she was going to Prague to find the devil."

"Actually," Rowan chose his words carefully. "She's looking

for a missing page from the Devil's Bible. When you're older, I'll tell you the whole story."

"We read the bible," Henry said. "And the Torah … and the Quran. Is that like the Quran?"

Rowan did a double take. He could not believe this kid. Henry was so smart for being such a little boy. He understood things kids his age could never imagine. "Something like that," Rowan said, mussing up his sandy-blond hair.

Rowan took out his phone and hit the speed-dial for his wife. The line rang and finally went to voice mail. "Hi, honey," Rowan chirped. It was hard to be cheerful when he missed her as much as he did right now. He did it for the boys. "Someone wanted to tell you hi."

He held out the phone for the boys. "Hi, Momma," Henry said.

"Momma! Hi! Momma! Momma, I *mith* you!" John Carter said with glee.

"Momma," Henry took the phone. "There is a nice man who is going to help you find that devil. It's okay. You can trust him. He's a good-guy." He handed the phone back to his dad. "Let's go, Daddy," Henry said, yawning.

Rowan stood, stunned; his mouth hung agape like a catfish on dry land.

11

Lauren woke up on her bed at the hotel in Prague with no memory of how she got there. She was still wearing the same outfit she'd worn to the museum, even her shoes. Her head ached, and her bladder was full. With caution, she pushed herself up onto her elbows, gaining her bearings. Once she was certain she wouldn't pass out or puke, she sat up and put her feet on the floor. She stood, surprised to find herself steadier than she'd expected. Lauren went to the lavatory and took care of her most pressing issue.

Catching a glimpse of herself in the mirror, Lauren scowled. Her hair was coming loose from its plait, and she looked like Hell. Her stomach growled and churned at the same time. She glanced at her watch and realized it was well after noon. Going back into the bedroom, she tried to gain her bearings.

Then, she remembered her purse … and her phone. The last time she'd seen either was at the café … her purse had still been on the back of the chair; her phone on the table. Searching the room, it surprised her when she found them both laying on the dresser. How they'd gotten there, she couldn't say.

She picked up her phone and found the battery had been drained. The charger was nowhere to be found. It wasn't in her purse, it wasn't by the bed, and it wasn't on the dresser.

Lauren picked up the receiver on the house phone by the bed, intending to call downstairs. The phone line was dead; no dial tone. She looked for the cord and followed it to the end. The cable was shredded. It had been yanked from the wall.

A wave of panic washed over her. She had used the phone to call room service before. The phone had been fine. *Why would someone do that?*

A mist of sweat broke out on her upper lip. Whatever was going on here, she needed to get home. Some stupid page from an ancient book no longer mattered. Rowan would be worried, and she couldn't put him through that. Not again. She needed to get home.

Lauren fumbled through the cash, counting it. Plane tickets here were cheap. She had three hundred dollars in her stash, but she also had her Mastercard. That was all she needed. Gathering up her things and cramming them into the suitcase, it took her only a scant few minutes to pack everything into her carry-on bag. She was an experienced traveler and rarely carried much. She tucked the passport, cash, and credit card into the leg pocket of her cargo pants and zipped it up.

She swung the door open with thoughts of home fresh in her mind. Lauren froze when she all but ran into a tall man in a brown trench coat with his hand lifted as if to knock. Two uniformed police officers stood behind him, their hands at the ready over their holsters.

Lauren yelped and took a step back, nearly tripping over her suitcase. He caught her hand, saving her from a nasty fall. "You scared me out of my skin." She gasped, leaning over with her hands on her knees as she caught her breath.

"Are you Lauren Pierce?" The man in the trench coat asked.

"Yes," she said, straightening. "Who are you?"

"Tomáš Kovač," he said. "Detective Kovač." He showed her his credentials. "Lauren Pierce, you are under arrest. You are being charged with murder in the first degree."

"Murder?" She stepped back. This time she did trip over her suitcase. The cops stepped in and caught her by the arms and before she knew what was happening, they had her pressed face first against the wall, with her arms wrenched behind her back. "This has to be some kind of mistake."

"You will have your chance to explain at the station."

THE *ADVOKÁT*, OR THE PUBLIC DEFENSE ATTORNEY ASSIGNED TO her case — a stern older woman with her dyed black hair pulled back tight — explained her rights to her after she'd been processed into custody. Now, she sat in front of the detective who'd arrested her, feeling numb and terribly afraid. The detective was of average height, not much taller than Lauren herself. He might have been in his mid-thirties or early forties based on the tinge of gray that framed his pitch-black hair at his temples. Those Slavic features were undeniable, from the heavy black brows to the wide bridge of teeth behind his congenial, but serious smile. His eyes were as blue as a summer sky.

"Ms. Pierce," he said in preamble, but she cut him off.

"*Doctor* Pierce." She corrected him.

"My apologies, *Doctor* Pierce," he said, emphasizing her title. "Can you tell me where you were yesterday afternoon?"

"Yesterday was a really bad day." Lauren sat back in her chair, her arms folded over her body as a shield. Her palm came to her face, and she rested her forehead in it. Her gaze went to his black patent shoes beneath the table. "It started out okay. I had an appointment at the museum to meet with Dr. Masa. He came to see me in Cairo a few days ago and asked me to come take a look at an artifact that had been surrendered to the museum some months back. When I got to the museum, I found out there was no one named Dr. Masa who worked there."

"Who did you talk to at the museum?"

"A volunteer," she said. "Vincent."

"Vincent Bača?"

"I didn't get his last name," Lauren said.

"Who else did you talk to?"

"The director, Dr. Kominsky. I think that was her name."

"Anyone else?"

Lauren shook her head, looking up at him.

"Did anything … unusual happen while you were at the museum?"

"Other than getting stood up by a guy who flew me from Cairo to Prague and put me up in a nice hotel with a driver for the week?" She scowled. "I did get sick while I was there, but no, the weirdness began after I left the museum."

"Sick?"

"I'm pregnant with my third child," she said. "I have been suffering from twenty-four-hour morning sickness. I … I passed out." The detective's brow lifted slowly. "I woke up in Dr. Kominsky's office."

"Did you speak to her before … or after you passed out."

"After," she said. "But now that you mention it …" Lauren swallowed hard. "I … there's a painting … just as you come in the museum. It … it looked like …"

"Like what?"

"Like me." Lauren held his gaze while he considered her.

Kovač sat back in his chair. He cast a shaded gaze at her with those bright blue eyes. She could feel him trying to burn through her to see if she was speaking the truth. Finally he sat up and opened the manilla folder in front of him. Inside was a picture. The image was a screen grab from a video. Lauren suddenly had a flash of déjà vu. "Do you recognize this woman?"

Lauren picked up the image. Her head swam as she lay it down. "That looks like … me," she said. "It must be me."

"Why do you say that?"

Lauren looked down. "She's wearing my clothes." The woman in the video walked toward the exit with the hotel's borrowed umbrella in her hand. Her wide stride suggested she was in a hurry.

He placed another picture in front of her. The grainy security camera image showed a man's back, mostly in shadow as he entered a room. The image was so poor, and the lighting so dim it was impossible to make out any of the features. "Recognize this man?"

Lauren studied the photo but shook her head, handing it back. "I can't tell anything from this picture. I can only assume it's a man, since you mention that it is."

"Is this your accomplice?"

"My what?" Lauren recoiled, the image falling from her hand.

"Dr. Pierce, where were you at approximately 4:00 pm yesterday afternoon?"

"I left the museum before noon," Lauren said. "The driver took me on a tour of the city. I wasn't hungry until later. He suggested a café he knew, and he dropped me off there. It was just a few blocks from my hotel, so I told him I would walk back when I was done. He insisted I call him if I changed my mind. I put his number in my cell phone."

"And what time did you go back to your hotel?"

"I didn't," Lauren said. "As I was drinking my tea, three men in black coats approached me and told me I had to go with them. I tried to …" She stopped. "They shoved me into the back of a van. I think … I think they must have drugged me. I don't remember much of what happened after that."

This new bit of evidence made his brow lift even higher. "Where did they take you?"

"I'm not quite sure." Lauren swallowed hard and folded her hands on the table in front of her. She leaned heavily on the edge. "I don't remember. I know the building was tall; ten stories at least. The room was basic … like this one. They asked me questions about why I was here. They showed me a picture of Dr. Masa and asked me questions about him. They accused me of lying when I answered them. I told them the same thing I told you … because it's the truth. But, I did not tell them about the artifact Masa brought me here to see."

"Which was?"

Lauren hesitated. She stood and turned her back on him a moment. It gave her a second to think. She didn't know who she could trust at this point.

"Dr. Pierce." He stood behind her. "I will give you a few moments to gather your thoughts. May I get you something? Some tea, perhaps?"

"That would be nice," Lauren said over her shoulder. "Thank you."

ROWAN HAD THE BOYS IN BED SHORTLY AFTER THEY GOT HOME. John Carter had fallen asleep during his run. Henry had dozed off but was wide awake. He got himself ready for bed, brushed his teeth and climbed into bed unbidden. "Will you read to me again tonight, Daddy?" he asked.

Rowan was exhausted, but he couldn't refuse. He barely got through a chapter before Henry drifted off.

Charles Pierce had been the one who introduced his son to Heinlein when he was a teenager. Normally, Rowan's dad preferred military dramas and legal thrillers, but knowing Rowan's love for sci-fi, he'd become a fan of the controversial author. *The Moon is A Harsh Mistress* had been Rowan's favorite growing up. He loved the character Wyoming Knot. She was tough as nails and helped lead a revolution. Everyone called her Wyo. Maybe that was why he liked Indiana Jones so much. *Indy. Wyo.* Both place names shortened. Both brave and bold, kind of like his wife.

Rowan went to the shower and turned on the water, letting it warm as he peeled out of his clothes. He was sweaty and the fact that he could smell his own funk was sufficient evidence that he needed to get into the shower before he collapsed into bed.

It had been a long day, but it had been a good one. The only void was the need to hear his wife's voice. At least once before he'd been visited by her in the night when he'd yearned for her. He yearned for her now and prayed she'd find him in the dark. Perhaps it had been a dream that one time in Mexico, but it was the dream by which all others were measured. He remembered every detail of her touch and how it made him feel. He also remembered the disconcerting feeling of waking up and discovering it was only a dream. There was no possible way she could have been there.

After he toweled off and pulled on his pajama pants he climbed into their king-sized bed and scooted over into the middle of it. She'd put clean sheets on it before she'd left, but her pillow still smelled of her and he clutched it to his chest as sleep came for him.

THE NIGHT WAS A RESTLESS ONE. HE TOSSED AND TURNED. More than once he woke up because he thought he heard the boys. He finally gave up some time before four o'clock. He stopped by the boys' room to check on them. Finding them both sound asleep, he left them to their peaceful slumber. He went downstairs to put on some coffee and make himself something to eat.

Rowan didn't have classes on Friday, but there were several reading assignments he needed to catch up on, so he fixed himself a sandwich and carried his coffee cup and plate to the sofa in the living room. Turning on the television, he adjusted the volume so as not to wake the boys. As he ate, he put on his glasses and picked up his textbook. By sunrise, the coffee pot was empty. He put on a second pot and returned to his studies while it brewed.

Rowan found himself nodding as he tried to focus on the pages. The words began to run together. Closing his eyes while he waited for the coffee, he thought about Lauren and decided to call her when it got a little later. She was probably still sleeping. Just thinking about her made a smile curl in the corners of his cheeks. He missed her, but hoped she was having a productive trip.

HENRY KNEW HE WASN'T SUPPOSED TO DO IT. HE ALSO KNEW he had to. His momma had a mission she had to fulfill. Still, he didn't like it. His father would be furious if he knew what Henry was capable of. It was bad enough that he left his room in the middle of the night, but he also left his own place in time. This was a risk, but one he had to take.

The monastery smelled old. It *was* old. The air was musty, damp and reeked of smoke and incense. Like most monasteries, the monks made their own vintages of wine as well as ale. The smell of fermentation wafted up from the cellar. Henry moved cautiously down the stone-tiled hallway, keeping to the shadows, hearing the sounds of music coming from the chapel. He didn't have his mother's gift for languages, but she'd been teaching him Latin and Greek, so he recognized the words of the song they sang.

The song was a prayer and the harmonious voices resonated through the building. Henry liked music, and he liked the blend of the men's voices. His mother didn't think of herself as a good singer, but his dad was. He could play the guitar, too. Henry loved it when he plugged in his electric guitar and played rock n' roll, but he didn't do that very often. Their neighbors didn't like it. The last time his dad had played his electric guitar had been at a party at the University.

"Well, this is odd," a voice behind him said softly, startling Henry. He froze. "I don't remember any of the brothers being so … short." Henry turned. A portly friar waddled up behind him, limping. "Who are you?"

"My name is Henry Jones Pierce, sir." The child bowed respectfully.

"Aren't you a little young for the brotherhood?"

"I'm almost six," Henry said. "But I'm not here to be a monk."

"Then what are you doing here, if I may be so bold as to ask, Master Pierce."

"I'm looking for a monk," he said. "One who's going to write a great book."

"Will just any monk do, or is this one monk in particular?"

Henry hesitated. "It's just one monk, sir. But … his name has been lost to history."

"There are over fifty brothers in service to Our Lord here, young master."

"We think his name was Herman. They called him Herman the Recluse. By chance, is there a brother here by that name?"

The monk's eyes crossed at the tip of his nose. "Well, young Master Pierce, my name is Brother Herman, but if they call me a recluse, they've never said it to my face … though I do prefer to spend my time alone, writing and making vellum."

"Oh," Henry said. The child blinked back his surprise. "I thought perhaps they had already walled you up."

"Excuse me?"

"You've done …or will do … something to get yourself in trouble and they're going to wall you up," he said, innocently enough. "At least that's how the story goes."

"I've done nothing." The monk sank down onto his heels to get to Henry's level. "I have strived to live a pious life. My confessions are quite boring, if truth be told."

"The story says you wrote a book with all of human knowledge contained within, in a single night…" Henry said.

"A single night?" The monk scowled. "I have been working on just such a project since I entered the religious life, but … I would have to sell my soul to the Devil to finish it in a single night, even with what I have already completed."

"That's what the story says you do," Henry said.

"I would never," the monk sputtered. "I am a man of God."

"I can help you," Henry said. "But the story has to be passed down through the generations, or we'll mess up history."

The monk considered him for a moment. "How is it that you know this? You are just a child."

"Jesus said great words come from the mouths of babes?"

"It's from the book of Psalms." The monk did a double take. "You're not a witch, are you?"

"Think of me as more of … of a messenger … like Gabriel," he said. The monk seemed satisfied with his explanation. "Can you show me how much of the book you have finished?"

The monk rose. "I am a man of faith, and something in my heart tells me, I must have faith and trust in you."

"I will do everything I can to help you, but I won't ask for your soul in return," Henry said. "I just need you to add one thing to your book."

"Do you know how many years it will take to complete the task at hand? Are you considering the sacred life, young man?"

"I have studied all the faiths of the world but, I kinda want to be a scientist like my parents, when I grow up. But, I have some knowledge of *science* now that will help us complete our task before I have to get home in the morning. But you can't tell anyone. Can you do that?"

"I believe in miracles, too." The monk nodded. "Come, let us go to my study."

"HEY." A SMALL VOICE WOKE ROWAN. HE SAT UP, STARTLED. "Hey, Daddy?" He looked around the room, feeling foggy headed.

John Carter crawled up in his lap and sat down in the middle of his textbook. "Daddy? Are you *sweeping*?"

Rowan was suddenly awake. "Yeah, buddy." John Carter made himself comfortable in his lap. Rowan pulled the book out from under him. He put his arm around the boy, leaning down, kissing his head. "You're up early."

"You, too." He tugged at the feet of his footie-pajamas. "I *hungy*."

"You're hungry?" Rowan said. "I fed you yesterday." It was a running joke.

"I *hungy*," he moaned, a giggle in his voice.

"So, what do you want?"

"Food!" That was Lauren's standard response.

"My favorite." Rowan's said as he kissed his son on the head. He looked so much like Lauren.

"Pancake, Daddy?" John Carter asked. "*Pwease* make pancake?"

That did sound good. "I think I can manage pancakes." Rowan stood and put his youngest up on his shoulders. John Carter loved it when he did that. He liked being tall. "What else?"

"*Eggses!*"

"Want bacon, too?"

"Yes!"

"Sounds awesome."

ROWAN HAD JUST SAT DOWN WITH A COLD CUP OF COFFEE AND a plate of steaming hot cakes when his phone chirped. *Finally!* He went and picked it up off the coffee table. The alert identified it as a text from Lauren. *Thank God.*

Made it to Prague. Nice city. You'd like it here. Miss you. Kiss the boys for me. Save one for yourself.

"Well, it's about time," he said more to himself than anyone. He sat back down across from John Carter. The toddler had quite the appetite. He had a huge pancake half devoured. Rowan looked down at his own plate and realized, it was *his* pancake the boy had absconded with.

"Hey," Rowan scowled playfully. "Where'd my pancake go?"

"*Heny* eats it," he said with a full mouth. It took a moment for Rowan to translate.

"Henry ate my pancake?" Rowan looked at him dubiously. John Carter could eat. They teased that his middle name was *What Else Can I Have?*

John Carter grinned as syrup dripped off his chin. "More pancake."

"Yeah." Rowan got up. "I'm going to have to make more pancakes."

The next batch was ready when Henry came down the stairs dragging his favorite blanket. He looked groggy. "Hey, slugger," Rowan chirped. Two pots of coffee had him pinging off the walls. "Want a pancake?"

"Sure." Henry fell face first onto the sofa, pulling his blanket up over him.

"Hey, what's up?" Rowan asked, hesitating.

"I've been up all night." His voice was muffled when he didn't lift his head to speak. Rowan had a hard time understanding him.

"Bad dreams?"

"I had to do something for Momma," Henry said, sitting up. "That woman." His exasperated tone sounded familiar. At least once in his life Rowan had said it himself. *Okay, maybe twice.* Henry shook his head. "I hope there's coffee."

"Coffee? Since when do you drink coffee?"

"I'm starting today," he said. "How do you put up with her?"

Rowan scowled. "What are you talking about?"

"My momma," Henry got up and dragged himself over to the table, climbing up into his chair. "If I ever have a wife, she's going to be a lot less trouble."

"Henry," Rowan started to snap, but he caught himself and took a deep breath. "Please tell me what on earth you are talking about."

"You know." He shrugged. "Taking care of *Momma stuff.*"

Yeah. *Momma stuff.* He knew all about that. "Did you talk to your mother? Did she call?"

"Yeah." He yawned, reaching for a piece of bacon on a plate in the middle of the table. He had to get up on his knees to reach it.

"Is she okay?"

"She's fine," Henry said, shoving it into his mouth. "But she's got some explaining to do."

Rowan stood with his hands on his hips, gazing down at his bare feet. "Doesn't she always?"

12

L auren paced in the narrow cell. Her brain was throbbing in her skull and her body ached. She couldn't get comfortable sitting or lying, and she was too agitated to do either, so she walked the floor, hoping her headache would abate.

She chewed her thumbnail down to the quick and was no closer to figuring out her plight than she was hours before. A rattle of metal-on-metal grated on her raw nerves. It drew her from her thoughts. She turned on her heel. The detective stood at the door. "Detective Kovač?"

"I just got the lab report back," he said, signaling the guard to unlock the door. "There was no blood on your shoes, or your clothes."

"No surprise here." Lauren forced a smile. "I swear. I'm sure there's been some kind of mistake."

"We checked the video camera at the café where you said you were abducted."

"And?"

"The video shows you sitting down with a cup of tea, but the film appeared to glitch and when it was restored you were gone."

Of course it did. "If you need proof of where I was, I need my purse."

"Your purse?"

"I took a tour at a cathedral before I stopped for tea. My ticket is in my purse. I think it had a time and date stamp. It'll prove I'm not lying. I did not go back to the museum, and I didn't do whatever it is you think I did."

"Come with me, Dr. Pierce," he said. "I want to show you something."

The door groaned as it swung open. Lauren had to fight the urge to bolt from the cell. She followed him calmly. Lauren was disappointed when he led her back to the room where she'd been questioned earlier.

"Please, be seated." She wanted to stand but complied with his request. He made a *request*, rather than a demand. If he was going to offer her any courtesy, she was committed to reciprocate. He took the tablet out from under his arm. "I have seen your work, Dr. Pierce. I suspect you are not easily upset by disturbing images?"

Lauren was a bit taken aback when he set a tablet in front her and cued up a video with a tap. She muttered, "No. Not usually."

The images came from the security camera system in the museum, and she realized where the earlier screen grabs had come from. She recognized the backdrop at once. The images were relatively clear, considering the source.

The video showed her walking into the museum, shaking out her umbrella. She set it aside as she continued through the front hall into the main gallery. It showed her stop at the painting, then her encounter with the volunteer in the lobby. A second camera view caught her in the hallway headed to the ladies room, and even her spell of sickness. She didn't remember that part. She certainly didn't remember being carried by the security guard into the director's office. It also showed her leaving the museum after she was denied access to the document she'd been summoned to see.

Lauren turned her gaze up to him as he stood watching over her shoulder. "Keep watching." He nodded as he stood watching her response. A third camera view caught her as she entered the antiquities examination room. The door remained ajar and only part of the room's interior was visible. A moment later something moved as shadows passed across the doorway inside. Suddenly there was a gush of blood that sprayed across the room with an unreal force. The lights flickered, and even the camera seemed to suffer the same type of failure as the image blinked with interference of some sort.

Everything seemed to go dark. The lights came back on, and it appeared that she walked from the room with a wooden box under her arm. The spectral version of herself even looked at the camera with a wry grin as she stopped at a mirror and ran a thumb across her face, smearing what appeared to be blood across her cheek. Then the camera flickered, and the image froze.

Dots danced in her eyes. She blinked back the euphoria. Her brain knew that it wasn't her, but she saw it just as clear as anyone else. She knew now why she'd been arrested. "It wasn't me," she managed, just before she bolted from the chair and collapsed over the trash can, heaving.

DETECTIVE KOVAČ MADE HER A CUP OF HOT TEA AND GOT her a cool cloth. She sat up from where she lay on a cot in the detective's lounge. She moved slowly to keep the room from spinning, taking the cup. He sat down in a chair beside her and pressed the cloth to the back of her neck. "I'm very sorry if I upset you," he said.

"The only thing that upset me was seeing someone who looked like me ... do something like *that*." Lauren blew on the hot liquid to cool it, welcoming the warmth that seeped through the Styrofoam to her ice-cold hands. "I don't know who that woman was. Someone …someone is trying to make it look like I did … something I didn't do."

"You don't happen to have a twin sister, do you?" Kovač moved the cloth to the exposed skin on her back. The cool cloth felt good even as she chilled.

"I have brothers," Lauren said. "But no. No sisters." Her brother had asked her to treat Kitty Donovan as a sister, and Lauren had, but she was currently assigned to DC to work with the UN on the Great Peace Accord. No one would ever confuse Kitty Donovan for Lauren Pierce.

"Are you sure?" Kovač asked, bringing her out of her thoughts. He tried to laugh, but even Lauren could sense it was an empty joke.

"Yeah, I think I'd know if I had sisters." She took the cloth from his hand and pressed it to her face, holding her head a moment.

"Better?" he asked when she lowered the cloth and turned her attention back to the tea.

"Yes, thank you." She took a sip; the tea scalded her tongue. Still, it was comforting.

"Tell me more about these men you said took you from the café? What did they look like?" he asked, looking dubious.

"They didn't look like cops," Lauren said. "I have a friend in the FBI. They didn't look like Feds either, that's for sure."

"Describe them," he said as he stood and walked over to a table nearby. He sat down and took out his note pad and his pen and waited for her to start.

"One was tall, with pale blond hair, pale skin, blue eyes. One was shorter, stockier. Balding. The other was older but slender. He looked more like a teacher or a salesman."

"How about their clothing?" He jotted notes.

"Pretty nondescript. Dark pants, black shirts … black jackets."

"Were their clothes all the same?"

Lauren paused for a moment thinking. "Pretty much."

"Like a uniform?"

"Perhaps." She shook her head skeptically. "But not like any uniform I've ever seen."

"How did they speak?"

Lauren shrugged.

"An accent?"

"Maybe, yeah," Lauren said. Her gift of the ancient All-Language — an ability that helped her understand all human language — made everyone's speech sound familiar, so she had to really think about accents and vocal mannerisms. "At least one stood out, but I couldn't place it. But how they spoke was …very formal now that you mention it. Not Czech … maybe German or Swiss. Highly educated, at least the one that was the ringleader."

"Did they say what they wanted?" Kovač was a patient inquisitor.

Lauren told him everything she'd told them to the best of her recollection. She didn't know why they were interested in her, or how they knew her, or why they wanted to talk to her. She also didn't know how she'd gotten back to her hotel.

"I think they may have drugged me," she said. "I was barely awake when you showed up and arrested me."

"You mentioned that," he said. "Did you eat or drink anything while you were …"

"No," she said. "Not that I remember."

"Let me see." He reached for her sleeve and pushed it up her arm, inspecting her skin, looking for signs of a puncture. Lauren rolled up the sleeves of her shirt to aid in the search. "I don't see anything."

"Other than a bad case of cottonmouth and a brain-splitting headache, I feel okay."

"Aside from the morning sickness," he said, eyeing her as he shook his head sympathetically. "I'm going to have the lab tech come up and draw blood for a tox-screen, just in case; for your safety … and that of your child."

Lauren didn't protest. She realized she hadn't allowed herself to be concerned for the safety of her child. The fact that whatever they did to her might hurt her baby was more than she could bear to handle at the moment. Thinking on it now left her with a lump in her throat and butterflies in her gut.

"Tell me more about this document, this doctor …" He paused to look at his notes. "Dr. Masa who brought you here."

"I'm going to tell you something I didn't tell those thugs." Lauren wasn't sure why, but she felt like she could trust him, even though he seemed to doubt her every word. He was kind enough, even refilling her tea while she talked. "The document was alleged to be a lost page from a book known as the Devil's Bible."

The detective looked up from his notebook. The features of his face went perfectly placid. His lip twitched and she noticed he had dark circles under his eyes and his five o'clock shadow seemed to darken with his mood. "The Codex Gigas?"

"So, you've heard of it?"

He swallowed hard. "Few here have not."

"Then you know the legend?"

He nodded and laid his pen down. The detective sat back and crossed his arms, tucking them under his armpits. Taking a deep breath, he said, "And Dr. Masa told you the museum had a missing page?"

Lauren nodded. Clearly his gears were turning. She gave him time to process it.

"Did they have the page?"

"The Director said it was locked up in storage and she'd have to have the archivist bring it up," Lauren said. "She said it'd take twenty-four hours or so to get it." Lauren stood and paced a moment. "I was supposed to come back another time. She was going to call."

Kovač's brow twitched. "Wonder if they really had it?"

"I don't have any reason to think they didn't," Lauren said.

The detective eyed her for a long moment. "Dr. Pierce, please allow me to apologize for having to bring you in like this. Clearly, we have reason to believe you are involved, but I had to eliminate you as a suspect. While the video is damning, the evidence contradicts everything I've seen." He nodded to the tablet. "Video can be manipulated. I recognize that fact. Completely eliminating DNA evidence from the bottom of a pair of sneakers isn't that easy, especially for a neophyte. I hope you can understand why we had to arrest you."

Lauren had done DNA collection and certainly was no neophyte in its preservation, but not so much in the destruction of such evidence. "I do," Lauren said. She suspected this was a bluff to gain her trust, to get her to share a tidbit of information she wasn't willing to give up. She wouldn't fall for it. "So, may I go? I have children at home I need to get back to."

He reached out and caught her hand, and the look on his face made her sink back to the cot. "Unfortunately, someone wanted us to think you were involved, and if you're not a suspect … you could be a target. Clearly, they have no qualms about killing to get what they want, and I can't leave you in harm's way. I'm afraid I have no choice but to keep you in protective custody until we are certain that you are not in danger."

Oh, so he was going to play it that way?

13

"Mr. Pierce? A word?" Dr. Aziz stopped Rowan as he rose to leave the lecture hall. He had to wait for Tima so they could ride home together, and he could get the boys and take them home for dinner. This had become their custom since Lauren left. So far, every night dinner had been a "snack" at Tima's house. She always made too much.

The rest of the class filed out and left Rowan alone with the old codger. Rowan had been waiting for retaliation for his defiance at the Priestesses' tomb. He figured this was it.

"Yes, sir?" Rowan clutched his iPad and his textbook over his chest.

"I've received a call from a colleague at Tobruk University. His team is going on a dig in Libya. They found what they believe to be a 1,700-year-old settlement. They have room for an adventurer such as yourself. Would you be interested in joining the team? We can consider it part of your internship?"

"Sounds like the opportunity of a lifetime," Rowan said.

"He's leaving in two days," he said. "You could meet him in Tobruk tomorrow."

"Wait, what?" Rowan's gears started spinning. "Kind of short notice, isn't it?"

"Opportunity is not a lengthy visitor, Mr. Pierce."

Rowan shook his head, his mind racing. "I'm afraid I have to decline." Rowan didn't want to, but what choice did he have?

Aziz looked at him a moment. Abhorrent shock flooded his features and his face turned red. "No?" He began sputtering and spitting as he muttered something in his native tongue. Again, Rowan was convinced he would have an apoplexy right then and there. Clearly this man was accustomed to dealing with much younger students who did what they were told.

"Dr. Aziz, I am very honored that you would think of me for such a project, but …"

"You, Mr. Pierce, are the brightest student in my class, but you continue to confound me at every turn. Any of your classmates would jump at an opportunity such as this. It's a once in a lifetime chance."

"Yes, it is and I'm sure anyone else would love to go and should have that opportunity, Dr. Aziz, but … I have two little boys and my wife is in Prague doing research of her own. I can't go off and leave my sons. I have responsibilities." Rowan turned at the jangling of bracelets, not surprised to see Tima leaning on the doorframe.

"Ah, Dr. Badr." Aziz turned to his colleague. "Can you talk some sense into this boy?"

"Don't be foolish, Rowan, darling," Tima said. "I will keep the boys while you go. They have been with us off and on all week. What's a few more days?" Apparently, she'd been listening from the hallway. "Take your video camera. Go make some amazing discoveries."

Rowan wanted to protest, but he knew his Dean all too well. *Whatever Fatima wanted, Fatima got.*

~

"BUT, DADDY. I WANNA GO DIG, TOO," HENRY PROTESTED.

"Sorry, son," Rowan said as he packed his duffle bag. "But you get to go stay with Aunt Tima and the girls."

Henry sat back on his heels in the middle of his parents' bed. John Carter sat watching his dad intently. They'd done the same thing when their mother had been packing her bag. "I guess that's okay," Henry conceded. "When I'm bigger, I can go; right? I can go on a dig? Please?"

Rowan's heart swelled at the thought of his children joining in on their adventures. "I'm looking forward to it, son." Rowan went back to the dresser to find socks. When he turned back around, his youngest was pulling his cargo pants out of his backpack. "John Carter," he said, putting his hands on his hips, gazing down at his son. He had to laugh, even though the boy was essentially unpacking his bag for him. The dark-haired child smiled a toothy grin and giggled, delighted with this new game he'd discovered. "*No go,* Daddy."

"It's just for a couple of days." Rowan ruffled John Carter's hair. "You like staying with Tima and Shemi, right? I think Ahmose will be home from school this week."

"Almost?"

"Ahmose," Rowan said, over-enunciating her name. "She's one of Tima's older daughters. She's going to college in London."

"Do I know Ahmose?" Henry puzzled.

"You met her when we first came to Egypt. She's the tall one with the nose ring. Surely you remember *that.*"

The light seemed to come on as his oldest son's face lit up. "I remember her! I remember Ahmose! She made us cookies, except, she called them biscuits."

"Yes," Rowan said. "That's her. Tima said she'd be on holiday this week."

"I *yike howiday,* Daddy," John Carter said, climbing down off the bed, no longer interested in unpacking his bag.

"Why don't you go get your backpacks and pack up some toys to take with you? Henry, can you help John Carter?"

"Yes, sir," Henry said. "Come on, John Carter. We gotta take our stuff."

Rowan mused to himself as the boys left him to think. He finished packing his clothes, not that he needed many. He grabbed his hiking boots and his hat from the closet and set them by his duffle bag. He was a minimalist when he traveled. Only a few changes of clothes went in the bag. A bottle of shampoo would serve as both hair and body wash. A stick of deodorant was a must in the heat, along with a tube of sunscreen and he had enough.

Lauren would scold him if he got sunburned again. She always did. She didn't sunburn like he did. Her skin just grew darker. Rowan envied that. The thought also reminded him that she hadn't called today. The one text was all he'd gotten since she left.

He sat down on the foot of the bed and took his phone out of his pocket. He hit her name in his list of favorites and put the phone to his ear. He didn't realize how hopeful he was that she'd answer until it went to voicemail. Still, he found comfort in hearing her voice, even if it was just a recording.

"Hey, you know, you haven't called since you left, and I just got the one text. I'm kind of freaking out over here. That and I got a chance to go on a dig in Libya. The boys are going to stay with Tima so I can go. I should be home before you get back, but … I really just need to hear your voice. I hope you're okay. Please. Just call me."

THE DRIVE FROM CAIRO TO THE RENDEZVOUS WITH DR. VanHouten's team would take at least ten hours. Tima briefed him on her association with the Dutch professor before he left. Clearly, she thought highly of him. Rowan detected a glimmer of something in Tima's countenance when she talked about the man. He couldn't quite put his finger on what it was, though. Maybe she had a crush on him. Maybe he was just another of her adopted students, like he was.

By the time he got in the Range Rover and headed out across the arid landscape, he forgot about it completely. He wondered if maybe Lauren had lost her phone, or maybe she was in some fortified bunker studying the page and had no signal.

Rowan knew how easily distracted his wife could get when she was working. Focused might be a better word. She had an intensity he had to admire, even though it meant her attention wasn't on him. He didn't need to be her *every* waking thought. He knew he was her *first* waking thought, and that was enough.

If he could change anything about her, it would be her communication skills. She rarely called. She wasn't one to sit chatting on the phone often, not even when Bahati called. She kept the conversations brief and succinct. *Lauren, where are you? Why won't you call?*

Rowan stopped on the outskirts of Alexandria to fill up his gas tank and grab some food. He hadn't packed his ice chest before leaving the boys at Tima's because it was so early. He took the opportunity to do so now. It was brutally hot, and if he had car trouble or there were other issues, he needed to make sure he had plenty of water and supplies. He'd already been cautioned about the potential for delays at the border crossing into Libya, even in a time of rare peace, so he made sure he was prepared to be self-sufficient for at least twenty-four hours, if necessary.

The highway turned west as he set off for the border. Turning into the afternoon sun, he pulled on his aviator sunglasses and cranked up the air conditioner. With the Egyptian desert to his left, and the Mediterranean ocean to his right, he did his best to try and enjoy the journey. The view was spectacular.

He realized though, he was fretting, not only about Lauren, but over any issues he might face crossing the border into Libya. Like most countries in the Middle East, Libya was fraught with turmoil. It was better since the Great Peace Accord, but to hear Aziz and Tima talk, it was a tentative détente.

The Libyan and Egyptian authorities had restrictions on travelers over the past few years due to civil unrest. Dr. Aziz had arranged to get Rowan an emergency visa even before he'd tried to convince him to go on the dig. He would have to stop and register with the authorities in Tobruk before heading out to the site. Tima assured him Dr. VanHouten would vouch for him if there were any issues.

He had been cautioned not to carry any weapons. Even a pocket-knife could be misconstrued as a weapon rather than a tool. As a visiting grad student, Rowan was no threat to the security of the region but that didn't give him a free pass either.

Rowan couldn't get over how stunning the scenery was, and he was happy in his element. He loved driving and with less and less traffic, he soon had the roads practically to himself.

He nearly crashed the car, though when his ring-tone suddenly bellowed out the haunting refrains of Stevie Nicks', "Rhiannon." He regained control and his composure and pulled over the car as quickly as he could.

"Lauren?"

"Hi, honey." Her voice sounded chipper. "Sorry I haven't had a chance to call."

"I'm just so happy to hear your voice," he said. "Did you get my message?"

"No," Lauren said. "I've been without my phone for a while."

"Oh?" he asked.

"Silly me." She laughed. "I must have left my charger in the taxi when I went to the museum the other day. I didn't have a chance to get a replacement for it until today."

"Oh, no." Rowan ran his hand over his face. That wasn't the first time she'd lost her phone charger like that. "Well what have you been doing? I've been worried."

"I've been tied up here," Lauren said. "So sorry."

"Well? Anything exciting there? Have you seen the page?"

"Unfortunately, not yet," Lauren said. "But I'm working with a local investigator. He's been extremely helpful."

"But I thought Dr. Masa was going to show it to you?"

"He … got called away." She swallowed hard. "We're going to check out some of the local sites related to the Codex until we can get access." There was hesitation in her voice. "I may be out of pocket for a few days so please, don't worry."

"I feel better now that I've talked to you," Rowan said. "I'm on my way to Libya to a dig."

"What? Are the boys staying with Tima?"

"She and the girls are probably spoiling them rotten," Rowan said.

"Girls?"

"Ahmose is home on holiday," he said. "She might still be here when you get back."

"I might be delayed a couple of days more," Lauren said. "I'm so sorry."

"It's okay," Rowan said. "I'm a couple of hours from the border and I'll be on the dig for a few days. I'll probably beat you home."

"Just … be careful," Lauren said.

Rowan grabbed the steering wheel with his free hand. "You, too."

"Don't forget your sunscreen," she added.

"I have it."

"I love you," she said.

"I know." It had become a running joke since they'd introduced the boys to Han Solo and Princess Leia.

The call was brief, and he wasn't sure if he really did feel any better. At this point, he was grateful for a moment to talk to her. He got a bottle of water from the ice chest and cracked it open. He took a long drink before twisting the cap back on and placing it in the cup holder. Refreshed and renewed, he put the car back in gear, checked his mirrors and continued on his way.

Lauren handed the phone back to the detective. "Why do I feel like I've just lied to my husband?"

"You told him the truth," Kovač said. "Your phone *was* dead. I *am* a local investigator. I do need *your* help. You *might* be a few days longer than expected. All true."

"I have helped the FBI before," Lauren said. She shivered as a chill ran over her flesh. She hesitated and gazed up at him from beneath her long bangs. "You do believe me, don't you? That wasn't me."

He paused a moment, clearly considering his words carefully. "I know what I saw, Dr. Pierce," the detective said. "But whoever killed the director and the curator would have had to walk through the blood. And there appeared to be another man in the video. I didn't mention it because I thought perhaps … well, it isn't important." He stopped abruptly.

"Wait, what?" Lauren asked.

"Two people were murdered at the museum, Dr. Pierce. There are tracks in the blood; only one set. Yet, your shoes were pristine. No DNA evidence whatsoever. That is not easy to do, even given time to plan ahead. It's difficult for me to doubt what I see, but … the evidence doesn't match. So I'm willing to consider you may not have been involved … at least provisionally. I need more evidence."

He was a man after her own heart. "I am a trained investigator, skilled in evidence collection," Lauren offered. "Absence of evidence is not evidence of absence." She made the statement under her breath, her mind still spinning trying to figure it all out.

"Giving you a chance to assist me is completely self-serving. You have not been completely eliminated as a suspect. To your credit, you have been cooperative, and something tells me I can trust you. You appear to be a woman of your word."

"I swear, I will do everything I can to clear my name," she said. "I need answers as much as you." Gooseflesh raced down her arms as she swallowed hard.

Kovač rose and went to the coat rack in the corner. He pulled a jacket down and handed it to her. "Here," he said. "Put this on. I'm working to get a safe house arranged for you."

"A safe house?"

"We'll have to move you to someplace safe."

"You don't think they're following me? Those men?"

"Considering we don't know who they are, or who killed those people at the museum …"

"The page from the Codex." Lauren's voice dropped an octave as she realized what must have happened. "I think that's what was in the wooden crate … the one that the woman impersonating me carried out. It was the missing page."

"We don't know that," Kovač said. "Not yet anyway."

She knew in her gut she was right. "No, it makes perfect sense. I was … I was the bait."

"Bait?"

"Whoever wanted the page, they used me …" She turned. "If the page was locked up for security reasons, and they couldn't get to it, then whoever wanted to steal it needed it moved out of the antiquities vault. Who would have enough clout to get it moved other than a visiting scientist ... especially one as well-known as me?"

"What happened to your television show?" he asked.

"We're taking a sabbatical while my husband finishes his degree and ... while our boys are little." Her hand went absentmindedly to her belly. For a moment she felt like mice were doing somersaults in her pelvis. She knew from experience what that flutter was. Even though she was hardly showing, the life within her was making its presence known. A thought came to her. "Dr. Kominsky didn't seem to recognize my face, but I did notice her expression when she heard my name. She didn't tell me *no* when I asked to see the page. She told me she'd have to see about having it brought up for inspection and that it would take some time. Maybe she needed time to check out my story before she had the artifact moved."

"That's when the thief or thieves struck," Kovač said. "Having someone who appeared to look like you take the page was the perfect cover-up."

"The three men who nabbed me may have been in on it," Lauren said. "It left me without an alibi."

"And it leaves me with more questions." Kovač shook his head. "Who and where is this Dr. Masa, and why would he go all the way to Cairo to pull you into this game of subterfuge?"

"And why would they try to pin something like this on me?"

They both turned when there was a knock on the door. Kovač went to see who it was. "Lab results," Lauren heard the man say. He handed an envelope to the detective. He returned with it and wasted no time opening it. He pulled out the paper and skimmed over it quickly. He turned and handed it to her. Lauren's head swam and the words blurred on the page. "Midazolam," he said. "You were drugged."

14

"Have you had an ultrasound done yet?" the doctor asked as Lauren lay back on the exam table and peeled up her t-shirt. She unbuckled her belt and exposed her lower abdomen.

"No," Lauren said. "I haven't even seen an OBGYN yet."

"How far along?"

"Eight, nine weeks."

"Morning sickness?" the doctor asked as she took her tape measure out of her coat pocket.

"In spades." Lauren hiccupped.

"Your first?"

"Third," Lauren said.

The doctor measured her abdomen. Her brow lifted as her cheeks rose into a smile. "You're measuring closer to ten weeks," she noted, putting the tape measure back in her pocket, then palpated her abdomen. "Tomáš said you were drugged?"

"So it would appear," Lauren said, gazing up into the light fixture. She wasn't sure how much the detective had told the doctor, but she seemed to know him well enough to call him by his first name.

"Any lingering side effects?"

"Headache," Lauren said. "But that could be from a number of things."

The doctor took a small device from the other pocket and pressed it to the slight swell of her stomach. The rhythmic woosh of a rapidly beating heart echoed from it. "Baby's heartbeat is strong," she said. "140 beats per minute. Let's run an ultrasound just to be sure everything's okay with this little one." She patted Lauren's leg. It took a moment to get the equipment set up. After a few squirts of cold gel on her belly, the doctor ran the transducer over her lower abdomen. Lauren closed her eyes and took a deep breath.

"Is it too early to tell the gender?

The doctor glanced back at her with a light in her amber eyes. "Most likely," she said. "Twelve weeks is usually the earliest, but that's rare."

"Oh…" Lauren hesitated, turning to look at the screen as the doctor adjusted it so she could see. The image in grayscale was grainy and it was difficult to make out details, but as she moved it, Lauren could see the profile of her baby's face. A small hand was tucked up next to its face. "Probably for the best. My husband would have a fit if I found out without him."

"Of course." The doctor nodded. "I'll take some pictures so you can show him your baby when you get home."

"Yeah, let's do that." A tear ran from the corner of Lauren's eye. The thought of seeing the baby growing inside her suddenly made it real. It hadn't really sunk in until that moment, that she would soon be a mother of three. To think that she never wanted to marry, never wanted children. She had been so wrong. She knew that now. Life was better with a family than she could have ever imagined.

~

KOVAČ WAITED FOR HER WHEN SHE CAME OUT INTO THE LOBBY at the clinic. She had a white paper bag in her hand and a few black and white photos the doctor had given her. "Everything okay?"

"So it would seem," Lauren said.

"What's that?"

"Prenatal vitamins and something for nausea," Lauren said. "If it is what I think it is, it'll knock me out cold for a whole day."

"Will you take it?"

"At this point, yeah, probably." Lauren followed him out into the hallway. It was late in the day and there were no patients left in the lobby. "How do you know the doctor?"

"Oh, Katia is my sister," he said. "She's usually not that slow. I thought you'd be done in less than an hour."

"She gave me some IV fluids," Lauren said. "She said I was dehydrated."

"And the baby?"

"The baby is fine," Lauren said, handing him the ultrasound pictures. He took them and inspected them politely. He gave her a nod and a small smile as he handed them back. "As far as she could tell."

"She's a very good doctor," he said.

Lauren could see the pride written on his face. She also noticed the family resemblance once it was pointed out. "Now what?"

"The safe house is ready," he said. "I'll take you there and you can rest tonight. I have a security officer who will guard you overnight. I've got some questions to ask at the museum tomorrow then I'll come get you. I'll take you to see the monastery where the Codex was supposedly written, or what's left of it, if you want to go."

"I do." Lauren nodded. "What about my things, back at the hotel?"

"I'll send someone to pick up your belongings," he said,

holding the door for her. "If you need anything before then, I'll have it brought in for you."

"Thank you," Lauren said. "That's very kind of you."

"Have you eaten today?"

Lauren shook her head. "No."

"I'll make arrangements for dinner then," he said. "Any preferences?"

"Just something simple." Lauren shrugged. "I don't think I could manage anything rich or spicy."

"Noted," he said as they reached the car.

The sky was purple in the west as the sun set beneath a bank of clouds moving in from the south. Lauren could taste rain in the air. A bolt of lightning flashed in the sky and the immediate crack of thunder made her jump. She felt ill-at-ease and chewed on what was left of her thumbnail as she watched the city pass away as he drove into the outskirts of town. No words were spoken, but none were needed. The rain overtook them. The detective flipped on the headlights and the wiper-blades before reaching for the defroster. It always occurred to Lauren when she traveled, how other parts of the world were so similar to the United States. She had driven on many long and winding roads, in all sorts of weather. Other than a few climatological differences, most countries were very much like another. Some buildings were older than others; some countries drove on the left, others on the right. Still, cars were essentially the same. The buttons and knobs were generally found in the same configuration.

The road wound through trees as the landscape grew hilly, and soon, the car turned off the main highway to a long private driveway. She sat up in the seat when they came around a wide bend in the road, as a rising castle appeared over the trees. For a minute the thought crossed her mind that he intended to put her up in a real-life castle. Then he turned off and veered towards a smaller house just inside the stone fortification that surrounded the estate.

He pulled the car up as close to the house as he could. He got out in the pouring rain and came around and got the car door for her, holding his jacket over her head as they rushed to the house. The front door wasn't locked.

Puddles collected around them as they stood in the stoned entry way shaking the rain off their clothing. "Tomáš?" She heard a voice echo from the other room.

"We're here, Zuzu," Tomáš answered back.

An older woman came down the hall and into the entry way. She wore a heavy sweater and jeans. She was slender and slight, her features chiseled. Her silver-gray hair was knotted up on the back of her head. "Ah, Tomáš! It's good to see you." She came over and greeted him with a kiss on each cheek, taking his hands in hers as he reciprocated. He embraced her affectionately. "Zuzu, this is my friend, Dr. Lauren Pierce."

"Welcome, Dr. Pierce," she beamed. "Any friend of Tomáš is welcome here. Come in. Come in."

"Thank you." Lauren wasn't sure how to address her.

"My dear, you are soaked to the bone." She observed as she put her hand on Lauren's arm. "Let me find you something dry to put on." Lauren couldn't say no. "Follow me, I'll show you to your room."

The house was twice as large as the Pierces' bungalow in Hawaii, practically expansive when compared to their apartment in Cairo. She was led to a room was on the 2nd floor, down a long hallway from the top of the stairs. The walls were paneled in what appeared to be mahogany, and a great canopy bed sat in the middle. There was a fireplace and a bundle of wood beside it.

The chill of the room required a fire to be built, but now was not the time. As Zuzu went to find her something to wear, she inspected the furnishings and décor. She found a spacious bathroom off the bedroom, including a deep ball-and-claw tub, and she longed to take a hot bubble bath. Such a luxury would have to wait. Her stomach was protesting from emptiness rather than nausea and she wasn't sure which was worse. She returned to the bedroom, unsure of what to do. She paused at the foot of the bed and gazed up.

There was a portrait over the mantel of what might have been a long-lost ancestor, or perhaps some historical figure from the region that Lauren didn't recognize. He looked a bit like Kovač, in that the Slavic features were similar. Dark hair, bright blue eyes, fair skin. He was clearly someone of import by the cut of his clothing and his regal appearance.

Lauren was standing under the painting, gazing at it, when Zuzu returned. "Here you go, dear."

Lauren startled.

"Sorry to have frightened you." She apologized, noticing the subject of her guest's interest. "Do you know who this is?"

Lauren shook her head. "No. I don't."

"That is my great-great-great-grandfather, Jiří Antonin Kovač, he was the royal composer to King Charles IV, the Holy Roman emperor, the King of Bohemia."

"Kovač?"

"Tomáš is my son," she said, proudly. "He didn't tell you, did he?"

"No." Lauren turned and took the clothes she provided.

"These should fit you. Come downstairs to the kitchen when you're dressed. Dinner is almost ready. I need to check on the soup."

So he's leaving me with his mother? Great. The thought lingered in her head long after she was left to her own devices.

15

"A *salaamu alaikum*," the guard at the border greeted him. Rowan didn't speak Arabic, but he knew what that meant. *Peace be with you.*

"*Alaikum Asalaamu.*" Rowan put his hand over his heart and nodded, mirroring the guard's mannerisms. "Do you speak English?"

"American?" the guard asked, eyeing him warily.

"Yes, sir. I'm a grad student at the University of Cairo." He handed over his papers, including his student visa and passport. "I'm meeting with a Dr. VanHouten from the University at Tobruk."

"Wait here." He took the papers back inside the guard shack. Rowan tried to remain calm as he watched the guards gather around and discuss his papers. The last thing he needed was trouble. A placid façade was in order, and he knew it.

The man, who appeared to be in charge, turned and looked at Rowan. He saw the man's eyes widen. A broad grin brightened on the dark face as the man turned and made for the door, rushing over to the truck.

"Rowan Pierce?" He beamed. "*The* Rowan Pierce?"

"The only one I know." Rowan puzzled.

"I watch your show. I watch all your *show*. Where is your beautiful wife? Where is *Missus* Pierce?"

Rowan realized now he'd found a fan, and a sense of relief washed over him as the other guards filed out behind him. "*Doctor* Pierce is working in Prague this week." She would want him to correct the slight. She always did. She worked hard for her PhD, so why not?

The guard turned back to his fellows and enthused something in Arabic. Lauren would have known what they were saying but he was clueless. All the men, however, seemed to share in the guard's excitement. The one with his credentials came over and handed them back, offering his hand. "Welcome to Libya. It is not every day we get to meet a famous adventurer."

"Glad to know I have fans here," Rowan said, accepting his hand.

Each guard had to shake his hand, which meant really to clasp his hand between theirs, for an extended period of time. "*Asalaamu alaikum*," each of them said before turning loose of him. Rowan smiled all the way to Tobruk.

IT WAS LATE WHEN HE ARRIVED AT THE HOSTEL WHERE HE WAS scheduled to meet the professor. He could hear the call to prayer echoing over the city. The streets were empty, and he knew most had either gone to the mosque or prayed in their homes. The prayer ritual was over 1400-years-old and was repeated five times a day. It set a rhythm to the pattern of life in this part of the world, and while Rowan didn't practice the religion, he tried to be respectful of it. He waited in the car listening to the haunting song that lasted several minutes. When a group of young men finally emerged from a nearby building, he got out of the car and gathered his things.

"*Asalaamu alaikum,*" the innkeeper greeted him. "May I help you?"

"Hi, I'm Rowan Pierce. I should have a reservation," he said.

"Of course, Mr. Pierce." He nodded. "We have been waiting for you. Dr. VanHouten asked that you call him at this number when you arrive. He hopes you have not eaten dinner yet. He would like you to join him."

"No, I haven't." Rowan took the hand-written card the man provided. "Thank you."

"I will have your things taken to your room," he said.

"I don't mind taking it up," he said. "I need to freshen up before dinner."

"Of course." He handed Rowan the key. "You are on the 4th floor, room B."

"Thanks," Rowan said.

He called the professor on his way up. Dr. VanHouten said he'd be by to meet him in thirty minutes. *Plenty of time to get settled*, Rowan decided.

The room was more spacious than he'd been expecting from a *hostel*. With the university footing the bill, he'd expected minimal accommodations. He tossed his bag on the bed and stripped out of his sweaty clothes. The cool shower never felt so refreshing.

WHEN HE STEPPED INTO THE LOBBY DOWNSTAIRS A HALF-HOUR later, he had on a fresh button-up shirt and linen slacks. It was probably the nicest outfit he owned. It seemed fitting for dinner with his host. "Mister Pierce?" He turned at his name and found his host sitting in a large wingback chair reading the newspaper.

"Dr. VanHouten?" Rowan asked. As the man lowered the

newspaper, Rowan was taken aback. He froze as his brow clamped down over his nose.

"No need to be so formal. Call me Vilhelm." Jean-René did a perfect Dutch accent. No wonder Rowan didn't recognize him on the phone.

"What the hell?" Rowan welcomed his best friend's embrace and hearty slap on the shoulder, but he was dazed by his presence. "What are you doing in Libya?"

"I got diverted to a show here," he said. *"Libya's Forbidden Deserts."*

"But…"

"Don't look so shocked, Boss. The Network put out a mandate that we were not to contact you, and I couldn't come to Egypt. When my last project when to hell, I got word this show needed a videographer. I took a cut in pay to get here."

"What do you mean the Network …" Rowan puzzled. He realized he hadn't talked to either of his friends in months. He thought perhaps they were upset about them stepping away from the spotlight, and he'd been willing to give them time to … adapt. "So there's no Dr. VanHouten?"

"Maybe, but not here." Jean-René's face was stretched so tight into a smilc that his eyes were nearly slits. He'd earned some new wrinkles in the year since Rowan had seen him last.

"How did you get Dr. Badr on board with this?" Rowan was completely flummoxed. "She went on and on about this … Dr. VanHouten …"

"The last time we spoke, you droned on and on about Professor Badr like she was some kind of rock star. I called her to see how I could get you to Libya and she actually came up with the cover story."

"Did Dr. Aziz know about the ruse?"

"I've never heard that name." Jean-René shrugged. "Dr. Badr told me she'd take care of everything on her end. I'm just sorry I couldn't figure out a way to get Lauren here with you."

"Well she wouldn't have been able to come anyway." Rowan finally managed a deep breath. It steadied his shaking knees. He was happy, of course, to see Jean-René. It'd been over a year since cable TV's power-couple announced their intention to take a sabbatical and leave their life in the US behind. "Look, I feel like I should apologize," Rowan started.

"No need." Jean-René stopped him. "We've all had to do what we've had to do. But there's a side project I'm working on, and I need your help."

"Something new? A side project?"

"We do have a dig here, but I … we … Bahati and I … had something unusual happen. Something we got on video."

"Video? Well, come on," he said. "You can tell me over dinner." Jean-René nodded as Rowan put an arm around his shoulder. "I have news, too."

"Another one?" Jean-René sat back in his chair when Rowan told him about the baby.

"I know, right?" Rowan could barely contain his joy. "I have my fingers crossed for a girl."

"You get what you get," Jean-René said.

"Well, of course," Rowan sat back in his chair as the waiter came back with a plate of hummus and a basket of flatbread, along with a tray of couscous with stewed meats and vegetables. "We'll be happy either way. But I do hope we have a girl. Speaking of, how's Nyota? Bahati?"

"They're fine," he said. "Bahati is doing some copywriting."

"She's working? At the studio?"

He laughed. "She's just working from home."

"Oh, well good for her," Rowan said.

"Her hands are full." Jean-René pulled out his phone and scrolled through pictures before handing it to Rowan. "Look at how big our daughter is." He pointed as Rowan inspected the images. The little girl had light brown skin with springy curls tied up in pigtails and amber-green eyes. She looked mischievous in almost every picture.

"She's beautiful." Rowan handed the phone back. "Good job, my friend."

"You're two up on me," Jean-René said, shaking his head, putting his phone away.

"Better get busy." Rowan waggled his eyebrows.

Jean-René's smile faded, and he lifted his brow and shoulder simultaneously. "I wish it were that easy," he said. "Bahati's had some … difficulties. We lost one in the spring. It was still early on, but it hurt, nonetheless."

Rowan's expression mirrored his friend's. "I'm … so sorry to hear that."

"Me, too." Jean-René's expression seemed forced. "But the trying is still fun."

"So tell me about this video you took." Rowan sensed a change of subject was needed.

Jean-René cued it up on his phone. "Better just to show you." He handed the phone to Rowan.

He watched it, his brows creeping up higher and higher as the video looped. "Where is this?"

"Catalina Island," he said. "I finally got that sail boat I always wanted."

Rowan looked at him, a wry smile hooked up in one corner of his cheek. "Congrats," he said, turning his attention back to the video. "Who have you shown this to?"

"No one has seen it except Bahati and me." He swallowed hard. "I didn't want the Network to run amok with it. I thought it might be … you know, *Lauren's friends*."

Rowan looked at him sharply. "Friends … or …enemies."

"That was my worst fear," Jean-René said.

Rowan eyed him warily over the edge of the phone. "Glad you kept this one close to the vest."

"What are we going to do?"

"I'll call Lauren and see if she's heard from Michael, or maybe … maybe she can make a call."

"She can do that?"

Rowan shrugged. "Considering everything else she can do; I wouldn't put it past her."

"Valid point," Jean-René said, taking his phone back. He looked pensive.

Rowan nodded, raising his cup of tea to his lips. "So, are we still going on a dig or what?"

The happy light returned to Jean-René's amber eyes. "Oh yes, of course we are. But I … I can't let you appear on camera," he said. "The Network … they don't know you're here."

"Oh, well," Rowan said. "I wasn't expecting to be, so … it's all good."

"Good," Jean-René said, relief apparent in his manner. "Good."

Over the next hour Jean-René filled him in on the plans for tomorrow's expedition as they lingered over a leisurely meal. "We will need to leave early to beat the heat," Jean-René finally said.

Rowan glanced at his watch. "What time?"

Jean-René grinned. "0400."

Rowan's expression dropped. "That's like five hours away."

"You were military," Jean-René said, as if that were enough. Rowan remembered the early morning calls to duty.

"After driving all day today, I'm beat. I need some Z's."

"We've lingered over dinner long enough to be respectful to our host." Jean-René nodded towards the restaurant owner who stood at the podium near the entrance. "Come on, I'll walk you back to the hotel."

～

THE MEAL WAS SIMPLE, BUT GOOD. TOMÁŠ' MOTHER HAD made soup. The broth was clearly chicken, flavored with lemon and parsley, enriched with wild rice, vegetables, and chunks of white meat. A loaf of crusty brown bread, still warm from the oven, was slathered with butter. Lauren knew she shouldn't make a pig of herself, but her hunger got the better of her and she ate two bowls of soup and had several slices of bread.

"Did you save room for dessert?" Zuzu asked. "I made a lemon chiffon cake the other day. It's still moist and I can't eat it all by myself."

Lauren debated, then nodded. "Maybe just a small slice."

When they retired to the living room Lauren was stuffed and just wanted to sleep, but she didn't want to be rude, so she joined her hosts for a while.

"Tomáš," Zuzu said. "Did you tell Lauren about our arrangement?"

"I'm afraid there wasn't time," he said.

Lauren looked between the two of them in a wordless plea for explanation.

"My mother is a former government spy," Tomáš said.

Lauren's jaw dropped. "She's a… a s-s-spy?" She turned to her hostess. "Like … James Bond?"

"Maybe more like *Mata Hari*." She offered. Lauren's brow lifted. Lauren knew the name. It meant *the eye of the day*. Apt name for a female spy, she supposed. "I started my career in as a military police officer, then worked undercover in Russia for many years. I helped shut down several KGB operations in Estonia and Czechoslovakia during the Cold War. All water under the bridge now. I spent the past few years doing private security for international corporations, up until I retired last year."

"I've never met a retired spy before," Lauren said blankly.

"Few of us make it to retirement," Zuzu said. "You have to be very good or very lucky."

Lauren puzzled a moment on that thought. "Which one were you?"

"I was lucky enough to be good." Zuzu grinned, then laughed at her own joke. "You will be quite safe here," she added.

"My mother can hold her own against anyone," Tomáš stated.

"Are we the only ones here? Surely you have help keeping up with such a grand manse?"

"I have a groundskeeper that comes every other day or so," she said. "Trust me, I don't need help with security. That's my department and if I may be so bold, I'm quite good at it."

"I'll sleep better knowing that," Lauren said.

"Tomáš, will you be staying? I've got your room made up."

"I can't." He shook his head. "I have to be back at the museum in the morning to follow up on some of the information Dr. Pierce gave me today. I'll be back out when I finish up there."

"If no one minds, I think I'll turn in early," Lauren said, rising from her chair. Tomáš stood, too.

"Of course." Zuzu nodded. "I'm just down the hallway, first room at the top of the stairs, if you need anything."

"Thank you for your hospitality," Lauren said politely. "Dinner was excellent."

"I'm glad you enjoyed it," her host said. "Rest well."

"I'll see you tomorrow," Tomáš said to Lauren.

"Rowan Pierce, this is Greg Wilson from the University of Miami," Jean-René introduced him to the field archeologist. "Greg's in charge of cataloguing anything we find."

"Nice to meet you," Rowan said.

"Dr. Fazan is in the trailer," Greg said, pointing that direction. "We've been waiting for you to get started."

"Sorry we're late," Jean-René said. "Rowan needed coffee before the long drive."

"It's all good." Greg loaded some equipment up onto his ATV. "Go check in and I'll wait for you and take you over to the site."

"Thanks, man."

Rowan followed Jean-René to the trailer as the door open and a man in a long white shirt and pants stepped out onto the deck. The dark-skinned man had a red fringed scarf around his neck.

"Ah, Mr. Pierce. I am Dr. Fazan. We've been expecting you. You're late." He seemed irritated.

"Sorry," Rowan said. "Jean-René needed coffee." The two were teasing each other and having a good time at it. It'd been so long since they'd had a chance to poke fun at one another.

"Well you will regret it when the afternoon heat sets in. You will need water today." He pointed to the water cooler. "It will be extremely hot out at the dig. The team has water at the site but please, help yourself."

They loaded up on supplies and made sure they had their equipment and everything they would need for the day. Rowan slathered himself in sunscreen and pulled on his wide-brimmed hat, wishing he had a scarf like Dr. Fazan. They hurried to catch up with Greg and the team.

ATVs carried them across the already-roasting desert, down to the dig site. Rowan loved driving any kind of off-road vehicle, usually, but driving on sand was a bit of a challenge. The risk of rolling even a four-wheeled vehicle was ever-present. Fortunately, they didn't have any trouble.

∼

"So what are we looking at?" Rowan asked as they came up on the team working down in an excavation that was maybe twenty meters squared, and about four meters deep. The remains of a stone foundation and portions of a stone wall lay among the ruins in one corner. Workers on the other side of the excavation lay sprawled out on their stomachs with paintbrushes and small pallet knives.

"This is an ancient storehouse," Greg said.

"A storehouse?" Rowan asked as Jean-René set up the camera. "How do you know it's a storehouse?"

"Well, come on over and let me introduce you to Marco and Paulo." Greg grinned.

"Wait? What? Marco? Paulo?" The two men turned away from each other rolling over to look at him. "Am I seeing double? What's going on here?"

"We are twins," one of them said.

"I bet you guys got lost a lot as kids," Rowan snarked.

"Marco!" Jean-René chorused.

"Polo!" Rowan echoed. "Which one's which?"

"I'm Marco," the other chimed in, as he stood, wiping his hand on the seat of his pants before he stuck it out. "Dr. Marco Bianchi. My brother, Dr. Paulo Bianchi."

Paulo rose and repeated the gesture. "It's nice to meet you."

"So how do you know we have a storehouse?" Rowan asked after introductions were made. The two men stepped apart and Rowan saw what they were trying to free from the sands. "Pottery ..."

"Yes, yes." Paulo waved him over, and soon all three men were sprawled out on their bellies, examining the markings on the crumbling ceramic vases and urns. Marco used a paint brush to clear the sand away.

Marco handed him a fragment. He studied it with a keen eye. It had been stamped while the pottery was still uncured.

Tiny chicken-feet hatch marks told Rowan of its age and origins as well. "Is that Sumerian?"

"You read cuneiform?" Paulo asked.

"No, but I recognize it," he said. "My wife is the linguist."

"We found tablets nearby written in a form of proto-cuneiform," Marco said. "Those date back to about 3,000 BC."

"How old are these pottery shards?" Rowan asked.

"About 4,200 years old." Marco beamed. "One of the tablets we found tells us about the rations of beer, lentils and grain provided as a bride-price to a groomsman's family."

"A bride-price?"

"Marriages were arranged in ancient Sumer. The bride and the groom had little to no say once the contract was arranged," Marco said.

"However, if the arrangement proved unfruitful, the couple could divorce and each of them could marry a second time," Paulo added. "We've found markings on tablets and building stones pertaining to everyday life in this city. This is just one of the buildings we've identified with LIDAR. Are you familiar with LIDAR, Mr. Pierce?"

Rowan nodded. "Oh, yeah," he said. "I've used it a number of times."

Paulo looked at Marco and shook his head. "Rich Egyptian universities have all the good toys."

Marco said something back in Italian shaking his head and the two laughed. For a moment Rowan really missed Lauren. She would be able to translate it, and he was certain his hosts would be impressed with her ability to read the ancient markings. "Well, actually, I used LIDAR to map some cenotes and underwater caverns in Mexico near Chichén Itzà before I started back to college. If Cairo has access to LIDAR they don't allow mere students to use it."

"Ah." Paulo shrugged. "We need to finish excavating this

layer of pottery, catalogue them and then package them up for transport. We have much work to do. Here." He handed Rowan a pallet knife. "Have you learned how to do artifact recovery?"

"Archaeology 101." Rowan grinned. "Aced that class."

"Well, best get after it," Marco said. "We think there are more layers."

"More?" Rowan smirked. "Someone call my wife and let her know I'm going to be late for dinner. I got some digging to do." He held up the small pallet knife and looked back at his colleagues, puzzling over its size. "What? The Network wouldn't spring for something bigger? Like a back hoe? What about a garden spade? No?"

16

The chill had overtaken the bedroom. Lauren built a fire in the fireplace, and it began to warm quickly. Zuzu had brought several outfits earlier, including a thin white cotton night gown, a robe, and slippers. Lauren decided the bath was too much to resist. After a warm soak in the tub, she put on the gown and settled in for the night. There was no television, but she didn't need one. She read the label on the anti-nausea medicine — Phenergan — the doctor had given her and decided a proactive dose of the medicine might help the soup stay where it belonged. If it made her sleepy now, it wouldn't matter. She needed rest.

Once bathed, warm and properly medicated, she climbed into bed with a book she'd found on the shelf in the corner; Ulysses printed in Czech. She'd read it in English while still a schoolgirl, and more recently in Greek. It would be interesting to watch for cultural and linguistic differences of the various translations, but she could barely keep her eyes open long enough to get through the opening pages. Sleep came quickly and pulled her down deeply. It held her there long into the night.

~

DREAMS CAME AND BLURRED INTO ONE ANOTHER AS SHE slept. Wolf songs filled her ears as she found herself lying in a field of daisies overlooking a familiar lake in Yellowstone. A shooting star streaked across the sky and a wolf — one she recognized as Judy Blue Eyes — yelped. Lauren had named all the wolves in the pack after her favorite singers, Judy Collins, Joan Baez, Frank Sinatra, Michael Bublé, Josh Groban, James Taylor, John Denver … even Christina Aguilera. Lauren could pick out their voices in the night as they sang to one another across the wide valley where they hunted. She knew each of their voices well. Each had a distinct timber. Judy's was the highest pitched of them all, but this cry wasn't song, rather a yowl of distress; a yelp of pain.

Lauren sat up startled. Her heart raced in her chest. Another wolf — Christina — cried out in the distance. Something was attacking the pack.

In her dream, she jumped to her feet and raced out across the valley with the moonlight over her shoulder. Her hair flew loose behind her, and her lungs burned with the cold night air as she ran her fastest. As she reached the tree line, she skidded to a stop. Her blood chilled in her veins. The gray and white wolf she recognized as Frank lay in a crimson pool. Life gushed from the wound at his throat.

She staggered a few paces, finding Judy Blue Eyes in the same condition. *No! What was killing her friends?* She thought of them as friends ever since she'd come to Yellowstone to study them. That had been over a decade ago, and she couldn't possibly expect the whole pack to be alive today. That didn't really matter. They lived in her dreams. When she was working in the wilderness, she would lay at night listening for wolf song. Sometimes she thought she could hear them singing at night as they remained constant companions; watchers in the dark.

"Josh?" she called out, letting her voice draw out. "Joan?" Though she had named all the wolves that first summer, she never interacted with them. It was safer for the wolves when she kept her distance. She didn't know why she called to them now, but she was genuinely afraid for the whole pack.

"Did you miss me?" A wolf stood in the darkness between the trees; obscured by shadow.

Lauren turned, startled. "Who are you?"

"Don't you recognize us? It's Michael," he said. He looked oddly familiar, yet completely strange to her. His voice was even more so. He had a soft tenor with a cadence she couldn't quite place; a voice that seemed to echo.

A breath of wind lifted the wolf's coat, and it seemed to sparkle as the creature morphed into human form. "Michael?" The man stepped out from the shadows. It looked like her brother, but there was something different she couldn't put her finger on. He had a rakish, almost wolf-like gleam in his eye as he moved closer.

"You named a wolf *Michael Bublé*? That's what you called him."

"Michael? Something isn't right here," Lauren stated. "What's going on?"

"We have been watching," he said. "We are always watching."

She made to move toward him, but he held up a hand. She froze. The ground was wet and slushy. She felt the cold against her bare feet and her toes went numb.

"What are you doing here?" She panted, her breath hanging in the air around her face.

He nodded as he moved casually with a lithe grace she wasn't accustomed to. "You need us." He stopped and leaned on a tree.

"Why? What happened to the wolves? Am I dreaming?"

He glanced over at the bodies. "Well, there's trouble."

"Who would do that?"

"Who? Or what?"

"You're talking in riddles." Lauren's knees felt weak. Chills raced down her arms.

"We're under attack. Enlil and his armies are collecting and gaining strength, despite the Great Peace." He started towards her. "Now is the time for war. This is the task you were made for, my sister. The one the gods have brought you to." She noticed his foot prints in the soft ground were not human tracks, but those of a wolf. "The trickster comes like a thief in the night."

Trickster, indeed. She was immediately suspicious. Lauren's mind was racing. She felt deceived even as she stood there watching her brother — someone who looked like her brother — just a few feet away from her. He looked healthy, robust, his long hair loose. He didn't look like he'd aged a day since his — ascension. "I don't know what you mean." Panic raced through her. She tossed in her bed, her body restless, while her mind was unable to escape the nightmare. "Please, explain!"

"*The Great Dragon* fell from grace long ago, but he prepares to challenge those who are chosen by the gods. He is gathering his power and when his book is made whole, he shall take up his wings and rise to take arms against the heavens and against the very gods themselves."

Lauren's knees turned to rubber. She slumped to the ground, trembling. "The war ..." The words of Enki echoed in her head. "The war is coming."

"The war is here, sister. The enemy is at the gate," Michael added. "You will need to be strong of heart, and pure of mind and spirit."

"But ..." Lauren reached out as if a silent query to ask the questions she couldn't articulate.

"Beware the *Deceiver.*" Michael's voice echoed in her head. A cold mist of sweat broke out on her flesh, and she could feel the gown clinging to her body. "He will do everything he can to defeat you before the war even begins. Beware the Fallen."

Michael turned, seemingly moving in slow motion as he started back into the trees. "Remember the promise that was made. *You who have sought truth, found it, and used it wisely. You are to serve as our hand, our eyes. When the time comes, your role will require the greatest sacrifice.*" The words of the alien god came back to her. She felt sick and swallowed hard, but then the remainder of the promise found her. "*We will not ask more of you than you can give, and we will guard over your family, and your children.*"

"Michael," she gasped as he took a step back and turned. The fog came for him, but she clearly saw him morph back into a wolf before he disappeared, and the scene faded to black.

"Michael! Help me! Come back!"

"Lauren?" Zuzu's face appeared as she forced her eyes open. The woman's hands were on her arms, grasping her tightly. "Lauren, wake up. Are you okay?"

"Huh?" Lauren roused. She felt as if her bones had turn to lead. "What?" Her bedclothes were soaked with sweat. Her hair was in her face and clung to her neck and brow.

"You were crying out in your sleep," Zuzu said, sitting back. "I could hear you from the living room. Are you okay?"

"Where am I? Where's Tomáš?" Lauren ran a trembling hand over her hair, pushing it away from her eyes. A pale glow of daylight was beaming through the windows. "What time is it?"

"It's well after noon," Zuzu said. "Tomáš called and said he found something interesting at the museum and he wouldn't be able to make it out 'til this evening. I knew you said you were tired, but I was starting to worry when I couldn't wake you."

Lauren pushed herself up to her elbow and slid up in the

bed. "The medicine the doctor gave me must have knocked me out." Her voice was gruff, even to her own ear.

"Well, one way to avoid morning sickness is to sleep through the morning." Zuzu stood. "Do you feel better?"

"I'm not nauseous at least," Lauren said, licking her lips. Her mouth was dry.

"There's some soup left from last night," she said. "I'll heat it and bring it up to you."

"No," Lauren said with a wave of her hand. "I mean, thank you. But I'll get dressed and come downstairs. You don't need to wait on me hand and foot."

"I had four children of my own, Dr. Pierce. I know what it's like in those first few months of pregnancy."

"And did anyone wait on you hand and foot?" Lauren asked.

A bemused smile graced her features. "Now that you mention it, no."

"Give me a few minutes to shake the cobwebs out and I'll be down," Lauren said.

"Fair enough." Zuzu turned and paused at the door. "Take your time. I'll be downstairs."

LAUREN ROSE SLOWLY, HEAVY-HEADED, AND HEAVIER BONED. Her stomach seemed to sit like a stone in her pelvis. Mice did cartwheels in her womb, a sign of healthy life that made her smile as her hand went to the growing swell. She paused at the window in the borrowed nightgown, getting her first good look at the castle on the rise above. The castle was a gothic megalith of gray stone with tiled towers topped with turrets and spires. The blocks were almost the same color as the slate-gray sky.

Something moved in the yard below. Lauren's eye was drawn to it. At first, she didn't notice the figure until the breeze picked up and parted the trees. Lauren realized there was a man standing between two giant pines looking up at her window. Her heart skipped and she took a step back, pressing herself against the wall while her mind tried to process what she'd seen. Then she recognized the face that had been looking back at her even from a distance. When she looked back, he was no longer there.

"Christ!" She gasped, trying to force her heart to still. She wasn't sure if she should be frightened or not, but clearly her mind knew to be alert. Panic washed over her, and she forgot her state of undress as she rushed out into the hall and down the stairs.

Her hostess froze when Lauren appeared at the kitchen door, still in her bed clothes, with her hair tossed about. Lauren could only imagine the look on her own face as it reflected in Zuzu's.

"What is it, dear?" She dropped the spoon she was using.

"There was a man … in the trees …" Lauren gulped hard. "I … it … I don't know, but … I'm … frightened."

Zuzu put a hand on Lauren's arm and pressed past her. "Stay here," she said. Lauren never saw where the gun came from, but she had one in her hand when she got to the entry-way. As she reached for the knob, someone rapped on the door. Lauren flinched, but Zuzu stayed perfectly calm as she looked through the peephole. She seemed to melt, and the weapon disappeared as she turned and gazed at Lauren. She opened the door, throwing it back wide. "Tomáš!" She scolded him as she opened the door. "You nearly scared poor Lauren out of her skin. Come in. Come in. You know you don't need to knock."

Tomáš stepped in, looking sheepish as he clutched his hat in his hand. "Sorry to keep you waiting." He turned and looked towards where Lauren stood, partially shielded by the wall. His gaze narrowed and something about his look made her skin crawl. For a moment, those Slavic features made her think of etchings she'd seen of *Vlad Ţepeş* — also known as Vlad the Impaler, *Vlad Drăculea* — *Dracula.*

"We weren't expecting you for hours," Zuzu said. She didn't seem to notice the look in her son's eye.

Lauren stepped out into the living room, suddenly self-conscious of her attire. The nightgown she still wore was a bit thin to be gallivanting about in, especially in the middle of the day.

Tomáš stopped and looked at her cautiously. The chill of his eyes on her skin made the hair on her arms rise. Her stomach churned and she swallowed hard to keep anything from coming up. "Learn anything interesting?" Lauren forced a bright question as she wrapped her arms around herself.

"Nothing of any consequence," he said flatly. "But another page of that document you were looking for has reportedly been found in the archives at The Sedlec Ossuary. You need to go see it. I'll take you."

"We were about to have lunch," Zuzu beamed. "Come join us. Lauren needs to eat before she goes anywhere."

"Excuse me," Lauren turned towards the stairs. "I'll go change."

Upstairs she dressed quickly, pausing to brush her long hair and plait it hurriedly into a braid, which she knotted up at the nape of her neck and pinned into place. As she passed, she paused at the window looking at the spot where she'd seen the man in the yard. Her eye turned towards the drive, and she chilled when she realized the detective's car wasn't parked outside. She suddenly felt sick.

She turned from the window and stopped long enough to put on her socks and shoes, then raced down the stairs to find Zuzu in the kitchen alone.

Her hostess froze when Lauren appeared around the corner. "What is it, dear?"

"Where's Tomáš?" she gulped.

"I told you," she said. "He's going to be late. He found something at the museum."

Floating dots turned to stars in her eyes as the room spun. She caught the edge of the counter. "What is it?" Zuzu asked.

"He was here," Lauren said.

"Who was here?" Zuzu looked genuinely concerned.

"Your son," Lauren snapped. "He was just here."

"Last night, yes."

"No. Just now." Bile rose in the back of her throat.

"Are you sure you're feeling all right?" Zuzu caught her arm as the room tilted and a mist of sweat broke over her upper lip. "Your color has gone off."

The woman led Lauren over to the table and got a chair under her before her knees gave out. Lauren fisted her hands and pressed her elbows on the table to support herself. Her mind was racing, and her heart was rushing to keep up, barely able to supply sufficient blood flow to keep her from passing out.

"Here." A glass of water was pressed into her unsteady hand. Zuzu helped her lift it to her lips. She took a tentative sip before all but burying her face in the glass, gulping desperately. The cool water hit her stomach and churned like a whirlpool, threatening to come back up. Lauren pushed the glass away, pressing her cold hands to her hot face. Zuzu took a tea towel from the drawer by the stove and rinsed it in the sink. She pressed the cloth against her neck. The relief was almost immediate. "Do I need to call for an ambulance?" Zuzu pulled up a chair and sat down beside her, as Lauren sat back. Her hostess mopped her face with the cloth, and the spinning in her head began to abate.

"No," she said, but even Lauren wasn't convinced. "I don't

know what's happening … I've never been one to get sick like this."

"You're with child, dear …"

"I never had morning sickness with either of my sons." Lauren took the cloth and used it to mop her chest where sweat trickled between her breasts. "Something is wrong with me. I think … I mean," Lauren hesitated. "I think I may be losing my mind." She spoke the words she'd been thinking.

"Perhaps you're having an indigo child," Zuzu said.

Lauren looked at her blankly. "A what?"

"Surely in your line of work you've heard of indigo children?" Zuzu said. "A star child? Sometimes they are even called rainbow children. They present as difficult to manage, but it's generally because they have some energy … some force they are struggling to control or understand."

"Did you say star child?" Lauren swallowed hard.

"Some say they are reincarnated spirits who didn't have the slate wiped fully clean," Zuzu said, taking the cloth and rinsing it again before handing it back. "Since they come straight from a higher plane, their karmic debt is almost nil, so they are *blessed* with gifts."

"What kind of gifts?" Lauren asked.

"Some are especially sensitive to others, some can teleport, or use telekinesis. Others have the gift of foresight or prophesy; clairvoyance. Some can change their shape, or even escape the bonds of their own time and place in the universe. Because their spirits are pure, they're especially in tune with animals and can sense when a creature is upset, or suffering. They have a higher aptitude for the arts, especially music and drawing. Some say they can even hear the music of the cosmos."

Lauren's head lifted and the hand holding the dish cloth to the base of her skull fell to her lap. "So … do they carry that gift throughout their lives?"

"Yes." She nodded. "Unless they have it beaten out of

them. Most remain at least sensitive to the forces around them; good or ill."

"Good or ill?"

"Why do you ask?" Zuzu leaned in to inspect her, taking the cloth back and mopping her brow as she pushed aside a lock of hair that had come loose near her temple.

"There was a man in the yard …" Lauren's voice caught in her throat.

"What?" Zuzu started to get up. Lauren caught her arm.

"I already told you …" Lauren said. "You went to the door to see who it was … you had a gun."

"Of course I have a gun. I have several," Zuzu said. "I'm never more than ten feet from a gun in this house."

"It was Tomáš at the door …" Lauren forced herself to continue. "But … something wasn't right." Zuzu's brow knitted, and she appeared to puzzle over Lauren's story, clearly baffled by the tale. "There was something odd about the way he looked at me. His car wasn't here."

"What do you mean? I think if my own son were here, I'd know it." She stood and paced. "How did he look at you?"

"I don't know." She took a deep breath. "He looked at me like … like he was … hungry."

Zuzu's brows lifted. "Hungry? Like … *sexually*?" She nearly choked on the word as she sneered.

"God, no!" Lauren recoiled. "But his eyes were … devouring my flesh."

Zuzu looked dubiously at her. "I suspect you are an indigo yourself," she said. "Clearly you have been under a great deal of strain. Tomáš told me some of what has happened to you. The soup is ready. You need to eat, then you can go lie down until he returns. Maybe when you see him, you'll realize you were imagining ghosts."

"Ghosts?"

"This region is rife with them." She shrugged. "The

ancient spirits of conquerors and kings still roam the lands. If you are perceptive, perhaps you have met one of them."

Perceptive? Well, that was one way to put it. Yes. She had seen ghosts before. Lauren was still certain of what she'd seen that night at the Stanley Hotel, the night she and Rowan met. No one was within ten feet of her when someone — *something* pushed her down the Grand Staircase. Not a quarter of an hour before, she'd encountered a figure in the hallway outside of room number 428. She'd thought it odd when the man stepped out of the room and donned a wide brimmed cowboy hat. He turned and nodded to her. "Ma'am," he said, tipping his hat. He turned and took two steps and vanished. As sure as she lived and breathed, she'd not only seen him, but heard him, too. His voice came to her just as easily today as it had that night so long ago.

"Here." Zuzu put a bowl of soup in front of her and added a plate of bread. "Eat."

Lauren did as she was told. By the time she finished the meal, her hands had stopped shaking and her nerves were starting to settle. She tried to convince herself that she must have still been dreaming; a vision induced by dehydration and Phenergan.

17

Rowan dropped his tools into the wooden box at the edge of the excavation and went to the tent where Jean-René sat with a bottle of water. The Canadian's face was red. His shirt was dark with sweat, but his skin was dry. Rowan eyed him warily. "You okay?"

He muttered something in French. Rowan didn't recognize it as any of his favorite swear words. Rowan didn't feel much better, but at least he was still sweating. The heat could be brutal, even deadly. Rowan leaned over, inspecting him. His hand went to Jean-René's brow. He was burning up.

"Not acclimated to the heat," he panted.

Rowan turned to the cooler nearby. Someone was keeping it loaded with ice and bottled water for the team. He took a bottle and handed it to Jean-René. "I know it sounds crazy but take this and put it against your groin."

"What?"

"The inside of your thigh. You look like you're on the verge of a heat-stroke," Rowan said. "You need to lower your body temperature. The largest arteries run along the groin, and if you can cool the blood there, that's a great way to lower your body temp." He reached back into the ice chest and took out a couple more bottles, handing a second to his friend. "One on each side." He took a third and put it against the back of Jean-René's neck. The cameraman seemed to melt into relaxation, as the relief from the heat came quickly.

"I don't know how you do it, man," Jean-René said a short time later. "I was not made for the desert."

"I've been here long enough; been on enough digs to get used to it." Rowan drained a bottle of water and tossed it into the recycling bin.

"Yeah, well your neck is sunburnt," the Canadian mused.

"No surprises there," Rowan said. "SPF 50 is no match for the desert. As long as I don't blister, it'll be okay."

"Tell that to your wife." Jean-René chortled.

Rowan stood, continuing to monitor his friend, resting a hand on the middle of his chest. He traded out the water bottles for three more cool ones. "She won't be happy either way," Rowan said. "Hopefully, the burn will fade before I see her."

"Maybe," Jean-René said, taking a deep breath. Rowan sat back down beside him. After a moment, Jean-René spoke tentatively. "I probably shouldn't tell you this," he began, but paused.

"What?" Rowan looked over at him, matching his eye.

"Bahati was pretty upset when you and Lauren left," he said. "Especially after how the Network treated us."

Rowan pursed his lips and hung his head, leaning his elbows on his knees. "We never meant to hurt her, or you." He swallowed hard. "Lauren was overwhelmed with trying to care for the boys and keep up with Jacob's demands. She offered to keep up with a couple research projects, but Jacob just seemed to pile on more and more. Me getting accepted at the University was just an excuse for her to have some down time. We pleaded with the Network to take care of you both, but ... I suspect Jacob took out his anger at us on you, and ... I am sorry for that."

"Jacob is an ass," Jean-René said curtly. "We all knew that. I just never thought he could stoop so low."

"Nothing he does surprises me anymore," Rowan said.

There was a long pause between them. Finally, Jean-René asked, "Do you think you'll ever come back to work? Think Lauren will ever want to come back?"

Rowan shook his head, his eye going to the horizon where the sun cast a shimmering mirage on the sand. Heat made the image sway like waves on the ocean as it rose. "She's restless," he said. "I can tell. But …"

"But?"

"In six or seven more months, she'll have a third to keep up with. I can't imagine she'll be ready to go back to work any time soon." He hesitated. "I'm not saying never, but … while the kids are little, who's to say."

"Think you'll stop at three?"

"We have been doing everything *not* to have another." Rowan smirked.

"*Everything*?" Jean-René asked playfully. "Really?"

"Well, short of one of us going under the knife, nothing seems to prevent it." He shrugged. "Not that I mind." He sat back, smiling as he closed his eyes. "I love our boys. Being a dad is just the best."

"Yeah it is," Jean-René agreed. "I know Bahati would like to have more." He sighed, "But … I'm happy with just one. I like being able to spoil Nyota."

"Just don't forget to spoil Bahati, too." Rowan grinned.

Jean-René pursed his lips. "I'm afraid Bahati and I haven't …" He choked back the words. "We're not doing okay."

"What?" Rowan's brows reached for the brim of his hat as he sat up. "What's going on?"

Emotions washed over his friend's troubled face as he fought back his feelings. "Things haven't been the same since Nyota was born. I don't think … I don't think she loves me anymore."

"What? What are you talking about? Of course she loves you. Why would you think she doesn't love you?"

His jaw clenched and he looked up with glistening eyes. "When I reach for her in the night … she draws away. I try to show her … to tell her how much I love her, but … she pushes back. We fight all the time." His voice cracked. "I hired help so she could have a break, bought a sailboat so we could take romantic trips on the water, but … she seems so distant; so lost to me."

"Jean-René, I'm so sorry." Rowan put a hand on his knee. "I'm sure all the drama with the Network hasn't helped anything."

"I just want the love you and Lauren have," the cameraman admitted. "It seems to come so easily for you. You just look at her and she melts into you. When I look at Bahati … she turns to stone."

Rowan hated to see his friend suffering. "It hasn't always been easy for me and Lauren, you'll remember."

"Maybe, but … even when you two were fighting, she still loved you. You loved her."

Rowan sat back, swallowing hard, considering his words for a moment. "I'll admit, Lauren and I are … unique." He took off his hat and ran his bandana over his head, sighing. "Her soul and mine are bound by a force I can't explain," he said. "God, that woman …" He proceeded to tell Jean-René about the night in Mexico, when he'd had an encounter he could only explain as a dream. "I don't think that's just love," Rowan said. "That's some kind of ancient magic. She's had me under her spell since the moment I laid eyes on her."

That didn't seem to help Jean-René any at all. "I love Bahati more than life. More than … hockey."

"That's saying a lot." Rowan gave him a wry smile.

"Tell me, Rowan. Tell me how to win her back? I can't live without her. I don't want to."

"Have you told her that?"

"Not in so many words, but … yes." Jean-René's amber eyes searched his. "Tell me how you won Lauren."

Rowan shrugged as he shifted in his chair. "Well, you know we met at the Stanley Hotel, right? She was hurt, and I was the medic that responded."

"You drugged her!" Jean-René jabbed a finger at him as he seemed to come to the decision that Rowan couldn't have won her any other way.

"Well, I did give her morphine," Rowan said. "But … I'm not sure that was what did it."

"Go on," Jean-René insisted. "Go on."

"The next day, I went to visit her in the hospital. I took her a bouquet of wildflowers and English roses. I was afraid if I waited until she was discharged, you guys would pack her up and take her back to California, and I'd never see her again. I asked her out on a date … when she was able of course," he said to himself as he thought about how awkward he must have seemed. "She said no."

"Wait, what?"

"She said no," Rowan repeated. "I thought my heart was going to fall into my shoes. I wasn't used to pretty girls telling me no."

"So, what did you do?"

"I conceded but I asked her if I could do anything for her, get her anything she might need," he said. "She finally said she could use a book or something to read. I just happened to have a couple of books out in the ambulance. I went down and brought them up to her."

"What were you reading?"

"Edgar Rice Burroughs and Robert Heinlein," he said. "*A Princess of Mars* and *The Moon is A Harsh Mistress*." Rowan had to laugh, remembering Henry insisting he was ready for Heinlein. "But I didn't just give her the books," he continued. "I pulled up a chair and opened one up and started reading."

"That's how you won her heart? You read to her?"

"She fell asleep halfway through *A Princess of Mars*," Rowan said. "I fell asleep in the chair beside her. I woke up with her gazing into my eyes; with her smiling at me. She said, *ask me again.*"

"So, you did, and she said yes." Jean-René anticipated her answer.

He nodded. "A week later, with her leg still in a cast, I picked her up at the cabin she'd rented for the rest of the month."

"And what did you do on your first date?"

"I took her to a lodge for a nice dinner, and then took her to my favorite bar," he said. "Friends of mine had a band and played there on weekends. They let me sit in on a set and I played guitar and sang to her."

"I didn't know you played guitar," Jean-René quipped.

"Can't very well take it with me on a Bigfoot hunt, now. Can I?" He chuckled.

"What'd you sing?"

Rowan laughed. "*Rhiannon*," he said.

"Stevie Nicks?" Jean-René's puzzlement contorted his face. "Really?"

"Have you ever listened to the lyrics?" Rowan asked. Jean-René shrugged in a way that told Rowan he hadn't. Rowan sang a few bars. The lyrics described Lauren perfectly.

"You definitely won," Jean-René said, swallowing hard.

"You will, too," Rowan said. "You just need to find a way to show her. Bust your ass if you have to, but you have to put in the work. She'll appreciate it."

18

The trouble with humans was that they were curious creatures. Too curious. On the reverse side of the coin, they were weak, easily crushed beneath a god's heel, Enlil thought, watching the house. Assuming the form of the detective was easy, and now he knew he could enter the house without invitation. The owner had given permission … twice now. He waited until the guest went back upstairs before he returned to the door.

This little game of cat and mouse was a delightful diversion from centuries of tedium. While his forces gathered and he waited for the stars to align, he had time for such games. Still, there was important work to be done.

Long ago, he had been cast from the heavens into the Hell he now resided in. His patience could only carry him so long. This stupid global peace accord was burdensome, but he knew it could not last long. Peace was weak. He needed conflict to fuel his war machine. He would have to feed the chaos that gave him strength. This would be a good place to start.

Though his brother's forces had been trying to thwart him at every turn, his creation was nothing if not predictable. Mankind couldn't avoid war; conflict. They couldn't follow the

All-Father's rules; couldn't keep their hands off someone else's woman or property. While Faith, Hope and Charity were the All-Father's favorite virtues, Enlil relied on their opposites; Doubt, Fear, and Pride. Each of these anti-virtues fed what had become known as the Seven Deadly Sins.

Of those, Lust and Greed were his favorites. Hatred, an offspring of Wrath and Envy, took a little more work, but once it was initiated, it would smolder and burn long and hot. His own hatred had simmered in his core for centuries. Now was the hour of his great and terrible wrath. It gave him authority over the forces known to mankind.

Standing at the door, he assumed the detective's form, then reached for the latch. As he came in, the resident of the manor house stuck her head out of the other room. "Oh, Tomáš. You're here! Good. Come here. I'm very worried about your friend. I'm afraid she's—"

He was at her throat before she finished her sentence. He tightened his claws around her neck clenching his hand tightly. He gazed into her frightened eyes.

"Tomáš …?" she gasped, barely above a whisper. He allowed her to see his true form, just to feel the terror that raced through her. It delighted him to feel it quicken her pulse as his black wings unfurled and his horns pierced his skull. He wore his heavy crown well. The throb of her heartbeat beneath his claws made his own heart swell with anticipation.

Like the puny humans at the museum, her flesh tore with ease. The look on her face was one that brought the demon pure joy as her lifeblood coursed from her veins. Her knees crumpled, and she slid down. He caught her elbows and lowered her to the slate tile floors, though why he'd cared to ease her death any was beyond him. Maybe his centuries of banishment had made him soft. But now, the time was coming when he would have everything he needed to regain his full power. He would take his seat at the right hand of the god who had betrayed him so many centuries before. Better yet, he would usurp the All-Father from the throne and take his place of dominion over the Heavens and the Earth.

Death gave him the greatest power. It renewed his soul to feel a heartbeat quiver one last time; to see the light go out in a human's eyes. They fed him with their soul as it escaped the bonds of their mortal shell. He felt his vigor restored as blood pooled and then thickened.

But this wasn't the soul he wanted. This wasn't the soul he needed. It was the soul he could take, and it would bide him 'til he had the incantations and spells needed to face the *Chosen One*. The creature upstairs had the most amazing powers. She vexed him. He'd never encountered a human with so strong a soul. He just needed his book. He needed it to be complete, with all the missing spells restored. Then, he could overcome that troublesome creature and reclaim his rightful place amongst the stars.

It was only a matter of time. She would lead him to the pages if he could just be patient. Meanwhile, he needed to feed, and feed he did.

The detective parked his car in the drive and dashed into the house through the rain. It was unusual for this time of the year to see so much of it, and the day had gone dark and cold; the night, colder. He had spent a long and tedious day going through records and interviewing staff members at the museum. He'd met with the medical examiner and spent hours going over the findings. Then the long drive from the city had him bleary-eyed. He longed for his mother's cooking — whatever she'd made for dinner — he didn't care. After he ate, he'd be ready for a good night's sleep in his old room. He also wanted to speak with Dr. Pierce when she was able to be questioned.

Not sure if his mother and her house guest were still

awake, he came in quietly, unsurprised to find the door unlocked. The living room was dark, but a dim light was on in the kitchen. He shook off his raincoat as he peeled out of it and hung it on the peg by the door. "Zuzu?" he called softly. "I'm home."

There was no answer. Maybe she and Lauren were upstairs. Hunger and the latent perfume of his mother's cooking coaxed him towards the kitchen where he anticipated finding freshly baked bread and perhaps something more substantial. Liver and onions? Black sausages? He couldn't quite identify the mélange of meat, onions, and something he could only discern as blood.

He stopped in the doorway when the carpet at the threshold of the kitchen made an unusual squishing sound beneath his feet. He glanced down, finding a dark stain. He gasped and took a step back, seeing red prints on the ivory rug. His eyes lifted and went to the houseguest sitting on the floor, covered in blood with a terrified look on her tear-stained face. Her blouse was dark with it. One fist was wrapped tightly around a bloody knife. She held it out, weakly threatening him if he came close. The other was clamped around his mother's neck as she lay limp in the woman's arms.

Lauren's face was terror-stricken; her eyes wide with terror. His knees faltered and he sank down to the floor, his hand going to his mouth. The houseguest struggled to move away from him as her dark eyes seemed to grow darker. She held up the knife to ward him off, like a lioness defending her kill. She had the look of a frightened animal who knew she was cornered. He reached for her to calm her, not sure if he should be more afraid of her than she was of him. She cried out and flicked the blade at him. "Don't!"

The detective recoiled. That was the first moment he considered what must have happened here. Lauren Pierce had been accused of killing two others, and now ... *Christ! He'd left his mother with a suspected killer! What a fool he had been!* His mother was a trained killer in her own right, but she was older … too old to defend herself against someone who was a good foot taller, thirty years younger, and deceptively strong. *This whole pregnancy thing? Was it just a ruse?*

"What have you done to my mother?" Kovač roared as he fell back then scrambled to his feet. His brows knitted as tears built in the corners of his eyes, then rolled down his cheeks.

Lauren looked wounded, as if she'd suddenly realized what he must be thinking. "No!" She held up the blood-soaked knife, blocking him from touching her. "Get away!" Her hand holding the knife was trembling. Then he recognized the woman's other hand was clamped over a gaping wound on his mother's neck. *Had she hurt his mother? Or was she trying to cover the wound. Was she trying to protect her? To save her?* Kovač knew how much blood the human body contained; how quickly a body could exsanguinate. By the sheer volume of blood, he knew it was too late. He couldn't move.

Lauren's panic culminated in a weak, "Help us …" The knife fell from her hand.

But there was no help for his mother. She was gone.

19

Tima woke to the panicked cries of a child. She threw back the covers on her bed and rushed into the guest room where Henry sat up in the middle of the bed wailing. John Carter slept through the shrieks. Tima scooped up the boy and wrapped him in her arms and carried him back to her room, patting his back and making soft hushing noises to try and soothe him. She sat down on her own bed and rocked him. When his cries turned to whimpers, she sat him back and looked him over, making sure he wasn't injured. "What's the matter, sweet boy? Did you have a bad dream?"

"Momma …" He sniffled and set to crying again.

Tima pulled him back into her and ran her hand over his coppery blond hair, kissing his head. "She'll be home soon. I know you miss her."

"The Devil's trying to get her." He trembled as he sniffed.

"Aw, baby." She rocked him. "Your mother is a strong woman. The Devil would be a fool to try and take her on."

"I don't like that Devil." Henry snapped. "That Devil is mean."

Tima's heart broke for the boy. He had a vivid imagination, and his dreams clearly reflected that. He'd never been without his mother. She did her best to comfort him, but she wasn't Lauren. Still, she had to do something. "Well, don't you worry about your mother. She'll show that Devil who's boss. Come." She hoisted him up and put him over her shoulder. "Let's go find something good for breakfast. Are you hungry?"

"I *hungy*." John Carter came around the corner, dragging his blanket with his Buzz Lightyear toy under his arm.

"Of course you are." Tima chortled. "Come. How about some *knaffeh*? Have you had that before?"

"No, Auntie Tima." Henry said. "What is *knaffeh*?"

"It is better to show you than to tell you," she said.

By the time she set the plate of *knaffeh* in front of them, the boy's nightmare seemed forgotten. She plied them with scrambled eggs and warm chai until the main course was ready. The boys' eyes grew round as she served each of them a generous portion. The cheese pastries were the perfect combination of sweet and savory, creamy and crunchy.

Ahmose made an overt act of inhaling the aroma of her mother's kitchen as she came in and found the boys with their faces covered in syrup, pistachios, and cheese. "Mumma, what did you make? That smells so good."

"Come make a plate." Tima beckoned as she sat at the table sipping her tea.

"You made *knaffeh*? You never made *knaffeh* for me when I was little."

"I made it for you now," Tima said. "I've been practicing my baking skills lately. I love having little ones to bake for again."

"Well," Ahmose scoffed as she made a plate and came to sit with her mother. "Don't get any ideas about grandchildren from me any time soon."

"You know I am not in any hurry." Tima rose and refilled the boys' cups. "Henry and John Carter have been wonderful to have around. They are such good boys." She ran her hand over John Carter's dark hair, then did the same to Henry. "What shall we do today, sweet boys?"

"*Pway wockets!*" John Carter enthused with his mouth full.

Henry looked up at Tima with sad puppy-dog eyes. "I want to go dig with my daddy."

Ahmose rose and came over. "Have you ever ridden a camel?"

Henry's face contorted. "A camel?"

"Why don't we go out to the pyramids and ride a camel?" Ahmose picked up John Carter and tickled his tummy. "Then, Henry, if you want to dig like your daddy, I bet we can find some ancient Egyptian treasure." That seemed to perk Henry up a little. "Mumma? Will you go with us?" Ahmose said to her mother.

"Sure," she said. "I'll call my friend Dr. Novak and see if he's got a team working a dig. Maybe they have a place for a couple of junior archaeologists."

"So, when we finish our breakfast, we'll get cleaned up and brush our teeth, and we'll go."

"What about Shemi?" Henry asked.

"Why don't you finish up and you can go ask her if she wants to go?"

THE POLICE OFFICER THAT CUFFED LAUREN HAD TO physically lift her to her feet and hold her up. Her legs felt like concrete and the room spun around her as she was led outside. She stiffened and came to an abrupt halt when she came face-to-face with the three men who'd taken her from the café in Prague.

"What has happened here?" The ringleader demanded of the police officer.

"You'll have to talk to Detective Kovač." The police officer nudged Lauren to move, but the three men were blocking her path. The ringleader eyed her warily. Lauren was so numb all she could do was stare back at him.

"Kovač? Who is Kovač!" the man yelled over the other crime scene investigators, detectives and law enforcement people who milled around outside of the house, waiting for their opportunity to participate in the investigation.

Kovač walked out of his mother's house, feeling weak; drained of all energy. He stepped aside as the gurney with his mother's body was removed. He turned and glanced over at three men as they approached. "Kovač?"

He recognized the three men immediately, just from Lauren's descriptions of them. His eyes found Lauren as the police officer shoved her towards the police car. He wanted to go to her, but he was also wary of her, in light of everything that had happened. The evidence suggested she had been the one who killed his mother.

"May I help you?" Kovač asked as the men met him at the step.

"My name is Captain Bertram," the tall one said. "We're with the *Corps Gendarmerie*."

Tomáš' expression dropped. "Gendarmerie? The Vatican Gendarmerie?"

"We are from a *special* branch of the Vatican Intelligence Service, to be precise," he said, presenting his credentials. "We have been investigating the theft of several holy …and unholy relics. The implications of these relics falling into the wrong hands is a grave danger to us all."

"A *special* branch?" Kovač puzzled, inspecting the badge and ID. It was printed in Latin, some of which Kovač could read and understand.

"Yes," Bertram said. "We are ordained to protect ancient relics and are tasked with preventing any foreseeable apocalypse. We do not enforce the laws of man … we enforce the laws of God and the Holy See.”

“Aren’t you a little out of your jurisdiction?” The detective studied the two men over the captain’s shoulder.

“Ours is the jurisdiction of the Bishop of Rome. It is not a geographical jurisdiction,” he said patiently. “The Kingdom of God is our jurisdiction.”

That made Kovač do a double take. “That sounds like a load of garbage, Captain.”

“The Holy See is administered by the Roman Curia, that’s Latin for Court,” he said. “The papal bull that was our charter was signed in 1346. It is one of the Vatican’s oldest orders.”

The detective eyed the men warily. “Did you take my suspect into custody and question her a few days ago? Did *you* drug her?”

“Your suspect? Drugs?”

“Dr. Pierce,” he said, handing back the badge. He made a note to run a search through the department’s data base when he got back to the office. He’d call the Pope himself if he had to. All this cloak and dagger sounded like a farce to him. “She claims three men abducted her and held her for questioning before drugging her and returning her to her hotel. At the same time, two staff members at the university museum were murdered. Dr. Pierce was seen leaving with an artifact on video camera. She’s been in protective custody, and now the officer who was protecting her has been murdered in the same fashion.”

“I assure you; the VIS does not drug anyone we take into question.” The captain glanced back at one of his fellows. “This is quite troubling to hear.” He swallowed hard, shuffling his feet.

“She claims she was with you when the first two were killed. She has no alibi for the death of our officer.”

“We have reason to believe we know who may be responsible for these murders … all of them," Bertram said. "Is there somewhere we can speak?"

"We can speak here." Tomáš crossed his arms. "If you have information regarding the cases I am working, then I'm listening."

"Very well then." Bertram cleared his throat. "Are you familiar with the legend of the Codex Gigas?"

"Quite." Kovač snapped. He'd heard plenty about it from Dr. Pierce.

"The Devil has come to claim what is his, and he will stop at nothing to get the missing pages of the Codex, including murder."

Lauren sat in the small room, trying to force her body to stop shivering. She had been given a damp towel to try and clean up after the lab techs had finished their evidence collection. Her borrowed clothes were still sticky, and her hair clung to her skin. A foul taste lingered on her tongue. She'd been sick several times since the investigators hoisted her up from the floor after they'd taken pictures and collected Zuzu's cold and broken body from atop her.

She'd been photographed and had her fingerprints taken … again. In handcuffs, she'd been placed in the same holding cell she'd been kept in before. Several other suspects sat on the benches; their feet secured in shackles. She sat with her head hanging, avoiding the horrified gazes of those around her. She had to think they saw her as some kind of an axe murderer.

Soon, she sat staring at the same public defender she'd seen previously. The same sick feeling she'd had the first time they'd hauled her to jail left her retching over the toilet in the cell repeatedly before they hauled her back to the interrogation room where she sat now.

Detective Kovač paced the room with his arms crossed,

glaring at her. He was angry, she could tell. He'd been peppering her with questions for the last half hour, none of which she could answer. Her brain had shut down and it took every ounce of strength she had now not to pass out, throw up, or freak out. That same effort kept her from answering the sharp questions and accusations he threw at her.

Lauren just sat there. She felt numb. This was the third time in her life she'd ended up in jail. All three were unfounded. So far, she'd been cleared twice, but the law of averages were eventually going to catch up with her if things kept going like they were. The lack of blood on her shoes had been her *get-out-of-jail-free* card last time. This time though, she was covered in it. *What else was she supposed to do?* She'd walked in to find a twisted visage of Tomáš Kovač kneeling over Zuzu's body with his hands at his own mother's throat. Lauren had fought off the monster with nothing more than a kitchen knife and her unbound rage, which had quickly ebbed once the *creature* evaporated into thin air. She sat looking at the same face now and realized the slicing cut she'd made across the monster's face had left no mark on the real Tomáš Kovač.

He finally pounded his fist on the table. Lauren flinched, gasping. "You killed my mother!" he roared.

She looked up at him, her mouth open as she tried to make her brain form the words and transmit the information to her mouth. Her voice came out in a faint gasp. "No," she managed. She shook her head, and it made the room spin. "No." She tried again. This time the word came out audibly. "I tried ... I did ... I tried to ... save her."

"I don't believe you!" he yelled in her face. "Who killed my mother?"

"Detective!" The *advokát* protested. "You don't have to answer his questions."

Lauren recoiled, torn between her better judgment and his angry words. She felt the need to tell him the truth, but she feared he wouldn't believe her and anything she might say could be used against her. She knew she needed to listen to the *advokát*. A tear peeled down her cheek as she cowered, turning away.

"Who killed my mother?" he demanded. His hand pounded the table again and she suspected it was everything he could do not to strike out at her physically. Lauren turned, steeling herself against his anger, setting her jaw and pursing her lips as he demanded answer of her a third time. "Dammit! Who killed my mother, Dr. Pierce?" Kovač stood to his full height. His anger flamed red in his cheeks and he all but spat the words at her.

"Mister Kovač!" The advokát stood to move between the two.

"Who killed my mother!" He shrieked, rage turned his face red, and tears poured down his face.

"The Devil killed your mother," Lauren cried, her tears matching his as they escaped her eyes.

"Dr. Pierce." The attorney turned, catching her arm. "Don't speak."

The detective's knees failed him, and he collapsed into his chair, his eyes locked with Lauren's.

She held his gaze despite the waves of sobs that passed over her. "I'm sorry." Lauren finally turned to her legal counsel. She swallowed hard, her lip still trembling. "I need to talk to the detective … in private."

The advokát looked at her as if she'd lost her mind. "Dr. Pierce, I would advise you otherwise."

"You are dismissed," Lauren said. "Thank you for your services, but they are no longer needed." Her gaze returned to Detective Kovač's. "I will serve as my own advokát from here out."

"But," the advokát protested.

The detective stood and went to the door, opening it. The public defender glared at Lauren for a minute, her eye going to the detective at the door as she rose slowly. "You can call me back any time you feel the need for aid. You understand that, right?"

"I do," Lauren said. She sat back in her chair until the door closed behind the woman. The detective returned to his chair, waiting for her to speak.

It took her a moment to collect her thoughts. When she didn't take the initiative, his angry words came out with a calm restraint she hadn't expected. "Some time today, Dr. Pierce."

"I don't expect you to believe me," Lauren began.

"Who killed my mother, Dr. Pierce?"

"You did." She managed. "You killed your mother." She watched the color drain from his face. He sank back into the empty chair behind him, his gaze piercing into Lauren's soul, and she began trembling again. She hadn't realized she'd stopped. "But ... I saw the look in *your* eye ..." her teeth chattered. "Saw the rage ... the evil ... and I knew ... it wasn't *you*." His expression never changed. "Just like it wasn't me ... in the museum."

"I killed my mother?" he asked flatly, clearly not believing her.

"It looked like you ... at first ..." Her voice trembled as she closed her eyes against the memory. The face had been his, until his teeth morphed into fangs; his hands splayed into claws. She tried to explain the long forked tongue and the grotesque face. "But then it changed into something so horrific, so evil, I knew ... it had to be the Devil. It had horns, scales ... like a lizard ... it smelled like a reptile, like a corrupted version of something from a H.P. Lovecraft novel."

At that, the detective's features lifted from a scowl to a mocking smile. "You really expect me to believe ..."

"I know what I saw, Detective! Someone ... something ...this monster... is baiting us ... playing into our fears. I gazed into those eyes ..." She drew back, trying not to remember, but unable to put the vision out of her mind.

"Those flaming red eyes … pulsing with evil … hungry for chaos and death." She could hear her own voice going dark. "It could only be the Devil. Who else … what else could it be?"

"Do you realize what this sounds like? It sounds like the ramblings of a mad woman!" he snapped, glowering at her.

"It wants you not to believe me. It wants us at odds. I could sense it. It will use us … is using us against each other. It wants us to be confused. It wants you to believe I killed those people. It wanted me to think you killed your mother. It wants *you* to think *I* killed your mother."

"It." His jaw flexed. He stood, running his hand through the mop of blue-black hair, before he looked back at her over his shoulder. "It?"

"I don't know how to explain it without you thinking I've lost my mind. Hell, I'm not sure I haven't, but … I've seen things. I've experienced … *things*. Unreal things. I had a … I don't know … call it a dream or … a vision. I've been given a warning."

He ran an unsteady hand over his five o'clock shadow, his eyes never breaking contact with hers. "You have *visions*?"

"A trickster comes like a thief in the night," she quoted.

"A trickster."

"Do you know who else comes like a thief in the night?"

"Let me guess. *Death*?"

"No, the Bible says the Lord will return like a thief in the night …"

"So … we have God to blame for my mother's death?"

"This … *trickster* wants us to believe many things, but the last thing I believe is that this has anything to do with God."

"I'm even more confused."

"Have you ever heard of the ancient astronaut theory?" Lauren asked.

"Ancient … astronauts?"

"In short," she paused taking a deep breath. "Any time

you hear a story about God or gods, you substitute the word *alien*."

His brow arched slowly as his blue eyes widened. She could tell he thought she'd lost her mind, but she gave him his moment of incredulity. "So now it's … aliens? Aliens killed my mother?" His incredulity was overt.

"Uh, huh," Lauren said.

"God is … an *alien*? Or this … *devil* is an alien?"

"It's just one theory," Lauren said. "But … if … *if* it's true and the ancient gods from the heavens really were aliens, then the enemies of the gods might also be aliens too."

"The enemies of the gods?" he asked. "Is that why the Pope's secret police were at my crime scene today?"

Lauren could feel the blood wash from her face. Her jaw dropped. "What?"

"The men you claimed abducted and drugged you. They say they are part of some secret order of the Vatican's Secret Intelligence division. They are looking for the missing pages of the Codex Gigas. The same pages that brought you here."

Lauren stared blankly at the wall. Her jaw flexed but the words wouldn't form on her lips.

Tomáš sat back, tapping the table as he seemed to choose his own words carefully. "They told me the Devil killed my mother, too. They think there are evil forces at hand trying to restore the book, to restore this … dark power that some believe it to hold. They think you are somehow involved in this … plot."

"And … what do *you* think?"

He stood and walked over to the window. He ran a hand over his weary face. "I'm not sure what to think. I might have been a believer once, but … well, that was a long time ago."

Lauren stared at her trembling hands. Drying blood filled the cracks in her knuckles; around and under her nails, too. She cringed at the thought of the dried blood on her chest and neck. "I believe they might be right." She finally broke the silence. "Dark forces are at play."

"I think you need to tell me more about this book." He came back and sat down in front of her. "Dark forces? Are we talking about bad people with evil intentions? Or are we talking demons from the Gates of Hell here?"

Lauren's shoulder lifted. She had her suspicions, but she wasn't sure he was ready to hear them. "According to legends, the Codex Gigas included a whole page dedicated to a sketch of the Devil who aided the book's author with his task. Do you have your cell phone?" she asked. He humored her, pulling his phone out of his jacket pocket. He handed it to her. She pulled up the web browser and did a search. When she found the image she was looking for, she handed it back. "That's the sketch of the Devil from the Codex."

"Unnerving to say the least," he said, studying it. The creature was depicted as having claws, red tipped horns, small eyes with red pupils and two long red tongues. Its skin was green.

"It's unlike any other image of the Devil from that time period," Lauren went on to explain most medieval representations of the devil, and how this one differed. His eyes lifted to hers. "There are pages of the Codex that are missing …" She hesitated. "What if the Devil is working to collect all the pages? A completed grimoire may be needed to—" She stopped.

"That's what the men from The Vatican said." Tomáš held her gaze. "But in order to do what?"

"I'm not sure," Lauren said. "But I do know one thing."

"What's that?"

"If we don't do something, more people could die."

"The apocalypse?" He eyed her skeptically.

She froze. "Yes." The statement was so matter of fact that there could be no doubt she truly believed the end of the world was at hand. "Exactly. If I don't get those pages before the Dark One does, the world … and everyone in it … is doomed to the same fate; annihilation."

"If …" He shook his head trying to reconcile her words with those of the VIS. "If you're right … how do we stop it?"

"We? I. I have to find those missing pages before the enemy does. I have to find them."

Tomáš crossed his arms over his chest and seemed to be sizing up the lies she must be telling him. He understood the kind of work she did from their previous conversations, but this was too incredible for any sane man to believe. Or was it? "So let's say all of this cock-and-bull story is true. Any clue where to start?" he finally asked.

"I'll play the Devils' advocate, if I must," Lauren stated flatly. "Supposing I am telling the truth … because I am … I do have one clue," Lauren said. "Ever heard of the Sedlec Ossuary?"

"No." Tomáš shook his head.

"The monster that attacked your mother told me about it," she said. The detective's look-alike in her dream had mentioned the ossuary and that there might be a page to be found at the ancient bastion. Now the trick would be to get the page before the demon and make sure no one died in the process.

"If this is going to work," Lauren said. "I am going to need your help."

Tomáš' eyebrow lifted. Questions were written in his blue eyes that were clouded with grief. Lauren could feel his pain. "Why would I help you? Explain."

" I need you to trust me. I have to know I can trust you. I need you to understand that I was not the one who hurt your mother. I did everything I could to save her."

"Did you really fight off a … *monster* for her? With nothing but a steak knife?"

"I'm sorry I couldn't stop it." Lauren swallowed hard; her lower lip quivered; chills washed over her. The flashback played in the back of her eyes like a movie, and she was certain Kovač could see the fear on her features. "It was too late by the time I got downstairs. But … I couldn't let you … it … defile her. It never occurred to me it might turn on me."

Tomáš recoiled. "It didn't hurt you, did it?"

"I am certain it wanted to," Lauren said. "I don't think the knife would have stopped it."

"So what did?"

Lauren looked at the manacles around her wrists that were attached to the bar on the table. She wanted to stand to stretch out her sore back; to run away and go home to Rowan, but she knew it was futile. "You're going to think I've lost my mind."

"You said it yourself," he said. "We need each other. I need you to help me understand what's going on because I'm having an incredibly hard time buying any of this. I'm sure you can understand why."

"I can," Lauren said. "I'm used to people thinking I'm crazy. Hell, I'm used to thinking I'm crazy."

"Better tell me everything then," he said.

Lauren told him. She told him probably more than she needed to.

20

R owan crawled into the bunk in a trailer near the dig site. He was hot, sweaty, and filthy from wallowing in the sand all day. His shoulders and knees ached from the tedious digging. The back of his neck stung where he'd missed getting sunscreen on his flesh.

Jean-René groaned as he hauled himself into the bunk above him. Sand fell from the cuffs of his pant legs. "I'm getting too old for this, my friend," he said, flopping down on the bed, his leg hanging over the edge.

"You're only five years older than I am," Rowan grunted.

"Admit it," Jean-René scoffed. "You're feeling it, too."

"Hell, yeah, I am."

Jean-René laughed. "I knew it."

There was a long pause as they lay recovering from the day. "So, what do you think?" Jean-René asked. "I did you a solid, didn't I?"

"Hell, yeah, you did," Rowan said, grinning. "You are my best friend for a reason. Thanks for the invite."

"What are friends for?" Jean-René chortled. Again there was a long pause before he spoke, his voice heavy with exhaustion. "Did you reach Lauren today?"

"I didn't have a signal," he said, lying flat on his back. "I'll try again in the morning before we head out."

"Tomorrow, we're going over to the glass crater." Jean-René's voice trailed off to almost a whisper.

"Say what?"

A heavy snore answered him.

"Henry? Whatever is the matter?" Tima rushed over to him as he backed away from the large white camel who eyed him warily. The boy was wailing. It wasn't like Henry to be so affronted. Normally he was an easy-going child with a good nature, but he'd been brooding and unsettled all day.

"I don't like that … I don't like camels." He tucked himself into her and wrapped his arm around her neck as she knelt down beside him. "That camel is mean."

"But you didn't even go for a ride yet." Shemi came over with John Carter. "Is it just this camel? There's a brown one over there with the longest eyelashes you ever did see. Would you rather ride the brown one?"

"I *yike* the brown one. I yike camels," John Carter said, but walked over and started patting the white one on his shoulder. The creature balked and snapped at the boy. It frightened him so badly the next thing Tima knew she had two wailing boys in her arms. She scooped them up and carried them away from the camel. The man running the rides said something sharply to her and she responded back in kind.

"I don't *yike* camels!" John Carter wailed. "Bad camel!" He stabbed a finger toward the beast as it rose, and turned, huffing.

"Maybe we'll ride the camels some other time," Ahmose suggested. "Mumma, where was your friend from the museum going to meet us?"

"He's not due for another hour," Tima said. "I did pack us a picnic." She sat Henry down.

John Carter squirmed so she sat him down, too. The younger brother reached over and caught his brother's hand. "Don't *cwy, Heny*," he said. "Momma's okay." Then Tima remembered Henry's dream.

"Come here, Henry." Tima drew him into her as she knelt down beside him. "Sweet boy, you are not still upset about the dream you had this morning, are you?"

Shemi and Ahmose took John Carter over to look at a vendors' booth nearby.

"Uh, huh," he said. "Momma's in trouble. I'm afraid."

"You know dreams are not real, right? You miss your mother and it's natural for you to be worried, but there's no reason to believe there's anything wrong."

"But there is, Auntie Tima." Henry sniffed, his breath coming in ragged waves. "I know my momma. She's scared and she's sick. My daddy should be there with her … but he isn't. Can you call my daddy, please?"

"I can try, but he's in the middle of the desert. His phone might not work."

"Just try?" He sobbed. "Please. Try?"

She hugged him and patted his back. "Okay. I'll try." Tima took her phone from her small handbag and dialed Rowan's number. The phone rang several times and then went to voicemail. "Rowan, darling. Tima here. The boys were missing you and hope you are having fun on your dig and making new discoveries. Henry would very much like to speak to his father when you have a chance and get this message. Please call when you have time." She hung up. "So sorry, sweet boy. He's busy. I'll try again later if he doesn't call right back."

"Thank you, Auntie Tima."

She ran her hand over his hair. "Of course. Now, let's see about lunch and then we'll go look for mummies."

~

"THE SEDLEC OSSUARY?" BERTRAM FURROWED HIS BROW. "Of course, I've heard of it." Kovač had shared his doubts about the *so-called* Vatican Intelligence Service agents with his superiors on the drive back from the scene. His lieutenant had gone through official channels to have their credentials validated, and it all checked out.

Lauren turned to Kovač. "We need to find it. We have to go there."

The detective eyed her warily. He still had his suspicions about Dr. Pierce. He wasn't sure he was ready to trust her; not yet. His mother was dead, and his heart was broken by her loss. But Lauren Pierce claimed she didn't do it — just like she had claimed not to have killed his victims at the museum. The evidence supported her claims about the murders at the museum, but the evidence of his mother's killing was still being analyzed. She couldn't refute the blood evidence. She was covered in his mother's blood. The medical examiner was checking for DNA evidence from his mother's nails as well. If Zuzu Kovač had put up a fight — and he suspected she would

there should be DNA evidence beneath her fingernails too.

"*Hřbitovní kostel Všech Svatých.* I had to look it up. It's a small Roman Catholic chapel located beneath the cemetery at the Church of All Saints. It's where the bones of hundreds of thousands of plague victims are ... well, interred might not be the right word," Tomáš said nervously.

"I think that may be where a missing page might be hidden," Lauren said. "But my fear is that this ... thing ... this *demon* ... is trying to bait me into moving it so it can be taken like the page at the museum in Prague."

"If the page is safest where it's at," Tomáš said. "Let sleeping dogs lie, as they say."

"That would be the easy way out," Bertram said. "We have our orders. The pages must be collected and protected from being misused. Dr. Pierce, your expertise here will be invaluable."

Tomáš turned sharply. He couldn't believe he was saying it. "You realize you're asking her to place herself in harm's way, yes? To put her child's life in harm's way." Bertram froze, his gaze darting between his colleagues and back to Lauren before he looked at Tomáš. "You didn't know she was pregnant." It wasn't a question. At this moment, he couldn't care less about Dr. Pierce's safety, at least not on a personal level. It was his job, however, and he had taken an oath to protect and serve.

Bertram sputtered. "All the more reason she has to go with us."

"What are you talking about?" the detective snapped.

"There is a prophesy," he said.

"It was claimed by the disciples of Jesus that he was of Heavenly origin, with a human mother and God, the Father," the bald man picked up the story. "There are similar stories in other pagan legends, but all of the prophesies are the same. They all say there will be a child, a child of the gods, who will come to save mankind, sent to be also a teacher of men. The savior will have mystical powers. First the child must be purely born ... of virgin birth."

"That rules me out," Lauren muttered under her breath. She was quite sure she knew when this child had been conceived. Rowan had been gone for two weeks on a class trip to Morocco. She'd been happy to welcome him home appropriately.

"Second, it must be a *son* of a god, not a daughter. In every story, this savior will perform miracles, be crucified, and resurrected, before becoming the judgment of mankind. But, another skills of this *messiah* in legends, is the ability to cast out demons. *If* the Devil incarnate is here to reassemble his book and make a play to have his place restored in the heavens, the prophesied child who is sent to save mankind in our lifetime, if such a child is born, would have the ability to cast out demons."

Lauren had run through these abilities like a checklist, marking off the ones she didn't think applied to her. She couldn't mark yes to most of the list, but it didn't ease her mind any.

"Like Jesus," the detective muttered.

"There are sixteen stories about crucified saviors, Jesus being one." Bertram nodded. "Dionysus, Mithras, Osiris, Inanna or Ishtar, the list goes on."

"I don't see how any of this has anything to do with me," Lauren said.

"You are a mother," the oldest said. "Life grows inside you. This child could be the very salvation of mankind."

Lauren felt her whole countenance collapse upon itself. The child in her womb was no larger than a strawberry. While she was aware of its movements and had heard its heartbeat she wasn't sure if the child had any Divine blood. Knowing its parentage without a doubt, she had to wonder. Henry had gifts. Could it be Henry and not the baby in her belly? She could feel her brain whirring in her skull.

"All I know, Dr. Pierce, is we need you." Bertram reached for her hand, bringing her back to the moment. She didn't draw it away, but she did watch him warily as he took her hand in his. "If we fail … if the Codex falls into enemy hands, the Heavens could fall. It could trigger … the Apocalypse."

"Apocalypse?" Tomáš and Lauren both chorused their surprise.

"The End of Days." Bertram insisted. His fellows stood behind him. While they had been active participants in her questioning, they remained silent now.

Lauren's eyes went to the blond one who seemed less unnerving than he had before, but his icy blue-white eyes watched her cautiously, and it made her feel ill-at-ease.

Tomáš came up out of his chair. He paced behind the

table, rubbing his chin. He was grieving for his mother, and she was certain he was not yet convinced of her innocence. Lauren could also sense his gears turning. She was pretty sure he hadn't slept in two days, and he was pushing his grief over losing his mother to the back of his mind. She also knew he'd deal with that once he figured out who'd killed her; once her name had been cleared.

"I ..." Lauren started but stopped. "I don't know how I can help."

"You know where to look," he said. "Just help us find the pages."

"You realize what my source was for the next possible location of the Codex page, don't you? If I haven't gone crazy; if I haven't lost my mind, it was the ...that ... the *demon* himself who told me where to look. He's using me ... using me to find the pages. He led me to the first one, and now he wants me to find another one for him."

"You have something now on your side you didn't have the first time," Bertram said. "You have His Holiness' blessing. We are his hand, his sword and his shield; we serve you as well."

Lauren eyed the man warily. These were the men who'd nabbed her at the café. Her gaze lifted to the detective who appeared dubious. His eyes darted to each of the visiting agents, then back to Lauren's. Clearly the detective was suspicious of them, too. His eyes narrowed as he hesitated, then finally stood. "You may be her sword and her shield," the detective addressed the Gendarmerie. "But I'm her *hired gun*. She doesn't go anywhere without me." He turned to Lauren. "I don't understand what's happening here and I don't know that I believe in this kind of thing. But my mother is dead ... three people are dead ... and I don't trust you."

"You don't have to," Lauren started, not sure if she wanted to convince him, or let him keep her here in custody. She feared what was to come, almost as much as she feared another night in jail, but he raised his hand and cut her off.

"I have to find my mother's killer and put a stop to all this. So, yes, I do have to. You don't leave my sight. If you give me even the slightest cause to doubt you, I will have you in handcuffs and back behind bars before you can lift a finger. Are we clear?" Lauren looked a bit taken aback, but acquiesced. Kovač turned back to the Gendarmerie and sat back down. "It will take at least an hour to get there. That's if there are no traffic tie ups." He turned to Lauren, grimacing at her. "I'll have a female detective take you to the locker room. You can get cleaned up. I'll see what I can find for you to wear. Then we'll go."

Lauren nodded. She was exhausted and her skin crawled, still caked with dried blood. She had blood in places no one ever should. A long, hot shower was welcomed. The detective's locker room wasn't private, but it was clean and soon the steam filled the room and she didn't care that there were other women coming in off their shift to shower before they went home to their families. She stood under the needle-sharp jets, letting the hot water course over her hair and body. Her hand went to the swell of her stomach as if to offer a silent comfort to the child safely sleeping there. She made the gesture as an oath of protection, pondering Enki's promise to her on that space ship so long ago. The gods said they watched over her and protected her children. She had to believe that was true. She just had to.

As she went to work with a washcloth and soap, she knew how Lady Macbeth felt. *Out damned spot indeed.* She couldn't scrub hard enough to feel clean, and soon her skin was growing raw.

At one point, she realized the locker room had gone quiet and she was truly alone. A red puddle gathered in the grout around her feet before running off into the drain. That's when she hit her breaking point. Unable to guard her emotions any longer, she crumpled. As her legs gave out, she found herself sliding down the wall into the corner. Tears came in waves.

Her sobs echoed off the tiled walls and filled the shower room until it became deafening.

When Lauren finally lay spent of energy, she no longer cared that she was naked on the floor. The female detective found her. She turned off the water and threw a towel over her. She left but came back a moment later with Tomáš. He scooped her up off the floor. By then, her tears were spent, and she was a limp noodle no one could do anything with. The female detective made a pallet for her on the floor of the locker room from a stack of clean towels. She instructed Tomáš to lay her there. Once he left, she knelt beside Lauren and took another towel, using it to dry her skin and blot her hair. She spoke softly, and it took several moments before Lauren realized she was speaking Slovenian.

"You're not from here." Lauren finally found her words as she pushed herself up to sitting grasping the towel Tomáš had wrapped her in.

"You speak Slovenian." It wasn't a question.

"I'm a linguist," she said. She never called herself that, but in truth, that's what she'd become. "I pick up languages like people collect postage stamps." There was no humor left in her voice.

"You are the Hand of the gods," the woman said with a beatific smile.

Lauren's brow lifted inquisitively. "How … how did you know that?"

"There is a light in your spirit — a spark of the Divine. But you've got a dark shadow over you," she said. "It's a curse of being in law enforcement … we see when trouble follows someone."

An uneasiness filled Lauren. The woman was talking in riddles. "Yeah, it follows me plenty …" she muttered, then gazed at the detective with a critical eye. "Have we met before?"

She smiled. "We have," she said. "Michael sent me. You used to call me Judy Blue Eyes."

Lauren froze, almost recoiling. Her mouth went as dry as the Sahara. "But …"

"It *was* just a dream," Judy said. "But … also a warning."

"A warning?"

"The Dragon is gathering his forces." She put a hand on Lauren's arm. "The task before you is great, but you have a strength to your spirit unlike anything I've ever seen before. If there's anyone who can overcome this darkness and put trouble in its place, I think it must be you."

"I'm not so sure anyone else believes that." Lauren sighed; her eyes went to the door where Tomáš had disappeared. She sensed he was not far; perhaps listening at the door. "Least of all me."

"Don't let Tomáš put doubt in your heart," she said. "His faith was tested, and it failed him."

Lauren puzzled, contorting her face in confusion. "You mean … his mother?"

"Long before that," she said. "Though he is mourning her terribly, he was in the seminary, studying to be a priest when his father was murdered."

Lauren felt her stomach knot up and drop like a lead weight in her gut. "Murdered?"

"He was a police officer, too," she said. "It's a long story. Maybe he should be the one telling it. Not my place."

"I had no idea …" Lauren felt lightheaded. "He's lost both his parents?"

"Tragic, yes, but now is the time for you to be strong," she said, patting Lauren's hand. "Your strength is needed now more than ever. You will not be alone. *We* are with you."

Lauren heaved a heavy sigh and nodded.

∾

"THIS IS THE CRATER I WAS TELLING YOU ABOUT," GREG stood over a wide bowl created in the rising sand dunes. The entire depression sparkled like shimmering waves. "That's not water."

"No?" Rowan would have sworn it was an oasis.

"It's glass," he said.

"I thought that was some kind of metaphor." Rowan shielded his eyes to the rising sun. Already temperatures were pushing into the 90s and sweat peeled down his brow.

"Our geologists have dated the impactite found here at 26 million years old." Greg wasn't holding back his enthusiasm as he started down the sandy ridge.

Rowan glanced at Jean-René behind the camera before sliding down the sand dune. "Impactite?" He had to raise his voice. "How did it get here?"

"It's believed to have been caused by a meteorite. Hence the name." Greg paused and collected a sample. He picked through it finding a small treasure. He held it out for Rowan as he skidded to a stop. "There you go. Libyan Desert Glass."

Rowan studied the golden glassy nugget. He held it up between two fingers both for the benefit of the camera, and to catch the morning sun. "Beautiful." The rock was rather plain looking, until the sun hit it, then it sparkled like amber. He thought about taking some samples home for Lauren and the boys. He pocketed the nugget and followed his host through the crunchy sand.

"We have found artifacts at a dig in southern Libya that we have been able to trace through chemical analysis back to this crater," Greg said. "Like Native American trade-beads, sand-glass was highly sought in ancient times for jewelry. Even in structures west of here, we found the most immaculately crafted headdresses that were adorned with sand-glass."

"I can see why." Rowan had a pocket full of the nuggets at this point. The variations in the color ranged from an almost clear buttery yellow to tigers' eye gold. Each piece was unique, like a snowflake. He had already thought of drilling a hole in a couple of the larger pieces to make earrings for Lauren.

"Part of the team of anthropologists are examining the impact of the environment on this settlement. Weather patterns have varied greatly over the southern Mediterranean for the last several thousands of years. Mankind has had a role in that too. Gaddafi used the riches gained during the oil boom to build a large man-made river. It was the largest water engineering project in the world. Unfortunately, in a climate that is 93% arid, sustainability of such a project has been an issue."

"Where do Libyan's get their water? Is it from that river? Surely not the Mediterranean?" Rowan asked.

"There is a finite cache of fossilized groundwater," Greg explained as they circled the crater. "It's a leftover from the Pleistocene era. Unfortunately, there's not enough to meet the demand of local farmers who would use it to irrigate crops. The same was true back when the city complex here was in its prime. We suspect there is a well somewhere among the ruins, but we haven't found it yet. There are desalinization plants along the coast, but they barely provide enough water for the cities."

Rowan's interest was piqued more and more with everything he learned about this site, the ancient people, and their culture. "So where are we digging today?" They started back up the slope.

"There's an underground structure not too far from here," Greg said. "We'll go check it out."

"Base to Field Team 1." A radio squelch nearly startled Rowan out of his sand-filled shoes.

"Go ahead, base." Greg snickered as he responded.

"We're monitoring some weather to the south," the site safety officer back at the base trailer came over the radio. "Looks like it's moving in pretty fast. You guys need to get to shelter."

"Haboob?" Greg asked.

"Affirmative," she answered.

"Thanks, Liza," he said. "We're about forty minutes from the trailer."

"You've got thirty," she said. Concern was heavy in her voice.

"We'll head to the underground structure where the crews are digging," he said.

Without a word of instruction, the men bolted for the ATVs. Rowan's four-wheeler didn't want to start. It took several attempts to get the engine to turn over, and by the time it did, Jean-René and Greg were far enough ahead of him that he felt abandoned. To make matters worse, the winds quickly picked up and the sands began swirling around them. In the distance, an enormous wall rose like a tidal wave, bearing down on the team. The storm seemed to swell, even as he gunned the engine and skidded down the dunes in pursuit of his party.

The ATV fishtailed in the sand, and he felt the two uphill wheels lose contact with the earth. One minute the vehicle was safely beneath him, the next minute, he was rolling with the craft on top of him. Just as abruptly, the craft was back on its wheels, and he whipped his body against the roll. The vehicle recovered as the wheels caught traction and spun in the sand, propelling him forward as if nothing had happened. He gunned the engine, confident that whatever had just happened, wouldn't repeat itself.

He couldn't have been any more wrong.

21

Kovač glanced up as Lauren returned to the conference room where they waited for her. He locked eyes with her. He was standing at a window down the hallway watching as the sun made a slow crawl to the west. She met him halfway. "Are you okay?"

Lauren nodded, swallowing a lump in her throat. "Thank you for the clothes." She glanced down at the haphazard attire he'd rummaged from lost-and-found. The jeans were too big, too short, but slung low beneath her belly and held together with a rubber band on the button; she'd made them work. The faded black sweatshirt was torn at the bottom, but otherwise decent. The bra was a cup size too small, and she felt like she was about to spill out of it. The shoes pinched her toes, but they would have to do.

"Sorry, that was the best I could find," he said.

"I'm not even going to ask where they came from." She tugged at the hem of the sweatshirt.

"I will promise you; they are clean."

She forced her brow to soften. "Well, at least there's that."

"You must be starving," he said. "I had some food brought in. We'll eat and then head out."

"What about the *three amigos*?" She nodded towards the office where the Gendarmerie waited.

"My superiors contacted the Vatican and verified their credentials," he said. "It all checks out."

Lauren nodded, tucking her hands in the pockets of the jeans. She shivered. Kovač's hand

went to her arm, but quickly withdrew as he took a hesitant step back. "Are you sure you're okay?"

"Food and a cat nap and I should feel better," she said.

"You can sleep while I drive," he said. "Come on. The food is getting cold." He turned, but Lauren caught his arm this time. "What?" The detective's eye went to her hand. Worry was etched into the features of his face.

"Are *you* okay?" she asked. She caught his hand in hers. His blue eyes swam in grief, but he held back. "I am so … incredibly sorry …"

His lip trembled. She could see his jaw flex as he fought back his emotions. With pursed lips he managed a nod and turned, leading her to the other room where a meal had been set out.

The three officers from the Vatican stood when she entered, and she realized they'd been waiting for her before they ate. She made a faint apology as she sank into the empty chair. The grease-laden redolence of Chinese food greeted her. It made her mouth water. She'd started to reach for the rice. "Allow us to bless this meal?"

She withdrew her hand and nodded, bowing her head. Kovač sat and lowered his own as well.

"Our Heavenly Father …" The man's voice provided a comforting warmth that washed over her. Her muscles relaxed and the ache in her joints faded. Her stomach calmed. "We thank Thee for Thy bounty." Lauren peeked out and realized the blond one was watching her. He gave her the creeps. He was the one that had been so rough with her on the street in the café, and his angry gaze — one that never seemed to abate — burned into her. She closed her eyes and lowered her head in reverence, but also to break the shared gaze. "Bless the hands that prepared it, and those who provided for our providence in this hour of darkness. Allow our bodies to be nourished and provide Thy infinite protection from the perils before us. And if Thou so chooseth to call us home, may we be welcomed into Thy loving arms … blessed by Thy mercy and Thy grace. Amen."

"Amen," Lauren said. She waited while they crossed themselves before, she reached for food.

"I hope this won't trouble your stomach any," Tomáš said as he passed her a cup of egg drop soup.

"Me, too," she said. "It smells so good; I'd hate to have it come back on me."

"I have your medications …" he said. "If you need it."

She shook her head. "It knocks me out, and all it does is make me woozy."

He nodded as the container with the egg rolls came around. Lauren took one. She didn't care if it did make her sick, she was going to have one. This was one of her favorite meals though one she didn't indulge in very often.

She made short work of the rice, the egg roll and the soup and sat back in the chair feeling satisfied. When the overwhelming exhaustion hit her, she yawned, feeling drowsy beyond all measure. The feeling of exhausted euphoria that overtook her reminded her of the thirty-two-hour boat ride they'd made home from Pitcairn Island in the South Pacific. From there, it had taken full day just to get to Spain where they had a thirteen hour layover. It was their goal to scout the *Alcázar of Segoviao* before the last leg of the trip home to San Diego. She hadn't caught more than a few hours of restless sleep the entire trip home and didn't think she'd ever been more exhausted in her whole life; until now. Unfortunately, she had to wait for everyone to finish their meal.

"Dr. Pierce will ride with me," Kovač announced when he

pushed back his empty containers. "You don't leave my sight, are we clear?" he snapped at her.

She didn't even perk up at the mention of her name. "Sure," she muttered her agreeance. Lauren sat with her head resting in her hand, half asleep.

"We'll meet you there." Kovač added.

"We'll be right behind you the entire way," Bertram said.

Kovač put his hand on Lauren's shoulder just as she nodded off and her chin slipped off her palm. She startled but recovered quickly. "Huh?"

"Let's go," he said, collecting their empty containers, carrying them over to the refuge bin.

"Yeah." She rose slowly. "Sure."

"Feeling okay?"

"I just need to sleep." She yawned.

He held out a borrowed jacket for her to put on, and she wrapped her arms around her body as she followed him to the elevator. It led the way down to the car park where his SUV was. The nip of the cold night air found its way even down to the parking garage. He started the vehicle and soon, the warmth of the heated leather seats worked its way into her core. Even before she buckled her seatbelt, she peeled out of the jacket and rolled it up to make a pillow. She reclined the seat and yawned again.

"Dr. Pierce," he started.

"You can call me Lauren," she said, her eyes still closed.

"Lauren." He hesitated. He was a trained investigator. He had been taught to spot lies through body language. A suspect usually gave themselves away within five to fifteen minutes, but the clusters — multiple nervous tics and cues he'd been trained to watch for — were absent. She wasn't throwing off the signs of someone who was being deceptive. Even if she had killed his mother — and he wasn't convince yet she hadn't — she hadn't given herself away yet, at least not in her body language. She was either being honest, or she was an exceptionally skilled liar. He started over. "I want to tell you something so that we're perfectly clear on how this is going down."

Her brow lifted as she peered out at him through heavy lids. "Oh?"

"If there's any trouble, I mean anything. I need you to get down or get behind me, because I have no problem shooting anyone who appears to be a threat. I'll deal with the repercussions later. I don't care if it's the Vatican police or Vlad Dracula himself. I have a duty to protect you while you're in my custody. If you'll trust me, I will do my job. If you truly are innocent in my mother's death, so be it. If not, I will see you brought to justice, and will deliver you to the courts uninjured if I can."

Lauren opened her eyes and turned to him. "I trust you."

"Good."

"But you need to know something, too," she said. "I will do anything I have to in order to stop whatever evil forces human or otherwise — stand in the way of preventing whatever disaster may befall ... by whatever means I have at *my* beck and call."

Kovač considered her for a moment, then simply nodded his agreement, buckled his seatbelt, and put the SUV in gear.

Lauren closed her eyes, and let sleep have her.

THE LAST THING ROWAN REMEMBERED WAS THE overwhelming feeling of falling. He came to flat on his back, with a helmet full of sand. The grit blinded him, filling his eyes, and permeated his mouth, and just about everywhere else sand shouldn't be. He'd landed hard and had the wind knocked out of him when the ATV flipped and began tumbling down the dune. The sudden stop at the bottom — well he didn't remember much about that.

Now, he found himself in the dark. Rowan sensed he was

underground; the loud blasting of wind and sand was deafening above him. In the darkness, he couldn't see what had happened. He pushed himself up onto one elbow, his shoulder screaming in pain as the muscles knotted and protested. The handlebars of the ATV had his leg pinned. As he moved, the sand seemed to fill in the void around him, and it slithered into the back of his pants.

He shook the grit out of his helmet as he peeled it off, tossing it aside. Sand skittered down the back of his shirt, and he could feel it everywhere now. Even his shoes and socks seemed full of it. It took all his strength to lift the overturned ATV off his ankle and he was left with a throbbing ache in the bone, right along the same line where he'd fractured it in Nepal so many years ago. As he moved it, and unpinned himself, he realized his pack was still lashed to the back of the four-wheeler.

He rummaged through it, finding his mag-light. He switched it on and got his first look at the void he found himself in. Overhead, a bridge of sand had him socked in, rivers of the fine grains peeled down the edges, and he blinked away the grit as he swung the light around and realized he was in some kind of an underground structure. The *ceiling* was at least forty feet up, but a bank of sand that collected around him was several feet tall — high enough for the ATV to have tumbled down; deep enough to soften the impact at the bottom.

Rowan grabbed his pack and worked himself out of the sand. Skidding down the dune to a stone floor, he struggled to gain his footing. Testing the ankle, he found it sore, but not broken that he could tell. He worked his aching shoulder, testing it, and decided a muscle strain might be the worst of it. He had other aches and pains, but he concluded he wasn't severely injured. The raging wind he could hear above him told him the storm had overtaken him. He was probably going to be here for a while.

Going through his bag, he found a bottle of water. He used it to rinse his face to remove as much of the grit as he could from his nose, mouth, and eyes. When he was satisfied, he drained the bottle. He had several more for later.

Once his eyes were clear, he was better able to focus his attention on the chamber he found himself in. The walls were made of stone bricks of epic sizes. He studied the chinks, examining the mortar. He'd learned in some of his earliest classes that gypsum mortar was most commonly used in building the Great Pyramid at Giza. But it wasn't an easy process. The gypsum had to be dehydrated through heating, which took large quantities of wood. This was believed to be a contributing factor in the deforestation of the region.

These stones were every bit as large as the blocks used in Giza. How ancient pyramid builders moved stones such as this, remained an eternal mystery of the region. Theories abounded, ranging from using wooden rollers, lubricating the stones with oil or water to make them skid, slave labor or even alien architects.

Journals from the ancient writer Herodotus in the 5th century explained that the pyramids were completed by workmen who used short wooden logs as levers to raise the stones up into the stair or step structures that stood still today. But even Herodotus was only speculating, and much was left unexplained.

Rowan studied the stones, deciding they must be limestone, like the ones in the pyramids. He walked along the wall, scanning with his flashlight, stopping when he realized there were carvings in the wall high above. He took a few steps back and heard a hiss that made him jump and turn. A dark, black snake coiled in the corner, waving ominously as it spread its hood. "Jesus!" His heart leapt. "Why does it always have to be snakes?" He'd never run into an Egyptian cobra before, and he secretly prayed that he never would again. The two squared off, in a cautious dance, as they moved around and away from each other. The snake was just as fearful of the man as the man was of the snake. Rowan gave the snake a wide berth and kept it in the corner of his eye as he moved along, now watching his step a bit more carefully. The snake found a hole in the stones and made a hasty retreat, disappearing from the void.

Once safely away from the snake, Rowan allowed his gaze to lift to the stones above. From this angle, he could better see the chisel marks and make out the figure of an elephant carved into the rock. The markings had worn over time, and Rowan couldn't be sure, but it appeared the artist might have painted the markings to enhance the image. It was faded, so it just as easily could have been a patina left by time and the intrusion of water.

He went back for his pack, keeping a cautious eye out for the snake to return, or others to cross his path. Rowan retrieved his camera. He wanted to document the cavern. After he did so, he continued, finding a narrow hallway that led to a second chamber.

The next vault was smaller, but it was full of antiquities. Rowan's jaw dropped. Ancient pottery gilded in gold rested in niches carved into the stone; pristine. There was what appeared to be a stone mausoleum that was in excellent condition, despite the layers of sand collecting on its surface. Rowan ran a hand along the top of it, seeking cracks or chisel marks that might suggest tomb robbers had tried to break in, but there was nothing of the sort. He realized there was etching on the surface. Remembering the tools he'd stowed in his bag, he went back and rummaged for them. In the dark, he snagged the sharp edge of the pallet knife with his finger. He snatched his hand away, holding it under the light. Blood coursed down his hand. The nasty little cut was deep but nothing life threatening. He had a well-stocked first aid kit, and with all the skill his military training had provided, he cleaned up the wound and patched it with a bandage. It was a minor annoyance. He was more careful the second time he went to take out the pallet knife and brushes; tools of the trade for an archaeologist. With his flashlight in hand, he went to work at one corner of the stone coffin and began brushing away the sands of time, revealing the interesting markings.

While he worked, he was able to put away his concerns about his current situation. He had cause to worry for his friends, not sure if they'd made it to safety, or had tried to come back for him. He prayed Jean-René would go to shelter and trust him to manage on his own. He was trained. He could survive anywhere. The desert was nothing new to him. Two tours in Iraq and Afghanistan had served him well in situations like this.

Then, it occurred to him that his cell phone was still in the pocket of his jacket he'd stuffed into his bag when they'd been preparing to head out that morning. He stopped and found it. His battery life was still good, but there were no bars — no cell tower nearby to pick up the signal. It was possible the underground shelter was also blocking his signal if there was a tower somewhere out in the middle of the Sahara.

Rowan set the phone to low-power mode, to preserve the charge on the battery until he desperately needed it. If the storm ever stopped raging outside, he might be able to dig his way out and make a call for rescue.

He put the phone back where it had been and returned to his work. It took a long time to clear the sand with little more than a putty knife and a paint brush, but Rowan finally got it where he could study the symbols.

While Rowan was no linguist, he could recognize Egyptian hieroglyphs as well as cuneiform. He could tell the difference between Korean and Maya glyphs just like he could tell the difference between French and Spanish. Little good any of that did him now, but he was certain of one thing. This was a form of writing he had never seen before. *God, he wished Lauren were here.*

LAUREN WOKE UP STARTLED, BATHED IN SWEAT WITH HER heart hammering in her chest. She looked around and realized where she was. She lay back in the seat, glancing over at Tomáš, who took his eyes off the road only long enough to check on her. She realized his hand was on her arm.

"Are you okay?" He quickly turned his attention back to the road, which was a twisting, winding path through dense forest and high hills.

"Yeah," she managed. "Bad dream."

"Get those a lot?" he asked.

"Too often," she admitted, raising her seat back up. "More so now than ever."

"Tell me," he insisted.

The road was dark, damp. Lauren shivered. Kovač reached up for the knob and she could feel the warmth rising from the seat. She melted back into it, the tension in her back beginning to ease. "They're the Watchers in the dark," she said in preamble. "When I was a grad student, I worked as a researcher for the television program Nova. I studied wolves in Yellowstone National Park. I got to know the pack. I gave each of them names. Lately, I've been dreaming of them."

"You named wild wolves?"

"After famous singers," Lauren said. "You should have heard their voices."

"Wolves are native to the region," he said. "I've heard them sing here."

"The other night, I dreamt the wolves were attacked. Frank and Judy Blue Eyes were killed. Then Michael spoke to me." She didn't mention her relationship with the *vision wolf*. He might assume it was Michael Bublé or Michael Bolton, she didn't care.

"You talked to a wolf?"

"They talk to me." She shrugged, wrapping her jacket

over her shoulders. "Why is it so hard to believe I would talk back?"

"Fair enough," Kovač said. "What did he say? Michael was it?"

"He said we were under attack …" she said. "He also said he would be with us. He would protect us."

"Are you familiar with the Catholic saints?" Kovač asked.

"Some of them," she said. "My favorite is Saint Marie-Bernarde."

"Bernadette Soubirous?"

"You know her story?"

"Who doesn't?" Kovač asked. "A child who saw the Blessed Virgin."

"The Queen of Heaven." Lauren said wistfully. "A girl who saw visions and wasn't afraid to tell the world." She wasn't a singer, but she took a chance and tried a few lines of the Leonard Cohen song, Song of *Bernadette.*

"You have a lovely voice," he said. "She had her faith tested more than once."

"I can relate." Lauren said.

"Why do you say that?"

"I've been tested before." Lauren rolled her head and gazed at him a moment. He glanced at her. "If people knew what I could do … if they knew how I could do it … they'd call me crazy. Just like they did her." She took a deep breath and told him about some of her more bizarre experiences; the Bigfoot shaman in Washington State and the gift of the ancient All-Language included. She wasn't convinced he believed her, but he had to know what she believed to be the truth if he was ever going to trust her again, and believe her innocence in his mother's death

"Perhaps you are a miracle incarnate, too." His eyes returned to the road; his voice almost bitter.

"Well don't file a petition for canonization just yet," she said. "I don't want to die for my cause."

"I won't let that happen." He set his jaw. His hands flexed on the steering wheel. His knuckles went white. "No one has to martyr themselves to prove their faith …or their power. Not to me. Not to anyone else. I am a man of faith, Dr. Pierce. I believe in miracles."

A wave of relief washed through her. She didn't know why, but she needed to hear him say that. She didn't know what had convinced him, or how he'd come to understand. She was just grateful that he had.

"But I am also trained to follow the evidence. My father gave his life for a cause," he said, seemingly out of the blue. "I talked to his partner before he retired. He told me everything about the man who killed my father."

"I'm so sorry …" Lauren wasn't sure what else to say.

The detective was silent for a long moment, the hum of the tires on wet pavement the only sound between them. When he finally spoke, his voice was dark. "He was investigating a break-in at the cathedral where our family has worshiped for generations. He was shot and killed by the intruder."

Her hand went to his arm this time. "I'm so sorry." She meant it, too. "How old were you?"

"I was eighteen," he said. "Because of what they did for a living, I grew up in constant fear of losing one or both of my parents. My faith was the only thing that helped me cope. My great aunt was a nun cloistered there, at the church where my father died. I would go and visit her when I was troubled. She died a year after my father … she was extremely old and exceptionally wise."

"Did they ever catch the guy? The suspect?" she asked. "The one who shot your father?"

"His partner worked the case for years. An arrest was never made, and an artifact that was stolen was never recovered." He drew a breath in through his nose. His nostrils flared as his jaw tightened. "He tried for years to solve the crime, but … I don't know that he ever …" Tomáš said.

"What was stolen from the church?"

The detective nodded. "A sacred document," he said. "That's all I know."

Lauren chewed on this for a long while. "Sacred document, hidden in a church, huh? Sounds familiar."

Kovač turned and looked at her, startled. She could see the pieces coming together.

2 2

The Sedlec Ossuary was illuminated from within as they arrived. The small chapel rose high over a cemetery full of tombstones that seemed to huddle around the building as if they were chicks gathering close to the mother hen. The ancient stones glowed in the moonlight, as fog gathered between them. Lauren stepped out of the car and pulled the jacket around her to ward off the chill. The cold climbed up her leg like a snake, wrapping around her flesh, constricting the muscles. She took a step and tried to shake off the feeling. She could feel the warmth off his body when Tomáš came around behind her as she gazed up at the chapel.

"You okay?"

"There's an old expression in English, one that isn't used anymore," Lauren said, tentatively. She hesitated a moment before she continued. He leaned in, waiting for her to finish. "This place *gives me the morbs…*" she said it first in English then translated it for him, demonstrating the abilities she'd told him about.

He considered her a moment before sticking out his lower lip. "It's an appropriate expression."

"Wait 'til you see it inside." Bertram was at her elbow before she even knew they were there.

Lauren didn't move. "Tell me more about this place?"

"This is an ancient site," Bertram said. "In the time of the Crusades, Henry, the Abbot of the monastery here was sent to the Holy Land by the King of Bohemia. He returned with earth he'd collected from Golgotha, where Jesus was crucified. He scattered the soil here. Word got out and this became among the most desirable cemeteries in Central Europe." His voice added to the chill that was seeping into her bones. "When the Black Death and the Hussite Wars took their toll, thousands were buried here, and the cemetery had to be expanded. The cathedral was built in the 1400s with a lower chapel to be used as an ossuary for the mass graves that had to be unearthed during its construction."

Lauren could almost envision the story as it was unfolding. The fog became a scene of the images of the workers, placing the stones and digging the bones from their resting place. Angels and demons swirled in the mist, battling each other for authority over the sacred land. Skeletal warriors rose from the black soil and took up arms for the Armies of Good and Evil.

"In the 1500s, a half-blind monk was given the task of exhuming the skeletons and stacking their bones in the chapel," Bertram said. "Today, the largest collection of skeletal remains rests here. Some claim there are more bones here than in the catacombs of Paris. In truth, a full inventory of the dead here has never been completed."

"What time is it?" Lauren turned to Kovač.

He glanced at his watch. "It's just after 11:00."

Her gaze was held by the cathedral and the path leading to the arching doorways. "It's probably closed." She hesitated to move.

"We're expected." Bertram pressed past her and started up the path.

Kovač started to follow, but when Lauren didn't move, he turned back around. "What is it?"

She pursed her lips as her scowl created a wrinkle between her eyes. She looked up at him with a hesitant gaze. "I'm afraid." Her voice sounded distant and small, even to her own ear.

Tomáš took her hand and held it between his. "*Where your fear lies, there is your task*," he quoted. "Do you believe in God, Dr. Pierce?"

Lauren opened her mouth to answer as her eyes lifted back to the cathedral. "I believe there are more things under the heavens than I can ever explain without a belief in something greater than ourselves." She swallowed hard.

"And that is what we call *Faith*." He turned, her hand still in his, and led her to the cathedral.

Bertram and the others waited for them at the door. "The monk here has taken a vow of silence," Bertram said. They entered the ossuary in reverence. The cathedral was lit by little more than candles on the wall. Their light was obstructed by the towers of bones that led the eye up to the ceiling where the geometric patterns of carefully arranged bones appeared like warped spinal columns. Jawless skulls perched on what might have been an arm bone, or perhaps a leg. They alternated: skull, bone, skull, bone. The gruesome image was accented by a chandelier of leg or arm bones as well. There wasn't anything in the cathedral ceilings, other than the flickering candles that were of a different color than the aged skeletal décor.

The place smelled ancient, musty. Lauren pressed her sleeve to her nose, trying to force her stomach to remain calm. The bones had long since dried, but the faint, sweet tang of death was heavy in the air. It coated her tongue like grease and her stomach threatened to protest.

In the middle, there was a stone altar with a window behind it and a towering cross above it. Lauren noticed the pious paused upon entering to cross themselves respectfully. She realized Kovač had taken a rosary from his pocket. He turned back to her and pressed it into her hand. "Keep this," he said, softly. "It'll protect you."

Lauren wrapped it around her wrist several times and clutched the crucifix in her palm. The crystals were cool but quickly warmed in her grasp.

The monk motioned for them to follow. Kovač nudged her and she moved ahead of him, falling in line behind the others. She stumbled, her foot catching a loose stone. She caught herself by putting her hand on the blond man's upper arm and he turned as if her touch were lightning. "I'm sorry. I don't even know your names," she said softly.

Bertram paused and turned back. "My apologies, Dr. Pierce." He kept his tone low as well. "I didn't even think to make introductions. This is Simon Betancourt," he introduced the blond man to Lauren. "And this is Lucca Campagna."

"Madame," the second one bowed. Meanwhile, the blond one, Simon, only gazed at her with that look that made her skin crawl. "We do beg your apologies for our … methods when first we met you. We feared you already had the missing page," Lucca said.

"You drugged her?" The Detective accused.

"We did no such thing," Bertram defended. If Tomáš believed him, he gave no sign.

The monk motioned for them again, more insistence in his mannerisms this time. Lauren nodded her forgiveness to the Gendarmerie and fell in behind the monk. He led them along a hallway to a stone staircase that spiraled down. Braziers flickered on the walls as they passed in near silence — only the clap of leather soles on stones announced their presence. Lauren's borrowed sneakers made no noise as she studied the bones that lined the stairway. Dead, empty eye sockets with wicked jawless grins met her gaze. She swallowed back a wave of nausea as a mist of cold sweat broke out on her upper lip.

She felt Tomáš' hand snake into her arm as he moved even with her. He had to duck to pass under a curtain of bones, bringing his eyes to her level. "You've gone pale," he said.

Her only response was a shivering nod of her head as she hesitated before the next step. She lost her footing, but with his arm in hers, he kept her on her feet and saved her from a terrible fall down the stone stairs.

"Dr. Pierce?" Bertram noticed her distress.

"I'm fine."

The monk finally came to the bottom of the steps and took out a ring of metal skeleton keys. For a moment, Lauren mused over the irony of it, but pushed back the thought as the door swung open and the monk turned with a hand up, indicating they should wait. He entered the vault, disappearing into the dark gloom. Lauren leaned against the cool stone wall as she could hear a lighter being flicked. A glow brightened the space. A moment later, the monk stepped out and gestured for them to enter.

Lauren swallowed her fear and stepped through the portal, with Tomáš right behind her.

The room was much larger than she'd expected. The walls were lined with a configuration of tiny bones arranged like mosaic tiles. Carpals and metacarpals were mixed with tarsals and metatarsals. In the center of each of the patterns, vertebrae lay flat. More braziers cast shadows on the eerie spectacle. Shelves lined the opposite walls, like mortuary benches she'd seen in the Tibetan monastery near Everest. Except here, instead of mummified corpses, there were relics. Ancient pottery, copper cups, wooden boxes, and ceramic tablets with carefully scribed text in ancient Egyptian.

One wooden box in particular caught her attention. It appeared to be ebony wood, carved with ancient symbols; spells of holy protection. Lauren was immediately drawn to it. She knelt, pushing her hair back over her shoulder as she studied it. The monk came over and took a pair of cotton gloves from somewhere in his robes. He donned them, then lifted out the tablet from within the box to allow her to study it.

"Do you know what it says?" Kovač asked, gazing over her shoulder.

"It's …" she seemed breathless. "It's from the Book of the Dead."

"The Egyptian Book of the Dead?" Bertram scowled.

"I'd say it's a spell from one of the later chapters," she said. "It says here, *having been tested by Osiris, the spirit having been vindicated assumes its rightful place in the heavens … as a god.*"

"That's fascinating," Tomáš said.

"But this isn't right." Lauren shook her head as the monk returned the tablet to the shelf.

"What do you mean?" Bertram lifted an inquisitive brow.

"The Book of the Dead was actually a collection of the many spells on papyrus that were gathered together … only some of the exceedingly early ones were on tablets found in Egyptian tombs. But this is from the later period."

"How is that possible?" Tomáš asked.

"I'm not sure." Lauren stood fast, pondering how a tablet from ancient Egypt had come to a gothic chapel in Central Europe. "These spells were designed to ensure the soul of the deceased made it safely into the afterlife. This appears to come from the Judgment scene. The heart of the deceased was weighed against the feather of Ma'at, the goddess of Truth. If the heart was lighter than the feather, they were admitted safe passage. But if the heart were heavier, because its owner were wicked, it would be devoured by Ammit …" Lauren's voice trailed off. She'd heard this story from her husband's professor. Dr. Badr had told it to her one afternoon when they'd gone to the market. She could hear Tima's voice now as she spoke. "If their heart was devoured …they died a second death. Their soul would be gone from existence, obliterated for all eternity."

"I can imagine that would be a fate worse than death." Tomáš smirked.

"To disappear in a *poof* versus a lifetime of eternal torture?" Bertram questioned the detective. "I say better to be gone than to burn."

"In a society where you lived your entire life to earn your eternal existence in the afterworld, annihilation was the worst thing the ancient Egyptians could imagine." Lauren pointed out. She'd learned as much from Rowan's studies — and his professor — as he had. She'd sat in on some of Tima's lectures, too. "To be forgotten, to suddenly have never lived. Their view of purgatory was far different from those of the Christian faith."

"How is this going to help us stop the dark forces?" Simon snapped impatiently. That dark scowl that made his blue eyes radiate made Lauren recoil. "We need the lost pages from the Codex."

The monk nodded and lifted a hand a moment, then went over to another wooden box on the same shelf. He picked it up and carried it to the table. The VIS agents followed him over. Lauren hesitated a moment, glancing at the detective before she moved.

This box was roughly three feet long and appeared incredibly ancient. The rosewood might have been pristine at one time but appeared gnarled from age. There were cracks that suggested water intrusion, along with tiny worm holes where wee beasties had once feasted.

The monk reached under the neck of his robe and revealed a leather thong with a crude ceramic crucifix and a single iron key. He lifted it over his head and handed it to Lauren reverently.

The metal warmed against her hand, but she chilled as she lay one hand atop the unadorned box. She placed the key into the lock. Taking a deep breath, she turned it. The ancient tumblers resisted moving at first. Twisting her mouth with determination, she added to her effort and the lock clicked open as the mechanism surrendered.

Feeling light-headed, Lauren moved back. The monk stepped in, taking over. As the lid opened, the dank aroma of rot melded with the mélange of ancient magic that filled the air. Lauren tried to breathe calm into her thundering heart, but to no avail.

The monk lifted the large vellum scroll from the chest and lay it out, unfurling it as they gathered around. The animal hide had dried and was riddled with worm holes. It flaked as the monk gingerly unfurled it.

Curiosity now guided Lauren and any fear was pushed to the back of her mind as she stood gazing at the cursed text. She put her hand over her mouth in fear that the words might escape her lips and call evil to her even in this holiest of places.

"What does it say?" Tomáš asked.

Lucca started to translate the text that was written in Latin.

Lauren reached out and caught his arm. "Don't."

He looked at her with shock written on his face. "Don't what?"

"Don't read the spell," she said. "You don't know what it will do."

"And I suppose you read Latin, too?" Simon scowled.

Lauren and Tomáš exchanged cautious glances. "Yes, as a matter of fact she does," Kovač said. "So, it is a spell?" He turned to her.

"Not like *bubble, bubble toil and trouble*, but …" she returned her attention to it. "In its simplest terms, this page speaks of the end times. It speaks of the *one who should not be named* and *his* return …" She was intentionally being vague. She hesitated and felt the blood drain from her face as she read on.

"What is it?" Tomáš asked. "Lauren?"

"It speaks of a child … *a child of the gods* who will be sent to destroy the Dark One. This tells how the Deceiver might be able to destroy him."

"As I said, it is a common theme in myth and religion," Bertram said to her.

"The Dark One? *He-who-must-not-be-named?* Like …" Tomáš' face screwed up in confusion. "Like, *Voldemort?*" His tone lowered as did the volume of his words, as if speaking the fictitious name would bring evil upon them.

"Oh, the page names him, but no good will come from reading this aloud." Lauren turned and took a step away. "Most people think of the Apocalypse as the second coming of Christ. But this … calls it the second coming of the *anti-Christ.*"

"We have to get this somewhere safe," Bertram said.

"What place could be safer than this?" Tomáš argued.

"I agree with Bertram." Lauren turned to Tomáš, stepping away from the table, leading him aside.

"I thought you said this was a trap … to bait you into moving the page so it can be … reclaimed?" Tomáš crossed his arms. His brows knitted over his ice blue eyes that flickered in the candlelight.

"If we can be deceived, anyone can." Lauren's thumbnail went to her teeth, and she realized there was nothing left. Instead, she tucked her hand in her pocket, trying to break the bad habit. "But I think there's a way …"

"You can't take it off sacred ground without exposing it to risk, isn't that what you said? That's why they got the first page from the museum, right?"

"Maybe we can't take it off sacred ground, but we can take sacred ground with us."

The three Gendarmerie turned sharply, glaring at her. "What?" Bertram gazed at her curiously.

"If Henry the Abbott brought soil from Golgotha, I'm going to need a sample of it."

The monk walked over from the place in the shadows where he waited patiently for them to finish their examination. He managed a beatific smile and curled his finger at Lauren for her to follow.

23

Hours passed as the storm raged. Rowan explored as much as he could, documented what he found, then settled in to wait out the storm. All the thoughts he'd pushed aside initially came flooding in on him. He was worried about Jean-René and Greg, and he missed his wife and children.

Rowan wondered if he tried extremely hard if he could make Lauren appear. He was starting to understand what he thought of as her *magic*, but neither of them really knew how it worked. Somehow, she had gotten to Mexico unaided in time to save his life, and hers as well. Then the little *magic tricks* in South Africa had aided her brother in his quest. He'd seen the truth of the events that had occurred then. He understood the magnitude of his wife's power, but Rowan didn't know how it worked. He was sure he had nothing to do with it. He wasn't the one who called her to him. She'd done it. It was all her. It was weird. It freaked him out. But he trusted her and was in awe of the powers she had; powers that appeared to be growing with each passing year.

Their son had powers, too. Henry, it seemed, was somewhat instrumental in Lauren's abilities to teleport — translocate — or whatever it was called. Raising a child with such powers made it difficult. They'd had to lay down rules for him. Lauren had been coaching him to make good choices, not to disappear unexpectedly, or go somewhere he wasn't supposed to.

He forced his thoughts back to the present and the space he occupied. He'd made rubbings of some of the markings on a scroll of butcher paper with a charcoal crayon he carried in his field kit. He hoped he had enough that Lauren would be able to make something of it when she had a chance to see it. He'd send the pictures as soon as he could. He studied the markings by flashlight, trying to make sense of the symbols.

When the light began to flicker and fade, Rowan realized his battery was starting to die. He found his small Sterno camp stove in his supply kit and lit it, deciding he might as well make something to eat while he could. The Sterno would run for a while, long enough, he hoped for the storm to pass. If nothing else, he could put his flashlight away and conserve his battery. With snakes a known hazard, he needed enough light to be on the lookout for cobras.

HENRY WOKE UP SCREAMING AND FRANTIC. AHMOSE ROLLED over and pulled him into her. She'd let him come crawl into bed with her sometime before midnight, and now, the pink haze of dawn illuminated the room. She cuddled him and patted his back, trying to soothe him as her mother had done a few days before.

This wasn't how she'd intended to spend her holiday from college, but she was happy to be able to get the little boy to curl up against her as he whimpered and drifted back to sleep. Anyone else's kid she'd have been less interested in, but she thought highly of Rowan and Lauren Pierce. Rowan was adorable beyond measure, and Lauren was everything Ahmose wanted to be when she grew up. She didn't care much for the idea of being on television, but she wanted to be a doctor like Lauren. Maybe when she was older, she would find a tall husband, too.

If truth be told, Ahmose had a bit of a crush on the American archaeology student. *Who wouldn't?* His charming smile and his witty repartee were two of his best features. He was handsome and a great conversationalist. And he made beautiful babies. That made her smile as she petted Henry's hair.

"Ahmose?" Henry's voice almost startled her.

"Yes, baby?" She kissed his head.

"You can't like my daddy," he said. The little boy looked up at her with an angry scowl. "My momma wouldn't like that."

"What?" Ahmose asked, perplexed. "Are you reading my mind, Henry?" The boy just scowled at her. She didn't know how he knew what she was thinking, but she tried to reassure him. "I do hope someday to find someone like your daddy. But what I like best about him is how much he loves your momma. I would never come between them." Henry nodded, but his sour expression didn't abate. "Are you all right? Another bad dream?"

"Daddy found a cobra," Henry said. "It wants to bite him. The cobra likes to bite people."

"Oh, my!" Ahmose scowled. She placated the child, since she couldn't convince him dreams weren't real. "What is your daddy going to do?"

"He's stuck in a hole," Henry said. "I think he'll get out, if the snake doesn't bite him first."

First, he's wailing because his mom is fighting the Devil, now he's worried about a snake biting his daddy. What a vivid imagination this boy had. She also suspected there was a theme. But where would Henry have heard about Devils and snakes? Maybe he'd been watching his dad's favorite Indiana Jones movies.

~

"MORE BAD DREAMS?"

"Snakes are after his dad," Ahmose said as she staggered into the kitchen and found her mother at the stove.

"Oh?" Tima arched a brow. "That child has a vivid imagination."

"Yes." Ahmose made herself a cup of tea. "He does."

"Today we will go to the market," Tima decided. "The boys will like that."

"My friend Ishan is having a party for his nephew," Ahmose said. "Maybe I will take the boys this afternoon."

"They would like that," Tima nodded.

Henry came in dragging his blanket looking like a lost Linus in a Snoopy cartoon. "Auntie Tima?"

She scooped him up and sat down with him in her lap, turning in her chair. He lay his head on her chest. "Did my daddy call back yet? Did he?"

Tima's heart broke for him. "No, not yet," she said. "Ahmose has a friend who's having a birthday party for his nephew this afternoon. Would you like to go to a birthday party?"

Henry didn't perk up, but he did ask. "Will there be cake?"

"Egyptian birthday parties are very much like parties in America," Ahmose said. "We call it a *hafla*. We eat a lot of food, and we sing Egyptian songs. There is cake, but it's a little different than in America. There are other desserts, too."

"I can't go to a party." Henry sighed sadly.

"Why not, sweet boy?" Tima kissed his head.

"I don't have a present to take. I can't go without a present. It isn't nice," he said.

"Presents aren't required," Tima said.

"My momma wouldn't want me to be rude," Henry said. "We always take presents to parties."

"Well, we have to go to the market today; we can shop for a present."

"I wouldn't know what to get him," Henry said.

"I'm sure Shemi and I can help you pick something out," Ahmose said.

JOHN CARTER LOVED THE MARKETPLACE. IT WAS CROWDED, but the energy of the surging bodies was exciting to the little boy. Henry didn't seem so moved. He held on to Tima's hand tightly, while Shemi and Ahmose took turns carrying John Carter in fear he'd get lost in the crowd too easily.

"What kind of presents do little boys in Egypt like?" Henry asked, standing in front of the table loaded with dried figs, dates, and mangos. Tima bought a few small bags of each. The vendor offered a large slice of dried mango to each of the boys, smiling a toothless grin at them. Henry took it and said, "Thank you."

"Whatever toys little boys in America like," Shemi said.

"I don't even know how old this little boy is," Henry said.

"Braheem is going to be six," Ahmose said. "Not much older than you."

Henry nodded, taking a bite from his piece of mango. He walked ahead studying every object he saw along the way. Each of the booths had something different. There were baskets, clothing, jewelry, and all kinds of things to eat. He paused to study the wooden carvings of Egyptian sarcophagi and the ceramic canopic jars. Clearly, he was interested, but even he knew these were knock-offs, trinkets for the tourists. "I don't see any toys."

"There's a shop up ahead," Shemi said. "We're almost there."

"Auntie Tima! *Yook!* *Yook!*" John Carter squealed. "*Yook,* Shemi. Ahmose. *Yook!*"

The girls stopped to see what he was pointing at. A man operating a large puppet — a camel — was moving through the crowd. The camel was wearing a red fez with a gold tassel and had big lips, a moustache, and large eyelashes. It was a funny puppet. John Carter giggled with delight as the puppeteer came towards him, working the controls to make the camel blink. The long eyelashes waved as the camel lowered its head and bowed in front of the crowd that paused to watch the show. A crier followed singing a sales pitch, encouraging people to come to Jumbo's Toys.

"Henry, look at the puppet," Tima said, as she turned back to where the boy had been standing. Henry was nowhere to be seen.

HENRY FELT DARK EYES ON HIM THE MOMENT THEY ENTERED the marketplace. He'd been vaguely aware of them at the pyramids the day before. At first, he wasn't able to identify the source, or recognize the threat, but today, he finally began to put the pieces together. The Devil had come to Egypt.

He stood, oblivious to the puppet that had enchanted the crowd and searched the spaces in between for the presence of the Devil. He knew he was there; knew he was watching him. He shifted his own position between time and space even though he was strictly forbidden to do so. The monster that had been stalking his momma had come for him, and might even hurt him and his little brother, given the chance.

Henry sensed John Carter would have gifts of his own, some day. But for now, he was limited to being a perfectly typical two-year-old. Henry had never had that luxury. He had powers from the first moment he felt his mind form; powers that came with responsibilities. Even his momma and daddy lacked a complete understanding of the gifts he had been given.

His Uncle Michael was fully aware. Uncle Michael had powers, too. He took the boy under his wing and was teaching him how to control his abilities. When his parents were otherwise occupied, Michael took him to visit the sky gods, who taught him even more wonderful things. They stressed the importance of controlling his power, of thoughtful use and timing of any actions because anything he might do outside his own time could have disastrous results for the future.

He had been a studious pupil and had not made this shift lightly or without careful consideration. The Devil was there, watching, always watching; waiting. But he was good at the game and Henry couldn't *see* him, even though he sensed him. He shifted again, searching the cosmos both for his momma and daddy, while he was at it. He found his mother safe in a cathedral, and his father, safe in a cavern. Shifting again, he returned to his own place and time, before he got lost or stuck. Uncle Michael warned that could happen.

24

Lauren stood on the hill at the corner of the chapel. The moss-covered gravestones were ancient, and they were crowded in so tightly that it was difficult to move between them. She found herself ignoring the monk and gazing out into the inky haze. Trees — gnarled and ancient — appeared as dark specters in the mist.

A tug on her pant leg drug her from her paranoia. The monk knelt with a small spade at her knee and turned over the soil. He held up the shovel of dark earth. Lauren knelt beside him. "This is the soil from Golgotha?" Lauren asked. He filled her cupped hands with the dark earth. "How can you be sure?"

He just gazed at her, his eyes going to the sky above in answer. He then made the sign of the cross over the soil and mouthed a silent prayer to further bless it. Lauren asked no more questions. She was grateful for any blessings she could get at this point.

Tomáš stood nearby, watching the woods just as cautiously as she had. She rose from her knees, carrying the handful of soil carefully back inside, and down into the vault beneath the chapel.

"Think this will work?" Tomáš asked as she spread the dirt across the bottom of the empty box.

"I'm not sure," Lauren said.

Bertram carefully rolled up the page of the Codex. He returned it to the box. The monk brought the key and gave it to Lauren. She turned and locked it, pocketing the key.

The monk took up the wooden chest and placed it in her hands. He took her by the arm and guided her politely back up the wide spiral stairs. She expected him to turn her towards the door, but instead, he led her over to the altar and motioned for her to kneel. She hesitated a moment and he made the gesture again. She lay the chest on the prayer rail and did as he indicated. He went to the altar and took up a small cross. He brought it over and seemed to mouth a prayer, though he respected his vow of silence. Lauren bowed her head as he did, sensing her escorts gathering behind her.

The silent holy man took the cross and returned it to the altar then came back with a small dish of water. He dipped his finger into it and drew a cross on the surface of the box, then repeated the step, drawing the cross on Lauren's forehead. His thumbnail grazed her skin, and a droplet of water ran down the side of her nose like a tear. He rested his hand on top of her head and continued in his silent prayer as she closed her eyes. A warmth spread through her core that lasted long after his hand moved from her crown.

She rose feeling fortified, not sure it was from the prayer or the power of the scroll inside the chest, tucked under her arm. She turned to the detective as his head lifted from prayer as well.

"Here." Tomáš moved to take the box.

The monk lifted his hand and shook his head no, pointing at Lauren.

"I have to carry it," she said, reading the gesture. "I appreciate the offer though."

Tomáš nodded in understanding. "Now the only question is, where do we take it?"

"No," Lauren said. "The important question is, where do we find the rest of the missing pages."

The monk raised a hand and gestured for them to follow. He had a small office just off the entryway. There he dug through a stack of papers, finding what appeared to be an ancient map. He studied it for a moment, then ran his fingers down to a red dot. He pushed the paper towards his guests and tapped the page.

"What's this?" Lauren asked.

The monk pointed to the box, then pointed to the map. His face seemed to light with a hint of a smile, perhaps pleased that he could contribute to their important work. Lauren could only assume that someone had given him directions to allow them to take the page, but that was just a presumption on her part.

"There's another page there?" Lauren asked. The monk nodded, then shrugged, giving her mixed signals. "Oh. You *think* there's another page there." Lauren understood him perfectly. He nodded, turning to his books on the shelf behind him with a wave of his hand. Lauren stepped around to study the spines on the ancient tomes. One was titled *Missing Relics: Holy & Unholy* in Latin. Another was titled *Antiquities Lost* in French. A third was titled *The Devil's Bible – A Complete History of the Codex Gigas* in English. Lauren picked up the first book tentatively. She was encouraged by the monk's expression. She lay the book on the desk and thumbed through the pages. A few pages in, she stopped and read carefully, then whipped her head up at the monk. "Really?"

He nodded.

"What?" Tomáš asked.

"The Foreskin of Jesus? From his circumcision? It's a missing relic?"

"Well, he was Jewish." Tomáš retorted.

Lauren looked at the monk again. "Do *you* know where it is?"

The monk shrugged with an expression that looked suspicious, then he pointed over her shoulder to the bottom of the page.

"What does it say?" Tomáš asked, as Lauren studied it.

"The story goes that an old Hebrew woman saved it, and then at one point it was the property of Charlemagne the Great ..." Lauren translated.

The monk scowled and shook his head. He pointed lower on the page.

"Oh," Lauren said after reading it. "In the 1900s the Roman Catholic Church issued a stern warning. If anyone talked about it, they would be excommunicated." The monk nodded. "Good thing you've taken a vow of silence." That made the monk smile.

Moving on, Lauren paused to study each of the pages. The Holy Grail, the Arc of the Covenant, The True Cross of Jesus Christ, the Lance of Longinus that pierced His flesh were among the most written about. But there was also the Ring of St. Edward, and even the singed heart of Joan of Arc. "Her heart was the only thing to survive the flames, according to French lore," Lauren went on to explain the text.

Amongst the cursed relics was the Devil's Bible, but also the shroud of Judas, a cat-o-nine-tails believed to have been used to scourge Jesus before his crucifixion, the Witches' Grimoire, the Ring of Saladin, and other objects that were used for demonic purposes.

"You've been looking for the missing pages, haven't you?" Lauren finally said to the monk. *What else was he going to do but escort guests, maintain the grounds and pray for several hours a day?* The monk nodded vigorously. "These other objects, too?" He nodded again. "You think it's in Slovenia then?" Lauren continued her interview.

"So, we're going to Slovenia next?" Tomáš looked dubious.

"We're happy to take it from here if it's an issue, Detective," Simon snarked, taking up the map.

"Why? Is that far?" Lauren asked, returning her attention to the men gathering around the map.

"It is." Bertram shook his head. "It's quite a long drive."

"Not if we take the Autobahn," Tomáš said, turning to Bertram. "I told you, she doesn't leave my sight."

Lauren turned to the kindly monk. "Thank you for your assistance."

He reached over and touched the hand she had laying on the wooden box. He bowed his head, taking it and kissing her knuckle, then returning it to the case. He smiled and turned, leaving them without a word.

"Slovenia, huh?" Lauren looked at the map uneasily.

"We'd best go," Kovač said. "Lauren, your job is to figure out what we do with the pages once we have them."

"That's assuming the monk is correct." Simon countered harshly. "Let me take this one and secure it. I can get it to the Vatican before you can get to Slovenia."

"No," Lauren wrapped her arm around the case. "It's my job to protect it. I won't let it out of my sight."

"What makes you think …" Simon started, but Tomáš stood and blocked him.

"We can do this with or without you, but I will not allow you to interfere."

Simon raised his hands in surrender and stepped out into the hallway, rolling his eyes as he turned.

Tomáš took out his phone and snapped a picture of the map. "Come on," he said to Lauren.

She nodded. She gave one last glance at the monk as they passed, along with a silent thanks for all his aid.

Into the night, they moved as the mist parted for them to pass. A night bird's song broke the eerie silence. Lauren turned sharply in that direction. Something moved in the shadows. Lauren's companions froze as she held up her hand. She scanned the trees, remembering the shadow of the man she'd seen just before Zuzu had been murdered.

Lauren turned to look over her shoulder, her eyes lifting towards the sky. There, an object hovered 50 meters above the surface of the ground. The fog-shrouded moonlight gave it a shadow and illuminated one edge of the triangular shape. As they stood, mesmerized, the craft shot straight up into the air and hovered a moment as if it had stalled, then rolled over and descended in freefall, a vapor trail building behind it just before it disappeared behind the rise of a hillside in the distance. Lauren anticipated the concussion as the craft crashed to the earth, but no sound came, and the craft never reappeared. Lauren shivered, remembering the vessel she'd witnessed; first in Peru, then in Washington State. This one was different. The others had appeared first as three individual vessels that merged together into a dulcet orb that throbbed with a soft blue-white glow. This craft was triangular, sharp, and very dark. There was no light emitting from it.

"What the hell?" Kovač's voice was weak with awe.

His words sent a chill through Lauren's core. "Hell, exactly," she muttered. "We need to go."

"But what was it?" Bertram, his eyes still fixed on the sky, was frozen even as she turned to press past him.

Suddenly, she took a step back, looking back over her shoulder towards the trees as she moved closer to Tomáš.

"What is it?" he asked.

"There was a man … in the trees, watching …" she said. "The day your mother was killed." Kovač stiffened as his gaze followed hers into the trees. Lauren continued, "I feel those eyes on me now."

"All the more reason to make haste," Bertram suggested.

"But …" Lucca caught her arm, pointing back to the sky. "What was *that*?"

"I don't know, but … nothing good can come from it."

Kovač took her arm and led her to his SUV. He opened the door and helped her in. He reached up and caught the seatbelt and latched it for her, so she never had to take her hands off her precious parcel. He turned to Bertram as the car door closed and said something to him Lauren couldn't hear. He came around and got in the car, buckling his own belt before starting the engine and putting the car in gear. "You know about the Autobahn, right?"

"No speed limits? Yes."

"But we must drive to conditions," he added as he pulled out. Lightning flashed in the distance as if in answer.

Lauren was still cautiously watching the trees, bristling when the thunder reached them. "Do you suppose there's a McDonalds on the Autobahn?" She swallowed back a nervous titter.

"I'm sure we can do better than that." Kovač snickered. "I know a great place for breakfast in Austria, if you can wait a few hours."

"Mmm … breakfast." She closed her eyes, inhaling deeply as if she could smell the sausages and coffee. "I can wait."

"Gives you time for a nap," he said. "I know you must be exhausted."

"You must be tired, too." Lauren observed as they pulled out onto the main road.

"I'm accustomed to long days and odd hours," he said. "Though, I might find a coffee after we cross the border."

"Wake me up if you stop," Lauren said. Just the smell of coffee lately had made her nauseated, but now she craved a creamy cup of the bitter brew. Tomáš nodded, as he stopped at the traffic light. She wrapped her arms around the wooden box and sighed, closing her eyes. She listened to the hum of the tires on the road as he picked up speed. It didn't take long before the gentle sway of the vehicle lulled her into an exhausted sleep.

~

"Dad?" A small voice found him in the dark. "Wake up, Dad."

"Huh?" He stirred.

"Don't move." There was caution in Henry's voice.

Rowan thought for a moment that his son was sitting beside him on his heels. Rowan had the flashlight, and he clicked it on. At the same moment, he could hear the skitter of something moving entirely too close to his leg. His heart immediately pounded out a raucous rhythm. The cobra was just inches from his knee. It turned and drew up, spreading its hood. It hissed at him in surprise. Rowan froze. The snake seemed to do the same. Finally, it lowered and calmed, then turned and slithered away, leaving a curving zigzag pattern in the sand as it passed. Rowan sat up on his elbow and noticed the patterns made an intricate weave around him.

Thank God he'd slept still and peacefully. The warm sand under his back had made a decent nest, but now his back itched. He pushed himself up to his feet and scratched, shaking the sand that crept down his boxer shorts trying to get it to run down his leg.

"Henry?" He turned, swinging his flashlight around. There was no sign of his son. *Why would there be?* The child was home in Egypt with his Aunt Tima and the girls. *Had he dreamt of his son's presence? What other explanation was there?*

He heard something else moving in the sand above, but he couldn't tell what it was. He realized the storm no longer roared. The sand began to skitter and fall down like rain. Then, he thought he heard a voice. "Jean-René!?" His heart began racing again. "I'm down here!" His voice echoed in the cavern. "Hey! Down here!"

The shuffling of running grains of sand told him they were digging. He turned his light towards the sound overhead, side-stepping the shower of sand as an opening appeared and daylight flooded in, blinding him. "Rowan?"

"Thank God," he said. "I'm here."

Jean-René slid in through the narrow opening and then skidded down the slope of sand. He reached for Rowan and instead of a hearty handshake, pulled his friend in for a manly hug. "I thought I'd lost you, buddy."

"You kind of did," Rowan beamed. "But I'm okay."

Greg appeared behind the cameraman. "What'd you find here?"

"Oh, you are not going to believe it," Rowan said. "I think it's a tomb." Greg pushed past him to explore, using his own flashlight to illuminate the carvings on the wall. "Watch out for the cobra."

"Cobra?" Jean-René gulped.

"He's a nice cobra," Rowan said. "He had plenty of chances, but he never bit me."

"*Nice* cobra?" Jean-René shook his head. "I didn't know there was such a thing."

"What? You don't like snakes?"

"You do? Even your hero, Indiana Jones, was terrified of snakcs."

Rowan just shook his head and followed Greg back to show him the tomb and other artifacts he'd found.

Jean-René went back for his camera and returned with a light bar, too. "Here, help me." He handed the light bar to Rowan. They fell in behind Greg as he inspected the tomb. Jean-René filmed. Rowan felt out of place behind his best friend. He was used to being in front of the camera.

"Oh my God!" Greg exclaimed as he inspected the illuminated tomb. "This is amazing!"

"Can you read the language?" Rowan asked.

Greg turned his attention to it. "Hmm." He paused, puzzling over it. "It's not Egyptian. Not Cuneiform. I think that's a Sumero-Akkadian version of cuneiform. See this glyph here? It looks like an arrow, and that one that looks like a three-legged stool? There are three stars… those symbolize the Pleiades."

He had Rowan's full attention. Even Jean-René turned and said over his shoulder, "Lauren needs to see this."

"Yeah, she does." Rowan agreed. "I took pictures. Get some video too, would you?"

"I'm on it," Jean-René said. He moved in to get a video inventory of the chamber from every angle.

"Rowan," Greg came back over and stuck his hand out. "Congratulations," he said. "You have discovered a previously unknown burial chamber. Well done, my friend." Jean-René caught the exchange on camera, though it was unlikely anyone else would ever get to see it. He certainly wouldn't let the Network get wind of Rowan being here.

"Thanks, but … what is this place?"

"That remains to be seen, but we had no idea this was here."

"So what happens next?"

"Next we bring the crews over to catalogue and document the find. We'll get a paleo-linguist to try and translate and maybe we can figure out who's buried here without opening the crypt."

"We're not going to open it?" Rowan sounded disappointed.

"In the old days, archaeologists would get a pry bar and pop that thing open without any thought of how much history they were destroying in the process. Today, we try to gain as much knowledge while still preserving the scene. We'll use GPR, x-ray, snake-cams, or whatever we need to try and see inside the tomb. If we don't have to, we won't violate the burial."

"So how long will you spend on a site like this?" Rowan asked, his role as a television interviewer kicked in.

"We've been out here on the other sites for about five

years," he said. "We'll do an initial survey here, but we prioritize our work, and we'll secure the scene so others can't violate it until we get back to it. It could be a lifetime of work at a single site. It's among the various reasons we invite visiting archeologists. We can't do this all by ourselves."

"So it's possible I could come back out here and visit when you're actively working the site?"

"You'll always be welcome," Greg said. "But you've still got a few days here before you have to leave. You can help with the initial survey. Right?"

"Heck yeah," Rowan beamed.

"HENRY! OH GOOD HEAVENS! THERE YOU ARE!" TIMA HAD been a nervous wreck trying to find the boy in the crowd. They found him in the back of the toy store hiding behind a cage containing balls of all sorts. He had his hands over his head. He looked like he'd been crying. Tima snatched him up and wrapped her arms around him, kissing his cheeks and hugging him fiercely. "Are you okay?"

"Yes, ma'am," he said, hugging her back. "I'm sorry. I'm sorry."

"You scared the life out of me," Tima said. "Where did you go?"

"I thought you were behind me, but I couldn't find you," he said, avoiding her gaze. He knew he wasn't supposed to lie, but he also knew Aunt Tima would never understand what he had done, how he'd done it or why. His daddy wouldn't either, but his momma would. She had friends to help her. While Henry was worried for her, he knew there wasn't much he could do. His daddy, well, that was something different.

His momma usually saved his dad's fat from the fire, and she couldn't. Someone had to keep the cobra from biting him. Henry was glad he made it in time. He was also glad he made it back to his own place in time before he got in too much trouble.

"Oh Henry! There you are!" Shemi came around the corner with John Carter riding piggyback. "Ahmose!" she called back over her shoulder. "We found him!"

John Carter squirmed and Shemi let him slide down to the floor. He walked over to Henry and stuck his finger out, putting it at his brother's face. "Momma's gonna be mad at you, *Heny*."

"It's okay, John Carter," Tima assured him. "We were just afraid Henry was hurt or lost."

Henry scowled at his little brother, a silent cautionary gaze that brought an end to the discussion. "Can we find our present now?" he said to Tima.

"Yes, of course," she said, turning loose of him.

25

Less than thirty minutes after they'd stopped for breakfast, Lauren ordered Tomáš to pull over. He could tell by the urgency in her tone that she was not joking. He complied, getting over as quickly as he safely could. The SUV hadn't even come to a stop before she flung the door open and leapt out, barely making it to the grass before she puked. She hadn't been sick in over twenty-four hours, but her record was now over.

By the time the Gendarmerie pulled up behind them, she was doubled over, leaning on the side of the car. Tomáš came around and put a hand on her back. He had a bottle of water in his other hand. He pressed it against the back of her neck. It was cool and felt good on her skin. "You okay?"

"Yeah," she said. Lauren straightened and glanced up at the trees. She felt her face turn to stone as she locked eyes with the spectral images she found there.

Tomáš turned. "What?"

The shadowy figure that reminded Lauren of the vampiric Dr. Masa stood in the dark place amongst the trees; eyes glowing red, like flickering flame, in the dim light. Around the fallen one a demonic entourage gathered. They seemed to rise from the ground; multiplying exponentially as their forces seemed to swell. Larger demonic entities backed Enlil up. Their eyes glowed as their master's did.

She knew then the Gates of Hell had been flung open wide. These were the minions of the Dark One. Hellhounds, wendigo, succubae, horned reapers, ogres, Chupacabra, banshee, and many more creatures she had no names for, stood prepared to take on all-comers. Smaller orders of beings made the ground crawl; beetles, worms, maggots writhing on the damp surface around the edge of the forest created a deafening cacophony of mutterings. The reek of rot and brimstone made her stomach churn.

"He's here …" she said in a voice that was icy cold.

Tomáš turned again, scanning the tree line. He didn't seem to see the danger or sense the threat.

With no warning Lauren found herself standing on the top of a high mountain. Cold air buffeted her flesh like icy needles as the wind tore at her hair. The monster she'd encountered in Zuzu's kitchen had her by the arm. His claws burned her flesh, and she writhed, trying to free herself. She felt dizzy, disoriented. Her stomach churned, incensed by that same nauseating stench of the foul serpent.

But Enlil let her go. He moved in a slow, slinking circle around her. The tail she hadn't remembered or noticed before drug along the rocky rise. She struggled to move away, but her feet held fast, not responding to her panic. "Do you see all the kingdoms of the world and their glory? Do you see these things the All-Father has made? While my brethren have been cast aside and forgotten, he has allowed you to reside in a place I have been denied; a place that was given to *me*! A place that was made for *me*!" The Dark One's voice was angry, deep; bone chilling. Lauren couldn't move. Couldn't respond. She couldn't cry out. Tears hovered in the corners of her eyes as if frozen; unable to fall to her cheeks. "All this I will give *you*, if you will fall down and worship *me*."

Lauren felt the fluttering of wings at her shoulder, as a comforting hand came to her elbow. The demon's hold on her released. "Resist him, sister. Remain firm in your faith in the All-Father. The Devil is a deceiver. He feeds on fear and chaos. War is his great buffet; an altar of gluttony." Michael's voice found her ear as a whisper. "His power lies in bringing death. After death comes *judgment*."

"Bow before me." Enlil turned. If he saw her brother behind her, he gave no sign.

"Resist," Michael urged; his voice barely above a whisper.

"Bow!" Enlil roared. "Prostrate yourself at my feet!"

"Resist."

"I will not." Her voice came out strong; her words resolute. "You have no dominion here."

"WHAT IS IT?" BERTRAM ASKED, MOVING BEHIND HER TO PEER over her shoulder.

"Lauren? What did you see?" The detective moved to block her from any danger that might present itself. Her frightened eyes lifted to his as he caught her arms to keep her from falling backwards. That dizzying sense of displacement made the world spin around her. "Was it the same thing you saw outside my mother's home?"

She moved past him, pushing him aside as she fell to her hands and knees and vomited again. Her body heaved again, and again, before she came up sputtering and spitting. Tomáš took the bottle of water from the cup holder in the car. He opened it, handing it to her. She rinsed her mouth and spat again. Bertram offered her a hand up. Tomáš caught the other arm when her knees threatened to fail.

A sense of urgency seemed to overtake the detective. "Come on." Tomáš led her back to the car. "We need to keep moving. We need to get to the church in Slovenia."

"Can you make it?" Bertram asked.

Lauren nodded. Her gaze went to Simon who stood by the Gendarmeries' car. His gaze went to the trees, and he seemed to have a wicked smile on his face. For a moment she thought perhaps he saw the army of Enlil, too. He turned, realizing she was looking at him and scowled at her. Kovač gave her a nudge. She let them help her back into the car and lay the seat back, closing her eyes. "Keep going."

"We'll meet you there," Bertram said, turning to the others. "Brothers, she saw something. Lucifer himself may be here. We need to try and stop him here if we can. Get our equipment."

That was the last Lauren heard before Tomáš closed the car door. He rushed around to the other side and got in, making sure they both had their seatbelts buckled before he checked his mirrors and drove off.

When Lauren finally got the courage to open her eyes, certain her stomach had settled, she glanced over at the speedometer. He was going nearly 200 kilometers per hour. She swallowed hard, raising the back of her chair. Tomáš glanced over at her cautiously.

"I'm better," she said.

"Good," he said. "But your color is still a bit off."

"I'm fine." She swallowed hard, turning her gaze to the road. "At least it's not raining."

"For now," he said, pointing towards dark clouds off to their right. "Storms are coming."

"Oh, brother," she groaned.

"I'm hoping I can get ahead of it," he said.

There was a long period of silence as the detective kept his focus on the road, moving in and out of traffic, increasing speed as he took the outside lane.

"Have you been to Slovenia?" Lauren asked so she didn't have to talk about what had just happened. In truth, she wasn't sure what had happened. *If Enlil was the deceiver, he could have made her imagine the whole thing, right?*

"Yes," he said. "I studied there ... before."

"Before?"

"Before I was a police officer," he said. "Before I made detective."

Lauren didn't need to ask but felt compelled. Judy had been correct. It was his story to tell. Lauren wondered if he would tell it; if he could. "Was that when you were studying to be a priest?"

"Yes, I came to study Theology," he answered, but offered nothing more. Lauren allowed the silence to fill the void between them and didn't prod. She closed her eyes and tried to fight off the replay running in the back of her mind's eye. Nearly five miles down the road, he spoke again. His voice remained deep, almost haunting. "My faith was tested, and ... it failed me ... maybe I failed it. I don't know."

"I'm sorry." Lauren wasn't sure what else to say.

"I was gone from home when my mother needed me most."

"What could you have done?" Lauren asked.

"I could have been there," he said. "My father was shot, and I know I couldn't have stopped it ... couldn't have saved him, but ... maybe I could have been there for my mother when she needed me. Maybe I could have prayed with my father before he went to work that day. Maybe ..." He stopped, his voice cutting off as he focused his full attention on the road. "I wasn't there when my mother was killed either. Maybe I could have ..."

"No, you weren't there ... but I was," Lauren said. "And ... even I couldn't save her."

~

ENLIL STOOD, IN HUMAN FORM ON THE BRIDGE AS CARS whizzed past below. Humans were always in such a hurry; as if time really meant anything. The Dark One knew time was a concept their simple brains could not comprehend. To them, it was linear. A one-way road with no turnarounds.

He could sense the presence of that insufferable woman; the *Chosen One*, as the car neared, even at the break-neck speed it traveled. He wasn't sure where they were going, but he intended to find out. All he needed to do was plant a seed. A seed that would grow into a hunger that would gnaw on even the strongest soul and take his quarry where he could extract the information he needed. Then he would have time to plan his attack and then he could get his spells. Once all the pieces of the puzzle fell into place, he would make his move. Just one thought was all he needed . He planted a seed in the woman's mind ... *hunger*.

~

"PULL OVER!" LAUREN ORDERED.

"I can't." There was a large box van running alongside them as Kovač tried to pass.

Lauren didn't hesitate. She rolled down the window and stuck her head out. Tires squealed behind them as cars swerved to avoid the shower of vomit. She had no control to prevent it as she got sick again ... and again.

The look on Tomáš' face when she finally collapsed back in her seat and reached for the bottle of water was nothing short of horror. She rinsed her mouth, then leaned out the window again to spit. "You're going to need a car-wash."

His lip curled up as he glanced back over her shoulder at the passenger side of the SUV. He'd never had anyone puke out of the window at nearly 200 kilometers per hour, but the cars behind them were running their windshield wipers, which gave him an indication of the impact of such an event.

"I need petrol soon too," he said.

"I'd kill for a cheeseburger right now." Lauren sighed dreamily.

"Really?" He glanced at his violated back windows and cringed. "*Now* you want a cheeseburger?"

"Well, that was the last of breakfast …" she said, looking at him coyly.

"What guarantee do I have I won't end up with a burger and fries on the side of my car?"

"I did ask you to pull over …" she said sheepishly.

"*Co ve jménu … Zabíjíš mě.*" He swore under his breath. With reluctance in his voice, he added, "I know a place …"

"DID YOU HAVE FUN AT THE BIRTHDAY PARTY?" TIMA ASKED when the boys came racing back into the house.

"They had a great time!" Ahmose fell into the sofa. "Wish I could bottle up all their energy. I'm exhausted."

Tima lay down her book as the boys ran around, jumping and chattering about all the fun things they did at the party.

"Slow down!" Tima beamed. It was good to see Henry happy again. John Carter seemed to feed off his brother's enthusiasm. "Tell me about the cake."

"We had *fondant* cake," Henry said. "No frosting. Have you ever had fondant cake, Auntie? And it had smashed up figs in it. I never had figs in a cake."

"Did you like it?"

"I *yoved* it!" John Carter enthused. "I *yoved* fondant cake."

"It was very good," Henry said. "I had two pieces."

"He did, too," Ahmose sighed.

"And did Braheem like his present?"

"They played with the LEGO sets we got him for hours," Ahmose said, closing her eyes. "I told them we'd go get some more LEGOs tomorrow."

"I *yike* yegos," John Carter said. "I made a *wocket*."

"You do like your rockets." Tima beamed.

Henry climbed up in her lap, leaning on the edge of the sofa. "That was a really good party, Auntie Tima."

"I'm glad you had a good time, sweet boy," she said.

"What are you reading?" He picked up her book and inspected it.

"Your daddy loaned it to me," she said.

"This is a good book." Henry nodded. "*The Hitchhiker's Guide to the Galaxy* is one of Daddy's favorites. Mine, too."

"Did your daddy read it to you? Or did your momma?"

"I read it all by myself," Henry said.

"You did?" She knew she shouldn't be surprised. Lauren intended to home school the boys. Henry was just old enough to start kindergarten. "All by yourself?" She hadn't waited. She'd been teaching them as they became interested in things. They were both curious and bright.

"Yes, ma'am." Henry opened up the book and began to read.

"Well, look at you," Tima praised him.

"I think digital watches are a pretty neat idea too," Henry said, in reference to the passage he just read. "Daddy says when I'm ten I can have a digital watch."

"Ten? Why ten?" Tima asked.

Henry shrugged. "I *dunno*."

"I overheard you reading *Where the Wild Things Are* to your brother last night and thought maybe you had it memorized. I didn't realize what a proficient reader you were."

"I want to read every book in the Library of Congress," Henry said.

"That's over five million books, Henry." Tima shook her head impressed more and more with her student's family. "And the number is growing every day."

Rowan set an excellent example for his boys. He scored an A on every assignment and every test. It was hard not to give him extra credit for his hard work. He had a work-ethic unlike any student she'd ever had. If anyone could achieve that goal, it would be Henry. He was just like his father.

"I would have read all the books in the Library of Alexandria, but they had a fire," Henry said.

"How do you know about the fire?"

"Momma is still mad about it."

"Still?" Fatima laughed out loud. *This child was a wonder.*

"It's all Julius Caesar's fault."

"Henry, do you know how long ago that was?"

"I know it was before my momma was born." He yawned.

John Carter, curled up in Ahmose's lap, was drifting off. Ahmose was, too.

"Yes, it was much longer before that," Tima said. "But we're not sure who burned it down. You know that, right?"

"I do," he said. "But Mommy blames Caesar."

"I think," Tima began. "It was Caliph Omar."

"Who's that?"

"He was the chief of the Muslim army who took the city of Alexandria in 640 AD. When he learned the city had a library with all of the knowledge of mankind within, his generals asked for instructions. Caliph Omar said, *they will either contradict the Quran, in which case they are heresy, or they will agree with it, which makes them superfluous.*"

"That means it's extra," Henry said. "I know that word. It's my favorite big word."

"Yes, it does," she said. "So, he ordered all the books to be destroyed. Some even said it took over six months to burn them all."

"I love books." Henry sighed. "It makes me sad that someone would burn them."

"Me too, sweet boy." She kissed his head.

"That's why my momma needs to find the Devil's book," Henry said. "Some of the books that were destroyed are in it."

Fatima's brow lifted. "How do you know that?"

"I looked at it," he said.

"Did you see it on the internet?" she asked. "Did your dad show you?"

Henry yawned but didn't answer. Instead, he curled up into her and sighed heavily. Fatima decided the boy was done talking about it. He'd had a long day. "Do you want to read some more, or shall I read to you?"

Henry read until his eyelids began to grow heavy. Tima took over and read until he was sound asleep. She might regret later letting him nap so late, but he clearly needed it. She glanced over and found Ahmose and John Carter both sound asleep.

26

By the time Tomáš pulled off the highway, Lauren was ravenous. She hadn't been this hungry since before she found out she was pregnant. All she could think about was a big fat juicy cheeseburger and maybe some fries.

Much to her dismay, Tomáš went in search of the petrol station first. She stayed in her seat as he got out at the gas pump. To distract herself from her hunger, she thought about the words in Slovenian. *Bencinska črpalka … gas station.* She let the words roll around in her mind before trying it out. She'd never spoken Slovenian before. The Slavic languages were interesting. She found she liked the feel of the words in her brain, and on her tongue. The words were melodic, but the consonants slurred into one another. The vowels often seemed to be added as after thoughts.

Americans said *gasoline*, most Europeans said *petrol*, while the Germans had to be the odd man out calling it *benzene*. The Slovenians called its *bencin*, and their word for gas pump referred to it as *benzene,* too. Perhaps their close proximity to Germany influenced the choice of words.

"The burger place is just up the way," Tomáš said without

preamble when he got back in the car. He started the engine and pulled out of the drive.

Lauren forgot all about the words for gasoline and let her thoughts return to a fat burger. She hoped there would be pickles and yellow mustard, maybe a nice ripe tomato. Her stomach growled at the thought of it.

"This is it?" Lauren asked when he pulled up in front of what looked like a cross between the old Dairy King across the street from her high school and a log cabin. *Okrepčavalnica "Rocky"*, the vinyl sign announced. *Bistro Rocky*

"Trust me on this one," Kovač said with a grin as they got out of the car. "The cook is from Toronto."

"Let me guess ... Rocky?"

Tomáš just smiled.

❦

THE DARK ONE SLIPPED PAST THE CROWD OUTSIDE, UNSEEN. He came around to the back of the burger shop and rapped on the screen door. "Delivery," he called out.

"Bout damned time!" The cook groused without looking up from the grill where he was flipping burgers. "Bring it in already!"

When Rocky came to check the order, the Dark One wrapped his hand around the chef's throat and silenced him with a fiery gaze and a wicked grip. The cook's eyes bulged in their sockets as the Deceiver crushed his larynx, then assumed his form. He shoved the stunned victim into the small supply room. He slammed the door and left him to die.

He took over the man's work, grinning wickedly to himself as he watched the front counter out of the corner of his eye. A few moments later, his quarry stepped up to the cashier. He watched as they placed their order.

The woman made his blood curdle. An aura of goodness stained her image and he sneered as he gazed through the service window at her. He could take her out here and now, he decided, debating if he should poison her food or lure her away from her escort and rip her throat out as he had the old woman. She'd come after him bare handed in a terrified blood rage, trying to protect the old woman. He had tried to finish her then, but she had powers he couldn't overtake. He'd knocked her over the island in the kitchen and she'd come up with the knife and came slashing at his eyes. She would not be easily defeated. He would have done so then, if he could, but just touching her burned his flesh, and he'd retreated; unprepared for the battle.

"Lahko naročim Cheeseburger, krompirček in Coca Cola?" the woman said, gazing over at the menu. She spoke perfect Slovenian without a hint of an accent. The Devil was impressed. The woman had skills, skills that came with a foul taint of Holy magic around her countenance. No, he would not defeat her easily. But he would defeat her. Somehow, he would.

The detective turned and looked directly at him. "Hey, Rocky! How's it going?" The Deceiver stared at him a moment before he remembered his role. He nodded and saluted him with the spatula before flipping the burgers again, smashing the meat into the grill. "Long time, no see."

How would the chef respond? He pondered a moment. "Been a while," the cook answered. "Welcome back." The words came out in Slovenian, with a distinctly Canadian accent. It surprised even the Devil himself.

The detective nodded, but said nothing else, which relieved the Devil who watched the woman out of the corner of his eye. He smashed the burgers against the grill, still paying little attention to what he was doing.

～

Tomáš finished ordering and paid for the meal. Lauren turned and went to the refrigerated cooler, taking out two bottles of Coca Cola, popping the tops off, before handing one to Kovač. He led her over to a picnic table under the portico. It was raining lightly. The day had gone cool. The sky was gray and growing darker. Their breath hung in clouds around their faces, and Tomáš's cheeks had gone pink.

The smell of meat, grease, and fried onions permeated the small semi-outdoor dining space. "This place smells so good," Lauren said, as they sat down to wait.

"I got us an order of poutine," he said.

"Poutine?"

"It's Canadian. French fried potatoes with cheese curds and gravy," he said. "Ever had it?"

"Never," she said. "I usually stick to salads and grilled chicken. I don't know what's gotten into me. I rarely crave a hamburger, much less one with cheese."

"Just promise me you'll try to keep it down?" He glanced back over at his car. A light mist began to fall, and he hoped it'd rain hard enough to save him a trip to the carwash.

"I don't know what came over me today." Lauren shook her head. "I wasn't even the least bit nauseous, then all of a sudden … *boom*! It hit me. Twice."

"I realize, I haven't been around that many pregnant women, but I thought this kind of thing only happened in the mornings."

"Huge misnomer." Lauren shook her head, reaching for the cold bottle of soda.

"*Tukaj je tvoja hrana.*" The chef came out with their order on a plastic tray. "I hope you are hungry."

Lauren suddenly turned green. She bolted from the table. She disappeared behind the building but there was no doubt in his mind what had happened.

Tomáš shook his head. "I think she got some bad *Chlebíčky.*"

"Too bad." Rocky shrugged. "Shame for all this food to go to waste."

"It won't all go to waste." Tomáš reached for the basket of fries slathered in gravy, topped with melting curds of cheese.

"Should I wrap up her meal for later? Looks like you are traveling. Might be a while before you get where you're going," the chef said, prodding for the information. Surely someone would give him what he needed.

"No. I'll give her a chance to eat it," Tomáš said. "She swore she was starving."

"But you have many miles to go, yes?" Rocky insisted.

"Not so many," Tomáš said. He stabbed his plastic fork into the dish and took a bite. He'd been anticipating something he'd had so long ago that was wonderful. Sadly, it didn't live up to his memory. Something was … *off*. "Did you change your recipe?"

"Huh?" the chef looked affronted. "You don't like it?"

Tomáš wiped his mouth on a paper napkin. "No, it's good. Better than I remembered." He realized he might not have come off as genuine.

"Bah!" Rocky grunted in a deep voice, slapping away the comment with a wave. "I'm not here for the five-star reviews. *Vsi so kritiki!*" *Every one's a critic.* He turned, scowling over his shoulder as he went back to the kitchen, keeping a wary eye out for the woman. She was the one he wanted, but he just couldn't seem to get close to her. Maybe he needed to get the cop out of his way.

The Dark One waited at the doorway, watching to see if the woman returned. When she finally did, he hoped to eavesdrop on their conversation. She sat back down and took a long drink from the bottle of soda, then picked up the burger and took a huge bite. Her companion stared at her in disbelief.

This is never going to work, Enlil decided. *I have to get close to her.* He needed the man out of the way, too.

Quietly, he went behind the building and moved swiftly, reappearing in a new form as he came around the other side.

❧

LAUREN GLANCED UP AS SHE HEARD THE SOUNDS OF A CHILD crying. A little girl came around the building wailing. Lauren leaned over the railing and called her over. "What's the matter, sweetheart? Are you okay?"

"I lost my puppy," the child sniffed.

"Do you need help finding it?" Lauren started to rise.

Tomáš caught her wrist and cast a wicked glare at her. She sank back to the bench, looking wounded.

"I'll help," he said. "You, eat … while you can."

Lauren stared at her food for a moment, suddenly wondering if she could. She glanced at the little girl, who seemed angry. Lauren couldn't tell why. Her attention returned back to her stomach as it churned momentarily. She wanted to be sick … again. Forgetting the child and the detective, she sat with her face in her hands. The food that had once smelled so good now turned in her stomach.

She opened her eyes to inspect it, and gasped, nearly falling off the back of the bench as the burger seemed to writhe with maggots that fell out from beneath the lettuce leaf and the bun.

"Sheesh, Lauren," Tomáš shook his head at her sympathetically. "You said you were starving, but you look like you're about to—"

She flung herself from the dining area a second time, rushing away, collapsing near a tree as her stomach revolted again, and then again. *God, what unholy torture was this?* Even as she vomited, her hunger reminded her of the need to nourish her body and feed her unborn child.

Tomáš followed the little girl the other direction, glancing back over his shoulder at Lauren. She shrugged, pathetically, as she leaned against the tree. He turned and shrugged back. She waved him off as she managed to stand on unsteady legs.

Wiping the sweat from her brow, she stumbled a few steps then managed to make her way back toward her seat. She fisted her hands on the table to steady herself as she hesitated to glance down. The aroma of the food made her mouth water. She lifted the bun off the bread and was stunned to find there was nothing wrong … nothing there but grilled meat, onions, mustard, pickle, tomato, and lettuce. *I must be losing my mind.* She sniffed at the food. Still, her guts twisted in her abdomen. She turned away, her eye searching for Tomáš, finding him and the little girl wandering down the street. She could hear him whistling for a dog that never answered.

After a moment, her stomach settled, and her hunger returned with a vengeance.

WHEN TOMÁŠ CAME BACK, HER BURGER WAS GONE, ALONG with all of the poutine. He gazed at the empty basket, then at his ward. She looked up at him sheepishly, wiping her mouth with the paper napkin.

"Did you find it?"

"No," he said. "I sent her home to get her mother to help." He glanced back in the direction the girl had been heading, but no longer saw her. "I'm always suspicious when a child claims to have lost a dog. Even more so when the dog can't be found."

"Why so suspicious?"

Tomáš looked at her sternly. "That's the oldest trick in the book," he said. "Human traffickers use children to lure their victim … usually a sympathetic woman … away from their companions. Once they get them out of sight of their friends, there's usually a van waiting to snatch them up and whisk them away, never to be heard from again. You've got *mark* written all over your face, you know."

"What?" Lauren snapped. "Are you serious?"

"I've worked dozens of missing person cases with the same M.O.," he said.

"You're forgetting one thing," Lauren said.

"Oh?"

"I've already been kidnapped and shoved in a van," she said. "Fool me once …"

"Shame on you." Tomáš chuckled. "I guess you liked the food?"

"Loved it." Lauren beamed. "Poutine, huh?"

"Yeah," Tomáš nodded.

"Best stuff I ever tasted. Slovenian food is good."

"Canadian." He reminded her. "But, it was better the last time I was here. Rocky must be having an off day." Tomáš shrugged. "We need to hurry up and get a move on."

"I'm done," Lauren said. "Just waiting on you."

He picked up his burger and made short work of it. He polished it off in five bites. "Come on," he said, wiping his mouth on his napkin. "We're not far from the church."

Lauren tipped back her bottle and drained it. She stifled a belch as she gathered up their trash. Tomáš took the tray to the trash can, dumping it in the receptacle, leaving the tray and the baskets on the shelf. He glanced back at the chef in the kitchen and gave him a wave.

The church? What cursed church? Enlil seethed. That insufferable woman was more torment than Eve ever dreamt of being. He'd been successful in tempting the first woman, but this …creature … there was something about her he could not pinpoint. She was the *Chosen One*, he was certain of it. She had to be. He hadn't been able to witness the defeat of his

Estonian agent first hand, but he suspected she had been the one who had taken out his most powerful human minion. He needed humans. Needed them to serve him, to intercede on his behalf and ensure the propagation of chaos, hatred, and war. Fortunately most were easily plied, and more than willing to cooperate. His current minion would be most helpful when the time came, he was certain of it.

Not that woman, though. She had rebuked him without hesitation on the mountain top. He'd been afraid of that when he saw her picture in the media. He knew his brother Enki had been conspiring with a human. The peace accord the humans were using to try and drain him of his powers wouldn't work. This woman was a known accomplice with the ambassador that was leading the American task force and the United Nations to push the accord off onto other smaller nations. *Bullies!* They were all bullies and cowards. Well, maybe not this woman, but she had an audacity about her. He sensed it.

He stood in an assumed form in her living room and eyed her down. He knew from the moment he'd laid eyes on her that she would be his salvation — or his destruction. He suspected now it was the latter, but he had no time to ponder on it. He needed to figure out which church they'd been speaking of. There were many churches in the region. Some were grandiose, others were as plain as a church could be. Ancient religions were not entirely dead here. Christianity was relatively new in the area.

Before Catholicism rose in Slovenia, the region was heavily ruled by paganism. *Those were the good old days!* In the 10th century, Christian texts were first written in the Slovenian language in monasteries by monks. By the 16th century, Slovenia was over taken by the Protestant reformation, thanks to the ideas of Martin Luther. Around the same time, Turkish armies occupied Slovenia for more than 200 years, yet the Turks never managed to conquer the whole of Slovenia. Still, there were signs of their presence in the mosques that remained.

The greatest dark victory of the modern era came when the Islamic community in Ljubljana struggled to build a mosque for nearly 40 years. The Dark One played a hand in preventing it, if only passively. While the official reason for its delay had been an issue with the planned location, 9/11 made the world so xenophobic, the city council officially pulled the plug on the project. *No, they weren't looking for a Muslim church.* 72% of the region remained Catholic. The Holy Roman Church had the most consecrated ground in the country. It *had* to be a Catholic church. It just *had* to be.

The Dark One stood on a hill overlooking the town, watching as cars passed on the roadway. He wasn't sure what he would do, but he could feel the pull of that woman on him as he stood thinking on her. The dark SUV seemed to have an aura around it as it rounded the bend and came into view. *Aha! There she was. Now, where was she going?*

There were dozens, if not hundreds of the All-Father's temples in this region. Churches stood for centuries, despite his best efforts to bring them down. But as the Dark One stood on the hill, he gained a sense of her thoughts. She'd dropped her guard and allowed him into her. He only needed a second. But, he didn't like what he learned. No, not one bit.

27

Tomáš parked in the small lot that sat at the bottom of the hill where the ancient cathedral perched. Candlelight gave the holy place an inviting glow. The Vatican Police's SUV was already parked nearby, but no other cars were anywhere near the holy temple.

Bertram approached and opened the car door for her. The Gendarmerie had arrived before the detective and his charge. Lauren had the wooden box wrapped in her arms when she got out. The Vatican Police gathered around her as Lauren's gaze went to the tree-line over their shoulders. Tomáš came up behind her and hooked his arm under hers, steadying her.

"We've already done a preliminary search of the area," Bertram said.

"Did you find anything back on the Autobahn?" she asked. Bertram pursed his lips, glancing at the others nervously, but shook his head in the negative. She looked back at the detective. She shrugged and swallowed hard, her eyes going to the surrounding trees.

Tomáš had sensed her unease when they reached the small town where the cathedral stood. Now, he recognized the symptoms of her wariness that manifested into a swirling queasiness and general feeling of dread; it was written all over her green face. He was starting to think it had nothing to do with morning sickness. He suspected she could sense the Dark One's presence. The Dark One — if such a demon truly existed — was close. Perhaps he'd been close to her before. It confirmed his suspicions that the child at the restaurant might have been a lure. Maybe their enemy had been poised and ready to pounce.

Tomáš' hair stood on end. She hadn't said anything to him or the others. She didn't have to. They all felt it as well, he was sure of it.

If it weren't for his arm on her as he led her towards the church, he suspected she might have turned tail and run. As it was, she was shivering, but it could have been the plunging temperature. Not even the warmth of his body, nor that of the Gendarmerie around her, seemed to help.

Just steps away from the stone wall and wrought iron gate, indicating the transition to hallowed ground. Lauren froze without notice, turning to gaze at something across the meadow.

"What is it?" Tomáš asked, his eye following hers.

The mournful howl of a wolf was answered by another from deep within the woods around the cathedral. "The Watchers," Lauren muttered.

Michael, are you there? Lauren thought, and a familiar wolf-song answered. *Yes! That was him.* She felt immediately comforted knowing her brother and his *friends* were close.

"Look!" Lucca's voice behind her drew the attention of the others. Across the empty meadow, a deep hum thrummed overhead.

Lauren's head tilted back as a triangular craft hovered above the tree line. The air beneath it trembled in waves like a mirage on the desert. The bottom of the craft opened, and a beam of red light split the sky, illuminating everything with a scarlet glow. Trees erupted into flame. Sparks caught in the wind and hovered between the timbers, igniting their neighbors. The smell of ozone and woodsmoke filled the air. The fire spread quickly, as silhouetted figures of wolves raced behind the flames, blocked from the safety of the sacred ground. Michael and his forces seemed trapped. It reminded Lauren of a fire that had broken out in Yellowstone when she lived there. The wolves had panicked as the flames raced through their territory. Lauren had struggled between capturing footage of their plight and trying to help them. Before she could respond, the wolves found an outcropping of rock to use as an escape platform and jumped the line of flames. The wolves now, had no such opportunity for escape. They were cut off.

From the craft came a black spectral form Lauren could only think of as a *wraith*. She turned as it flew over the field, then came up behind her as she turned to run. She spun around, falling, just as the specter reached out and clawed for the box. She recoiled instinctively to wrap her body around the rosewood chest.

As the specter's claw connected with Lauren's skin and a white-hot fire screamed from the wraith; its cry crackling like lightning. An ungodly pain shot through Lauren's bones, racing down her arm and into her core. She could feel an opposing force rise from her soul, pushing back against the demon specter's. The force of the conflicting forces knocked everyone from their feet except Lauren. She curved her body around the box. She shielded it despite the agony written on her face. The scream that raged from her chest could have broken glass.

The specter surrendered in the struggle for dominance and possession of the scroll within the box. It seemed to weaken as it was cast back by the unseen force Lauren had generated. Without warning, the wraith flashed into dark bits of ash that fell around her like black snow.

Tiny bastions of Hell, like those she had seen on the Autobahn, seemed to appear from the fragments like rats boiling through a sewer. They skittered towards Lauren and pounced. Their fangs tore into her flesh. She rose weakly swatting them away; elbowing one that came over her shoulder and looked as if it might sink its teeth into her throat.

Recovering from the wraith's attack, Tomáš regained his wits about him. He swatted and kicked at the small demons, trying to save Lauren from their attack. It seemed futile. There had to be hundreds of them. But, with each blow of Lauren's hand, the demonic creatures disappeared into nothingness.

Bertram raised a holy cross, while Lucca began shouting prayers. All the while, Lauren's screams never abated. Her lungs had to be burning. "I cast thee out, minions of Lucifer!" He prayed aloud, but it seemed to have no effect on the horde.

"Master," Simon gulped, and fell to his knees. Kovač and the other's froze as they realized what was going on.

Enlil appeared across the expanse where the craft first scoured the ground; a dark shadow against the burning land-scape. The Devil transformed from first one visage to another, each more horrific than the last.

"Master?" Kovač squashed one of the demons beneath his boot and kicked the last one away. It landed on the other side of the fence and erupted into flame before flashing out into nothingness. He snatched Lauren to her feet, inspecting her. She was frantic; terrified. She could hardly function as she clutched the case to her chest. A wound on her cheek bled freely, and there were other minor bites and gashes, but there was no time to tend to them. "Get back!" He shouted to the others. He moved back past the gate, onto sacred ground. "Get back! Get back!"

With insouciance composure The Dark One sauntered across the field drinking in the power of the conflict; lifting his arms as he consumed it. A dark aura of energy wrapped itself around him as he found human form.

"That's him! That's Dr. Masa," Lauren said to Kovač.

As the others made for the safety of sacred ground, Simon stood and bowed as the Dark One neared, his eyes glowing with a wicked fire. Behind Enlil, his hellions gathered, seething and ready for the fight. "Bring me the pages of my book," Enlil ordered.

Simon bowed again. "As you command, my Lord," he said, then turned.

Lauren stiffened, freeing herself from Kovač's grasp. She limped forward, ready for the minion of Enlil to charge. She had faced one of the Dark One's minions before and had defeated him. She clutched the box containing the scroll to her chest but raised her other hand expecting her own energies to build in her core and push him away. She'd done it without thinking before and expected her own magic to work in a similar fashion this time — but nothing happened. Simon grabbed her arm, trying to wrench the box from her hands, but she recoiled at his touch and cried out. He leaned into her, his nails digging into her flesh. "I drugged you." His lips curled as he sneered. Lauren struggled, fighting to free herself from his grasp.

Tomáš roared, "I've had enough!" He struck the Vatican officer, heedless of the danger to himself. He knocked the man from his feet. Simon tumbled away, striking his head on a rock. Tomáš regained his footing, catching Lauren under the arms. "For the love of God!" he shouted. "Get into the church!"

The combined screams and the din of Enlil's minions were deafening. It drove Tomáš past his breaking point. Still, he persevered. He caught her arm and all but dragged her away from the approaching danger.

He hit the door of the cathedral with his shoulder, but it didn't budge. A grunt erupted from his throat. He fumbled for the ancient latch. With a frantic jiggle, it surrendered. He all but fell through the doorway and across the threshold. Lauren tumbled to the floor, the case skidding away from her grasp.

Frantic, Tomáš slammed the door behind them with his foot, popping up long enough to secure the bolt. He collapsed on the floor, leaving the others to their own devices. He wasn't sure now whom to trust or what had just happened. Simon, at least, had betrayed them; of that, he was certain.

Lauren struggled to find her footing but stumbled and fell at the altar. She held her hands out in front of her as she tried to press herself against the prayer rail, as if that might offer additional protection. Her breath came in ragged gasps, turning into weak whimpers. Her fingers curled in pain as the tendons visibly tightened and spasmed beneath her pale skin. Tomáš rushed to her side.

"Are you hurt?"

"My blood … is boiling …" she panted hoarsely. The features of her face were contorted into the most desperate example of agony Tomáš had ever seen. The rosary he'd given her remained wrapped around her left wrist. He took her arm to inspect it, finding the skin scorched beneath.

Tomáš glanced up through the narrow leaded glass windows around the doors to check on the battle outside. He could see Bertram, standing with his cross raised. Lucca read from the Bible, and a fury resounded around them as the Dark One tried to cross the invisible border between the dark night and sacred ground. The Dark One's fury raged and the screams of a million damned souls rose from where they were buried beyond the walls of the churchyard. They were rising from their graves to join the battle. It was deafening, even from within the ancient temple.

Tomáš glanced back at Lauren. He froze when he saw the wounds developing on her skin. Her color had faded to a pale off-white and her eyes had gone as dark as midnight; reddened around the edges. Tears stained her face. "I don't believe it," he muttered, dropping beside her. "The … stigmata …"

Lauren's gnarled hands trembled as a pool of thick, dark blood collected in the cups they formed. Puddles collected on the marble floor beneath her. Her breath came in a panting whisper. He could feel her pattering pulse in her wrist as he took her arm. "What … is that?" She gasped.

"The marks of our Lord's suffering." He crossed himself hastily. "I have read of this phenomenon before, but I never …" He glanced up at her, realizing she had growing marks on her forehead, as trickles of blood ran down her cheeks.

He came to his senses as Lauren leaned against the prayer rail, fading quickly. Her skin was now ghost-white; her lips near-blue. "Let me see." He reached for the hem of her shirt. She was too weak to fight him. Beneath her ribs, a red stain marred her ashen skin. He probed for the wound but found no sign of it. "What the hell …?" His gaze followed the blood to the tops of her sneakers that were torn. Blood coated the laces.

"I've never believed …" He gazed up at the effigy of the Blessed Virgin on the altar above her head. The Madonna's holy smile seemed to be fouled into a horrified gaze. What appeared to be blood flowed from the statue's eyes. Her hands showed the same wounds Lauren bore now. He glanced back at Lauren as she slipped down. She pinched her eyes shut, fighting back tears from the agony of the minion's touch. A red tear rolled down her cheek. "All five signs?" He crossed himself and began to pray under his breath. "Lauren," he started.

"Help … me … Tomáš," Lauren's faint cry was barely more than a whisper.

"Lauren?" He reached for the hem of his oxford shirt and ripped a piece from it, folding it into a bandage. He held it to the wound on her torso, applying pressure as the blood seeped between his fingers, despite the lack of a visible wound. "How?" He panted. "How could a that man's touch … cause … the wounds of Christ?"

"That was no man," Lauren panted. "A minion … an Agent of Enlil …"

"But, how?" Kovač insisted.

Because thou art holy.

Lauren heard the voice like the fluttering of a sparrow's wings by her ear. A comforting warmth spread through her as the world around her seemed to fall away. Time and place no longer mattered. She felt drawn into a new plane of existence. The nexus of the universe coalesced into a glowing orb that filled the space around her with a comforting light.

She could hear Tomáš calling her name, but his voice became a distant echo as she felt herself lifted to her feet, bathed in a radiance that was almost blinding. She levitated above the floor, her arms lifting out, her feet crossing over one another as she matched the pose of the Christ on the cross. Where the statue of the Virgin Mary stood above the altar, the orb of light pulsed in the same tempo as her waning heartbeat; the world she knew was lost.

Lauren gazed numbly as the ghostly image of a woman appeared. She glanced down, realizing her own body lay crumpled on the floor in front of the altar.

Her gaze returned to the apparition before her. All pain, now gone. "Am I ... dead?"

"You are *transformed.*" The voice was as soft as a prayer. "The gods have smiled upon you and find favor in you."

"But ..." Her hand went to her stomach.

"We will not ask more of you than you can give, and we will guard over your family, and your children ..." Enki's words came back to her, though they came in the angelic voice of the apparition before her. "The child within you is guarded by the All-Father himself. Have courage."

"Henry?"

"The gods do not make promises they do not keep," she said. "He is blessed with all the abilities he will need to play his role in this battle. You must trust in him, as he trusts in you."

Lauren felt a peace washing over her unlike any she had

ever known. She looked down at her scarred hands that were now healed. No stains of the minion's touch marred her flesh or stained her clothing.

"You are the Hand of the gods," the voice spoke softly. In the span of a quickening heartbeat, she realized this specter was not a demon, nor one of her guardian angels who came with her brother to aid in the battle that raged outside the cathedral. This was *The Lady. The Queen of Heaven.* But this was not the Blessed Virgin of the Christian faith. This was the Sumerian Queen, Inanna herself. The *bright queen of the sky,* a goddess associated with not only love and war, but Venus as well. She appeared with a radiant glow as her dulcet face lifted. Lauren felt herself fall into eyes that were deeper than the universe.

Lauren's feet found the floor and her knees buckled as she sank with her hands outstretched in supplication. Her head lowered in reverence, and she felt a comforting warmth pass through her. The rosary wrapped around her wrist, entwined in her fingers grew warm as the Lady stood fast before her.

"Blessed Champion of the Heavens and the Earth, Hand of the All-Father ..." Her soft voice thundered around Lauren. She could feel it in her core and felt fortified by it. "You have been chosen above all other women. Do you willingly accept your place among the stars? Do you wear the crown of this burden of your own free will? Do not answer in haste, as your burden will remain great throughout your days. But your blessings will be many."

"I have welcomed my fate even when I did not understand it." Lauren's voice seemed so faint compared to the Lady's. "I ... I will do what must be done."

"Ah, *Faith,*" the Lady sighed beatifically. "The greatest of all virtues after Love."

"I fear my faith will not be strong enough." Lauren swallowed hard. The aura of joy seemed to ripple around her body. The hair on her arms stood on end.

"It will be enough. But Love? Love will cost you dearly," she said. "It will break your heart … but … it will save the world."

"I will do whatever is asked of me." Lauren's voice sounded like an echo in her own head. "But I would ask … please … tell me what that is …"

"Maiden, mother, goddess," the Lady said softly. "Father, Son, Holy Ghost."

"I don't understand," Lauren took a step back, trying to collect her thoughts.

"To everything there is a season under Heaven." She smiled, sweeping a hand down to graze Lauren's cheek. "Do you recall the painting at the museum in Prague?"

A vision of it came into her mind's eye. The woman still looked like her, but she noticed more than just the demons clawing at her legs, shredding her gown. She saw the urn the angel carried in one hand against her abdomen, as the other hand was raised to ward off a winged minion who came at her. It was like a miniature version of Beelzebub himself.

"This," the Lady stood beside her in the museum gallery. Her hand moved over her abdomen and a warm glow came from it. "This is your mission. As other women before you were so chosen, so are you. Blessed is the fruit of thy womb." Lauren realized the urn was a chalice, held over the angel's womb; the angel who looked like her.

Lauren stood, slack jawed and mesmerized for a long moment. "I'm … I don't feel worthy," she gulped when she found her voice. She turned thinking of Tomáš and the soldiers of the Gendarmerie, but the world she had known remained veiled. She was aware of the fury raging around the cathedral. This was an epic battle of good and evil; one she knew she would have to engage in, sooner or later.

"What you seek and what you need … you will find here, beneath my feet," the Lady said with a beatific smile. "Take it, and see it safely returned to pair with its source. Go with the gods, for you are favored."

The altar became clear to her. Her own apparition moved without effort to it. Lauren knelt and lifted the drapes that covered it. There, she found a box like the one she'd brought with her. The skeleton key the silent monk had given her was still tucked into her pocket, and she took it, slipping it into the slot, turning. The case opened; five more pages were contained within. She reached for the case she'd brought and took the pages, combining them into one bundle. In haste, she re-rolled them tightly, so they'd all fit in one box. She didn't even bother to look at them. She sensed there wasn't time.

"There is one more gift for you." The Lady turned to the altar and took hold of the gilded cross that stood there. Like Arthur drawing Excalibur from the stone, she drew a glowing sword from the cross, and held it before Lauren. "Kneel, Champion of the Heavens, Hand of the All-Father."

Lauren dropped to one knee, as the blade came down on one shoulder, then the other. "Take this holy weapon." The blade found its way to her hand. "Rise and smite the demon and end this coup against the gods in Heaven." She lifted her head and paused. "Peace be with you," the holy vision said as it evaporated into a shimmer of light.

The peaceful shroud that had enveloped her fell away, and Lauren found herself restored, standing in the middle of the cathedral. Tomáš knelt at the altar, sobbing. A puddle of blood spread out from the place where she had lain before the vision took her away. She glanced at the box in one hand, and the small sword in the other, trying to figure it all out. She took three paces and knelt beside Tomáš. He looked up, startled, then fell back onto his rump and scrambled away from her as if she were some horrible specter that had awakened him from a nightmare. His eyes frantically searched the void where her body had lain, then looked back at her in abject terror.

His hand rose to cross himself, numbly, as his breath came in ragged gasps. "L … L… Lauren?" His eyes narrowed into glowing blue slits, framed in red beneath his dark lashes. "But … but … you … you … *died* …" He seemed to choke on the word.

"This isn't time to mourn," she said, as he reached for her hand, snatching it, and turning it over. His fingers went to the scars in her palm that were miraculously healing. He looked up at her and paled. His jaw dropped as he scrambled back against the prayer rail. "Blessed are they who have not seen and yet believe." Lauren wasn't sure where the words came from, but they flowed from her lips without effort, as she reached out and caught his limp hand that now hovered in the air between them. She pulled him to his feet and stood eye-to-eye with him.

He studied her as he stood, visibly trembling. "But …" He stepped back, and his eyes ran down the length of her. She knew he was struggling to comprehend. She lifted her shirt to show him the blood on her side was no longer there. A faint line of scar tissue faded before his eyes. His hand went to it, as he tentatively caressed the mark. His eyes lifted promptly to hers. "I don't understand."

"Believe," she said, her voice soft as the flutter of sparrow's wings. "But there's no time to delay." She turned to the barred door, aware of the conflict that raged outside.

Without hesitation, she threw back the bolt effortlessly, the ancient door creaking as she flung it open. Tomáš rushed to catch up to her as she stepped outside. Winds like a zephyr met her and threw back her hair, which seemed to unwind from its plait and wave behind her like a cape.

The conflict seemed to pause at her appearance. She turned, drinking in the scene. The howl of wolves met her. Michael and the Watchers — in both angelic and wolf form — battled the minions from Hell, who raged on unconsecrated ground outside the walls of the cathedral. Lauren was unfazed by the skeletal warriors who rose from their graves beyond the church walls, clawing from the unblessed soil. Any remaining tissue fell away as they broke branches from a gnarled old tree and wielded them like clubs or swords against Michael's forces.

Michael ran through the fray towards his sister as he morphed from lupine into human form. He came to stand at her side. "Sister," he said.

"Brother." There was no time for embracing. A nod was all that passed between them as they turned to face the fury before them.

The entire company of wolves came up behind him, making it to the relative safety of hallowed ground. Each transformed into what Lauren could only describe as angels. Even Michael was caped with dark wings that lifted to catch the air. His brethren moved to stand at Lauren's side, as her eyes lifted to another dark wraith that hovered above the hallowed sanctuary. Michael rose to face it.

Bertram and Lucca were battling to hold it off with their holy symbols and prayers of exorcism. She sensed, however, that their strength was waning.

Enlil volleyed dark magical spells at the cathedral — his force seemed dispelled by the prayers and efforts of the Gendarmerie. In the span of a quickening heartbeat, however, Enlil turned his attention from Vatican's agents to Lauren.

Seeing him, she turned and handed the wooden box to the detective. "Stay on sacred ground," she ordered. "Enlil cannot harm you so long as your feet remain on holy soil and the pages must be protected." Thomas started to protest, but she didn't give him a chance.

Lauren lifted her sword, turning to the battle. Like Joan of Arc, commanding the French armies to charge, she used all the authority given to her by the *Queen of Heaven*. It created an aura around her. It provided a shield to protect her from the evil energy Enlil volleyed at her. His assault rained down.

Enlil transformed into a hideous monster that Lauren recognized as the Sumerian twin hero god … or more properly, anti-hero. This was the form he had taken in Zuzu's kitchen. He wielded a weapon of his own; a mace with two lion heads facing opposite of each other, a diadem between them, the sign of a ruler, but not a heavenly one. Not even an earthly ruler; this was the staff of the ruler of the Underworld. This was the Mace of Nergal, which was just another of Enlil's many names.

As Lauren slashed her blade, cutting down minions who dared challenge her, the assault of Enlil's barrage of wicked magic made her stumble and her courage waned in a fleeting moment. In the crowd of battling angels and demonic minions, Lauren caught sight of a familiar silhouette against the burning forests. She forgot about the battle around her as the shadow appeared to stagger. He looked disoriented.

"Rowan!" she screamed. He froze, locking eyes with her, unabashed terror was etched into his features.

Lauren knew he was in danger. He couldn't be left unprotected. She leapt over the stone wall, turning her eye to the writhing ball of small rat-like minions that boiled up the rise, surging towards Rowan. She charged, slashing with her blade, cutting the monsters between them down. Each dissipated in a puff of smoke and the acrid tang of brimstone found its way to her nose. "Rowan! Look out!" she shouted, as a covey of succubae spotted and charged him. In the same moment, the ground began to tremble and heave, splitting apart as a great red dragon broke from the ground between them. Rowan fell. Lauren heard him cry out, as she hacked her way through the fray.

The dragon, as wicked as Smaug from the Lord of the Rings movies, took to wing and arched into the sky, swooping back down, casting a curtain of flame from its throat. The line of fire cut across the field, and blocked Rowan from her gaze. It turned towards her as it lifted and arched again. Her eye went to where Rowan had been, seeing the image of a burning man staggering across the field, fighting the flames. Screams —— familiar screams — found their way to her ear and her heart froze in her chest. She stopped in her tracks, realizing it was too late. She couldn't save him. His eyes were the last thing she saw as the flames consumed his flesh and the cinnamon locks of hair ignited and turned black. A half-hearted cry of agony found its way to her ear and the burning man fell to his knees. Frantically, he tore at flesh as it fell away, collapsing into a heap; writhing and growing still. "Rowan!" Her heart shattered.

"Lauren!" Michael, now in the form of an angel, swooped down before the dragon could do the same to her. He caught her in his arms, and she turned, burying her face in his chest. Peals of sobs split the heavens as the entire army of demons converge on the spot beneath Michael's feet. The winged beasts made for them, but Michael called out the name of the All-Father. They fell back, tossed from their feet, or cast to the ground as his wings carried them back to the protection of hallowed ground.

Lauren's sword slipped from her hand and fell to the ground, imbedding itself into the stone walkway at the foot of the steps to the cathedral. Like Excalibur, it bore deep into the soil, quivering as it grew still. Michael held tight to her, even as he sat her down. "It was Rowan … she whimpered into his hair. "The dragon … it killed him …" she wailed, tears pouring down her cheeks.

"Sister," Michael said, trying to soothe her. "Enlil is the Great Deceiver." His voice found her, and she stopped weeping, looking at him blankly. "He knows your strength lies in your heart and he uses it against you. He *wants* you to believe your husband has fallen."

That seemed to calm her. "Are you sure?" she asked, refusing to look for herself. She'd seen the look in Rowan's eyes as he stumbled and lost his feet. She saw the flames;

smelled the charred flesh. Tears rolled down her cheeks even as she tried to convince herself it was just an illusion; a cruel trick.

"Yes," Michael said, taking her hand. "Rowan isn't here. He never was."

She melted into him, sobbing now with relief.

"Lauren," Tomáš was at her side, the case safely tucked beneath his arm. "Are you okay?"

"Fine," she managed, brushing him off as she wiped her eyes.

"Now, Lauren! You must cast out the Dark One!" Bertram met her on the other side. "I will tell you what to do."

Lauren looked to him, uncertain, then turned to Michael.

"Do as he says." Her brother spoke firmly. "This is the only way to restore the balance of power. You are the hand … the voice of the gods. Your words have power."

"Tell me what to do," she said, gathering herself.

"Confess your sins!" Bertram shouted above the fray. "It's the first step to casting out the Dark One!"

Lauren didn't understand why she needed to do it, but she took a leap of faith and trusted him. She knelt before her sword and crossed herself. "I am an imperfect being!" Her voice rose over the din. "Bless me, All-Father, for I have sinned. I have lied to my husband, and my friends. I have done so to protect the Truth, and to protect those whom I love and would not see harmed."

Bertram moved to face her, praying over her, while Lucca cast holy water in her direction. "I absolve you of your sins."

The Devil threw another bolt of dark energy towards her. She fell to her rump with a grunt. Tomáš caught her and helped her to her feet. Michael charged with his sword, but a wave of the demon's weapon sent him tumbling, cartwheeling across the ground. He sat in a stunned heap, shaking his head; disoriented. His wings fluttered, shaking his flight feathers back into place as he got to his feet. When Lauren was sure he wasn't injured, her attention returned to her work, assured Michael would buy her time to do what she needed to do.

"Bind the demon!" Bertram called.

"All-Father in Heaven! Hear my plea!" Lauren wasn't sure where the words came from. Before she could finish, a hand caught hers, and small fingers wrapped around her hand. She glanced down to see her fair-haired son looking up at her with fear in his eyes. "Henry?"

"Momma," he said. "It's not safe here." He tugged on her arm.

Lauren pulled him into her arms to envelope him. *Was this another act of deception?*

"What are you doing here?" Lauren suddenly remembered the line from the ancient text. *A child of the gods who will be sent to destroy the Dark One…*

Lauren suddenly no longer saw the world around her. Instead, an ancient scene played out in the back of her mind.

The priest waited until the moon was dark and the gods had left the human race to their own devices. He draped a robe of alpaca wool over its surface, hiding an obsidian blade beneath it. He took a wooden bowl from his basket and filled it with water from the sacred pool behind him.

Then he turned to prepare the grave. The floor of the cavern was damp, but the ground was not easily broken. He used a flat stone to gouge out the soil. Time passed slowly, and it seemed to take hours to carve out little more than a depression big enough for the body.

When his back began to spasm and his knees burned, he sat back on his heels and decided that would have to do. He could do no more. Once he could, he rose and took the brazier he used for light with him to the edge of the pool. The water was as clear as glass and the light sparkled off the mirror-still surface. The priest peeled out of his now-filthy clothing and lay them aside, stepping into the icy water. He bathed, purifying himself with the cleanest water known to the tribes.

Once cleansed, he prepared a compound in a stone mortar and pestle. He took the leaves of the muña plant and tore them into smaller pieces. He took a twist of dried palo santo and lit it in the brazier. He waved the smoking herbs over his naked body and cupped it into his hands to catch the smoke, fanning it towards his face as he inhaled, then held it over the mortar, letting the ash fall into the receptacle. He added a few drops of canula oil before taking up the pestle and grinding the whole mixture to a fragrant paste. Once the leaves were fully macerated he added a generous portion of ground ochre and thick palm oil. Satisfied with the concoction, he set to work painting it onto his chest and face. Normally he would sing prayers to the gods for their blessing and for the spirit of the sacrifice. But, he could not sing those songs; could not call attention to his deception.

The godchild climbed up on the alpaca blanket and watched the entire affair with those large dark eyes. The priest had forced himself to ignore the being, lest the creature peer into his soul and know what was about to happen.

Little did the priest know, the godchild knew everything.

Lauren witnessed the entire scene, and came back to herself, gasping, as the demon transformed into the man she knew as Dr. Masa. "You!" She gasped, pushing Henry back behind her. "You tricked the priest into killing the godchild. You're a … a … murderer!"

"It wasn't hard," the man-formed demon's voice found her ear, the battle still raging around them. "Human hearts and minds are weak." He raised his hand as Simon came and stood beside her. Something wicked flickered in his eyes. Lauren recoiled, now assured the Vatican police was a double agent. She'd sensed there was something about him before, but now, she realized the full magnitude of it. Tomáš acted as if he might tackle the man again, but Simon grabbed the child and tore him away from his mother. Lauren didn't hesitate, she turned on him. Striking out, she could do little to harm him. He turned with a heavy arm, the blow knocking her to the ground. Henry broke free and ran back to his mother, wrapping himself around her as she pushed herself up.

Tomáš stepped between the two of them, his weapon drawn. The turn-coat stood, a trickle of blood running down his chin from a cut in his mouth. Lauren's attack hadn't been entirely in vain. He laughed at the detective. "You are as foolish as your father," he said wickedly.

"My … father?" Tomáš took a step back, his finger going to the trigger of the weapon.

"I knew your father," Simon said. "It was only for a brief time, but it was I who knelt over him as he drew his last breath. He thought he could stop me from taking a page of the Codex from the cathedral in Prague, just as you think you can stop me now." His words were laced with malice.

The detective's grip on the weapon tightened and it was everything he could do not to pull the trigger at the man's words. "You?" He drew the word out as he realized his father's killer stood before him. "Why?" His voice began to tremble, even as his hand shook.

"He suffered from a fatal flaw … vanity." Simon laughed. "He was vain enough to think I could be stopped; that he could stop me. Just as you—"

The gun went off, and the whole battle seemed to stop. The traitor looked down at his chest, then looked up at the cop as smoke wafted up from the barrel of the gun.

"The only thing I suffer from is an overinflated need for revenge," Tomáš said, then fired his weapon again.

Lauren's arms wrapped around her son shielding him from the scene, her entire attention now on him. "What are you doing here, baby?"

"I came to save you," Henry sniffed. He clung to her, wrapping his arms around her neck.

"You need to go home," she said. "You shouldn't be here."

A hissing sound came from above, where Enlil hovered. His lips curled into a terrifying smile that spread across his hideous face. "Such a foolish boy … especially for a *star child* …" a deep chuckle followed. "I have been defeated by a child before … you could see why I had to destroy the godchild in Peru. I cannot allow a *child* to foil my plans again; not a godchild, not a star child."

Henry slipped around from behind his mother. "You will fall, and you will fail, just like you did the last time … and the time before that!" he shouted. "You couldn't defeat the godchild without placing fear in the hearts of those sent to protect it. But you weren't expecting the gods to catch you in your game! You better not hurt my momma, either! My daddy will cut your eyes out with his knife. He will—"

"Henry!" Lauren snapped. She grabbed him and pulled him back. "Get out of here! It isn't safe."

Henry surprised her, grabbing her hands, and pinching his eyes shut. At that same moment, her breath caught in her lungs. Fire consumed her flesh and the stench of brimstone that had filled the air was gone and she could smell the burning aroma of ozone in the air.

28

Lauren found herself lying down, gazing up at an industrial light fixture above her. "Henry?" She demanded weakly, sitting up, finding the child sitting cross-legged beside her. "What have you done?"

He looked mortally wounded. "I … I … I saved you," he said. She realized he had the wooden chest containing the pages of the Codex inside. "I saved the pages from the Devil's Book from falling into Enlil's hands."

"But …" Lauren sputtered. "How … why … where are we?"

"This is the place where the rest of the book is kept. *The Lady* … the *Queen of Heaven* … she told you it would be safe here, right?"

"How did you know about *The Lady*?" Lauren took the case from his hands.

"She talked to me, too," he said. "She came to me in a dream. She said I had to help. She said I had to. She told me everything I had to do. I did everything just the way she said … just the way Uncle Michael taught me. I didn't mess anything up. I did what I was told."

"Uncle Michael?" In her confusion, Lauren struggled to

admonish him, but the words wouldn't come. Finally, she managed, "Where are you supposed to be right now?"

"Taking a nap at Aunt Tima's."

"You have to go back," Lauren said. "I have to go back to Slovenia. It's more than just seeing the pages safe. I have to stop Enlil."

"But ... Enlil will be hard to beat," Henry said, almost in tears. "I don't want you to get hurt. Momma, please. Momma we need you. That Devil will hurt you if he can."

"Hurt me? No, sweetheart. I'm the only one who can defeat him. Remember when we were with Uncle Michael? They told me I had a mission, that ... that my sacrifice would be great, but my children would be protected. You don't have to worry. You and your brother are safe, but you have to do your part. You have to stay where you belong and keep an eye out for your brother."

Henry threw his arms around her neck and held onto her for a long moment, burying his face in her hair.

When he let her go, Lauren balled up her courage and got to her feet. "So, where are we?"

"This is the big Library at Stockholm," Henry said snaking his hand into hers. "The rest of the Codex's pages are in there ... in that vault." Henry pointed to a thick door. "This is a safe place to leave the pages. The sacred ground you put in the box will keep Enlil from getting it."

"But ... the page that was stolen in Prague ..." Lauren said, trying to wrap her brain around everything.

"The man the police officer shot had it," Henry said. "I couldn't get it from him."

"I'll get it." Lauren dropped down in front of him. "You have to send me back."

"I don't want to." Henry pouted. "Momma, you don't know what he can do."

"I know what he'll do if he's not stopped." She reached for her son and pulled him into her arms. "You need to go home. Stay with your brother. I'll be home as soon as I can."

Henry clung to her. "I'm scared for you."

"Sweet boy, I have armies of my own," Lauren said. "Well … not exactly *my* army, but Uncle Michael's army fights at my side. Send me back, Henry. I have to do this. I'm afraid Enlil may try to use you to defeat me. If you and John Carter aren't safe, I can't do what I have to."

Henry considered her for a moment. The child looked so like his father when he was being serious. Reluctantly, he did as she commanded.

WHEN THE EUPHORIA OF BEING DISPLACED BEGAN TO ABATE, she found herself whisked back into the fray. The battle had continued in the scant moments she had been gone, and when she became aware of her surroundings, the dark forces appeared to be winning.

"Lauren!" Tomáš was at her side before she could act. "The pages of the Codex?"

"Safe," she said, inspecting him. A horrific wound spread across his forehead, as if he'd been clawed by a hellhound. A creature she couldn't identify lay smoldering at his feet, it erupted into flame and was quickly consumed. Tomáš' own blood mingled with her dried blood on his shirt. Lauren forgot the battle and pressed her hand to his forehead, closing her eyes. A heat seemed to pass from her hand to his flesh and the blood faded as the wound disappeared.

He swayed but steadied himself. They leaned on each other a moment. Michael swooped down and landed behind her. "Is Henry okay?"

"Yes." Lauren turned and threw her arms around her brother, hugging him fiercely.

"We invoke the Queen of Angels that she grants her

guardians to keep your children," Michael said. "But now it's time. You have work to do."

Lauren nodded. She looked for her sword, finding it as it had been when she'd been swept away. She struggled to free it.

"You won't need that," Michael said. "Leave it there to bear witness, a sacred cross … a holy weapon. I am your Champion."

"And I am your hired gun," Tomáš reminded her.

She turned to Bertram, drinking in the scene. The demons, wraiths, and other twisted creatures were held back by an unseen force that rose around the churchyard, yet they still flung themselves towards the sacred ground. Like the one that had attacked Tomáš, occasionally one broke through the barrier, only to burn up like a vampire in broad daylight.

Michael's army passed through the shield unfettered, meeting the demons in the air and on the ground. Enlil now stood in the middle of the car park, their vehicles tossed aside and crushed like toy cars. He seemed to be fading, struggling to stand his ground as he faced off with the Vatican police. Bertram shouted prayers. Lucca had run out of holy water and lit incense in a thurible. The perfume of frankincense and myrrh blended with the stench of rot and brimstone that rose from the corrupted ground. Lauren could no longer smell the forest fire, even as the smoke rose above the distant trees.

"Bind him! Now! Lauren!" Bertram instructed, his cross glowing red as Enlil focused his attack on the holy symbol. The Gendarmerie and the Watchers had held him at bay in her absence, but they lacked her strength … and her gifts.

She moved over to Bertram and to the Demonic being poised to strike. "All-Father in Heaven, by your command, I serve as your Hand. I bind these minions of Darkness, these demons and wraiths who battle for authority over the heavens and the earth. I bind all the foes who stand against me and our allies!" She threw out her hand and a wicked white light sent a shockwave towards the heavens. It rolled across the fields around them, and into the woods, quenching the fires. Demons and tortured souls screamed a blood-chilling cry at her words. "I bind all the wicked spirits of the New World Order. I bind you demons of Enlil's kingdom! I bind you, the Dark One himself; Lucifer, Deceiver, Fallen Angel. I bind you, Enlil!" Her throat burned with the force of her words. "I loose legions upon legions of the All-Father's forces to minister to the needs of believers; to cast out the evil that overtakes men's hearts."

The ground beneath her feet trembled and the trees bowed and waved with the force of the battle. She placed her hand on the pommel of the sword in the ground as she prayed. The hilt grew hot against her flesh, but she continued as Enlil roared with fury, now appearing in his true form. It was the horrible being found in the Codex.

The sketch in the Codex Gigas had been stunningly accurate, as the winged beast snarled and threatened to charge, his crown of horns appearing as lethal as his sharp teeth and wicked claws. His wings flayed out behind him, with sharp spurs.

Undaunted, Lauren continued. Her knees ache and the muscles in her back and calves cramped. Her head throbbed. She forced back the pain of her body as she pressed on. "I unleash the spirit of understanding and wisdom, the spirit of counsel; the might and the power of Truth. I call on my beloved Archangel Michael, Chosen of the Most-High," she called. Her voice thundered in her own ears.

"Chosen?" The Demon roared, whipping towards Michael. "*You* are the Chosen ..." It seemed surprised; stunned in fact. "No!"

Michael stood beside his sister now with his hand on her shoulder. "My sister is the Hand of the All-Father. *I* am his Chosen Emissary."

Enlil took a step back, stumbled over a rock, but regained his footing.

Lauren continued, finding Michael's voice joining hers. "May the Most-High god's will be done on earth as in the heavens! Satan, Lucifer, Devil, Asmodeus, Mephistopheles, The Dark One, The Dragon … Father of Lies … Beelzebub … Enlil, and by whatever other names you are known as, we cast you back into the depths of the fiery pit from whence you came! In the name of the Queen of Heaven and the All-Father, Anu; by the authority appointed me by the ancient gods, I cast you out, Satan."

Michael charged forward, wielding his mighty blade, he struck, but the weapon fractured with a metallic chord as it contacted the monster's scaly flesh. A menacing laugh erupted from the Dark One. "You have no power over me!" Enlil roared.

"No, but I do," Lauren snagged her sword from sacred ground. It yielded and she rushed past her brother who fell aside. The Dark One matched the swing of her sword with his mace. Her blade cut through the gopherwood staff. The diadem — a precious ruby — fell onto holy ground. It shattered with an unholy scream and burst into smoke before disintegrating into nothingness.

A second strike of her blade contacted Enlil's flesh and pierced his black heart. All the wickedness contained within his evil soul escaped with a force. The wooden box containing the last missing page of the Codex fell to the ground from the void left by the disintegrating soul.

The shockwave of the Dark One's destruction knocked Lauren from her feet. She fell into Tomáš, who landed hard beneath her with a grunt. A stillness followed, as she lay stunned, the last of her energy drained. Her breath came in panting gasps as she gazed into a gray and empty sky. No angels, nor demons remained. The fog had faded, and a dulcet moon appeared briefly, before blossoming cumulonimbus clouds built quickly. A drop of rain fell on her forehead as it began to sprinkle.

Bertram dropped beside her, his hand going to her shoulder, as he gazed down into her eyes. He ministered to her soul, praying over her as he made a cross on her forehead with the raindrop.

"Michael! Tomáš!" She couldn't even form the words fast enough before the form of Simon, looking more like a zombie than Gendarmerie, staggered back into the churchyard. He stood holding the missing wooden box. He ran his hand over the case with a lustful look in his icy blue eyes.

"Drop it." Tomáš stood with his pistol drawn. It had been worthless against the wraiths and demons. "Your master has been destroyed."

Simon's brow lifted and a laugh escaped from his chest, blood sputtered at his lips as he stumbled, and then righted himself. The front of his shirt was damp with his wanning life-force. A pistol hung in his hand. "You have no authority over me or my master." The man coughed. "I am … an Agent of Enlil himself. Your father thought he could turn me … save me …"

"My father was a good man," Tomáš stated flatly.

"He offered me a chance to repent, to return the page … but my master would have none of it. I did as I was commanded. I could not be stopped."

"You *have* been stopped," Tomáš said, anger at the man's betrayal was evident.

"But, Detective … your weapon … is empty." Simon laughed, blood gurgling from his mouth as he coughed. "When my master's book is remade, I shall see him restored to his rightful place among the stars, and no one can stop him; not even you." Simon stumbled a step, redirecting his pistol towards Lauren's head. "Foolish mortal …" he sneered, staring her down. Lauren froze, prepared to meet her end. But a stunned expression appeared on his face, and his icy white eyes widened in shock. He looked down at the fragment of the blade that pierced his chest, catching the bloody end of it, as if to steady himself.

"Foolish demon spawn," Michael said. His broken blade protruded from the man's chest. The man sputtered and hissed, writhing as an unholy scream pierced the sky as his form was twisted into a demonic creature that was hideous to behold. The tang of brimstone and sulfur filled the air as he collapsed. Smoke rose around the corpse as it erupted into flame. A stench of fetid rot joined the putrid odor. Lauren wanted to turn away, but her eye remained fixed as the Dark One's minion began to seize then immolate into ash. The unscathed wooden box was all that remained in the scorched mark on the fouled ground.

Michael took the wooden box and pressed it into his sister's arms. He gazed down at her and ran a hand over her cheek. "I cannot stay. I am no longer needed here. Balance has been restored."

"But ... why ..." Lauren started, but stopped, trying to think about how to ask what she needed to know. "Why did Enlil seemed surprised that you were the Chosen One?"

"Because of the prophesy ... in the Christian story, the son of God is sent to become a teacher of men ..." he said. "But in the Akkadian legends, the child of *The Chosen One* will be the savior of men ..."

Realization hit her like a punch to the stomach. "*Your child?*" She muttered. "Not ... not *mine?*"

Michael smiled beatifically. "*My* child ..." He nodded. "Call Kitty when you can. She has news."

Lauren felt her spirit lighten when she realized what this meant. "Michael, wait," she said, but before she could continue, he shimmered into nothingness.

"Lauren?" Tomáš was pinned beneath her. His gaze lifted as the victorious cries of the other wolves, now restored to their canine forms, found their way to them. She could feel Tomáš' arm wrap around her, as he pushed himself up to his elbow. "Lauren?" He gasped, sitting up. Lauren's gaze remained fixed on the sky above. She could feel her body sprawled out like a starfish. Her bones felt leaden, but her heart light. "Lauren?" Tomáš caught her hand. Bertram patted her leg. Her name repeated in echoes around her.

"It is finished."

29

Henry woke up in bed next to Tima. He'd slipped out after the rest of the house had gone to sleep and had returned in the wee hours of the morning once his mission was done. He hadn't had time to accomplish this last objective to help his mom during naptime. He didn't think the girls would ever go to bed. Tima had stayed up reading late into the night.

He went back to the National Library in Stockholm. He wasn't sure how or when anyone might find the box they'd left behind, but he knew it was important for everyone to know what his momma had done. The world didn't need to know everything, but he wanted them to know *she'd* found the pages. She'd figure out a way to explain how they had made it here. She was clever like that.

As he tucked the card into the rosewood box, he decided his mother might be able to assume he left her business card, but he was fairly sure he wouldn't be in too much trouble for it. *Well, maybe just a little.*

Still in his pajamas, Henry hurried back to Aunt Tima's and stood by her bed watching her sleep. She yawned and rolled over, her eyes opening as she matched his gaze. She lifted the covers drawing them back enough he could slip in underneath them.

The bad dreams that had plagued him for the past week were gone. He yawned dreamily as he rolled over and snuggled up next to his auntie. She sighed and put an arm around him as he nestled his head in her silvery hair. His mother often slept with her hair down, making a pillow for his head from it. It always made the little boy feel safe and loved. Tima's hair smelled of the spices and exotic oils she rubbed in the long silver-streaked tresses, different than his mother's but no less comforting. Content he drifted back into dreamless slumber.

SHEMI HAD THE TELEVISION ON WHEN HENRY WANDERED INTO the living room later. He climbed up onto the sofa beside her. Ahmose and John Carter were playing on the floor.

"Mumma!" Shemi said, picking up the remote, turning up the volume as the news came on. "Mumma! Come quick!"

Tima came in. Henry exchanged a cautionary glare with his little brother. "Officials at the National Library at Stockholm announced this morning, that a number of pages missing from an ancient tome known as the Devil's Codex were discovered outside the vault where the book is secured. Tucked into the box of precious relics was the business card of none other than famed television show personality Dr. Lauren Grayson, former host of the Exploration Channel's *The Veritas Codex* series." Henry pinched his lips at John Carter who looked startled to hear his mother's name on the news.

"She did it ..." Tima gasped. Her hand went to her mouth. "Oh boys! Your momma did it! She found the missing pages."

The report continued. "Dr. Grayson has been credited with the discovery of a number of relics, most notably a new Calendar of the Ancient Maya and a fortune in gold and treasures. A request was made to the Exploration Channel in the US, who indicated Dr. Grayson was on sabbatical in the Middle East and was unavailable for comment."

Cheers erupted from the girls and a broad grin spread over Henry's face. John Carter followed his brother's lead, and stood up on the sofa, jumping on the cushions in elation. "Does this mean Momma's coming home?"

"I'm sure she'll be here as soon as she can," Tima hugged him. "We should have a party."

"Will there be cake?" John Carter asked. "I *yike* cake!"

"You bet there will be cake!" Ahmose picked him up and bounced him on her hip. "It'll be the best cake you ever tasted!"

"Will it have frosting?" Henry asked. "I like frosting better than fondant. But I like the figs in the middle."

"We can do figs and frosting, whatever you think your momma would like best." Tima beamed, her bracelets rattling as they all celebrated the news.

"Momma *yikes waspbewies*," John Carter said. "I *yike* waspbewies too."

"Raspberries?" Henry scowled at him. "Since when have you had raspberries?"

John Carter shrugged. "I dunno. I *yike* waspbewies."

"We can make two cakes then," Tima said. "Maybe by the time your momma gets home, your dad will be home too."

"Maybe." John Carter shrugged.

LAUREN WOKE TO SUNSHINE IN HER FACE, AND THE STALE STING of antiseptic in her nose. She blinked and shut her eyes against the blinding light as she stretched lazily, finding no aches or pains, just the comforting heaviness of the tiny babe who stretched under her hand as it came to rest on the swell of her belly.

"Dr. Pierce?" A familiar voice found her. She opened her eyes. Tomáš' sister stood at her bedside, with a chart in her hand.

"Dr. Kovač?" Lauren pushed herself up onto her elbows. "Where am I?"

She turned as Tomáš came in carrying a bouquet of flowers. He glanced over his sister's shoulder and leaned over her and kissed her cheek, then leaned down and kissed Lauren's forehead. "Feeling better?"

Lauren's brow knitted over the bridge of her nose, as she looked around. "What happened? Where am I?"

"You don't remember?" he asked, his eyes shifting towards his sister nervously. "You solved the mystery, found the pages and returned them to their rightful owner. The story has been all over the news for the last few days."

"Days?"

"Dr. Pierce, this is the second time I have had to treat you for exhaustion. I don't think I need to tell you that this is just not good for you or your baby. You need to focus on your health from here on out. Do I make myself clear?"

Lauren lay back. "Perfectly."

Katia turned to the computer, her attention on Lauren's chart and the readings from the fetal heart monitor attached to her belly. "The baby is healthy. I took the liberty of running a second sonogram while you slept." She reached into her pocket and handed Lauren a sealed envelope.

"What's this?"

"If you and your husband decide you want to know the sex of your baby before it arrives ..." Katia offered with a shrug. Lauren looked at the envelope as if it were the greatest gift anyone could have given her.

"Thank you." Her voice trembled, and she sniffed back a tear.

"How are you feeling?" Tomáš asked.

"I'm fine ..." She pushed the tears off her face. "But what

about you?" Lauren reached for Tomáš' face and he leaned in to let her touch. "No marks?"

"Just a flesh wound," he said softly. "The cut healed as soon as you touched me."

Dr. Kovač turned to her brother. "Tomáš, I'll call you tomorrow. Will you be home?"

"Yes," he said. "At some point. Will Dr. Pierce be able to go home soon?"

His sister looked at Lauren for a moment. "If she'll go home and go to bed, I'll consider it tomorrow afternoon. That's if she's doing better. She's awake now. That's a start."

"I'll make sure of it," Tomáš said. "If I have to take her home myself."

"I'm a big girl," Lauren said. "I can take myself home."

"Mm-hmm," they chorused, doubtfully, both crossing their arms as they gazed back at her.

Lauren blanched, feeling appropriately admonished. She deserved that.

"Talk to you tomorrow, *bratr*," Katia added, before returning to her rounds.

When they were alone, he turned, and looked down his long straight nose at her. His blue eyes cut into her a moment.

"How did I get here?" she asked.

"Does it matter?" he asked, sitting on the edge of the bed. "You defeated that monster, Enlil. You saved the world."

Lauren scowled a moment, drinking it all in as the memories flooded back. "Yeah, well … the Devil had it coming."

"He certainly did," Tomáš beamed.

30

"Momma?" Henry took the phone when Tima handed it to him. "Momma? Is that you?"

"It is," she said, feeling her heart leap in her chest. Her phone battery had finally charged sufficiently overnight to allow her to call. "How are you doing? Are you being good for Auntie Tima?"

"Yes, ma'am," Henry nodded as he spoke. "John Carter is being good too. I kept him safe."

His little brother held up his toy rocket he had made from LEGOs as if his mother could see it. "I made a *wocket!*"

"And I'm sure it's a terrific rocket," Lauren praised him. She addressed Henry. "Has your father made it back yet?"

"No ma'am," he said. "He's still at his dig."

Lauren sighed. She knew Tomáš was serious about delivering her to her husband, but she wanted to see her boys first. "Well, I'm finished in Prague. I'll be home soon," Lauren said.

"Daddy needs to see you," Henry said. "He has something to show you."

"He does?" Her brow arched.

"Yes," Henry said. "You should go see Daddy first. When you come home, we can have a party."

That made Lauren smile. "I'll look forward to it."

"Momma." John Carter grabbed the phone. "Do you *yike* figs or *waspbewies* bestest?"

"Huh?" She puzzled, then realized what he'd said. "Oh, raspberries? Yes, I like figs, but I do like raspberries better."

"I *tole* you so," John Carter said, tormenting his brother. "I *tole* you she *yikes waspbewies*."

"John Carter be nice to your brother. Listen to Auntie Tima and the girls. I'll see you soon."

"Yes, ma'am," the boys chorused.

She hung up the phone as Tomáš and Katia came in together. Katia was carrying a paper shopping bag. Lauren was sitting on the edge of the bed in a blue floral hospital gown.

"Here you go," Katia handed her the shopping bag. "I hope everything fits."

"Thank you," Lauren said. She found a brand-new outfit in it. There was a pair of low-cut jeans with a blue maternity top, undergarments, socks, and a new pair of sneakers. There were some hair clips, too.

"I guess this means I can go home?" Lauren's brow lifted optimistically.

"You have to promise me you'll go straight home and go to bed for at least another week. No skipping meals, get plenty of fluids, and I'll discharge you."

"Can I make one quick stop to see my husband before I go home?"

Katia looked as if she might protest.

"I did promise I would deliver her to her husband," Tomáš spoke up for her. "I don't care where he is, that's where she's going."

"Fine," she said. "But my conditions remain firm. You rest. No hard work, no stress. You need it. Your baby needs it."

"I promise." Lauren crossed her heart with her finger.

∽

Henry had been reading quietly in the blanket fort he'd made with some of Tima's linens. While no one was paying attention to him, he slipped off to go see Herman. He found the monk at the work table in the library at the monastery. He was standing on a small step ladder, struggling with the bindings on the massive book he and Henry had finished some nights before.

"You don't have to tie it so tight," Henry said, startling the holy man.

"Ah, young Master Pierce," the monk regained his composure. "I wasn't expecting you to come back." He climbed down the ladder, then stepped back and admired the tome. "Isn't it spectacular? A complete copy of the *Vulgate Bible, Josephus' Antiquities of the Jews ... De bello iudaico,* Isidore of Seville's *Encyclopedia Etymologiae,* the *Chronicle of Cosmas of Prague;* medical works, and two books by Constantine the African ... just to name a few."

"Did you include the section I asked you to put in it?"

"Yes," he said, finishing the bindings. "Yes, of course" The monk struggled to open the massive book, but he found the page where he'd hidden the boy's message. In carefully penned Cherokee Syllabary he'd written, *Tsi stu wu-li-ga' na-tu-tu'n une'gu-tsa ge-se'i.* "But, what does it mean?"

Henry climbed up on the step ladder and had to stand on his tiptoes to see it. "My mommy tells us a story about how the Rabbit was the leader in all the mischief," he said. "She'll recognize it when she sees it. But ... you didn't write her name ..."

"I thought perhaps you might like to help me with that," Herman said, giving the boy an encouraging smile.

"Could I?"

"Do you know how to prepare a quill? Mix ink?"

"No sir," Henry said.

"Let me teach you then," he said, and helped Henry down, leading him over to his desk. He took out a collection of quills and ink powder, and showed him how to mix the ink first, then, took out his quill knife. "You must be careful with a knife."

"My dad lets me use his pocket knife sometimes. He taught me how to be careful."

The priest showed him how to do it. Henry made the cut, carefully. He handed back the knife when he finished. "How's that?" He held up the quill.

"Nicely done," Herman said. "The ink is easy to smudge, so as soon as we print the letters, we will dust it with sand and leave it to dry."

The monk climbed back up on the stepladder as Henry brought over the small pot of ink and the sharpened quill. "Ow!" Henry flinched as he handed over the tools. He held up a thumb where blood dripped from a cut caused by the sharpened tip on the quill. Normally, a quill wouldn't be strong enough to cut an adult hand, but the skin on the little boy's finger was much thinner.

"Are you hurt?"

"It's just a scratch," he said, embarrassed at having cried out. He climbed up to hand him the pot of ink. The ladder wobbled and he threw out a hand to catch himself, a smear of blood stained the vellum page. The priest inspected it and shook his head. "I will need to bandage that wound," he said, starting to climb down.

"No," Henry scrambled down. "Finish writing Mommy's name. I need to get back to Auntie Tima's."

"Dr. Lauren Grayson-Pierce, PhD," the monk said, planning each letter, and inscribing each with the greatest of care. "There we go."

Henry climbed back up; his finger wrapped in his t-shirt. "Perfect!" he beamed, happy with the end results.

A rumble of what sounded and felt like thunder resounded

around them. Henry jumped down. "Remember the story," Henry said to the monk.

"What was that?" The monk gazed up, trying to pinpoint the sound and figure out what it was.

"The monastery is under attack," Henry said. "You have to protect the Codex Gigas."

"The *Codex Gigas*?" The monk looked to him blankly.

"Oh, that blank page near the back? You have to draw a big scary devil. You better hurry. You don't have much time."

"Wait!" The monk clambered down from the step ladder with ink and dusting-sand still in hand. "You're leaving?"

"I'll do everything I can to protect you so you can finish, Brother Herman. You've helped me. It's the least I can do." He hesitated. "But you have to do what you must to protect the Codex … and preserve its lore." He knew the monk's true fate. He would not be walled up, but the curse of Cassandra was upon him. No one would believe he had completed the book in one night. No one of this era would understand the abilities of a child to pause time — to allow the monk to finish his work — even in Henry's own time. No one would believe Herman, but it was a secret he could never tell … and that was okay.

EPILOGUE

Rowan stood on the ridge of the sand dune, a lone shadow against a setting sun. He'd spent all day underground working in the cavern that had been hidden beneath the shifting sands. The team had discovered what appeared to be a hidden room behind a false wall. They had plans to open it in the morning, but he wasn't quite ready to call it a day.

In the distance, he could hear the hum of an ATV approaching the site. As the four-wheeler slowed and came to a halt at the tent the teams had set up as a command post, he recognized the long braid that emerged beneath the helmet as she peeled it off. Startled by Lauren's unexpected presence, he broke into a run and met her pulling her into his arms, swinging her around, then remembering himself as he sat her down. "Sorry," he said, stepping back to admire the swell of her belly that had grown since he'd last seen her.

"It's okay," she said, pulling him into her to kiss him. "Mmm. I've missed you."

Rowan beamed brightly as her companion came up behind her, peeling off his helmet. For a fleeting moment, Rowan felt a pang of jealousy wash through him. "Tomáš Kovač." He stuck out his hand. "You must be Rowan."

"In the flesh," he said, sizing up the man. He was a handsome specimen, even Rowan had to admit, but he lacked the dimples Rowan knew his wife preferred. He'd put his dimples up against that Slavic look any day. "Thanks for bringing her to me." Rowan put an arm around her and held her close.

"Wild horses couldn't keep her away," he said in his thick accent. "I understand you've had quite the adventure here. What did you find?"

"Well, we aren't entirely sure," Rowan said. "There is a burial in the last chamber, but we haven't had a chance to collect enough data to know who it might be. What's really fascinating is we found a hidden chamber. Honey, I can't wait for you to see."

"Well, let's go have a look," Lauren enthused. "I want to see it."

He knew how she felt about caves. "It's pretty spacious," he reassured her. "It's nothing like the cavern in Peru."

She nodded. "I can do it." She hoped she could.

"Watch your step," Rowan took her hand and helped her down the ramp that had been constructed in the last couple of days. Once they reached the bottom, the two new visitors were introduced to Greg and his team. Light towers had been set up and the hum of the generators powering them echoed in the distance. Lauren stood at the bottom, with her hands on her hips, gazing up at the inscriptions on the walls. A look of wonder lit her features. He anticipated the response he knew would follow once she recognized the ancient markings.

Her hand went to her mouth as she walked towards the banner that seemed to stretch the width of the false wall. She hesitated, her knees threatening to give beneath her. Rowan caught one arm and realized Tomáš had the other. The two exchanged cautious glances in the brief moment before she turned to Rowan. "You aren't going to believe it." Lauren's color rose in her cheeks, her excitement evident only to him in her placid features.

"What does it say?" Rowan asked.

"*Mouseion of Didymus*," the words came out as a gasp as her hand clamped over her mouth, as if they were verboten.

Greg came over and caught her elbow. "Did you say *Mouseion of Didymus?*" He glanced up at the writing. "Are you sure?"

"It's an ancient dialect of a proto-Byzantian language branch," Lauren said.

"What does that mean?" Rowan asked. "Clearly it means something to the two of you."

"*Mouseion* is an ancient word. The root in Greek is Muse," Greg said. "It was part of a project first suggested by Didymus Phalerum."

Lauren grinned brightly now. "A project known as a Universal library." She turned to Rowan. "The Library of Alexandria was only one library in the universal library system in antiquity. This ..." She turned back to the entrance. "This is the entrance to the *museion* ... a library ..."

"Do you realize what that means?" Greg was feeding off her excitement.

"I do," she said, glancing over Greg's shoulder as a familiar form sauntered into from the smaller ante chamber. "Jean-René? What are you doing here?"

She broke out of Greg's grasp and rushed to meet her old friend, holding out her arms to him. His hand went to her belly. He patted it as he drew her in for a hug, his camera on the other shoulder. "Getting fat, Boss. Better lay off the sausages."

"Shut it, you." She giggled. "Don't make me flip you off in front of all these people."

"Maybe some other time, then." He laughed, hugging her a second time. "Bahati sends her love.

"Why didn't she come with you?"

"Long story. Just call her," Jean-René said. "She's been missing you terribly."

"I've tried," Lauren said. "I thought she was mad at me."

"We had orders from the Network to leave you alone." Jean-René shrugged. "But that doesn't matter now. I'll explain later."

"What are you doing here, though?"

"I had to go around Jacob and pull a little prank on your husband to get him here," Jean-René said. "I had video he needed to see. Glad you could join the party. You need to see it, too."

"Video? Hm. Sorry I'm late." She grinned, hugging him again.

"Solve any great mysteries?" he asked her as Rowan, Tomáš and Greg came over to where they stood.

"Yeah," she said, reaching into her hip pocket. She handed an envelope to Rowan. "I think this is another mystery you'll be happy to have solved."

Rowan took it hesitantly, not sure if this had something to do with the Codex Gigas, or the *museion* that she was convinced rested behind that false wall. He paused, looking at her, seeing the anticipation on her features as she bit her lower lip and looked at the envelope before looking at him impatiently. "So ... what is this?"

"Open it up, silly." She nudged him. He stared at her for a long moment.

"Is this what I think it is?" he asked.

"You're the one that always wants to know."

Rowan's eyes narrowed and he glanced back at her. He took the envelope and tucked it in his shirt pocket. "Let's wait until the boys are there to hear it, why don't we?"

That caught her off guard. She had expected him to rip

the envelope open and shout it from the rooftops. Instead, Rowan's eye went to her belly, then his hand followed as he dropped to his knees, pressing his ear to her stomach. He leaned in and turned to kiss it, then spoke into her belly like an antique telephone. "Hey, you! It's your dad," he said, glancing up at Lauren with a glimmer in his eye. "See ya in about five months, m'kay? Quit giving your mom a hard time."

"I just realized something," Tomáš said, out of the blue. Rowan rose and turned to him.

"What's that?"

"Lauren hasn't lost her lunch in three days now," he said.

"That means you can finally wash your car." Lauren laughed.

Rowan did a double-take with perfect comedic timing. "Huh?"

"I'll explain later," she said. "When are we going to crack this puppy open?" She turned back to the magnificent stone wall.

"Tomorrow," Greg said. "First light of dawn."

"Well, I guess we better get a good night's sleep," Lauren said. "I can't wait to see what Didymus left for us to discover."

"Speaking of books, did you find your missing page?" Rowan asked.

An angelic smile passed over Lauren's features. She and Tomáš exchanged a knowing glance and she nodded. "*Pages.* Yes. We did."

"I can't wait to hear all about it," Rowan said. "Congratulations."

"Psh." She waved her hand like it was nothing. "Just an ugly old book filled with mean pictures and boring tomes of forgotten lore. True knowledge is waiting for us right behind that wall. This …" She raised her hands to the façade in front of her. "*This* is the real treasure … I can tell."

Rowan puzzled over this for a moment, glancing at his

watch. "What the hell?" he started, looking to Greg for support. "Let's crack this puppy open."

Greg grinned, picking up a power tool with a wicked looking blade. "Somebody plug this bad boy into the generator. Everyone else stand back."

It took hours to remove each block one at a time. The tool included a dust collection system and Greg had to stop every twenty or thirty minutes to clean out the filtration system. Soon enough, he had an opening just big enough for Lauren to get through. Rowan insisted they check the air and was glad they did. It was stale and lacked sufficient oxygen. After a few hours of pumping fresh air in, he finally verified it was safe to enter. Of course, by then, a few more blocks had been removed, and he and Lauren entered one after the other. Greg and the camera crew were close behind. Tomáš followed, too.

Long benches had been carved into the sandstone walls, and the shelves were filled with tablets, parchments, vellums, and earthenware vessels containing linen scrolls. More documents from antiquity were stacked in rows up and down the room, as if placed there in haste. Lauren studied the inscriptions on the wall over the shelves while Rowan and the others focused on documenting the initial positioning and conditions found within.

"Oh my goodness," Lauren gasped, slowly panning the beam of the flashlight along the rows and rows of shelves. "It *is* a library!"

"What does that say?" Tomáš came up behind her, pointing to the engravings over the shelves.

"It says, *Memento Alexandria. Scientia sit potentia.*"

Greg turned, hearing the words. "Latin?"

"Yes," Lauren said. "It says, *Remember Alexandria. Knowledge is power.*"

"Truer words were never spoken," Greg mused. "I wonder if these were rescued from Alexandria before the library was destroyed."

"Is that even at all possible?" Lauren asked.

"There were some legends that the keepers were able to spirit away some of the texts before they were all burned." Rowan scratched his beard with his pinky.

"Henry's going to be so excited," Lauren said.

"Indeed." Rowan put an arm around her. She leaned into him.

SHEMI AND AHMOSE SAT ON THE FLOOR WITH THE BOYS, cutting flowers, stars, and other pretty shapes out of tissue paper. The Pierce's Egyptian household was festooned with streamers and bouquets of flowers. Ribbons curled at the corners of the doors. The essence of the exotic spices wafted through every corner of the house. Tima had spent the entire day cooking after she'd spent most of the night baking. A beautiful three-tiered cake sat in the middle of the dining room table. The vanilla cake had been covered in a thick layer of white frosting. The bottom section was layered with raspberry filling, the middle had the fig layer Henry preferred. Tima had found fresh apricots at the market and decided to fill the top layer with them. Marzipan fruits of all kinds had been used to decorate each layer.

"Mumma," Ahmose said. "It's almost eight. How long do you think it will be before they get here?"

"Any minute," Tima said, plating the couscous and turning her attention to the pita bread dough that was ready to go on the griddle. "Boys, can you help set the table? Your momma and daddy should be here soon."

John Carter and Henry both responded with the appropriate "Yes, ma'am."

Tima had already set out the plates, and all they had to do was put them in place. Tima's phone bleeped, and Ahmose snatched it up. "It's Lauren. They're just getting off the highway."

"Perfect!" Tima said, pleased with herself. She'd have everything ready as they walked in the door. She hadn't told them about the surprise celebration, just that she'd have the boys tucked into their own beds tonight so everyone could get a good night's sleep and they could all be home together.

"Set everything on the table," Tima said, flipping the first batch of pita bread, and preparing the second batch. "Boys run upstairs. Wash your hands and faces. Make sure your hair is combed and pick up your toys so your mom and dad will see what good boys you are."

"Yes ma'am!" They chorused and hurried along to do as they were told.

"ARE YOU SERIOUS?" ROWAN FINALLY SAID, AFTER SHE'D briefed him on every moment of her trip to Prague and into Slovenia. He'd been driving, eyes fixed on the road while she spun the fantastical tale, not leaving out a single detail. He'd assumed, and she'd never corrected him, that Kovač had been with the museum and that he was helping her track down the missing pages. He didn't realize that Tomáš was a detective with the police department in Prague. He chewed on the long hair at the bottom of his lip as he drove.

When he finally took his eyes off the road long enough to glance at her, they glistened in the fading light of day. "You faced Enlil." It wasn't a question. "Without me?" She nodded, not sure what else to say. His hand snaked over and caught hers, pulling it into him. "I'm so sorry I wasn't there."

"I'm kind of glad you weren't," Lauren said. "I'd hate to think what could have happened …" her voice trailed off. He could tell it was everything she could do to remain detached from her feelings. It'd taken her two days to get to the point where she could tell him all this. He suspected she didn't want to rain on his parade either.

"So what happened with the last pages of the Codex?"

She didn't want to tell Rowan about Henry's involvement, but she decided he needed to know. "Henry? Henry returned the pages to Stockholm? He knows he's not supposed to … you know … *poof.*" He waved a hand like he was casting a magic spell.

"Don't be mad at him. He's just a little boy."

Rowan knew his son had … abilities. His wife had abilities, too. "We have to find a way to keep him from doing stuff like this," he said.

"I'll work with him," Lauren said. "You know, you need to thank him, right?"

"I do?" Rowan's brow clamped down over the bridge of his nose.

A wistful smile crossed Lauren's face. The lights of the city came up as the sky faded from pale blue to indigo. "Do you remember the cobra?"

Rowan's features went slack, and he turned to cast a curious glare in her direction. "How do you know about the cobra?"

"Henry told me," Lauren said. "Not in so many words, but … I don't always need words to communicate with my son. It's just this sense of knowing."

"Does John Carter do this?"

"No," Lauren said. "It's just Henry. I'm not sure why."

Rowan shook his head. His hand tightened over hers. "After what happened in Africa, I tried to convince myself it couldn't possibly be Henry. It took me a while to come to terms with your powers, and it's going to take me some time to come to grips with his." He drew her knuckles to his lips and kissed them. "I trust you … both."

"Now, that is faith," Lauren said. A heavy sigh escaped her throat as the baby kicked against her stomach. Her free hand went to the spot, rubbing it. Rowan turned her other hand loose and let his join hers on her abdomen. "And this is love."

~

He pulled up in front of the house and gave her a long glowing gaze. A wave of joy washed through her that was accompanied with a sense of profound peace. She'd been through Hell and back and knew there wasn't anything they couldn't get through without a lot of each. They had faith in each other and there was more love than any two people should ever know.

Rowan opened the gate for her, and they walked arm-in-arm up to the front steps. "I hope you're hungry," Lauren said pausing at the door.

Rowan puzzled. "So, you're psychic now?"

"No, I can smell the cumin and the garam masala," she said. "Tima's cooking."

"Well, you don't have to be psychic to know that," Rowan chortled.

The door was flung open and two little boys jumped up from the sofa and screamed, "Surprise!!!"

~

The festivities lingered long into the evening, despite Lauren and Rowan's exhaustion. Tima and the girls took care of all the work, and John Carter and Henry were patient waiters, passing out plates of cake, each one had a small slice from each of the three layers of cake; a sampler.

Rowan made coffee in his Turkish press, and Lauren indulged in a small cup. Tima sprinkled spices over the cream-laced brew, which she knew Lauren liked.

"Which one do you *yike* better?" John Carter pointed his

fork at her as he leaned his elbows on the table, sitting on his knees so he could reach.

"The raspberry is my favorite, but I like them all."

"I *tole* you," John Carter turned to Henry and gloated. "I *tole* you she *yikes waspbewies*."

"How did you know I like raspberries?" Lauren tried to remember when the last time she'd eaten raspberries, probably in Virginia before John Carter was born, if her memory served her well.

"Do you remember how many quarts of raspberries you ate a day when you were pregnant with that one?" Rowan asked. A mischievous light made his eyes glow in the soft lighting.

"I *wemember*," John Carter said.

"Raspberries and cream, raspberry crumble, raspberry jam," Rowan said, taking a bite of the cake with the apricot filling.

Lauren glowered at her husband, then let her features soften as she turned to John Carter. "You really remember that?"

"Uh huh," John Carter said.

"Huh." Lauren huffed and shook her head, starting in on the fig-filled slice. It was better than she expected. She'd never had figs that she could remember, not before coming to Egypt. "I called Bahati before we left Tobruk," Lauren said to Rowan. Thoughts of Virginia reminded her to mention it. "She and Jean-René are going to come for your graduation."

"Oh, that reminds me," Tima said. "I had the Bursar's office run a degree audit for you, Rowan, dear."

"A degree audit?"

"Turns out, all these extra projects you've taken on have counted for additional credit hours. All you need is a physical education class and you can graduate."

"Physical education?" Rowan screwed up his face, glancing down at his stomach. He ran three to five miles a day.

He ate a balanced diet. What more of an education did he need? "Like what?"

"Swimming, yoga ..." Tima started.

"Underwater basket weaving ..." Lauren chortled at her own joke.

"First aid/CPR ..." Tima finished.

"First aid/CPR? I'm an EMT for the love of Pete," he scowled.

"He renewed his Instructor's certification before we came to Egypt," Lauren added. "He used to teach all the television crews' refresher classes."

"Do you have a copy of your certificate?" Tima said, lifting her brow.

"I can have the Network email a copy," Rowan said.

"Get it to me and I'll see if we can use that in lieu of the last class you need."

"So, would that mean I can graduate at the end of the semester?"

"If the college will accept it," Tima said.

Rowan turned to Lauren. "How do you feel about going back to work?"

"Now that I'm not throwing up every time I smell coffee or eat a cookie, I'm ready to go," Lauren said. "We've got a couple of months before I'm as big as a house and have to take some time off, but I made it work when I was pregnant with Henry and John Carter. This one doesn't have to be any different."

"I guess Jean-René and Bahati will need to plan to visit sooner than expected," Rowan said. "Hope the Network doesn't give them too much grief."

"They don't have to know," Lauren said. "While Dr. Masa might have been a wolf in sheep's clothing, I checked the bank account before I left Prague ... the check cleared. We can afford to send them their tickets."

A toothy grin spread over Rowan's face and his dimples deepened. "That's great!"

"Uncle Jean-René and Aunt Bahati are coming to visit?" Henry asked. "Are they bringing Nyota with them?"

"Of course," Lauren said. "I'm sure they will."

"That reminds me," Rowan said, turning to the boys. "Do you want to know if you're having a brother or a sister?"

"Do you know?" Tima looked up sharply. The girls looked to one another, and the boys began shouting. "Well, spill it."

"Hey!" Rowan's voice raised to a warning tone, and the boys settled. "Do you want to know?"

"Yes, please," Henry said. John Carter nodded.

"In about five months, you're going to have … a new baby brother."

Henry's excited features faded. John Carter's did, too. "Oh."

"What?" Lauren asked, surprised by their reaction.

"I kinda wanted a sister," Henry said. "I already have a brother."

"Me, too," John Carter parroted.

"Well, maybe next time," Rowan shrugged.

All four of the women chorused, "Next time?"

AFTERWORD

Thank you for reading *The Monk's Grimoire*. If you enjoyed it, please post a review where you purchased it.

The next book in the series is *The Lost Templar*. Watch for it!

SNEAK PREVIEW OF THE LOST TEMPLAR

Southern France – 1308

"*By the blood*, Brother Wolfgang. I bid you welcome." The French Templar stood watch at the castle gate. He had been expecting The Enclave to arrive for the past month, but the Teutonic soldier was the first to arrive. "How was your journey?"

"*Through His Blood we are saved*, Brother François. I have been too long on the road," he said, answering in French as he reined back his warhorse and slid out of the saddle. His sword caught on the saddle bag, but he freed it with minimal effort. The soldier landed on the damp pathway with a heavy thud. His tangled hair caught the pale moonlight; even his rusty beard had a glow to it.

"*Bienvenu au Château de la Fleur*." François caught his forearm, clasping his hand as the guest returned the gesture.

The warrior appeared as if he had come from the field of battle. The back of his leather coat was damp from the mist. The garment was torn along the shoulder. The fur lining around the neck, matted with blood — blood that was not his. His tabard beneath was equally stained and torn; his chain mail was visible beneath.

"Are you injured, Brother?"

"Not so much as the enemy I left behind on the road from the Holy Lands." Wolfgang chuckled. "Have I arrived too late?" He panted, his breath hanging in the cold night air.

"The Enclave is not yet assembled," François said. "Several of *The Order* have yet to arrive; Brother William and the Lady Elisabeth from Scotland among them. We received word when they reached the coast; there has been no message since they made it to Mount St. Michel."

"How long ago since his last missive arrived?"

"Three days' time." François said. The visitor moved to unloose his saddlebag. "We are growing concerned. He traveled under a Flag of Truce signed by the King himself."

Wolfgang hesitated. "Am I to assume the English will send no envoy?"

"They will not," François said soberly. "I can only hope his promise of truce was not a ruse to deceive us."

"And what of … the *holy relic*?" Wolfgang asked, glancing over his shoulder as he lowered his tone.

"Brother William and the Lady Elisabeth protect it at all costs," he said. "At this point, we can only pray for their safety."

"May God offer his protection," Wolfgang said, crossing himself. François did the same, putting a hand on his comrade's arm. "Come, Brother. You must be tired and hungry. There is food and bed prepared for you. Until all are assembled, best we tend to the needs of the body."

"God bless you, Brother," Wolfgang said, handing the horses' reigns to the stable boy. He shouldered his saddlebags, reaching inside. "I have brought the gifts of my house; if you will take ale."

François smiled brightly, accepting it and inspecting the dark glass bottle. "Ale would be most welcome."

"A gift for your House," Wolfgang said, brightly.

"I shall have a bottle of our finest wine brought from the cellar for you, in return."

"And we shall drink it together," François replied.

The autumn night had gone bitterly cold, and the long journey had been made all the more difficult by the early change of seasons. It had rained; snow was still a few months off. Wolfgang's wool cloak had provided some protection and served to hide the silken tabard of his order. Not everyone on the road was a friend. He was grateful to have made it to the safety of the Château and ready to accept his Brother's hospitality.

Shouts from the road outside the castle walls met them just before they made it inside. François stopped, as others raced from their posts to see what was amiss. Horses approached on the road in the darkness; a sorrel stallion and a white mare. The rider on the stallion slumped over the pommel of his saddle; limp. The white horse was riderless. Sweat from the animal's flanks turned to mist around the anxious horses as the stablemen caught the reigns. Wolfgang and François both raced to meet them as the horses were lead into the courtyard where the brasiers illuminated the horrific scene. The white horses' coat was matted in something dark; something that could only be blood. The white horse pranced in agitation and blew snot from her nose. The other seemed to limp but calmed at the gentle hand of one of the grooms.

"Brother William?" François raced around to the other horse, lifting the man's head. His face was bruised, his eyes swollen, his upper lip cut. The broken shaft of an arrow protruded from his leg. Blood caked around the wound and stained both saddle and horse. "William?"

"*Nous avons ... terminé*," William gasped. "*La rose ... est tombée.*"

"Where is your traveling companion?" François gasped, tears filling his eyes. "Where is your *sacred missive?*"

"My wife…" he gasped, sliding out of his saddle. He was a dead weight in his comrade's arms. "We were … beset … she carried the *treasure* …"

"François!" Wolfgang shouted; the injured man's boot caught in the stirrup. "Help me get him down."

It took more than the two of them to free the limp form of Brother William from his horse. "Call for the physician!"

"The stallion's hoof is split," the groom said as the knights inspected the horses, looking for clues to what might have taken place. An arrow pierced the saddle of the white horse, and remained lodged at the base of the pommel in the fine-tooled Scottish leather.

A rider on the path bolted through the gate and drew back his reigns as he saw something was amiss. "What has happened?" Brother Alwar asked, doffing his cloak as he landed; his boots clapping on the damp ground as he strode over. The Spaniard's white tabard was emblazoned with a cross, embroidered in gold. A red rose at the conjunction of the lateral and horizontal arms.

"Brother William was attacked on the road," François said, without the formal greetings of their order.

"And … the *Sacred Heart of the Rose*?"

The two men had no words, but their faces spoke volumes. Alwar took the shaft of the arrow in one hand, bracing himself with the other; straining with the effort to free the arrow. He carried it to the firelight to inspect it. The other's followed. "I recognize this." He pointed to a mark on the shaft, just beneath the fletching. "I saw such marks during my time in Aleppo. It's the mark of *The Asāsiyyūn's Guild*."

"*Asāsiyyūns*? Here? We are thousands of miles from the Holy Land. The Infidels could not have infiltrated so far into France."

"They are like maggots that infiltrate our flesh while we sleep. Their numbers swell as they burrow into the darkest recesses of our realms. We must launch a counter attack," Alwar insisted. "Why do you cower in this fortress like nuns? Are we not Soldiers in the Army of God?"

"Brother William lies on his deathbed ..." François gestured toward the castle as he started to explain.

Alwar was incensed by his lack of urgency. "If you will not go after her, I will."

"Wait," François caught his sleeve, realizing he, too wore his mail beneath. He'd come dressed for battle as well. "We must wait for the others of our *Order*."

"Wait?" Alwar gasped. "Wait? While the Asāsiyyūns ride with *the Sacred Heart of the Rose*, what of Sister Elisabeth? It may already be too late, but I made an oath upon my life to defend and protect my brothers, and by virtue, his lady. I will not let the act of these *Asāsiyyūns* go unanswered. I will fight them all ... with or without the support of a full Army."

Wolfgang looked to François. "I will go with him," he said. "Vauquelin, fetch my horse!"

Alwar nodded, clearly pleased to have the Bohemian's aid. "If we find *The Asāsiyyūn's Guild*, we will send word. When the rest of *The Order* arrives, we may need aid."

"How will your message find us here?"

"My falcon," Alwar said, pointing to the shadow at the peak of the roof above the entryway. "She is well-trained and carries letters for me in times of urgent need. She will return to her roost. I will mount it here in the courtyard." He went to his saddle a took a long post from a sheath. It might have appeared as a longsword, but the Spanish knight took the post and buried it in the compacted soil with one mighty blow. The falcon flew down and landed on it, before moving to her master's arm.

François nodded. He made the sign of the cross over each of them. "I pray, by *the Blood*, may you go with God."

Alwar bowed. *"Through His Blood we are saved."*

The warriors returned just before sunrise, though the day had gone gray, as was so common this time of year. François never made it to his chambers. Instead, he felt compelled to pray and kept a vigil over the fallen soldier. When he heard the beat of hooves on the bridge just outside the fortress that protected the chapel, he crossed himself then made the same sign over the patient. He rose and went to greet his brothers. He didn't get far.

The body of Lady Elisabeth had been found on the road, a dozen miles away. An arrow had pierced her heart. She wore a bloodstained overdress that looked like a fine silken a tapestry bearing a pattern of similar gold crosses and embroidered red roses.

They had shrouded her in their own tabards and brought her body to be properly entombed with her husband if he did not survive. She hadn't yet been cold when they found her, but the last warmth of life was fleeting; her flesh still pliable as they collected her from the back of the horse.

François peeled back the shroud to study her face. Despite the cold pallor of death, he could see she had been a beautiful woman. She was young, fair-haired, and bore no marks or bruises on her ghostly face.

"Take her to her husband's chambers," François instructed, moving her body to Vauquelin's arms. The man was not young, but he was robust; a form built by decades of labor.

"Why? What are you doing?" Alwar asked.

"The ancient wisdom says true love cannot be separated, even by death. If such things are true, and if the magic of my order holds, there may be salvation for them after all."

"But the *Sacred Heart of the Rose*?"

"Another reason to take her to her husband," François said.

William stirred as they carried his lady into the chamber, his eyelids fluttered. The   monks moved a second bed into the room, sliding it close to the one upon which he lay. The body of his beloved wife was lain beside him and draped in a gossamer shroud. Brother Vauquelin brought holy water and sacred oils, placing them on the table beside the Lady's bed.

"Brother William?" Wolfgang knelt at his side, as François knelt beside the Laird's wife. "*By His Blood*, can you hear me, Brother?"

William rolled his head towards the man's deep voice, he muttered something that they could only assume was the counter to their blessing. It was also a message *The Order* used to identify one another. *Through His Blood we are saved.*

François reached over and took the man's hand and lay it upon the shrouded hand of his wife. "She's been gone too long," Wolfgang said, keeping his voice low.

"Be of faith, Brothers. Pray with me," François said, bowing his head and lifting his hands like open cups to the heavens. Vauquelin stood back, crossing himself, then clasped his hands beneath his chin.   "Father of the Ancients," François began, dipping his finger in the dish of sacred oil, anointing the Lady's head through the shroud. "God of Abraham and Isaac, Father of Christ, First-born from the Dead. Alpha and Omega. By all Thy Names, hear our prayers. In the Name of Love, we have come beseeching that these two souls be fully restored. Open their eyes wide that they may serve at Thy command. You, O Lord, who opens graves, who heals the sick, and raises the dead; O Lord, we beseech that Thou restore life and health to these mortal bodies. Through the Spirit that dwells in Thee, loose the pangs of Death, and awaken Thy warrior's bride to everlasting life that we may bring glory to Thee and rescue *the Sacred Heart of the Rose*, and see it safely delivered from the hands of our enemies; as Thou has bidden. Mend these broken bodies to fully glory that their acts may magnify Thee.

We ask this, our blessed Redeemer, as You raised Your Son from the grave, bring forth our Sister from the dead."

François breathed in a deep breath and let it out slowly. An unseen surge of energy seemed to pass through his body, lifting his hair and sending goosebumps across his flesh. William too, drew in a deep breath. He gasped and cried out, "Elisabeth!" His voice was weak, but the word was unmistaken.

As if the windows had been thrown open, a gust of wind swirled into the small chamber; brasiers and candles flickering. A deep huffing echo came from the fireplace and ashes blew from the bed of coals; sparks erupted like fireflies on the summer air. They swirled and danced, coalescing as they hovered above the shrouded body.

The luminaries stopped short of contacting the linen that draped the lady's delicate features. They seemed to throb with a heartbeat all their own. The *lub-dub* of it echoed loudly; repeatedly. François noticed William's hand wrap around the smaller one of his wife. A gossamer voice found its way into the room.

"What God has joined together, let no man put asunder …" The words, that came from nowhere and everywhere, were soft like the prayer of a small child. Just as soft was the sigh of the Lady St. Clair as her chest rose and fell, then rose again. The sparks twinkled into nothingness; the shroud pulled from her form, as if by unseen hands. It fell to the floor beneath the cot.

William rolled over, reaching for her cheek. "My beloved," he buried his face in the tumble of golden curls that lay on her shoulder.

"You came back for me," she said, weakly. An angelic smile curled in her cheeks as her hand went to husband's head.

Alwar stood in the door, a gasp. "We could not leave you to our enemies, Lady Elisabeth." He crossed the room and fell to his knees beside François, taking her other hand. He kissed her ring in reverence.

"They road with us in the guise of friends … we were … betrayed." William said.

"Did you see who it was, Brother William?"

"I did not recognize him at first. But … it was my beloved wife who discovered it was Lord Henry de Lacy." He lay back, his hand still entwined in his Lady's. "The … Third Earl of Lincoln. The … seneschal of King … King Edward himself."

Sharp glances passed between François, Wolfgang, and Anwar.

"But … I did not detect the deception quick enough. I fear God is not pleased." Lady Elisabeth said, faintly. "We have enemies of the Faith in the Kingdom."

"Enemies that must be defeated," William said. "We must find and retake *The Sacred Heart of the Rose*."

The sound of hoofbeats could heard outside the chamber. "The rest of our Enclave has arrived." François made for the door.

William struggled to rise. "Good," he said. "Bring me … my horse. I will … lead … the charge."

Elisabeth caught his arm. "Husband," she said. "You are not yet mended."

"And I am … not yet done taking … scars to secure … the *Sacred Heart of the Rose*," he said, struggling to rise. "Scars I … will gladly bear."

Elisabeth reached for him as his hand clutched his wounded side. She moved to rise as well. "So be it, my love. Brothers, saddle our horses."

ABOUT THE AUTHOR

Betsey Kulakowski has thirty years of experience as an occupational safety professional and recently completed her degree in Emergency Management. Betsey and her husband live in Oklahoma and have two grown children. She has been writing since she could, and created her first book at the age of six cardboard cover, string binding and all.